MATT TOPFER

INTERVENTION

INTRODUCING ALEX WARD

To Mum, thanks for encouraging (forcing) us to read!

Prologue

NOVEMBER 15TH, 2022 is a bellwether day in the history of our planet.

It is the day recognised and consequently 'named' by the United Nations as the 'Day of Eight Billion.'

While we could argue as to whether the UN really applied itself in the naming of this significant milestone, it is nonetheless a day we need to acknowledge, to reflect on and to consider the future-shaping implications. It is the day (the clue is in the name!) the United Nations acknowledged the world population reached eight billion people.

In 1950 - very recent history - and living memory for many - there were an estimated two and a half billion people on the planet. As of today we are well in excess of eight billion. In just seventy-two years, a single lifetime for our parents or grandparents, the population has exploded by a multiple of three. And while the rate of population growth is slowing, we are nonetheless, still growing. Nine billion is on the horizon. Ten billion is expected by 2050.

Population growth can be pretty popular. I live in Australia. We have political parties that have actively campaigned on policies that drive higher migration and encourage - often incentivise - natural population growth. Economists and politicians almost universally promote a growing population. They lay out an evident association with economic growth. More people. More spending. More development.

More. More. More.

And isn't economic growth the most fundamental objective of our governments and our broader socio-economic collective? It is generally proposed as the single measure of the prosperity of a country and the capability and performance of the government in charge.

Population growth may be great for the economy. But it is terrible for the environment. The linkages between population growth and environmental destruction are without question. And they are linear. More people, more devastation.

Let me preface this by saying that I am no eco-warrior! I struggle to understand what can be recycled and which of the four rubbish bins our council provides, I should be using. I definitely should do more! Nonetheless, it seems there is little attention or discussion addressing the obvious - the relationship between population - the sheer mass of humanity - and the ongoing and possibly irreversible destruction of our planet.

We have well-documented environmental degradation. Pollution in the air, on our land and in our seas. Holes in the ozone, manmade landfill mountains and oceans clogged with plastic. Air in many countries is barely safe to breathe and water, in places, is no longer safe to drink. Resources are being stripped from the planet to fuel productivity and lifestyle. And it is all a consequence of people.

The World Wildlife Fund reported in 2022 that between 1970 and 2018, global wildlife populations fell by sixty nine percent. That's two-thirds of the world's wildlife wiped out in less than fifty years! And the place is heating up. Because of the way we live. And if we cross the much-publicised 1.5°C threshold we risk even greater environmental and ecological impact including rising ocean levels, more frequent and severe droughts, heatwaves and rainfall.

The Kyoto Protocol adopted in 1997 was the first attempt to focus the world's attention. The intent was to get developed countries to reduce emissions to pre-1990 levels and to keep them trending down. It failed. The US signed on in 1998 and would later withdraw its signature. The Paris Agreement followed in 2015 - a renewed and historic commitment by signatory countries to set emission reduction targets. Lots of commitments and action plans.   However, a Stanford University report published in December indicated that in 2023 we had reached record global emissions.

The weight of informed opinion - by some measure, is that if we continue unchecked, the future for the planet and for the people that live on it - is dire

Chapter 1

ALEX WARD STEPPED up her pace. She wanted to push hard for the last half mile of her six-mile run. Actually, she corrected herself, it was the last kilometre of ten - her adopted country had been metric for decades!

This part of the coast was stunning. The return into Avalon - a beautiful town on the northern beaches of Sydney, made her feel blessed to call this place home. She'd just descended the rocky headland that jutted out to the Pacific Ocean, following a rarely used trail that took her right across the top and then dropped down a rock and grass slope towards the village. It was a precarious descent. Particularly at speed. The gradient of the slope and the loose soil and rocks meant she had to keep her head down and each foot strike put pressure on her knees and her quads.

But she loved to run and to suffer. This slippery slope was often about as exciting as her day would get.

Now and then she would take her eyes off the trail, look up and take in the breathtaking expanse of the Pacific Ocean in front of her and in her peripheral the beautiful homes that graced the coastline. Subconsciously she appreciated the skill of the architect as the houses seemed to perch untethered over the beach below.

She slowed her pace a little as she bottomed out from the descent and came closer to the coastline of Avalon. This was home, along with her Australian husband. Just the two of them. Alex shut down her podcast and removed her air buds, zipping them into her bum bag - a rather amusing Aussie term - as she ran along the foreshore. She tuned into the cadence of her feet hitting the ground, aware of waves breaking over the rocks, exploding into the air creating a salty mist that softly cooled her skin.

Paradise found.

Several days a week Alex would run with the local triathlon group. The camaraderie and the challenge of fit and competitive athletes pushed her a little harder. But running alone was her therapy. Where she recalibrated. Her mind turned inward as her body found its groove. An opportunity to reflect on her day, to cherish what she had and to consider the days ahead. Relaxed and at peace.

Though even when relaxed her eyes behind the reflective lens of her Oakleigh sunglasses constantly scanned.

She missed nothing.

She had fallen in love with this place as soon as they'd arrived. This part of Australia was truly beautiful and less than an hour's commute to Sydney for those days when she had to work in town. Avalon was where her husband had spent his childhood and they had settled here a little over a year ago.

With the sun a fiery orange ball low in the sky Alex turned away from the coast and headed up the hill towards her house. It was a place they'd bought sight unseen while they were still living in the States. A leap of faith they had both committed to in relocating to Australia. A demonstration of their desire for permanency and stability. Perhaps more in hope than with a clear plan. But it had worked out brilliantly. She was so pleased they had trusted their collective intuition and backed what was for both of them a snap decision. She and David were both thriving.

The elevated location of their home caught the breeze and offered beautiful views over the ocean.

And it appealed to her innate need to find the higher ground.

Chapter 2

THE SCREEN DOOR slammed.

David Mitchell called out, 'Up here.'

Ward kicked off her running shoes and socks and stepped lightly in her bare feet up the stairs and into the kitchen. The run and the coastal humidity had her glistening with sweat. Turning from the cooktop David looked at his wife across the counter. She even seemed to sweat elegantly. He noticed - as he did as often as possible, how good she looked in her short shorts and cropped running top. Her dark, almost black hair was pulled back in a single ponytail, accentuating her sharp cheekbones and strong jawline.

She had always been fit and driven but the move to Australia and particularly to the coast had her catching the triathlon bug and she'd leaned down even more. Her tanned skin and the definition in her arms and legs gave her a long and athletic form. It suited her. This place was having a wonderful effect. On Alex and on him. He tried to capture and hold these simple moments in his mind.

Ward caught the look of her husband. He turned back towards the kitchen conscious of his attention being noticed. He was not one for overt displays, tending to favour what she had come to realise was quintessential Aussie understatement. Deflection was second nature. She found it cute. She moved around the bench top and into the kitchen, giving David a kiss and grabbing a bottle of water from the fridge.

She asked, 'When are you going to come running with me?'

'When I can keep up.'

'I'm going to grab a shower.'

'Want company?' he paused briefly as he quickly looked her over, 'I can soap your back,' he offered, 'Or your front, if you prefer?'

'Haha! We don't want to spoil that lovely dinner you're working on. Give me ten and we can have a beer on the deck.' She smiled as she teased her husband and walked out of the room.

'It's a date,' he called after her.

Chapter 3

RECENTLY ELECTED US President James Charleston picked up his cut crystal tumbler from a side table and settled deeper into the overstuffed leather chair. Outside the Brownstone it was a freezing late November night in Washington and he had the room warming with an open fire. The soft yellow glow was complimented by carefully placed, subdued lamps.

He was alone - which was very unusual these days. And he was enjoying the relaxed familiarity and comfort of being in his own home. He looked into the mirror across the room that sat above the low fireplace and considered the person who looked back at him. The full head of hair, rare at his age. With a little cultivated silver at the side and a soft tan on annoyingly smooth features. Throughout the campaign, he had aspired to the trusted news anchor image and thought he'd achieved it quite nicely. As President he wanted to exude calm and confidence and project authority - a face people would trust. An observer might see this as superficial, particularly given the importance of his position. But for Charleston the perceptions of the American public were important. Politics could often be a superficial game. First impressions and the way in which one presented themselves was unfortunately more important than the substance beneath. And he really didn't like people looking too deeply.

Charleston took a moment to reflect on the first months of his administration. He contemplated whether his Presidency was in a good place. He'd taken office as the COVID pandemic was gaining traction. Initially, he'd hated the damn Chinese virus. Thought it a trumped-up and overblown version of the flu. A big distraction. And getting way too much attention.

Then he realised COVID-19 was a godsend. The virological equivalent of an international war. This was his nine-eleven. He was on TV and streaming services constantly. Leading and guiding the country through unprecedented challenges. And he had free rein to spend. To throw money at the problem and to fuel the economy through ever-increasing debt. It would be political suicide for his opponents to challenge how he was protecting the country and assisting those most affected. He'd never had such favourable polling numbers.

He rose, and carrying his drink, walked closer to the mirror. He looked intently at his appearance, pulling at the loosening skin that covered his Adam's apple. He needed to instruct the White House kitchen to cut back on the carbs. Well, he thought as he settled back into the leather chair, if this virus kept running as it seemed it would, his re-election in a little over three years would be a shoo-in.

Charleston had decided to take tonight's meeting at the Brownstone in Washington rather than the White House. Despite having spent most of his adult life dreaming about and scheming to get into the Oval, he was not comfortable there with some of the more personal meetings. He didn't really trust that there wasn't always someone listening.

At the Brownstone there was only his long-serving maid and the lightest Secret Service detail permissible. The place had hardly been used and had all but been empty since the inauguration. It was about as off the record as he could make it. It suited the nature of the coming conversation.

And it suited his other plans he'd arranged for later that night.

Chapter 4

CHARLESTON'S STUDY WAS heavy on the masculine. Intentionally. This room was a sanctuary that contributed to his already engorged sense of confidence. Like the Oval it projected power upon its occupant. And when people met with him here, it had an impact. As a Senator, he'd set the office up at considerable cost, moving two walls to make it larger than the Oval. He valued subtle cues and symbolism and ensured they were designed into the room. His study had been decorated by his wife Arabella. Under his strict instructions. The rest of the three-level townhouse in the Georgetown district in Washington was all Bella and straight out of Vogue Living. This was his room. He'd rejected all of her suggestions when she looked to improve his design. He wanted none of her feminine touches.

Not that he'd experienced any of her feminine touches lately. In fact not for a while. And he didn't care. They'd had enough forced time together during the marathon that was a Presidential campaign. Particularly the intensity of the public spectacle surrounding the inauguration and the tradition of the new First Family moving into the White House. This was a welcome break for them both. She was on an extended visit to her parents in Georgia with their daughters. He reflected that the last time they'd been together was his fiftieth birthday celebrations almost a month ago.

He was happy to be left alone - except those occasions when he needed her as his First Lady. Such as the coming weekend. They would be traveling together for the first State Visit of his Presidency. He'd have preferred an international tour earlier in his first year but COVID had required he stay domestic. Travel had become a bitch even for a President. In fact, particularly for a President. His PR people said it would be poor optics.

Whatever. He was now looking forward to what would unfortunately be a brief trip. He had some debts to pay.

Charleston found himself at times contemplating life without Arabella. To be free to do what he wanted, when he wanted and with whom he wanted. It was an indulgent, satisfying, albeit fleeting fantasy. His ambition always triumphed and as he had learned of himself there was no sacrifice too great. The public liked a married President.

Especially one married to a beautiful and wealthy southern blonde. Besides, theirs was an arrangement that over his political career had satisfied them both. He got her family money and status and the extensive connections of the Deep South. While she shone under the spotlight of one of the country's most influential and revered power brokers. Her desire to be First Lady matched his to be President. Theirs was a true partnership and she really wasn't interested in what he did on his own time. He'd been doing what he wanted for years anyway and planned for that to continue as President. He figured the office and the scrutiny it brought certainly hadn't hindered many of his predecessors.

He'd removed his jacket and tie pulling on a well-worn heavy sweater. The President refilled his glass with more ice and a double measure. He wanted the right tone. The right message. Chummy. The inner circle.

He'd seat his guest closer to the fire and have him sweat a little.

Chapter 5

THE PHONE OF the lone agent sitting in the driver's seat of a plain silver sedan vibrated in the pocket of his lightweight tactical cargo pants. He'd been discreetly parked for some time in the coastal town of Avalon under a Norfolk Pine on the hill just down from Alex Ward's house. He answered the phone by tapping on the Bluetooth earpiece and kept his polaroid-covered eyes firmly on the target. He knew who would be calling without looking at the screen.

'Hello Boss how are things back home?'

The woman's voice on the other end of the secure line cut straight to the point, 'Do you have eyes on?'

'Yes. I have a nice elevated position near the house. She's inside.'

'You are cleared to make contact.'

'Copy. Any non-friendlies around?'

He didn't expect any trouble. This was a quiet corner of the world and Ward had been off grid for months having been here now for over a year. But he hadn't lasted this long by taking anything for granted. In her office, the woman consulted the screens in front of her. Like her operator in Australia, she also didn't expect anything in that part of the world. Also like her operator, she was taking no chances. She hated mistakes. She looked up at the drone operator sitting across her desk -

'Anything?'

'Negative.'

The operator kept working through his screens. He was running two high-altitude drones deployed to provide overwatch and intel. He thought it was a lot of tech and a lot of money pointing at this part of the world.

Seemed like overkill. Nothing had ever happened here. But this place seemed to have limitless money. And it was not his job to question.

Out of habit more than concern, the man under the Norfolk Pine checked the slide of his Glock and adjusted the tactical knife in the sheath at his side. He prompted; 'Any final instructions?'

'Call me when it's done. And don't fuck this up.'

Chapter 6

GAZING INTO THE fire, James Charleston considered the coming meeting. Robert Marshall had called to say he wanted to see him. In private. As a Deputy Director of the CIA, Marshall was a very useful confidante and Charleston had let him believe over many years that they were friends. He knew Marshall didn't have any real friends. People from both sides of the political spectrum couldn't stand him. He was opinionated and grumpy. A stickler for rules and process and often out of touch. But Charleston realised early in his political career that he could nurture Marshall. Position himself as friend and confidante and supporter. It served him well in the Senate and during the campaign and particularly the first few months of his Presidency. Marshall was his eyes and ears into what was going on behind the closed doors of the CIA. Charleston didn't trust any of the fuckers running the place.

The hierarchy in their relationship had been as subtle as it was evident. Their conversations were frequent. And always private. Ultimately their relationship as Charleston believed the best relationships always were, was mutually self-serving. Or so he made Marshall believe. Marshall was an invaluable inside source. So it was important Charleston made him feel needed and valuable and to continue to want to please him. Marshall had a bulging conscience and he used Charleston to unburden himself. Believing he had both a sympathetic listener and an equally committed true believer. Robert Marshall also wanted to run the CIA. The new President could make that happen. And Marshall without a shred of self-awareness was convinced he was the only person that could do it right.

The President briefly considered yet again whether Marshall would be a good appointment. And then as always quickly rejected the idea.

Certainly they were close and his access and authority with the CIA would improve. But Marshall was a stickler for the rules and process. Too straight and unbending for Charleston's style. For a long time, Marshall had been of the view that there were people in the CIA acting outside their remit. Operating internationally without oversight and domestically when it was illegal. A small and completely unaccountable group of senior CIA staffers. In fact the most senior. People who felt they were the only arbiters of right and wrong and who felt the end always justified the means. Whatever the means might be.

This railed against Marshall's values and deep and self-important sense of what was right. Even if the rogue senior leadership at the CIA were regularly proved correct regarding threats to the United States, in his view their extreme, violent, often unauthorised tactics could not be justified. There had to be appropriate oversight and accountability. Charleston had always projected empathy and when together, shared Marshall's outrage. It provided him a brilliant confidante and an easy patsy to manipulate and agitate within the walls of Langley. But that might not be the case if he was put in charge. Charleston actually liked having a CIA that was willing to operate close to the edge. So long as they followed his agenda. Besides Marshall would probably drive everyone nuts and they'd lose half the people at the agency.

Robert Marshall had asked for this meeting. That probably meant he wanted to yet again press his case for replacing current CIA Director Kristen Thomas. Or he had news to share. Or both. And news normally implied a problem. Something that he needed Charleston to solve. Which he generally found a way to do. He would, as always indulge Robert his time and his sympathetic ear.

He just hoped this meeting would be quick. He was expecting company.

Chapter 7

DEPUTY DIRECTOR ROBERT Marshall was driving his own car. Something he didn't do all that often. He ideally wanted this meeting off the record - any record. His informal meetings with James Charleston over several years had been invaluable to him when James had been a senior Senator. They'd kept their personal relationship as quiet and invisible as possible. An experienced and influential Washington insider with values aligned to his own had proven rare. Charleston's counsel and his quiet support had been important on many occasions. Now as President, it was almost impossible to have the same discreet interaction. But he didn't want to lose what they'd developed. And he had never found anyone else he could trust as he did James.

Some time ago he'd had the car computers modified to enable him to switch on and off the GPS and trackers. And he'd left his CIA-issued cell at his office - which was against protocol, but almost no one ever called him this late. He had a burner and that was it. He knew the capability of America's intelligence network to track and trace and to listen and record. He also knew that despite his efforts if they wanted to watch him they could. He was a senior member of the intelligence community and understood their capability. He had helped build it. He took these measures anyway. It would make it a little harder. And he didn't really want to have to explain himself if he could avoid it. Despite his paranoia, he really didn't think he was of interest to anyone. Deputy Director of Support at the CIA was not seen as a high-risk or high-level target.

Despite having a more back-of-house role he was surprisingly well informed and regularly briefed. Need to know was balanced with entrenched organisational redundancies to ensure continuity in the senior ranks if anything went wrong. And he heard things.

Driving into this area of Washington still felt foreign to Marshall. Beautifully kept and presented homes. Pale street lighting that guided him down wide tree-lined boulevards with seemingly effortless interconnected gardens. It felt clean and peaceful here. Unlike most of Washington. Old money met new money. He had neither. His family had been blue collar and had worked hard to give him and his brother opportunity. He had secured a scholarship to Yale and was the first in his family to attend an Ivy League College.

An excellent student, multi-lingual from his mother's European heritage and a fierce advocate for the conservation and protection of American values, even as a teenager - he had come to the attention of America's intelligence recruiters, particularly the CIA. So he had knocked back the lucrative offers from Big Corporate in favour of adventure and service. He'd taken the invitation from 'Campbell', his CIA recruiter and become an analyst straight out of college. Not suited to the subterfuge and compromise of a field agent, he was a brilliant back office operator, serving in numerous embassies and at home in the US and had risen steadily through the ranks.

The history of the CIA had only ever seen the Director appointed either from Operations or Intelligence - or from outside the agency. And it was this that he felt had led them to where they were today and needed to change. Too many cowboys. It was up to him to take the agency into a new era - he just needed to get appointed.

Chapter 8

THE MAID HAD been asked to stay late. She didn't mind, her job was pretty easy these days and she wanted to keep it. It was quite a step up to be working for the President. Her friends were all jealous and wanted to know what he was like at home. He'd asked her to greet his visitor and show him in. Charleston wasn't going to answer his own door. He knew it was a trivial little ceremony given even a Deputy Director needed to be cleared by the Secret Service to see him. But he liked these subtle little plays and reminders.

'Welcome Robert. A drink? Rosie - bourbon with ice for the Director. And I could do with a top up.'

Robert Marshall only now removed the surgical mask he wore almost constantly as a defense against the raging coronavirus, 'Hello, Mr President and as you know it's Deputy Director.'

'Haha, Robert - it's just a matter of time. Thanks, Rosie - if you're all done, you can go home now.'

The maid furnished the drinks and left the room. Charleston continued, 'So Robert, an off-site meeting between the President and the Deputy Director - it has me intrigued! Sit by the fire and tell me what's up at Langley!'

'Mr President...' started Marshall.

'Please Robert - how many times have I asked you to call me Jim when we're alone? We've known each other for years.'

'Of course. Is the First Lady here with you?'

'Not at the moment. Just you and I. And my Secret Service detail.' He smiled at the office door.

Marshall settled into the stuffed leather chair and contemplated his glass. He felt the immediate heat from the close flames. His eyes paused briefly on a framed photo of Bella Charleston taking pride of place on the President's desk. A First Lady the American people loved. He'd been in this room many times but was always impressed. And a little over-awed. It was a man's office - full of leather and wood, warmed and fragranced by the open fire. He considered his own cramped and cluttered office at his modest suburban home. Not for the first time he found himself jealous of the easy luxury and privilege James Charleston enjoyed.

But the news he brought tonight may rattle him.

Marshall continued to look into his glass, 'Jim I wanted to meet you alone and off the record. I'll get right to it. My colleagues at the agency have commenced an investigation into foreign involvement and manipulation of the election. I'm not quite sure how expansive the investigation is, my briefing is limited. The one aspect I'm aware of is that they have strong intel from one or more former Cambridge Analytica employees and seem to be taking it seriously.'

He looked up from his glass and across towards the President and continued, 'It goes without saying this frustrates me no end as it is in direct conflict with the CIA remit and official charter. The CIA should not be active on US soil without justification. This should be handled by domestic agencies. My concern is the agency will act without oversight and without concern for the legalities involved.' As an afterthought he added, 'It's also a direct affront to your integrity as President.'

Charleston looked across at Marshall working to keep his expression impassive, while emotions began to swirl. Typical of this fool, his main concern was whether the CIA followed the rules. But if Marshall's intel was right and an investigation as he suggested, had commenced it could be a problem. He'd barely warmed the seat in the Oval. The last thing he needed was scrutiny over the election. He determined to get as much out of Marshall as possible without tipping his hand.

'Robert, as usual, you waste no time on small talk. Take a good sip of that bourbon. That's Pappy Van Winkle Twenty Year old. I keep the best stuff here at the house. Relax. Take your time. You have my attention. Are you talking about electoral fraud - at the ballot box - there have been rumours of vote swapping.' Charleston wanted Marshall to lay out the details.

'Actually, I'm not sure of the specifics. There may be concerns in that regard. My understanding at the moment, though is that the focus is on a foreign government being involved through massive manipulation of the media. No specifics, but we know who the foreign government would be.'

The President stayed quiet. He was contemplating the implications. And he knew Marshall needed to vent.

The Deputy Director continued, 'The focus of the investigation is not really the issue. In fact, if there was any foreign involvement, I completely agree it should be investigated and dealt with. I'm sure you feel the same. But by the right agencies and in a rightful manner. My concern is that my agency should not be involved. At all. I have shown you in the past where they have clearly overstepped. They seem to think they answer only to themselves. Now that you are President I wanted to bring this to you and have them brought to bear. Enough is enough.'

The President looked at Marshall, who was still yet to make eye contact, 'What are you suggesting I should do Robert? I mean this is your agency. You're a Deputy Director. Are they not doing their job if they suspect foreign intervention? Do they have any proof of illegal behaviour?'

He took a long pull from his glass.

Chapter 9

STAYING CALM AND considered on the outside the President was feeling decidedly unsettled. This is not the conversation he thought he'd be having tonight. Just months into his Presidency and if Marshall had good intel, the CIA and god knows who else was investigating its legitimacy.

Marshall finally looked up, 'Nothing I give to you can come back to me. You need to promise me you'll be subtle in using this information. I've been confidentially briefed.' He waited for Charleston to speak. He only received a slight nod.

Marshal continued, 'Apparently the Cambridge Analytica whistleblower from the 2016 campaign, an online hacker named Thomas Brendt has been in contact with an influential political blogger. Brendt has been providing the blogger with information about the 2020 campaign - indicating that, like 2016, it too was corrupted. What Brendt doesn't know - what nobody knows is that this blogger is a source for the CIA.'

He paused and took a small sip from his tumbler. 'However, I really think that is beside the point. The point to me is the CIA - led by that bitch, is acting on American soil. If you were to put Kristen Thomas on the spot she would either have to admit to the investigation or lie to you. The President. That would be grounds for dismissal.'

'Whoa, there Robert. You and I both want change at the top but we can't go in guns blazing without thinking this through and having a clear plan. They are, by profession, the very best at covering their tracks.'

Marshall was unrepentant, 'Sir - it's time to make the change we've talked about at the top of the CIA. There is no oversight. No accountability. And no adherence to the chain of command. It's untenable. They use terrorism and national security to justify the means. Any action they want to take. This is just the latest in a long procession of activities that are borderline illegal. And this time they might be coming after you!'

The President considered the man across the room, 'Robert, you know I agree with you - we've discussed this many times. It is well overdue. And I want you running the CIA. But the timing and the optics of the change need to be properly managed. If I sack the Director while she is investigating foreign political terrorist activity on American soil, it won't wash. People will think I've got something to hide, that I'm in bed with the Russians or the Chinese or whoever else it might be. It will destabilise my Presidency as it will whoever is appointed to replace the Director.'

'Ah fuck James. That's all politics. We need the CIA run the right way. And fuck what the public thinks and fuck the optics! You're in charge now. It's been months. You need to make it happen!' Marshall was getting a real head of steam going.

Charleston felt his own blood begin to boil and fought to ensure he gave nothing away. This do-gooder prick sitting in his house was telling him what he should be doing. He was the fucking President! And at the same time denigrating politics! This Boy Scout was as political as anyone - trying to leverage his way into the Director's chair. He drew a deep breath and contemplated his bourbon as he assembled his thoughts. The frustration from Marshall was palpable. And he knew that the Deputy Director felt this was his time. Self-interest as always the most powerful force in Washington. But Charleston had to be smart about this. And get better intel.

Charleston focussed on managing the conversation and keeping his expression and tone even and reasonable. Inside he was anything but. Marshall was annoying but he could be managed. The bigger issue was the idea of the CIA and who knows who else sticking their nose in. The last thing he needed as he settled into his Presidency was an investigation into how he got here and who may have been involved. This had disaster written all over it. It would bring into question every decision he had made. And it would shut down any prospect of a second term.

Forget the CIA, if the media got onto this and made the connection of foreign governments helping him get elected it would be game over. The feeding frenzy would be unstoppable. Of course, they'd used some pretty grey tactics in the election. It was part of the way the game was played now. Everyone did it. But even he wasn't sure how much of his election win was due to outside help. Mainly because he didn't want to know.

They had set up degrees of separation and everything had been coordinated and run by his Chief of Strategy. And they had literally limitless and hidden funding from the South African Hanse Kallis.

Charleston didn't really understand how it worked. He just knew that voters were influenced by what they saw and read and heard. Particularly if people they respected were visible advocates. Influencers!! Charleston thought of it conveniently as the evolution of campaign marketing. Hanse in South Africa was the cutout. Offshore and off the radar. And Charleston never spoke with him directly about the election. He had others that were hands-on. And who would take the fall if the shit hit the proverbial.

But if the CIA got rolling and started to uncover illegal activity and foreign connections he would at best be tainted by the association and at worst...well, he didn't want to contemplate that. He needed to shut off this rabbit hole the CIA was going down and stop them before they found something.

For now, he needed to play along. He didn't want Marshall to think he was concerned about an investigation into the election.

'Robert, thank you for bringing this to me. I am going to give it some thought and I will ensure action is taken. It is just another nail in Kristen Thomas' coffin. Let her chase shadows. There is nothing there! The sooner I get you in charge the better. Now - another drink. You're a Red Skins fan, aren't you? I can't stand their new name. The world is mad. I'll have to get

Mary and yourself along to a game. Guest of the President. Makes the hot dogs taste so much better...'

After another thirty minutes of Marshall bending his ear about the corruption of the CIA and the broader American democracy, the Deputy Director finally took his leave.

Charleston picked up from underneath a discreet side table the Nokia burner phone that had been connected the entire time and pressed it to his ear

'Daniel. Are you still on the phone? Did you hear all that?'

'I did Mr President.'

'Meet me at the house in Georgetown.'

'I'm already on my way.'

Fuck. Thought Charleston - his carefully planned evening had just gone pear-shaped.

Chapter 10

ALEX WARD WALKED into her bedroom catching the view on display through the full-height window overlooking the ocean off Avalon beach. Barefoot and still dressed in her running top and shorts, she had a bottle of water in one hand and her phone in the other. She tapped the screen and soft music started playing from recessed speakers. Distractedly scrolling on her phone, she kept walking to the bathroom, flicked on the light and turned on the shower.

The man from the silver sedan now faced a dilemma. Having 'let himself in' to Ward's home through the bedroom verandah, he could either make his move now or after her shower. From his vantage point in the bedroom's walk-in closet, he could only see one corner of the bathroom. He tried to improve his angle and only succeeded in whacking his head painfully on the wardrobe rail. He stifled the noise that threatened to escape as he rubbed his head.

A flash of skin appeared as Ward threw her tank top and sports bra at the basket. Decision made. Let the girl shower. She'd likely drop her guard in the sanctity of the bathroom. He caught a glimpse of a finely muscled back and highly defined rear end as she crossed the bathroom. The rest of her clothes were dropped on the floor and he heard her open the shower door to get under the water. He tried to improve his angle and hit his head again. He pushed back further into the walk-in closet and closed his eyes. The tanned skin, soft music and running water had him a little distracted.

He was brought back into clear focus when the sharp edge of a knife blade pushed painfully into his throat and water dripped down onto his boots. Or maybe that was his blood.

'Hello Mack. Fancy seeing you here. In my bedroom. Watching me take a shower. Is this how you get your kicks now?'

Mack Stewart was simultaneously pissed off and pleased. Pissed that he'd been caught off guard. Pleased that she had gotten the better of him. He'd thought 15 months out of the game may have her losing her edge. He wondered when she'd made him. He'd seen, in sharp relief, how she'd kept in shape. Perhaps in better shape than she had been at the agency. And clearly, her skills were still there. It was a good start. Though the blade was cutting painfully into his skin. Actually, he was mostly pissed.

Mack reciprocated and pushed his own knife softly into the bare, wet, stomach behind him.

'I thought you might have gotten soft in the last year Alex. You're anything but!'

He started to move his head to look back at her.

'Keep moving your head and this knife will give you a new airway.'

'Hey - I'm only here to talk.'

'Seems you were doing more looking than talking. People who just want to talk use a phone. Or knock on the front door.'

'Are you naked?' he asked making another effort at turning. He flinched as she pressed the knife a little harder. That one must have drawn blood.

'Why are you in my house, Mack? Breaking in and hiding in my wardrobe would suggest this is not a social visit. And make it very quick. I'm retired, I'm wet, and my dinner is nearly ready.'

'Wardrobe?' he mimicked.

'It's Australian for closet. Now - talk Mack.'

He took his blade away and she did the same. Though he thought the better of stealing a look down.

'Sure you don't you want to finish your shower first?'

Chapter 11

SURREPTITIOUSLY REMOVING A tiny wireless bud from his ear, Daniel Walker, Chief of Strategy for President James Charleston had been killing two birds with one stone. Simultaneously enjoying a cozy and potentially intimate dinner with Susan Simon, a wealthy widow who had become a mega-donor to their campaign, he was also listening to the President's meeting with the Deputy Director. And the latter was causing him to do a poor job of the former. The meeting he was listening to had completely distracted him, taking all of his attention. What he presumed was a typical play for the Director's job from that bore Marshall had taken a turn and unexpectedly dropped a grenade into Walker's world.

Walker now needed to extricate himself and orchestrate his exit. While he was happy to date as many beautiful women as he could, this one was a direct favour to the President and the campaign. He was taking one for the team. Which, he thought as he was preparing for the evening, was likely to result in him giving one for the team!

He'd been asked to show flattering interest in the middle-aged cougar-esque widow as a payback for funding and favours she'd provided to the President. Susan Simon had made some large contributions and organised several fundraising events. More importantly, she was on several big US-based pharmaceutical boards - positions inherited from her dead husband's substantial share ownership. Through her connections in big Pharma, Charleston had pressed Susan to get their South African benefactor Hanse Kallis lucrative contracts with both private and government accounts amplifying even further, Hanse's massive and highly profitable involvement in combatting the ever-growing pandemic.

Apparently, one good deed deserves another. And it was looking to Daniel a lot like he'd be doing the deed.

He'd expected he would only be tuned into the President's meeting for a few minutes to get the gist of the Boy Scout DD's current gripe and then focus his attention properly on the night ahead.

Sitting on the couch in Susan Simon's massive lounge, Daniel absently reflected that over the last few months, he and the President had settled comfortably into office and hadn't given the campaign a second thought. Once they won the election he'd felt supremely confident that their strategy of fake news and misdirection had evidently been lost in the sheer mass of mass media that surrounded presidential campaigns. They'd gotten away with it. And they'd won!

Walker and Charleston had seen how effective an orchestrated 'news' campaign could be in 2016 when the Senator engaged Cambridge Analytica and was re-elected against the odds and in defiance of the polls. When he'd decided to become a Presidential candidate they knew this had to be a key part of their strategy. And like 2016 they could neither do it alone nor with direct involvement. To become President would require a massive concerted, coordinated and costly effort.

In 2016 the strategy had been to use fake news and media manipulation to divide the populace and to present themselves as the answer. And it had exploded. Fake news was everywhere. It was new and it was well done. No one could tell fake from real. At least not the people who wanted to believe what they saw and heard. Then all sorts of allegations of Russian and foreign involvement started to get traction. But it was so murky and grey that it was impossible to know what was real and what wasn't - and who were the authors. Even when the Cambridge Analytica scandal broke the public struggled to understand what was happening or join the dots.

Daniel Walker and James Charleston figured the same would happen for the 2020 Presidential campaign. Controlling the narrative, controlling the stories people would see and believe and controlling how their opponents were regarded, would be integral to getting into the White House. There was no way they could rely on the Fourth Estate to present them in the way they needed. So when Hanse Kallis had come back to them and promised an invisible hand they had grabbed it. The CIA starting an investigation was a real problem. They needed to shut that down before it got anywhere.

'Fuck!' he muttered out loud.

Chapter 12

SUSAN SIMON STOPPED talking and was now staring at Walker. How long had she been looking at him? They were entwined on the luxuriously soft sofa in her Georgetown apartment. Housed in a beautiful, historic building, she'd had the apartment completely gutted and renovated while her husband was still alive. She'd married well. An incredibly wealthy older chap with a bad ticker. Now widowed, filthy rich and still in her early forties, she was determined to have fun and make up for lost time.

Simon had created a stunning open plan first floor which she'd shown Walker when he arrived. The bedrooms were upstairs. He figured that tour was to come later. They'd just finished dinner - which he was certain she'd had prepared by someone else. And they had been on the lounge for some time in front of an open fire enjoying a beautiful Californian Pinot. She owned the vineyard.

Simon had given up on trying to get the President to her apartment and had changed focus to the youthful, single and good-looking Chief of Strategy. She had invited Walker for a private dinner - ostensibly to discuss the President helping her with her charities. Walker had been flirting with her for months hoping to increase her support. It was an old game - but one that was still played in this town. They both needed each other. She wanted to be seen to be in the President's circle. It would elevate her social position and ensure invitations to her events were the most desired in town. Walker and Charleston wanted her money. And her access.

She prodded him with her bare foot, 'Hi there - did you just say something? Are you still with me or am I boring you?'

He needed to recover fast and minimise the damage. And then get out of here. There was work to do.

'Oh, not at all Susan. In fact, quite the opposite. I was thinking about how perfect this night is. I'm more relaxed than I've been for a long time. I haven't had a night off since before the election and definitely not in such beautiful company. Please don't mistake my relaxed state for boredom! Thank you. Tonight has been just what I need.'

She considered him for a moment, he was young and college boy good looking. Just what she needed! 'You lie easily. You're in the right job!'

'Seriously, Susan. This evening has been wonderful. I'd like time to slow down and the night not to end.'

She was sitting close on the sofa and had turned towards him, still holding her wine glass. She smelt wonderful and the silky blue slip of a dress was riding high on her bare legs. She was in better shape than most of the young interns he had churned through at the Senator's office.

She leaned into him and kissed him deeply.

Walker knew that if this went on any longer he'd have to take her to bed. No real hardship there. She spent her days at the yoga studio and her nights not eating. And he'd known the bedroom was where this night would likely end up. But he now had other priorities. Extending the deep kiss, he surreptitiously hit a preset number on his phone and moments later his pager went off in his jacket slung over the back of a dining chair. Breaking the moment she looked over at his buzzing jacket.

'What is that?'

'Oh God. Sorry. It's my pager. Only the President has the number.'

'A pager. How very 1990.'

'He insists - I have to be contactable at any time. He doesn't like that cell phones can be turned off. Let me see what he wants and I'll get rid of him. Stay right where you are.'

Walker got up and glanced at his pager.

'Fuck! Oh Susan, I'm so sorry. Apparently, he has something that can't wait. He wants to meet. Pronto. I'm going to have to take a rain check?'

She looked at him for a long moment. 'Sure.' She responded, 'I'll call you.'

That was a cold dismissal! Damn - she was too important. He'd have to make this up. He made a mental note to get one of the secretaries to organise flowers first thing in the morning.

He needed to get to the President. And he had a call to make on the way. This CIA problem had to be shut down. Now...

Chapter 13

DAVID MITCHELL PUT the dinner he was preparing on hold.

Mack Stewart, his wife's CIA recruiter, previous boss and mentor had appeared with Alex from upstairs a few moments ago and was now sitting at the counter in the kitchen. Seeing Mack had thrown him. He thought he'd seen the last of these people. Yet here he was in his house in the northern beaches of Sydney, thousands of kilometres from the US and Langley. This couldn't be good. Alex looked steamed.

He knew Mack pretty well and actually liked him. They had a common interest in Alex and a somewhat unorthodox relationship. Not by the CIA book. Mack had always found a way to quietly let David know Alex was OK when on assignments. No doubt breaching strict CIA protocol. Mack hid a driven and laser focus with a light-hearted veneer. David also suspected Mack was a little in love with Alex. But he was more of a father figure for Alex and their banter hid their mutual respect and complete professionalism. David knew he was CIA Director Kristen Thomas' most trusted operator. Smart and able to adapt, he was her eyes and ears, despite getting on a bit for a field agent.

David had always respected and believed in the work Alex was involved in. Though he hated the risk and not knowing where she was or when he'd see her, he also knew it was fundamental to her. She had already been recruited by the CIA when they had met in college, though it had taken him a long time to find that out. And until fairly recently her job was the most important thing in her life. He had always appreciated the small circle of people who were truly looking out for her.

He felt dread and his anger rising at the thought that these people were back in their lives. And that inevitably they would want something from Alex. Something that would very likely put her at risk. He also knew Mack would say nothing of substance in front of him. He'd have to make himself scarce and catch up with Alex later.

David looked across at his wife, 'This dinner really needs a nice Riesling. I'm going to walk down to the bottle shop. Back soon.

Chapter 14

THOMAS BRENDT PULLED on his Canada Goose Black Label Wedgemount Parka. Warm and slim fitting it was snug against his lean cyclist's frame. It was in the mid thirties with a freezing wind and misty drizzle in DC. He had checked the weather app earlier that morning and meticulously selected his outfit for the day ahead. A light black Reiss knit sat over black woollen pants, finished with understated Grenson Bobby boots. Zipping his jacket, he set the security alarm of his Navy Yard loft apartment and checked the Arlo security app to ensure the camera feed was working. He headed out of his building and towards his dinner venue on foot, pushing himself further into his coat against the cold.

A creature of habit he was both a food and coffee purist. His walks to The Insider were a pleasure and a daily - generally twice-daily ritual regardless of the weather. The Insider opened early and closed late. It wasn't the closest place to get a meal or coffee but it was the best. The chefs had been employed from a buzzing cafe in London and offered a progressive and mouth-watering menu. The two young baristas who shared running the place in morning and evening shifts were obsessed with finding and sourcing the most exquisite beans. And Thomas was obsessed with the best. Of everything. On a cold night like this, the air seemed to hold and accentuate and he thought he could smell the aromas from the kitchen still a block or more down the street.

The cold air filled his lungs and with Covid restrictions currently relaxed he enjoyed the small freedom of not wearing a fitted mask against the virus. It was past the evening peak when he arrived. He found one of his favourite spots on a bench seat against the wall looking through the glass as this buzzing corner of Washington seemed to fuse with the night.

He didn't need to order. Nikki working behind the LaMarzocco four group espresso machine had seen him arrive and was already preparing his ristretto. And she will have ordered him the evening pasta special. Brendt opened his MacBook to continue the work he'd started early that morning and had been focussed on most of the day. Smart to the point of genius and with quirks that betrayed his place somewhere on the spectrum he was happiest with the familiar. He rarely strayed from his routine. Brendt quickly became immersed in his online world, unaware he was at that moment, a person of interest.

Eyes discreetly watched as his coffee was placed before him and he took the first delicious sip.

Chapter 15

WARD STOOD ACROSS the kitchen bench from Mack. Waiting for him to speak. Theirs was a long and intense history. And a purely professional one. Mack had recruited Alex to the CIA years ago out of college. She was an ideal candidate. Super smart and a natural athlete she was already multi-lingual from her part Asian mother. They'd found she picked up languages easily and with the subtle mixture of her racial heritage could pass for several ethnic backgrounds.

Her dad had been part of the NYPD and having seen people at their worst, wanted to ensure his daughter could look after herself. She had revelled in the discipline of Tae Kwon Do and was a gifted and relentless distance runner. Ward had been offered several college scholarships on their various athletic programs and could turn her hand to most sports and excel. Talent and a highly competitive nature were amplified by her focus. She was fierce. Driven and determined. And this was the bit that made her truly appealing to the CIA. She was motivated.

Ward was just eight years old when 9/11 happened. Her dad was a first responder. He had run into the South Tower as others were running out. Like so many on that day, he was never seen again. They'd not even found his uniform or his badge. Nothing. He'd vanished. That's a lot for a young person to handle. The CIA had long valued the association between a traumatised youth and amplified determination. It was a combination the psych's at the agency found the most effective in their field agents. A combination their recruiters actively looked for in finding new talent.

Her fire was fueled almost equally by wanting to make her dad proud and by the unabated hatred she had for those who had taken him away. She had become single-minded in proving herself - to rise above those that had robbed her of her father and her childhood. She sympathised and identified with those that had also suffered on that day through the loss of loved ones. It had become her obsession. Researching and delving into the history of terrorism and its fanatical leaders. She was sickened by their ability to twist religion and history to brainwash and inflame their people against a common and often fictionalised enemy.

She was manna from CIA heaven.

Chapter 16

FOR A WHILE as a firebrand undergrad, Ward had become outspoken towards those that defended terrorism, sympathised with their plight or suggested the perpetrators be protected by the laws of the country they wanted to destroy. It had at times caused her to get into some intense arguments. At some point, she had tired of the ineffectual and incessant debating, deciding that rather than bring attention to herself she'd hold her views tightly.

But inside she never wavered. And she had been noticed.

Mack knew that Ward had had her demons when he recruited her. It was one of the reasons she was a compelling candidate. Her motivations were pure and her resolve was unrelenting. But he knew it was a balancing act. People like Ward could easily get out of control and misdirect their anger and intensity. Usurp authority, or develop issues. The line was not clear and crossing it was an easy step and a journey often without return. As he got to know her, his fears of her going off the rails subsided. She never lost her cool or her focus. She was fucking smart. He came to appreciate her resilience as much as her judgment. His real concern was how hard she pushed herself and the danger she was willing to confront. He had regularly witnessed actions from Ward that suggested she had no fear and a dangerous disregard for her own safety.

Mack applied his own rudimentary psychology to Alex and figured the memory of her dad and the vision of others like him running toward danger was deeply embedded into her DNA. A mother that had raised two strong and high-achieving girls on her own was a powerhouse with rock-solid values. The manifestation of both parents and of devastating circumstances was incredible.

As an agent, Ward always went forward. Never took a backward step. Attack was always her defense. She was relentless, she was fearless and she showed absolutely no mercy for those she considered the enemy of her country and more importantly who did not abide by her own beliefs on what was right and what was not. Variously underestimated or dismissed as a slight and pretty young thing she had been extremely effective. They knew they had lost a special talent and a special person when she left the CIA. But she had good reason. David had been diagnosed with a rare blood cancer and she wanted to be with him for every step of his treatment.

And now, Mack thought, here he was - tasked to bring her back. He'd resisted this assignment. Pushing Kristen for another approach. Partly because he thought Alex deserved the happiness she'd found. Mostly because he thought it was overkill and that they could handle this with their agents in house. But the boss had been persuasive. She had to have someone she could trust. Someone who wasn't on anyone's radar. And given what was at stake, Mack succumbed to the view that the boss was right.

Chapter 17

'TALK MACK. WHY are you here? No offence, but I'd be surprised if your visit is good for me. And why not the front door. Pretty peaceful around here. Not much need for subterfuge.'

Mack looked across at Ward as he took a long drink from the 'stubby' of beer she'd given him. 'Well to be honest I didn't want anyone to see me or know you'd had a visitor. And I wanted to see whether you were still aware and sharp.'

'Fuck off Mack. I stopped trying to impress you years ago. You might want to focus more on your own awareness. You seemed pretty distracted until my knife touched your turkey skin neck.'

Mack subconsciously stroked under his chin, 'Well regardless, you've passed so far. You actually look in better shape than ever!'

'Get to the point'

'Got another beer?'

Ward opened the fridge and threw a local icy Stone and Wood Pacific Ale to Mack and opened one herself.

Mack continued, 'Kristen sent me. She wants you back. Actually, we need you back. Temporary assignment.'

'Nothing is temporary with you or Kristen. In fact, it can often be very permanent. I'm pretty happy here Mack. Beach is down the road. Weather is awesome. David is making real progress. And no one has shot at me for over a year.'

Mack ignored the deflection, 'You're one of the smartest people I know. You've already figured I wouldn't be here on a speculator. This is big. We have a situation that runs to the heart of the country and the agency.'

Ward wasn't going to make it easy 'I know you're here for reasons that must be important and you're going to tell me all about. When you get to the point. Eventually. And I appreciate you telling me I'm top of the list because you trust me and I'm the smartest person you know...'

'Not what I said at ...'

'But Mack this is my home now and my priorities are here with David.'

He looked straight at her for a moment, his demeanour intensifying,

'We believe the President of the United States was corruptly elected. That he and his team worked with foreign countries - Russia to be precise - to manipulate and destabilise mainstream and social media. Effectively an orchestrated and wide-reaching Fake News campaign. At a massive scale. It divided people, it presented countless, blatant lies and completely fabricated stories, changing the outcome across numerous contests.'

He continued; 'The implications are beyond quantifying. The elected President is not of the people, by the people. He is there because another country - one run by a tyrant and not with our best interests at heart - put him there. The ripple through the constituency and legitimacy of both houses is unknown. We are at risk of not running our own country. Of favours owed, representatives compromised and strings being pulled from elsewhere. Russia is run by a madman and he may have installed a puppet in the Whitehouse. If it's true this will be catastrophic. It's an act of terrorism by the Russians. And it makes us compromised at the highest level.'

Ward put her bottle on the bench top, 'Quite the speech - not one to undersell are you, Mack...'

Mack went on without missing a beat, 'Social, mainstream and digital media were hacked and manipulated. Fake News became a buzzword during the campaign. The Russians were pulling the strings and paying for everything.'

Ward was starting to feel compromised. She told herself almost daily that her life here was good. Perfect. But deep in her DNA was the desire to serve. And to stop anyone that threatened what she fiercely believed in. Mack's speech was already poking the embers. She needed to shut this down.

'So - we got caught with our pants down. Seems to me it's happened before. Every election is a variation of manipulation. What is that to do with me? If this has happened wouldn't every agency be investigating this?'

Mack raised his intensity, 'It's a mess and a nightmare to trace. A small digital team can be located almost anywhere in the world and influence the public, plant fake stories and create fake news to divide and disrupt. Once they get it rolling others pile on and do their work for them. It builds its own momentum and it can be impossible to determine what's true and what's not or how to shut it down. It goes to the heart of our political integrity. It's the 21st-century online version of having our borders invaded.'

Ward interrupted, 'Surely this is on every acronym's agenda to sort out? FBI, DEA, CIA, the works...They all live for this stuff. You can't need me for this!' Alex said.

Mack responded, 'Terrorism is the CIA's wheelhouse. And this is terrorism.' He paused and took another pull on his beer. 'So far we are keeping our fears and the investigation very tight and very quiet. The CIA is leaking. Badly. We can't trust our own organisation. We must assume the leak runs to the White House and ultimately Moscow. If the investigation becomes known and those assisting us are identified, there will be targets on people's backs. The biggest possible stakes are in play. We have to compartmentalise. And we have to work fast.'

Chapter 18

ALEX WARD HAD zoned out, lost in her own thoughts. This was exactly why she had joined the CIA after college. To stop selfish pricks, terrorists and other countries trying to take what they had. Tyrannical leaders and governments with horrific agendas motivated by misplaced vendettas, or ego, or greed. Robbing average Americans of their right to live a free life. But she'd moved on. And out. Hadn't she? It was time for others to do the heavy lifting.

And to be the blunt instrument.

She refocused on Mack buying time to think, 'Bit late isn't it? The election is done. The new President is in the White House?'

Mack drained his beer and held the empty up prompting another one.

Ward raised her eyes, 'Might want to slow down a little there Cowboy. I've seen your silver ride out the front. Wouldn't want the local police to cuff an undercover agent driving over the limit!'

Mack held back a smile - so she'd made him that early! Even noticed the car. She really didn't miss anything. Still, the shower scene had been tasty!

He continued his pitch, 'People are pretty raw at the moment.'

'People?'

'The American people. The pandemic has them more uncertain than ever. About their country, their own jobs and incomes, their health and their future. Anxiety levels are through the roof. Drug and alcohol consumption is higher than ever. Domestic violence and relationship breakdowns are spiking. Getting in to see a therapist is a six-month wait. The place is a tinder box. It's ripe for un-friendlies to grab their opportunity. If we have a compromised President that owes them, or worse - is one of them - and opens our front door, the place could completely implode.' Ward passed him another beer. 'So sort it out. Get all those clever people and toys and weapons and fix it. If you know it's happened and the consequences are enormous, get it done.'

'Spoken like a true academic.' Mack retorted, taking a jibe at her post-agency career. 'Unfortunately, we're not there yet. We know it's happened but we don't know by who...'

'Whom!' she corrected.

'Fuck off. And if we use our internal teams we will tip them off. Somebody, maybe more than one person - is leaking at the CIA. We need to be surgical. We need to be fast. And we need the solution to be permanent.'

Mack made his final play, 'You're a geopolitical expert. Your new job is to lecture in geo politics so you are more current than ever. You know the implications. You're highly trained and from what I've seen still very capable. And you're off the radar. Nobody is watching you anymore. You retired and went away. You're not one of us anymore and that is what we need. Kristen trusts you. I trust you. The stakes are as big as they get.'

Ward met his intensity 'Now we're getting to the true story. You want someone that won't come back on the agency!'

Mack responded; 'No - we want someone invisible, completely committed and that we know will get the job done. Whatever 'the job' is. Just the way you like it. No cover and no rules.' Mack caught himself, 'Within reason. This is important Alex. This is terrorism happening in our country - your country - right now. We may have a President only in office because he sold himself to our enemies. The downside is beyond thinking about.'

Mack watched Ward for a few moments. He'd gotten to her. He knew he would. And so did Ward. This was fundamental to what drove her. She couldn't stand the idea of bad people winning and running over unassuming Americans. The idea that they couldn't trust the leaders they had elected. Or of their security systems and agencies failing. Bono had once said America 'is an idea' and the idea that was America was deep in her. And the people that she most identified with - the salt of the earth, hard-working, tax-paying and contributing families - like her own mother and father - were the people she wanted to protect and ensure could still raise their kids and chase their dreams.

Mack could see the emotions play across her face. And the tightened expression as she came to the inevitable decision. He was both pleased and saddened. Pleased because he needed her. Saddened because she was happy here and he had just blown that apart.

'You may want to let David know.' Mack suggested before she'd even spoken her thoughts.

'No need. I'm here and I heard.' David said.

Mack looked across the kitchen bench to the doorway where David now stood, 'I thought you were getting wine...'

'You seemed more like a beer man! Did you leave me any?'

Ward could see David's expression was bleak despite his lighthearted comments. He looked pale.

'Did you hear everything?' asked Mack

'Most of it, I was checking no one else was out there - either more of you, or that you'd been followed.'

Mack looked at him clearly offended at either option, 'There is no one else...'

But David Mitchell was no longer listening - he was looking at his wife.

Chapter 19

HALF A WORLD away from the tense conversation in Avalon, HANSE KALLIS was at his residence within the wildlife sanctuary he'd created in the Savannah region of his home country, South Africa. Contemplating the state visit of his friend and now President James Charleston. The Presidential visit would be the cherry on the pinnacle of his life's work.

Now a white-haired, tanned and weather-lined gentleman in what was likely his final decade, Kallis was the notional head of JHK International, the pharmaceutical business his grandfather had started. Encompassing a range of oncology, therapeutic and viral medicine, he'd built into a global and successful multinational over several decades. Kallis had been running the business during its most successful era and had created a massive, privately owned and diverse organisation.

Along the way, the company acquired a small offshoot business specialising in delivery systems for medication. And then the pandemic hit. And the requirements for safe, fast, low-cost syringes and applicators to vaccinate had exploded. It was unprecedented. The world was unprepared for the pandemic and every country was scrambling. Kallis had understood early that the coronavirus was a much bigger problem than most thought. Typical of the vision that had fuelled a lifetime of success he had backed his judgment and moved to scale the syringe business immediately. It had been a commercial masterstroke and had fuelled even greater growth - and profitability.

And it had presented him the opportunity he had been waiting for.

Now in his eighties and while still physically vital and mentally sharp, he had decided to pass the day-to-day operations to his daughter Meagan some years ago and she was succeeding beyond his expectations. He really shouldn't have been surprised. Meagan inherited the best of both himself and his now departed wife. The transition allowed him to focus on his true passion and what would become his legacy.

Chapter 20

FOR MOST PEOPLE, a large and largely happy family, a global and growing business, immense wealth and his personal contribution to restoring Africa's wildlife would be enough. Beyond their wildest dreams in fact. But Kallis had bigger plans.

Through the experience of his own eighty plus years and the history and heritage of his family, he knew firsthand the incredible detrimental changes the world had gone through and continued to go through at an ever-increasing rate. The stunning and abundant African habitat of just a generation or two ago was massively depleted. It was a sick and miserable result of man's ignorance and self-importance. He had witnessed firsthand the degradation within his own country. And he was seeing exponential devastation beyond the borders of his beloved Africa, across the globe. Unfortunately, all the signs for the future were pointing one way.

He had become one of the world's leading environmentalists and humanitarians, determined to use the time he had left and his immense wealth to bring real change. Generational change. It was his abiding goal and singular focus to properly kickstart restoring the world's environment back to the beauty he knew it could be. He took this on because nobody else was. He was sick of waiting.

Politicians talked a big game but did almost nothing. Often worse than nothing. Their only objective was popular appeal. And the changes needed to the way we live to reverse the damage were anything but popular. Certainly, the idea of helping the environment and the rhetoric it generated appealed to the masses. It appeased their collective conscience. And the world leaders all eagerly signed up to protocols and new emissions and restoration targets while the media filmed their staged ceremonies.

But the reality - the changes they would be required to make and the way their people would need to live to really make any difference was beyond the displacement they were willing to contemplate. It was a short-sighted and completely self-serving attitude. The fact that politicians made wide-reaching commitments on behalf of their country and then promptly did nothing to achieve them was, to Kallis, worse than doing nothing in the first place.

He had spent too long arguing and lobbying and cajoling for better. Early on, with the ignorant positivity of the zealot he had thought the words and commitments of governments and organisations were honest and real. But over time, through disappointment after disappointment, realism had been beaten deeply into him. The endless committees, debates and resolutions meant nothing. And changed nothing. He had invested in these people. With his time, his voice and his money. For no result. The world had not even stabilised. It continued to go backward.

A slowly growing cohort of scientists and independent organisations thought the destruction to our planet and our atmosphere caused by man's plunder and indulgent lifestyle was now beyond any ability to stabilise and reverse. That the damage was done. That we were heading for a multitude of disasters. Hanse Kallis agreed with them. The four horseman writ large.

Kallis believed COVID-19 was just another symptom of a sick planet - one so depleted and so affected, it couldn't fight anymore.

Despite the woeful history, the unrelenting trajectory and the depressing predictions, he remained hopeful that something could be done and retained the most burning and determined desire to restore the planet to a more balanced natural state.

He was determined to put a stop to the destruction. To make the necessary changes. To not just leave it to Mother Nature to sort out mankind's mistakes. It was a determination that had been building for years. A determination galvanised with each false promise and each ineffectual 'leader'. He knew these were not small changes. Would not be tolerable to most and would need a seismic shift from government and industry. To make the commitments stick would require the right leadership in place in the biggest economies.

He abhorred the world his children and grandchildren now lived in. And he feared for those not yet born. He pitied the unfortunate souls in underdeveloped countries living day to day, so focussed on their own survival they could not consider the bigger picture. He didn't blame them. But he did blame and he despised those that lived comfortably and in relative or real luxury. Those in the wealthier countries. These people should see that their environment was degrading and disintegrating before their eyes. And do something. Force their leaders to act. Or elect those who will. Because the numbers didn't lie. The current rate of ecological change and decline would see a world of hardship, intolerance and instability in just a handful of years. These people - our political leaders and those running the economy were too comfortable. Too soft. And too compromised.

So - he was taking it upon himself. And he had a plan.

Kallis had immense means but relatively little time. So he was willing to ignore convention and the laws that had served his country and others so poorly. And pay almost any price to force the changes needed. Manipulating elections and politicians and upending governments was a price he was very willing to pay. He wanted people in the biggest jobs to owe him. Actually, he wanted to own them. To ensure they were so completely compromised they would do what he instructed - what needed to be done. The picture he saw was much bigger than one government, one state or one country.

Chapter 21

FOR KALLIS, THE recent US election and appointment of James Charleston had been critical. He had worked tirelessly and spent massively to put in place a President that owed him. A lifetime spent cutting deals had equipped him with enough psychology and insight to know what makes people tick. He had used this to leverage Russia into applying its resources and influence to join him in getting the right candidate elected. Kallis and the faceless men in Moscow had agendas well served by a favourable US President.

Getting the Russians on board had been easier than he'd thought. The collective resource, technology, and, at times, blunt force that they brought to bear had worked. Now, he needed to keep Charleston in place long enough and with the proper focus to get done what he needed done. The world's largest economy and most influential country was critical to his environmental agenda. And he was just days away from taking a massive step forward.

The remote location of Kallis' Wildlife Park and the sweeping open vista that seemed to go forever were juxtaposed by some of the most advanced communications tech available. Disconnected but completely connected. It was where he could free himself to think, focus, and plan.

He was in his office. A massive room decorated in tasteful African style. He was putting the finishing touches to a multi-nation and multi-corporate two-day forum he was hosting commencing this Saturday and concluding Sunday.

The Global Intervention Initiative. Another forum, another talk fest by the talking heads. But this one was different. This time, the commitment would be real.

His private mobile phone buzzed. His American President was calling...

Chapter 22

WITH THE SOFT top down, Daniel Walker drove his BMW the short distance to the President's private residence. Fast. The cold Washington night was no place for a convertible. He'd driven it to Susan's place when the sun had been out and his ego needed air. Now, he was freezing and getting colder by the second. At least it was sobering him up. Getting him focussed. He knew the President would be working himself into a state. Charleston had initially resisted getting into bed with the Russians to 'support' his election. But Walker and Kallis had convinced him he was unlikely to win. Charleston's perception of his own popular appeal was highly inflated. And he had quite a few skeletons in quite a few closets.

With Walker running point on the campaign strategy and everything being managed offshore through Kallis, Walker had been entirely confident they were beyond challenge or suspicion.

But somebody had talked - at least enough to initiate what Walker thought was an unsubstantiated and possibly illegal fishing expedition by the CIA. The Agency was inherently suspicious - it was their job to be suspicious. So they were pretty happy to go looking under stones - particularly if someone showed them which stone. The problem was, legal or not, having the CIA asking questions and running interrogations and interviews would have the President paranoid.

In Walker's view, their best strategy was to ignore it and give it no oxygen. Or, even better, quietly shut down their avenues of inquiry, and they would soon move on. He figured the President could apply his considerable influence to distract the CIA from other areas of national interest.

He just needed to contain the President, get to the bottom of whatever the CIA was looking into, and sort it out.

As he drove, Walker reflected on the Cambridge Analytica scandal in the 2016 campaign and Marshall's mention of Thomas Brendt. During that election, Cambridge Analytica focussed on data harvesting and profiling to target advertising and fake news. It was very effective and the genesis of Walker and Hanse Kallis's strategy for 2020. They had seen how the public could be manipulated. How they could impact individual constituent campaigns and, ultimately, a Presidential election. Walker and Kallis had put together their own strategy. Cambridge Analytica 2.0. They would be a lot smarter and completely invisible. Running everything offshore.

In 2016, Cambridge Analytica was brought down by one of their own –Thomas Brendt. A boy genius coder, he was a rising star within their organisation and instrumental in implementing the whole strategy. Unfortunately, once he realised what he was contributing to, he'd developed a conscience and taken the story to the real media and told them the truth.

Walker knew that while Brendt's information and testimony had brought CA down, Brendt had not been celebrated as a hero of democracy. In fact, quite the opposite - and ultimately, had been entirely disillusioned by the fallback that had come his way. At some point, he'd given up the fight and disappeared. Too bad he'd found a conscience. Unfortunately, it seemed that conscience was still being purged. Brendt was a genius and they could have used him in Charleston's Presidential campaign for 2020.

The Cambridge Analytica scandal had been a real mess and nearly dethroned the then President. Walker was determined that the strategy he and Kallis had implemented would stay forever hidden. He needed to get on top of this CIA investigation. Even if it was just a throw at the dartboard.

He was minutes away from the President's Brownstone. With one hand on the wheel, he took out his burner phone and texted his contact based at the Russian Embassy. He wanted a meeting later tonight, somewhere discreet.

The reply pinged. 'Sorry, Daniel, tonight is not possible. Tomorrow morning is the best I can do. '

Fuck. Russian pricks. They were probably up to their eyeballs in cheap vodka.

'When and where?' he texted back.

Chapter 23

THE SECRET SERVICE detail greeted Walker as he approached the front door. The natural sneak in him hated having a record of their meetings; however, it couldn't be helped, and as the Chief of Strategy, he could always claim legitimate business. They waved him through.

'Daniel - In the study.' The President called.

Was the President slurring his words? He could do without having to handle him half-cut with bourbon. This was important. Managed quickly and well, it would all disappear in a day or two, and they could continue. A President intoxicated and emboldened would make things worse.

Walker was barely through the office entry as the President started his tirade. He quickly closed the thick door.

'What the fuck is the CIA doing taking an interest in some hacker connected to 2016?' Charleston half shouted.

'Mr President - your voice. Have you swept this room?' Walker said, trying to calm the President.

Charleston retorted, 'They wouldn't dare bug the President. '

Walker closed his eyes and consciously breathed in. He knew there were no such boundaries.

Charleston saw his reaction. 'Yes, I've swept it with that fancy device you gave me. Before - and after Marshall left. We're clear.'

He was definitely slurring. 'Still - The Secret Service is just outside.' Walker said.

'Focus Daniel - the CIA is now taking an interest where we don't want it. I'll call Kallis and you need to tell your Russian cronies they need to sort this out. I refuse to have my Presidency fucked over before I've even started.

I know the fucking Ruskies expect me to support them, and if they want my help as President, they need to clean their fucking house.'

Walker had noticed the half-empty bottle of Old Pappy Van Winkle that had fuelled the President's mood. It would do no good to pound the door of the Russian Embassy, albeit metaphorically. The situation called for a subtle hand: quietly closing the CIA inquiry down, raising no suspicion. Walker wanted to keep a working relationship with all parties. After all, there was a second term to consider.

'Mr. President, it's probably a storm in a teacup. The CIA is fishing. Thomas Brendt has nothing to do with us or the election. They clearly have a sniff of something and are just looking in every corner. I'll take care of Brendt. Once he stops feeding information to the CIA, they will lose interest. You need to consider how to re-focus the attention of Langley without raising any suspicion. It may be time to have one of our congressmen or senators start making noises about national intelligence inquires. We need someone favourable at the top of the CIA. And now might be the time to start the burn.'

The President looked at him. Ignoring the prompt to distract and restructure the CIA he asked, 'How will you get Brendt to be quiet?'

Walker grabbed a tumbler and reached for the Van Winkle while answering, 'He's a keyboard warrior. A few words from the right people will see him run off and hide like last time. I'll take care of it.'

Chapter 24

LATER, WITH WALKER gone and alone again in his study, the President checked his watch. It would be morning in South Africa. Kallis should be up. Too bad if he wasn't. If he had to wake Kallis he would. He needed a redundancy. Kallis was his real link to the Russians and he couldn't just rely on Walker to get this done properly.

He hit the preset number on the Nokia burner that Daniel updated every couple of weeks. Kallis answered on the second ring, 'Mr President, an early surprise.'

In fact, it was no surprise at all. Kallis had been alerted by his Russian contact when Walker texted the embassy. The Russians wanted to ensure Charleston was under control. They didn't yet know why Walker wanted to meet, but Kallis was the key to ensuring the President stayed focused, so they'd been in touch.

Daniel Walker was little more than an ineffective errand boy - occasionally useful in his own way. And a soft and easy target to take a fall if needed. For Kallis, having Charleston installed as President had been pivotal to his plans. But he could be a loose cannon. Too much ego and self-importance. Kallis didn't want him to lose focus or to come under scrutiny. There was too much at stake.

Kallis had decided to string him along; 'Are you calling about the Global Intervention Initiative? We're all looking forward to welcoming the President of the United States this weekend to lead our collective voices at the forum. You are personally crucial to our ambitious protocol.'

Kallis knew the buttons to push - it wasn't hard. It was like a big red EGO button on the President's lapel. Importantly, he wanted to ensure this conversation was about more than the President's immediate concern with his reputation. That would all be handled. More important was to ensure he was fully committed to the Initiative and aligned with Kallis' plans.

The President responded, 'Of course, Hanse. You know I'm completely on board. I'm looking forward to it. The Intervening Initiative will be game-changing.'

Kallis interrupted, 'Global Intervention Initiative, Mr President!'

Charleston quickly moved past his annoyance, 'Of course. Sorry. The public lapped it up during the campaign. Americans take the environment seriously these days. And we want to be leaders, not followers like my predecessor.'

Charleston paused, in his own mind frustrated. There was always a game to be played. Fucking greenie billionaire. They were all the same. They locked on to one big legacy project as they approached the end and it became all-consuming. He'd string Kallis along. He'd play the global statesman and sign the protocols. They were inconsequential agreements. Good for the cameras. The US was not going to compromise economic growth the way Kallis' crazy protocol demanded. He wasn't going to be the President that put the country into recession. Hanse had been invaluable through the election. But his ongoing importance was beginning to fade. And he was old. He might not even make another four years. He'd talk to Daniel about doing without him for the second campaign.

Chapter 25

'THANK YOU, JAMES', Kallis could hear the alcohol in the President's voice.

Charleston, barely tolerating the conversation, wanted to get to the point, 'I'll have my people send you a draft of my speech. But I could use your help, Hanse.'

Kallis replied, 'If I can, of course.'

The President continued, 'It seems our CIA is taking an interest in the election campaign. They are getting suspicious to, um...off shore involvement. Or at least that people may have been misled in some way.'

His attempts at subtlety were horribly amateur - unaware of his own fumbling words, Charleston went on,

'They've identified a former Cambridge Analytica hacker talking to some political news blogger. The idiot hacker doesn't realise the blogger is a CIA informant. Unfortunately, this hacker has provided detailed information about our election and is now being watched by the Agency. They are gearing up to initiate an investigation. I need you and our mutual friends to shut this off before it goes anywhere. I can work on it from my end and ensure their focus is elsewhere. But I fucking hate loose ends...'

Kallis wanted to calm the President.

'No one from Cambridge Analytica was involved in the campaign, Mr President. Certainly, not this Thomas Brendt character your Agency is interested in.'

Charleston was always surprised at how informed and across the detail Kallis was - mentioning Brendt should have given the President pause. But he was too impatient to think about it and wanted some action,

'I appreciate that and I know - it's a fishing expedition, but if they link this back to me and this Brendt gives them new information that links in turn to our friends in the East....Well, it's the type of thing the CIA and the FBI and the media take seriously. I really don't want any bumps on the Presidential highway.'

The inebriated Charleston was pleased with himself with that last analogy.

Kallis wanted to see how desperate Charleston was - and perhaps build on his leverage, 'Do you have anything specific you'd like me to do Mr President?'

Charleston quickly replied, 'Oh, I haven't thought that far out. I was hoping you and your friends would handle things quietly and make this problem disappear.'

Kallis figured this would be the response. Charleston had no stomach for the grubby stuff. He always thought he was above it.

'Mr. President, leave this with me. It is a trifling matter. Don't think of it again. Now, let's talk about the weekend. I look forward to welcoming you and the First Lady on Saturday.'

Chapter 26

FINALLY, OFF THE phone from the President, Kallis dialled another number. The call connected. Without waiting for anyone to answer, he said, 'We have a problem.'

Kallis ended the call after briefing his Russian contact on Thomas Brendt. He quietly reflected for a few moments. His plans for the Presidency and the Global Intervention Initiative had been in place and taking shape for months–years, really. Much was already in progress. He was just days away from one of the final pieces falling into place. But he knew no plan survived first contact. He had to act to ensure there was nothing that would disrupt what was so crucial to the world's future.

Chapter 27

MACK STEWARD PULLED the silver Volkswagen SUV the US embassy in Sydney had provided into the entrance of the private aviation section of Mascot Airfield. The trip from Avalon had taken a little over an hour. He glanced to the left at his passenger, 'We're here'.

Now late evening, Ward had used the time to read through the background package on the encrypted tablet. It was pretty skinny on detail. Mack had been bugging her the whole trip, clearly pressing to see if she was still up to operational capacity. She tried to tune him out. The briefing suggested a simple op, under the radar. But the seemingly simple ops were the ones that always worried her the most. People got complacent. Didn't do the homework. Ward figured this was a two-pronged strategy - to flush out the CIA leak and to get specific information about the corrupted election from this person Brendt. Once one or both were validated, Kristen would no doubt have a plan to deal with them.

As much as she would hate the prospect of an attack on their country, Kristen would really hate the idea of an inside mole. And Ward agreed. Kristen's job was incredibly difficult without the added challenge of being spied upon and undermined by her own people.

She looked up and out the window, 'A private jet! I thought we were going for discreet. You know - no agency involvement - off the books!?'

Mack grabbed their bags from the rear of the SUV and passed Ward hers, 'There is discreet, and there is fast. We need fast. It also means we don't have to worry about wearing masks or getting the virus. Kristen wants this followed up yesterday. Fortunately for us, it actually is yesterday back in the States!'

Mack paused for a reaction. Nothing. 'That was an international dateline joke! No? Ahh, well, time to go. Political terrorism and CIA leaks apparently wait for no man,' He looked across at Ward, 'or woman!'

Both Ward and Mack had only a duffle each and they carried them through the private terminal and onto the plane themselves.

Mack checked with the pilots and held up five fingers to Ward to signal how long until takeoff.

Ward took the time to check the interior of the jet. It was set up for pre-mission. In a series of built-in lockers, she found an assortment of street clothing for different climates and conditions, tactical clothing for ops and bags with observation and covert equipment and CIA state-of-the-art comms. She would grab what she needed before they landed.

No weapons on board. Not staffed but well stocked. Ward was famished, having had no time to enjoy David's dinner. She'd left him in their kitchen, sombrely putting away her plate and cutlery. She would call him when she knew more and had her own space. She hated to admit that she felt more than a twinge of excitement at being operational again, even for what looked like an easy and minor op. As the plane commenced its taxi, she started the coffee machine to be ready once they were in the air. The smell of the fresh beans hit her and made her stomach growl.

The pilot called them to their seats and told them to buckle up.

Chapter 28

'SO, WHAT'S THE plan? asked Ward as she dropped into an executive-style leather seat directly facing the seat Mack had taken.

'We are direct to LA. We'll refuel, and while on the tarmac, once we clear customs, we will get a weapons drop. Then across to Washington.'

Mack paused and reached into his backpack, 'Here's a fresh creds package,' he said, throwing an envelope to her. 'You have a new alias and full passport already stamped for your exit from Australia, residential details, occupation, backstory, photos of your cat - you're a committed cat person, sad and single. Lose your wedding ring. Everything you need to pass customs, police or security is in the pack. Spend time on the flight to memorise and get to know your new self. There are also credit cards and cash. This is off books, so no CIA credentials to be carried by either of us.'

'I'm not a cat person,' replied Ward.

'Not yet. Give it time, Pussy Galore.'

She looked at the creds pack. Her new name was Alex Susan Hole.

'Did you come up with this yourself, Mack? A. S. Hole!' She shook her head and then asked, 'Any additional assets?'

Mack responded, 'With the leaks at Langley, Kristen has kept a tight rein on numbers. There is a rotating surveillance team running shifts watching Brendt. As soon as we land, we will head to Navy Yard. All going well we should get there about 9pm Thursday Washington time. Brendt is under visual surveillance at all times, his loft is tapped and we are watching his online activity - although that bit is tricky. He's a world-class hacker and will have sophisticated security. We'll get an update from the team on the ground while we are in-flight to Washington.'

Mack looked through the dark porthole window of the plane as it taxied across the tarmac and continued with the briefing, 'The target, Brendt, is a raving hipster and a creature of habit. Walks to his favourite cafe every morning around nine or ten. And again at some stage later in the evening. He has dinner pretty late. His girlfriend works either a morning or night shift at the cafe. If she's not working they have dinner and they walk home together. He generally sits at one of two tables, has two coffees in the morning and an espresso at night and plugs away on his MacBook.'

Mack paused and brought his gaze from the window back to Alex. 'We will keep our initial contact subtle. Just us two. We'll meet Brendt at the cafe on Thursday night when he is having dinner. I'll intimidate and scare him and you talk to him.'

'Let's hope he's easily scared.' Ward said.

'Oh, I've really missed you! We'll take him back to his loft and find out what he knows. The information he's been feeding our blogger has been highly informed. We need to know what he knows and get detailed intel. Kristen does not want to officially dig any further and risk more leaks. The team on the ground are the only other operatives she trusts. We'll meet with Brendt, learn what he knows and report to Kristen.'

'Do I go home then?' she knew the answer but thought she'd push his buttons a little. The plane had commenced take off and the engines were roaring. She spoke above the noise.

He smiled, closed his eyes and tilted his chair back.

'You've really developed a sense of humour in the last year. Good to have you back on the team, Alex.'

Chapter 29

THOMAS BRENDT UNCLIPPED and removed his Sidi cycling shoes and lifted his Colnago C64 full carbon road bike onto his shoulder, carrying it up the stairs to his loft. The bike weighed almost nothing. Now a little before seven thirty in the morning, he'd been riding with a local cycling group for the last two hours in the dark and cold. While his bike was Italian, his riding apparel was French. Café Du Cycliste. He favoured the design and fit and the quality was second to none. It kept him warm and dry even in the depths of the Washington winter.

From time to time he thought that if his loft ever caught on fire and he could only save one thing, it would be the bike. Handmade in Italy to accommodate his long, lean frame. He had visited the factory in Camiago, the previous year when COVID was a minor story and well before travel restrictions kicked in. They had invited him to personally select the final build's components and they wanted to formally hand over the beautifully finished bike. Colnago representatives and technicians had spent several hours with him to ensure it was fitted correctly. He'd stayed in Italy for the next month spending the time riding along the Amalfi coast and Tuscany and into the mountains. Linking up with Nikki and other cycling friends at different times, staying at B&Bs and quaint hotels, enjoying the warmth of the people and the wonderful regional food.

He treasured these mornings, even in the cold and the dark. Brendt enjoyed having the normally busy streets to himself and his riding group, listening to nothing but the precise engineering of the bikes and the muted chatter of his friends. It made him feel truly alive as the world around him was still asleep or just coming awake. The rain had stopped late yesterday, and the early morning had been beautifully still and crisp.

Coming into the loft was warm and quiet. He positioned the bike on its wall hook next to an original 1968 Colnago Super. He placed his bike shoes in the rack, nudging them until they perfectly aligned with the five other pairs he stored there. Nikki had left while he was out to open the cafe. She was currently working double shifts, covering staff sick with COVID. Before heading to The Insider, she'd made him a fresh brew, black and strong and steaming hot in an Arian Brekveld carafe. It would fuel him until he headed to the cafe later that morning. Her soft, lingering scent and the aroma of fresh coffee were heaven.

Still in his Café Du Cycliste riding gear, he poured his first cup. At the same time, he checked his digital alerts and his position from the overnight markets. He'd created his own custom code to let him know if anyone tried to get into his online system. He was paranoid about security and wanted no one to be able to see into his digital world. Brendt had reinvented his life after the election debacle. He'd set up his own trading fund and spent his time investing in various markets and looking for start-ups and smart people to back. But he liked anonymity. He'd briefly experienced the sour taste of public and media attention back then. Once was enough. He went to a lot of trouble to stay invisible.

He closed his apps. Everything was precise and in order. As it had to be. Brendt needed to shower. Then to the Insider for some food and to see Nikki.

Chapter 30

BACK IN HIS convertible, the roof now in place, Daniel Walker exited the carpark of his apartment building into the dark, still morning of another cold Washington day. He was simultaneously exhausted and wired. He'd only been in his bed for a few hours and not much of that was spent asleep. Walker had been up for quite some time and consumed several cups of black coffee, which only exacerbated his fatigued and stressed state, making him particularly jittery and putting him in a volatile mood.

He was sweating both literally and figuratively–despite the freezing morning–contemplating the meeting with his Russian contact. He needed to get whatever interest the CIA had in the election under control before it gathered any momentum. He knew that in politics, little things could become big things if they ended up in the wrong hands. And election tampering was a big thing! If they hadn't already, the CIA would bring other agencies into the investigation if they thought there was substance.

The Russians were horrible but necessary bedfellows, and unfortunately, he couldn't delegate this task to someone else. They were fully invested in Charleston, thinking they had a puppet in the White House. Walker knew that at some point, the Russians would come for their pound of flesh–probably several pounds–no doubt believing Charleston would do their bidding to avoid the career-ending public shame they could cause. They would also be counting on Charleston needing them again when he nominated for a second term.

Walker had other plans. He was working on a strategy to isolate the Russians while positioning this modern President as the true manipulator. The leader that played them at their own game and won. Turning the tables on their historical enemy. The President would emerge as an American hero the country would love even more. But that was all down the track. For now, he was counting on them wanting to protect their prized asset. At all costs. Self-interest was a powerful motivator, so he figured they'd do what was needed. But they needed to manage this with subtlety.

Not the blunt approach their reputation predicated. He wanted it done in a way that would not lead to further investigation.

He figured, or perhaps hoped, the CIA would move on if they saw Brendt as a dead end. He just needed Thomas Brendt to be shut down and discredited as some grudge-holding whacko. Or to disappear. Walker was even considering getting the Russians to pressure and manipulate Brendt to start feeding a different story and misdirect the CIA. The Russians could definitely be persuasive. Once he had the Russian dogs focused on the task, he needed some time with Charleston. Walker and The President flew out later that evening to collect The First Lady in Georgia on the way to South Africa and he wanted the agenda for their first state visit tightly buttoned down.

He pulled up to the suburban strip mall diner. This was working-class America personified. His BMW convertible stood out here like the proverbial, but he thought he'd done a very commendable job dressing himself down to be less conspicuous. He'd removed his flashy Washington gold power tie and put on a plain, thick grey overcoat. From the parked car, he could see through the diner's window that his counterpart was already seated in a booth.

The prick probably had other people watching out here somewhere.

Chapter 31

'HELLO DANIEL.' The Russian had taken the last booth against the far wall.

'Boris', Walker offered without extending his hand. He pulled his coat more tightly around himself and slid into the booth opposite, his back exposed to the rest of the diner. It annoyed Walker no end that Boris knew his name and probably a lot about him, but he knew almost nothing about this Russian. It was almost certain Boris was not his real name. Walker's current, uninformed assumption was that Boris was the head of the SVR in Washington, which in turn meant the entire United States. But he wasn't sure. Boris had been introduced to Walker through Hanse Kallis. They had developed a tense and awkward working relationship through the long presidential campaign. Walker had grudgingly taken a pragmatic view; Boris was their man, and he got things done. The arranged 'marriage' had so far worked out exceptionally well.

Walker stared at the Russian for a moment longer. He often wondered if Boris had him watched? Was he important enough to them.....? Walker couldn't decide if he would be more offended if the Russians were watching him or if they weren't.

The waitress interrupted his distracted thoughts, asking for their order.

Boris smiled at the tired woman and ordered waffles with bacon and coffee.

Walker ordered black coffee and waved her off.

'Daniel, you should really order at a place like this. It's better to blend in. Not that your convertible outside and your slicked hair is blending around here. We'd prefer not to be remembered, you know!' Suggested Boris.

Walker self-consciously rubbed a hand through his hair and stared at Boris with his chin tilted a little into the air, hoping to convey disdain. It had no effect. This Russian was always unflappable whenever they met or spoke. He always came across like he knew things Walker didn't. Like Walker was missing information and out of the loop. Or just being played. And while Walker's confidence was always on the wrong side of arrogance, Boris unsettled him with his assurance and presence. He probably carried a gun.

Boris was dressed beautifully and appropriately for the wintry conditions. Deep and muted navy offsetting his styled black hair. What looked like a fine, close-fitting light merino wool knit sat over fitted dark navy trousers. It was understated and looked expensive. Not really fitting into working-class America either, Walker thought! Boris had a long, heavy navy coat on the seat next to him. And he always looked extremely fit. Like he'd just come from the gym or finished a spa session against some highly skilled opponent. He looked like he could as easily be heading to work to run some Euro auto company as he could be about to escort his wife to an exclusive restaurant.

It made Walker feel more tired than he already was to see Boris so fresh and alert. And his intentionally understated grey Brookes Brothers suit and white Oxford shirt felt a little rumpled and pigeonholed him to the stereotype he was. Walker felt himself shrink a little under the Russian's gaze and thought he should try to get to the gym more often. Maybe today. Before the flight. Or perhaps he could dig out his running shoes once he'd finished with the President. He'd been quite the jock at college and he hated feeling inadequate across from the Russian.

Chapter 32

IT FELT LIKE Boris could see right through him, and it brought out long-forgotten schoolboy insecurities. As usual, Walker overcompensated with bluster and self-importance. Boris' accent was a neutral European and American mixture, not the heavy Russian inflection and vowels that were typical. He figured Boris was well-travelled and may have been schooled outside of his homeland.

Boris picked up the conversation. 'How is the President of the United States - I hope his health is holding up? An election campaign and high office can be taxing, I would imagine?'

Walker looked at Boris momentarily, wondering if this was small talk or some version of a veiled threat.

'Boris - that's why we're here. The President needs you to finish a job that should have been taken care of well before now.'

Boris offered the slightest smirk, 'Really! I'm not aware I work for the United States.'

Walker stayed focussed; 'Well, we're all in this together. So let's cut to the chase, shall we!'

Now Boris smiled; 'Cut to the chase. Of course. America loves to cut to the chase! What chase would you like us to cut to this morning, Daniel?'

'Boris, you guys left a loose end from 2016 and it may just bite my guy's ass.'

Boris seemed to be enjoying himself, smiling across the table, 'Well, nobody likes having their ass bitten. Perhaps just slapped from time to time, hey Daniel.'

Walker blinked and checked himself, his face darkening a shade or two, fuck me, he thought - that's a little close to the bone - was this guy actually spying on him? He'd have to check his apartment for cameras again.

With opportune timing, Boris' breakfast arrived, giving pause to the conversation and a moment to re-gather. Walker asked for more coffee. In a voice softened to ensure it sat under the conversations around the diner, he continued.

'Boris, Langley is taking an interest in the election. They think you were up to your old tricks trying to interfere with how Americans think and vote.'

The convivial tone he'd affected now gone, Boris spoke with hushed intensity as other booths had started to fill. 'You want us to take on your Agency? That is more than a loose end!'

Walker matched his tone. 'Leave the Agency to us - we have people we can trust. But they are taking an interest in a former Cambridge Analytica analyst and hacker. As far as we know, he wasn't involved in anything, but maybe he was - you tell me Boris - Thomas Brendt - is he on your payroll?'

Boris chewed slowly on a bite of his waffle, swallowing, he said, 'His name means nothing to me, Daniel. He does not work for us. Perhaps he is involved in another interest if the Agency is poking about?'

'We don't think so. We think they are just chasing leads at the moment. But this guy was involved in 2016, and then he got a conscience and tried to tell his story. Fortunately, the people running the party at the time pumped enough fake news into the ether that his credibility was completely destroyed.' Walker poised and looked over the rim of his coffee mug as he took a sip. The refill was not an improvement on the first cup.

'But it looks like Brendt still holds a grudge and is talking to an investigative blogger who is actually an agency plant. If the Agency keeps pushing, his link to you and to us during the last election may lead them to this election and it will become a problem. For both of us. We want you guys to ensure Brendt loses interest.'

Boris sipped his coffee; 'What exactly would you like us to do?'

Walker could sense an old bait and hook. He had no interest in spelling out the details.

'Boris - this is what you guys do, isn't it? We don't want anything to interfere with the work of the new President. I'm sure you guys think the same way.'

'Of course', said Boris, 'We love covering your amateur mistakes and your President's chequered moral history.'

Walker wasn't inclined to bite, 'Boris - it just needs to be subtle with no link back to you or us and to have the Agency move on to other things. They need to see him as a washed-out hacker, no longer relevant. A dead end.'

Boris prompted Walker, 'How close is the Agency to him? Have they made contact?'

Walker pushed away his now tepid coffee. 'So far, only indirectly, as far as we know. Our sources believe they are getting close to pulling him in. So this needs to happen now.'

'Interfering with a person of interest under agency surveillance is inevitably going to look suspicious, don't you think Daniel? Is it not better for them to keep watching him or interrogate him and see that he is a nobody?' Boris questioned.

'No way. If he fingerprints our party or our candidate and they start digging further, then we'd have the prospect of a President under scrutiny. Too much risk.' Daniel was emphatic.

Boris sat back in his booth and looked out the window into the strip mall car park for some time.

'Ok Daniel. I agree. There is too much at stake. I will sort out the hacker. You take care of our President. The next four years will be of great benefit to both our countries.'

Walker riled at Boris again, calling him 'our President,' and reminded himself that he needed to ensure they started distancing themselves from these people.

Boris gathered his jacket and put some cash on the table.

Feeling a little more under control, Walker sat back in the booth, 'Do you want me to find out Brendt's location?'

Boris smirked slightly, 'No need Daniel. We know where he is.'

Chapter 33

CIA DIRECTOR KRISTEN Thomas glanced out the window of her elevated Langley office. The sun was rising and trying to find a way through the grey mist. Hers was a modern and functional space. A reflection of her personality, it was highly organised and devoid of distractions. Thick, reinforced and soundproofed walls. With an equally thick door. Bulletproof, tinted windows with an anti-surveillance electronic current running through twin pieces of glass. Filtered and cleaned air. Heavy, thick carpet. It all created a noiseless and unnatural vacuum. She compensated by playing soft classical music through discrete speakers. The music filled the void, calmed her mind and offered a final barrier to directional surveillance.

As Director of the CIA, hers was a complex and often opaque world. She had to simultaneously focus on singular and targeted threats to the United States while also connecting the dots to anticipate and repel forming enemies. At times, the threats were simple - evident once the intel was available and she could appropriately direct her team. Those were the easy ones to deal with.

More often, there were layered strategies connected across countries, cultures, religions and time zones. Where the United States was the common enemy, it brought together unusual, often incongruous alliances. More importantly and much more challenging was to anticipate threats before they manifested. To know and think like her enemies. So she could be proactive. To shut them down before they even started. Her job was to both monitor and, where necessary, control the geo-political landscape across the globe and to ensure no terrorism made it to American shores.

She dealt with the more typical and historical issues facing her country - from the ongoing turmoil in the Middle East, the always simmering conflict around Palestine, to the political and economic agendas in Russia, China and many other parts of Europe, Africa, Asia and the Americas. And she also dealt with the increasingly digitised and borderless threats to the American economy and people. Old-school terrorism was making way and was now complicated with new forms of political and economic destabilisation. Twenty first century terrorism was not restricted by borders. It existed in the fourth dimension. Their new enemies were faceless and could operate from anywhere. It was a job that required structure and prioritisation. Technology that stayed ahead of the others. And great people. Or it would quickly overwhelm. Her inner circle was small, incredibly smart and completely trusted. Beyond them, she trusted nobody else.

And she watched them all.

All of this was made more challenging when coupled with navigating the various egos and agendas around Washington. Particularly given the historical and now outdated charter and limitations placed on the CIA to manage foreign intelligence and avoid domestic issues or work on domestic soil. How could she differentiate the origin or location of the threat when it emanated from the cloud? The risk, if she did not stay diligent and pushed beyond what many were comfortable with - was that covert operations would constantly fall behind and fail to keep pace with the speed and technology that enabled their enemies. These people that wanted the CIA to contain itself to matters laid out in a mandate written decades ago were dinosaurs.

She was putting the final touches on the work her team had done on the Presidential Daily Brief. Either she or the DNI was responsible for delivering this to the President. At times, she would delegate to a Deputy Director if other matters took precedence.

The emerging dual security threat could not be included in the PDB, but her mind was partially consumed by the clear reality of a President elected through mass manipulation and beholden to Russia and the clear evidence of a high-level leak in the CIA. Each of these would warrant the Agency's attention on its own. To contemplate them concurrently and very likely connected was truly concerning. She needed to tread carefully and get her ducks in a row.

She finished her markups and sent them back to her senior analyst for finalising and delivering. As one of the most classified and sensitive documents in the country, very few hands touched, or eyes viewed the Presidential Daily Briefing.

Chapter 34

WITH A FEW precious spare minutes before her next meeting, Kristen sipped on filtered water and turned her mind to the domestic situation and how it had to be handled. She needed Mack and Alex to get proper intel on what was going on. A newbie President was challenging enough to manage. One also beholden to their enemies would be catastrophic! If the place started to unravel, the hardships forced onto the public would be immense. An already divided America, further distressed by the uncertainty of the pandemic, would turn on itself. Few people realised just how fragile was the house of cards they lived in. And God knows, they didn't need another idiot in the nation's most senior office. A knock at her door interrupted her thoughts.

'Morning, Kristen.'

'Come in, Tom.'

Tom Gillian was the Deputy Director of Intelligence. Both career spies, they had risen through the CIA together. He now reported to Kristen but was one of the rare breed not intimidated nor diminished by having a female boss. He knew she was good. They worked well together.

Tom dialled Mack and Alex in from the Gulfstream. Kristen brought the meeting to order. She looked across her desk. 'Tom, get us started, please.'

Typical of his no-nonsense style, Gillian jumped straight in, 'We've had eyes-on surveillance for several days. No change to Brendt's schedule. He has a very structured life. Fits his profile; he is undiagnosed but likely on the Asperger's spectrum. High-functioning intellect and genius level with mathematics, hence his ability with digital technology and coding. Highly introverted with no real close or regular friendships. He has a girlfriend who works at a nearby cafe and a cycling group he rides with, but it doesn't seem to extend into other social contact. Spends his days at his loft and generally his mornings and nights at the cafe.' Tom paused and looked up at Kristen, wondering if she wanted to jump in.

She nodded for him to continue.

'We deep-dived him online - social networks and anything published. He has no personal pages on Instagram, Facebook, LinkedIn, Twitter or other public socials. We have had the tech team look at hacking into his private files, but we have not cracked them, and given his expertise, he will more than likely know if we start to tamper. Filed tax returns indicate a seven-figure income from online trading each of the past two years. He has local and offshore corporate accounts, which we are looking into now.'

Gillian moved into the specifics of their interest. 'Given that he broke ranks with Cambridge Analytica and tried to be a whistle-blower five years ago, and that he has moved on personally and financially, it seems unlikely he would have returned to working on an election. Particularly considering the rough ride he had at the time.'

Mack broke in, 'So why are we targeting Brendt? Surely we don't need him now—we can work to ID and take care of those who are active in election manipulation.'

'Mack, hold questions until Tom is done,' Kristen said.

Gillian continued, 'Not much more really - his profile is conflicted - he is personally and financially independent, so he may not be tempted or interested. But ... he did work at and was a key operator at CA. He knows how it works, and he leaves no digital fingerprints. Our concern is that he may be disaffected from not being listened to previously. Mack, to answer your question, we don't think he is active again, but we want to be sure. More likely, he simply wants to bring down those who continually corrupt our elections. We think he's pissed that nothing has been done to stop this type of interference given what happened during the 2016 election. If he is not an active player and is actually an experienced information source, he could be a brilliant one - he has good knowledge. He may have latent leads from the previous campaign. He knows how to rewrite the internet, and we have seen strategies evolve from those he created in 2016 and activated in 2020. We want access to what he knows.'

Chapter 35

MACK SAID, 'STILL, it seems we're pretty limited - putting our stocks in one person to investigate the possibility of a President improperly elected and working with Russia!'

Kristen now took over. 'Mack, rest assured we are applying a full press on this. Intelligence is working with domestic agencies to analyse suspicious online activity across platforms and look for those behind it. It's taking time. Social and mainstream media have become so massive that the lines between real and fake news are almost impossibly blurred. We need actionable intel from the tech analysts.'

Kristen paused to reinforce the point and to ensure the next comments were noted. 'We have to be smart about how we manage this. We have a leak, and it goes directly to the President. If our interest is flagged too early, his team will run interference. The key is to build evidence quickly and quietly. We're taking on a President and a hostile sovereign entity. To do this, we need unequivocal intel. That's your task. And the task for your new partner.'

At this point, Kristen acknowledged the other person on the call for the first time. 'Good morning, Alex; nice to have you with us again.'

Ward replied, 'Not sure I share the sentiment, Director.'

'I understand,' Kristen offered. 'I'll catch up with you separately once we get a moment. Unfortunately, our own leaks necessitate involving only those we - or I - trust. That's you.'

As Director of the CIA, Kristen Thomas bristled at the thought her enemies may have jumped ahead of them. If Charleston was in bed with the Russians, there was almost no end to the horror that could cause her country. She would not waste a second and spare no resource to determine if it were true. And if so, deal with it.

Kristen continued, 'Alex, I want you to connect with Brendt. I think he will respond to you. Find out what he knows. You understand the landscape, and being off the books allows latitude. Shake the tree. And keep shaking until it all starts to drop.'

'What else do we have in play?' Ward asked.

Kristen decided to provide more context. Hearing Alex Ward on the line helped her breathe a little easier. A trusted, confident asset who would think for herself was reassuring because, like her, Ward did not stop until she had the answers.

'A lot of work has been done on vote security since the last election. We have confidence that voter fraud, vote tampering and issues at the ballot box are under control. But the infiltration and manipulation of people through media - both social and mainstream - is a beast. And we're highly exposed. The publishers are unwilling to self-regulate, censor or impose editorial control or author responsibility. Particularly the social platforms. The explosion in AI makes proliferation exponential. The availability of deepfakes and CGI technology is everywhere. As quickly as we move to monitor, investigate, and shut down, the perpetrators grow another 10 heads. Differentiating authentic, credible news from fake news is becoming more and more difficult. For some time, we have had a massive commitment to technology, and people across multiple agencies have all focused on this.'

'Are you telling me not to believe everything I read?' Ward asked with more than a touch of sarcasm.

Kristen added, 'Or see or hear!'

Chapter 36

THE PAGER DR Benita Morris carried on her hip started buzzing. An infectious disease consulting pathologist working at the Royal London Hospital, she felt exhausted to the core of her being. Since its first sporadic appearance some eighteen months ago, the pandemic had exploded and became the catalyst for the most horrible period of her career. The message required her to urgently attend the Covid ICU facility. Still in full PPE, she turned around, pushed back through the doors she'd just come through, and found the technician who had paged her.

'Doctor,' the technician said, 'we have a recent admission: a fifty eight year-old female, vaccinated and boosted. Presenting moderate virus symptoms, she has tested negative for COVID-19. Dr Visage has been attending and now has the results from a full blood workup and has requested your consult.'

'For mild symptoms and a negative test? It's not uncommon for vaccinated people to still be affected by side-effects or another virus.'

The technician looked as tired as Benita felt. 'That's all the information I have. Dr Visage has just finished with the patient and will meet you in pathology.'

Benita put her visor back in place, then washed, sanitised and applied fresh gloves. She entered pathology to find her colleague, Dr John Visage, reviewing samples using transmission electron microscopy.

'Hello, John.'

'Benita, thanks for coming back.'

'What's up? I've just had a brief summary and checked the patient's charts. Nothing too unusual?' she noted Visage had deep black shadows under his eyes. Everyone on the front line dealing with this horrific and relentless disease was deeply affected.

Visage did not look up from his reports. 'No, it's not the symptoms. At least not just the symptoms. Protocol requires us to test all fully vaccinated patients presenting with modest to extreme symptoms. Melinda Simpson, our patient, came in a couple of days ago to be tested and was found negative. Since then, her respiratory system has been progressively shutting down. Again, this is rare once vaccinated, but unfortunately, it happens. The issue is her blood work. It's not my specialty, but I don't think this looks like any Covid variants we've seen. And she's not the only patient presenting with this cluster of symptoms. There are more by the day. By the hour.'

Unfortunately, this had been the story of this virus. It evolved and morphed, and each new strain seemed more contagious and virulent than the previous.

Stepping up and placing her eyes to the viewer, Dr Benita Morris hoped this patient and the large number like her, was just another unfortunate exception having a vaccination reaction and that they were not on the cusp of yet another mutation.

Chapter 37

HAVING SEEN THE sun rise from her office that morning, Kristen Thomas was vaguely aware it was now setting as she was still immersed in her day's work. Her discipline, her team and a near photographic memory were crucial to her ability to do her job. But what really separated her was her work ethic. She never seemed to fatigue. She put it down to the strong-bodied farmers in her mother's Irish ancestry.

She checked her watch - Ward and Mack would be on the ground in Washington in four hours.

Chapter 38

DRIVING ONE OF the wilderness sanctuary's original Land Rovers back to the main house Kallis was accompanied by his oldest and most loyal dog, Nelson, a now-ageing Rhodesian Ridgeback. Kallis was on his way to meet with his Senior Vice President of Special Projects for a debrief following a multi-country trip from which he'd just returned.

Kallis had spent the early morning carousing parts of the sanctuary and reviewing the progress of the nurture programs implemented over many years. This was family land. His grandfather had acquired it as a private game reserve decades ago. Kallis had expanded, purchasing adjacent properties when they came on the market or more directly through proactively approaching the owners and making them offers they found hard to resist. He'd changed the purpose of the place from a safari and hunting park to a wilderness sanctuary. Now, in excess of fifty thousand square kilometres, he and his wildlife team had painstakingly restored native African flora and fauna. Taking almost extinct species and many with substantially reduced numbers and rebuilding them through both science and traditional land management.

The sanctuary was as large as some European countries - almost half the size of England and required aircraft to cover it. But he loved these relatively small, unchartered forays in his old Land Rover. He felt genuinely connected to the land and the myriad life it supported. As he drove deeper into the reserve, it was like wandering into an earlier century. Teeming wildlife, lush bushland and large healthy herds were testimony to the resilience of nature and its power of recovery once the damaging effects of man were removed. Balance had been restored.

His own efforts proved to him that the environment could rebound. They also proved that allowing nature to recover required isolation and the removal of the devastating impact of people. Humanity had gotten so out of balance and so dominating on the rest of nature that it caused almost irreversible destruction.

Herein was the essence of his remaining time–the legacy he intended to gift the planet. The forum he had put together–The Global Intervention Initiative–was only days away. It would bring together the sharpest and most articulate scientists and environmentalists, along with senior current and aspiring politicians and corporate leaders, to commit to one singular plan for the globe.

ONE COMMITMENT.

ONE PLAN.

ONE PLANET.

It was the theme that informed the forum and around which all of the protocols and targets had been built.

ONE.

The singular idea of ONE offered an important duality to Kallis. It represented something far more significant than a resolved commitment from the world's leaders. It occupied almost all of his thinking and his time. ONE was his ultimate goal. It would take them way beyond the protocols and targets he had proposed and practically demanded from those attending the forum he was hosting this weekend.

Unfortunately, while the stated intent of those attending was positive, history irrefutably demonstrated that when it comes to environmental commitments from business and politicians, they make for a lot of rhetoric and little substance. They just couldn't move away from the economic and commercial agenda that had driven every major decision since the Industrial Revolution.

Chapter 39

KALLIS, THE ENVIRONMENTALIST, was also a pragmatist. He had long ago realised that the single biggest issue facing humanity and the planet was not the issue governments and businesses were focused on–economic prosperity. The biggest issue they faced was quite clearly their own survival. But getting real commitment and affecting real change had so far proven completely elusive.

Pragmatically, he knew that the massive effort it took to create the forum–The Global Intervention Initiative–and the equally massive challenge of securing alignment from politicians and business leaders would, at best, result in minor change. They inevitably diluted their commitment to the environment and the health of the globe in favour of pursuing economic growth and avoiding the massive structural changes needed.

Forums like these tended to lead to a false expectation of progress and change. In an isolated environment with a singular focus and the evidence and energy presented by truly passionate advocates, the leaders and their representatives would jump on board and encourage others. It became self-fulfilling, and for a brief time, they all truly believed what they were committing to. But it lasted only as long as the flight home.

Despite the inevitability of commitments never being realised, Kallis still considered the forum crucial. He knew his would be different. And he had gone to massive expense and used all of his influence and political capital to assemble an unprecedented representation from around the world. In his view, there was only ONE issue - the health of the environment. Because money and wealth wouldn't matter if the planet and its people were chronically sick and dying. The forum was an essential means to an end. It galvanised much of the work he was truly intent on. It would give him the opportunity to have the people he needed, who were rarely located in a single location.

'ONE' was the mantra.

And for Hanse Kallis, there was only ONE answer.

Chapter 40

KIRIL ANTONOV HAD tried his best to dress to blend in to what he knew would be some yuppie hipster crowd at the Insider Cafe. This part of Washington was a world removed from where he lived and spent his time. His strong Slavic features and steroid-inflated upper body were competing with the intended subtlety of his all-black urban camouflage. And while tattoos were still de rigueur amongst the inner urban crowd of any large, modern city, his told an ugly story, started at his neck and finished at his toes and in a place like this, needed to be hidden.

Antonov was carefully sipping on five-dollars worth of sparkling water served in a glass so delicate he thought it might shatter in his massive hand. He was uncomfortable and wanted to get this job done and hoped his target would turn up soon. Antonov had been told the man arrived at the same time each evening and that the large crowds in the cafe and around the area would provide them with good cover. A low, flat cap covered his face and obscured him from the cameras all over this part of the city. He pretended to be immersed in the screen of his phone to complete the effect. His colleague Andrei was waiting outside in the car. Antonov wanted this to be quick and discreet, and they would just disappear into the night, having never really been here.

Chapter 41

MACK PARKED THE blacked-out, supercharged Dodge Durango in a vacant car spot half a block down and across the road from The Insider. He spotted the Tesla used by the CIA surveillance team, noting it blended well into this part of the city and was a few car spots closer to the cafe. One of the two agents exited the passenger door, headed towards them and climbed into the rear seat.

The surveillance agent spoke first, 'Good to see you guys. This one has been a complete bore. He does the same thing every fucking morning and night. Like a metronome.'

Mack asked, 'Has he arrived?'

'Not yet.'

'What's the sit-rep?' asked Ward.

'Same as yesterday. And the day before. Lots of twenty and thirty somethings in expensive puffer jackets carrying laptops. Though I'd like a piece of that cafe. It runs solid all day, and I can get three twenty ounce coffees from Dunkin' Donuts for what they pay for an espresso in there.'

'Exits?' Ward asked, ignoring the sarcastic observations.

The agent looked across at the source of the voice for a moment. The side profile suggested a young and very attractive female with dark hair protruding from a stylish woollen cap.

'Obviously, we can see the front door as well as another door off the back. That one is only accessible through the kitchen. Bathrooms are in an enclosed area with no windows. That's it. So, what's the plan?'

Mack offered a brief briefing. He and Ward had re-considered their original plan and figured a single agent would be less threatening to Brendt. Ward would go in initially alone. If needed, Mack could join her and dial up the heat. 'Agent Hole will go in and talk nicely to the target. She will encourage him to join us in the SUV, and we will take him to the staging house. While Hole is inside, I'll be in the car on standby. All going well, we drive quietly away. If he decides not to cooperate, I'll intercept him when he leaves and help him into the backseat. Either way, he is with us, and we will find out what he knows. You guys stay on surveil and provide support as needed and follow us to staging.'

The agent nodded. 'Anything else?'

Ward wondered if Mack could put any more emphasis on 'Hole'! Dickhead.

'Radios open but with operational silence - we will hear what Agent Hole hears and be ready.' Mack finished.

While Mack was going through the briefing, Ward attached the hidden earpiece. She looked across to the cafe. She could do with a good coffee.

Chapter 42

THOMAS BRENDT WALKED along the softly lit pavement as he approached The Insider. His head was bowed as he took pains to step precisely in the centre of each paver and avoid the cracks. The cool, damp night air carried the aroma of freshly ground Ethiopian beans. He had an AirPod in each ear and one hand on the strap of his Porter Yoshida Tanker Backpack draped over his left shoulder. He used his free hand to open the front door and looked around the cafe's interior. The place was busy. More than three quarters full. Pretty typical for this time of evening. The seats at the counter were crowded. He decided on a small, empty booth with a window looking back onto the street. Nikki would have already started making him his espresso. He removed the full-length Kiton parka and burgundy Ssam cashmere beanie. Brendt pulled his laptop from the soft padded section in the backpack. He opened his computer and squared it to align with the edges of the table, waited for it to connect to the wireless mesh system of the cafe, and settled in.

Completely unaware, there were now more eyes than ever watching his very precise movements.

Chapter 43

SO INTENTLY WAS Brendt focused on his laptop he almost spat out his first, delightful sip of espresso as the slim, dark-haired woman wearing a black knit cap silently slid into the booth across from him.

'Hello Thomas, how's the coffee?'

For a fleeting moment, he thought it was just another cafe customer looking to share his table—but she had said his name! 'I don't know you!' Brendt responded in typically unfiltered fashion.

'We'll get to that. First, I need to order. I'm dying for a real coffee.'

A young female waitress with a full-sleeve tattoo running down her left arm came over and Ward ordered a double shot espresso. She was aware that Brendt was staring at her and she met his gaze.

He stated again, 'I don't know you. We've never met. I would remember you.'

'That's very flattering.'

'It's not intended to be. I just remember everyone I've met. And I don't remember you.' Brendt stated.

'Oh, and here I was thinking you were being nice. Thomas, We need to talk.' said Ward.

'I don't talk to many people. At least not in person. Why do you need to talk to me?' Brendt asked.

'Not here, Thomas. Let's enjoy our coffee, and then we'll catch up elsewhere.'

Ward's espresso arrived, and she took an expectant sip. It was the perfect temperature. And it was delicious. She needed the caffeine. Ward savoured the coffee as she scanned the room. It was a habit hard-wired. She continued to move her gaze until finally settling back on Brendt, taking her time to try and get a read on him. Ward also knew that silence could be disarming, and she wanted him off balance. He looked pretty intense. Tall and lean - skinny, really. He seemed fairly composed, given the circumstances. Perhaps more displaced than anything as she had pushed into his space. His response fit the profile.

She took another sip. Her silent appreciation for the coffee not shared by Brendt, 'I really don't understand. Tell me who you are and why I need to talk to you? Are you saying you want me to leave with you? I'm not leaving with you. I don't know you. Are you with those guys in the Tesla outside?'

This caught Ward's attention, 'You're aware of the guys in the Tesla?'

'They have been watching me and following me for four days. Are they with you?'

Ward looked at him for an extra moment. 'Who do you think the guys watching you are?'

Brendt answered with a slightly raised eyebrow, 'I thought they might be media initially - reporters - but then they didn't do anything. They never approached me. So, I figure they are the government. Media people wouldn't just watch for long. So government. That makes you government.'

'Why would reporters be interested in you, Thomas?' asked Ward.

Brendt smiled tightly, 'Perhaps for the same reason the government might be.'

Discreetly, Ward placed her newly acquired government ID on top of the menu on the table and slid it across. She let him view the details and then pulled it back. 'My name is Alex. And yes, I do work for the government. We want to talk to you about the election. It's important. We think you can help us, Thomas. And yes, the people in the Tesla are with me.'

She figured honesty, or at least partial honesty, was the best strategy. He was clearly too smart to be oblique. She'd like him to trust her. It would help when they started talking.

Brendt was processing the conversation, 'The election! The one that we just had or the one four years ago? I tried to talk to the government in 2016. No one listened. You all thought I was fake news. Ironic. Why can't we talk here?'

'Better in private, Thomas. My car is outside.' She brought the small cup to her lips, tipped it right back and savoured the last of the espresso. She placed the empty demitasse on the saucer. 'Shall we?' Ward asked.

'Is this where I get to choose to come quietly? Or will you drag me out? Because I don't really want to go with you at all. I really don't care about 2016 anymore or 2020. I don't have anything to say to the government about it. The government didn't want to listen last time. I stopped caring or talking about elections after that fiasco. The whole thing is bogus anyway.' Brendt said.

'You're rambling a bit there, Thomas. Nervous? In fact, that's exactly what we want to talk about. And we know you've already been talking about the election. Albeit with digital obscurity. Someone has been sending veiled but very detailed information to a political blogger anonymously. That was you. And we want to know more.'

Ward was keeping an eye on the place while they talked. Her eyes constantly sweeping. She had a view of about half the room and was picking up reflections of parts of the rest. She'd scoped the people in the cafe when she entered. It was a mixed crowd, and she couldn't tell if anything was out of place. One of the baristas kept staring their way. She figured that was Brendt's girlfriend the surveillance team briefed them on. Nikki. Ward couldn't see around corners or properly behind her, and her little voice was talking to her. She always listened to her little voice.

Wanting to move, she addressed Brendt, 'Let's not talk here, Thomas.'

'I'm not involved. Nothing to do with elections in over four years. You guys are way off the mark.' Brendt stated. Though his demeanor was pretty transparent. Smart, thought Ward, but a terrible liar.

Ward looked across at him and put her hand on his forearm as he leaned on the table, 'Let's go.'

This chick wasn't going to give up, thought Brendt. He looked at her for a bit. Took another sip of his coffee to bide his time and caught Nikki's eye. 'How about my apartment? Can we meet at my apartment?'

'Sure. Let's talk at your apartment.' That was fine with Ward. She wanted him calm and wanted him to get moving.

'Do I need a lawyer?'

'No lawyer, mate.' She figured he was stalling now. He kept looking at the barista.

'Mate. You're calling me mate?' said Brendt.

'   Sorry. New habits. Time to move.' Her senses were tingling now; she wanted out of there.

'I need to use the bathroom. This is all a little unusual and the coffee is hitting me.'

She weighed him up for a moment. 'OK. Nothing funny. Leave your phone and laptop here.'

Chapter 44

WATCHING DISCREETLY FROM beneath the peak of his flat cap, Kiril Antonov was trying to understand the situation. The woman wasn't expected. Not part of the briefing. He'd been told the target would be eating alone. But that was not the case. He figured the briefing they'd received was not much of a briefing. Just a photo of the subject sent to Kiril's phone and details on where and when. Maybe she was his girlfriend. She was definitely good-looking. And tall. She could easily get a job dancing at one of the clubs he worked at. A little undersized up top. But plenty liked the boyish look. He saw the target, Brendt, get up and head to the bathroom.

Who cares. It was go-time.

Chapter 45

HER EYES TRACKING Brendt, Ward noticed the giant emerge from his seat tucked around a structural pillar at the cafe counter and follow Brendt towards the bathroom. He'd been obscured from her view until now. Her senses spiked, and without conscious thought, she started moving.

Ward spoke into the mic as she moved several metres behind, 'A really big guy in a long jacket has followed Brendt to the bathroom. I'm following. Mack, bring the car up.' She continued, 'Team One check surrounds for other operators and assume defensive posture. Provide cover to Mack.' She heard the click of the mic's in acknowledgement.

She was at the bathroom door - there was only one - a unisex toilet used by all patrons. Hipster cool or just frugal, she fleetingly wondered.

Ward reflexively felt for her Sig Sauer P229 in the concealed holster at the small of her back. But she wouldn't draw her gun. There were too many people around, and if the big guy was just reacting to his coffee and needed some bathroom time, she might have some explaining to do.

In a fluid, single movement, she pushed the door open, stepped in and quickly assessed the room. There were three stalls. Two had their doors sitting ajar and were empty. The giant had gone into the third stall where she assumed Brendt was. The door was still open, and he had his massive back to her. She couldn't see Brendt - the guy was too big. At the sound of her entry, the giant was trying to turn quickly in the limited space. As he moved, she caught a glimpse of Brendt in the stall being pinned down one-handed by the giant; she also saw the big guy had a hypodermic syringe in his other hand. His face showed a pissed-off expression as he looked at Ward, clearly annoyed at the disruption.

She called out to him; 'Drop that and let him go. Now.'

He grunted and did neither. The giant turned back to Brendt, disregarding Ward, seemingly intent on injecting whatever was in the syringe.

Ward lunged at him, grabbing the back of his jacket and yanked hard. Nothing. Didn't even move the beast. He let go of Brendt, reached back with his right hand, and swatted at her. The massive arm caught her, knocking her off balance, and she fell backwards out of the stall, whacking the back of her head on a hand basin.

He again turned his attention back to Brendt. He was pushing the sleeve of Brendt's knit top up his arm, preparing to inject the needle and plunge the hypodermic. Shaking her head to try and clear swirling stars, she needed to find a way to throw the giant off. She didn't want to shoot and cause an incident. And she had almost no time. She pushed herself back up and noted the giant's slightly spread legs and bent knees as he manhandled Brendt in the stall. She took one full step onto her left foot and then kicked with all her might with her right, aiming up from behind, between his legs, right at where his balls should be. Contact. A right foot David Beckham would have been pleased with. That got his attention. The giant grunted loudly this time, swayed a little and then turned and flung the syringe at her. She dived to her right across the bathroom avoiding the flying needle while registering the movement of his right arm across his chest and into his jacket. Gun. Fucker was quick for his size.

Ward heard the sound of a suppressed shot, and the ceramic hand basin behind her exploded into pieces. She tucked and flung herself the other way across the black and white tiles of the bathroom. Another muffled shot and impact into the mirrored wall behind her. Glass splintered and came crashing onto the bathroom floor. The time for discretion had passed. As she rolled she reached for the Sig behind her and fluidly cleared the holster, bringing the gun around in a fast, single motion, firing twice at the massive target. He was stationary and big and hard to miss. He went down onto one knee and, with a painful effort, brought his head up to look at her. He'd used his gun hand to break his fall and it was now slowly coming up. Ward fired twice more. One to the head and another at centre mass. And it was a lot of mass. Game over. This time, he went down, falling back into the cubicle, and stayed down. Ward was up and moving towards the fallen giant. Gun held low, directed at the target in a double-handed grip outstretched in front of her. She was vaguely aware of screaming coming from the cafe. Her Sig was not suppressed, and the noise of multiple shots in the confined space had been deafening. She kicked the giant's gun across the floor and then kicked his body. No movement. She saw why. The back of his head was missing. What the fuck had just happened?

Chapter 46

BRENDT WAS TRAPPED under the dead giant. Ward quickly holstered her Sig, the sounds from outside the bathroom now hysterical. She pulled hard at the body and shouted to Brendt to push himself out. The stall was cramped, and it was hard to find leverage. She had both hands full of the beast's jacket and was off the ground leg-pressing the wall across from her to get as much drive as she could. Finally, Brendt managed to push himself sideways across the tiles and get out. He'd collected some of the big guy's blood and brain on his face. She shoved him towards the remaining undamaged hand basin. 'Wash yourself.' She turned back to the beast; no need to check the pulse, she started working through his pockets. Ward found a wallet and an old-school Nokia and pocketed both. She also noticed the tattoos on his neck and hands and grabbed her phone. Ripping his clothes out of the way, she started taking photos.

Mack was now in her earpiece calling for a sit-rep.

She spoke into the mic as she snapped photos, 'Contact. One target down. I'm clear, and so is Brendt. We're coming out. Have the car ready and right outside. We need to move before the police arrive.'

'Copy' replied Mack.

Ward continued, 'Team Two. Watch for any friends this guy might have.'

'Copy' came the immediate reply.

She finished with the body and, turning around, noticed Brendt had disappeared. She pulled the door and went back into the cafe. It was mayhem. Unfortunately, people knew what gunshots sounded like. They were screaming and falling over each other to get out. Ward saw Brendt pushing past exiting people moving back into the cafe's interior! He was beelining the barista who was still behind the counter. Keeping one eye on Brendt, Ward rushed back to the booth where they'd had coffee and grabbed his laptop and phone. Brendt was now with the barista, grabbing her hand and pulling her towards the exit. Ward wasn't sure what he was doing and didn't care. She grabbed Brendt by the arm, broke his contact with the girl and pulled him towards the door. Through the glass, she could see their SUV stopped in front. People were spilling into the street, trying to escape the cafe. She exited with her head swivelling, looking for threats.

Chapter 47

THE DRIVER'S DOOR of a black BMW X5 parked across the street began to swing open and a guy who could have been the even bigger twin brother of the dead giant stepped out of the SUV, bringing to bear a compact polymer automatic submachine gun.

'Contact. Contact. Black BMW.' Ward shouted into the mic as automatic fire erupted and bullets hit the cars in front and the shop windows behind her. People started screaming again and running.

Brendt was exposed in front of her. She changed hands, held the Sig in her left, and pushed Brendt hard with her right towards Mack's SUV. She squeezed several shots off left-handed at the new target as she did. Glass flew from the BMW driver's door window and the windscreen and at least one shot must have struck as the massive body fell back into the car still firing his weapon, firstly towards the cafe and then into the air as he went backward. She desperately hoped no shots had found an innocent mark.

The fuck are these people? thought Ward. A busy evening in the hipster part of Washington, and they were blasting away. So much for her quiet chat with some internet hacker nerd.

Mack came out of the driver's seat of the Durango and grabbed Brendt, shoving him into the back. Alex momentarily considered running to the BMW and finishing the big guy but discounted the idea, instead prioritising Brendt as she raced to the Durango and jumped into the now vacant driver's seat.

Mack followed Brendt into the rear and closed his door. 'Go. Go. Go.' he shouted.

'Team Two, stay on the BMW.' Ward yelled into her mic as the 6.4-litre hemi's four tyres struggled to find traction.

'On it.' came the response.

The black BMW was already moving, screeching erratically away in the opposite direction. Fighting her instinct to turn around and give chase, she watched as the SUV disappeared in the rearview mirror.

Chapter 48

DRIVING ONE-HANDED and staying just under the speed limit, Ward reached for her phone and started dialing.

'Who are you calling?' Mack asked.

'Kristen. Shit just got real.'

'Wait until we get to the staging house - go left at the next lights.'

'Not happening. She needs to escalate this and get assets activated.'

Mack paused, 'I'm bleeding. Caught a stray from Hulk Hogan back there. I need to get it fixed and we need to recalibrate and get proper intel.'

'How bad is it?' She was pushing the SUV, the tyres screeching, still holding her phone.

'Superficial. Maybe a little more than superficial. Abdomen.Through and through.'

Ward finished dialling. 'Who is this?' Kristen Thomas answered the call.

'Kristen, your intel was shit.'

'Alex.' said Kristen calmly, 'Not many people have this number.'

'It's etched in my mind. Unfortunately.'

'Update, please.'

'The quiet chat with Thomas Brendt was a shit show.' Ward informed her. 'A massive dude straight out of central casting followed him to the bathroom as we were about to leave and tried to inject Brendt with something. I managed to run interference just as he was about to hit Brendt with whatever was in that hypodermic. His offsider was outside and opened fire on us as we exited with an un-silenced AKM. I think I wounded him, and he drove off. We have Brendt, who is uninjured and are now mobile. Mack's hit and has a wound that is bleeding and needs attention.'

Kristen immediately prioritised 'I'll get a doctor to the house for Mack. What is the status of the attackers at the cafe?'

'One dead. And one wounded that your surveillance unit is following. I have the dead guy's burner and wallet. And I have photos of his tattoos. He was covered in rough, hand drawn ink.' Ward stated.

'OK. I'll get a tech analyst to meet you at the staging house. They can see what the phone gives us and we can run down the tattoos and any other information. Call me once you're at the house, and we will assess and determine your next move.'

'Negative Kristen.' Ward was emphatic. 'I'll drop Mack there to get treatment, but I'm staying mobile with Brendt. Those guys were serious but sloppy. They were waiting for him. Somebody is a step ahead of us, and until we know what is going on, I'm staying offline. Plug your leak, Kristen. This could have ended a lot worse.'

Always the professional, Kristen was moving with the situation and the new information. 'OK, I'll get support assets activated and available to you. We're working on the leak. I'll call you in one hour.' She disconnected the call.

Mack, having heard one side of the conversation, commented from the backseat. 'I'll stay with you.'

'Negative mate. You're a liability injured, and you're a mess. Get sorted. And someone needs to work this from the inside.'

Ward caught sight of Brendt in the rearview mirror. He was slumped into the seat next to Mack and looked shell-shocked, his eyes fixed directly ahead.

Chapter 49

ARRIVING EARLY, PIETER Roberts was waiting in the large inner office at Hanse Kallis' wildlife sanctuary. He was taking the time to wander around the space that memorialised a life well lived—a life he himself had been intertwined with over several decades. Roberts had worked with Kallis for more than forty years, having helped craft and build a provincial pharmaceutical business Kallis' grandfather had started into what was now a massive multi-national company. He was Kallis' most trusted employee and, more importantly, lifelong friend.

Recently, once the operational management of the business was passed to Kallis' daughter Meagan, Roberts accepted the offer to work with Hanse directly. His title, Vice President of Special Projects, was intentionally vague to give broad scope. It was a wonderful way to bring his career to a close, working with a completely committed and visionary humanitarian. As much as Roberts had loved the intensity and reward in building a large commercial business, he was now finding that giving back and offering service was much more fulfilling. Roberts was meeting Hanse to debrief him on an expansive international multi-country trip from which he had just returned. A trip made all the more challenging with the many and varied travel and movement restrictions in place to manage the pandemic. It was amazing what private air travel and connections could accomplish.

When the virus first emerged, and it became evident the world was on the precipice of a truly global epidemic, Hanse had decided to support the inevitable mass vaccinations across continents and countries by manufacturing and supplying millions of syringes and other forms of vaccine dose applications at low or for some countries zero cost. It was a commitment he was both able to afford and one that was, in fact, now generating substantial profits. Hanse realised that many other big Pharma companies would compete to develop the vaccine and figured there was a gaping opportunity to help distribute and deliver it.

It had become Pieter Roberts' job to oversee rapidly scaled manufacturing and logistics and get distribution deals in place. Not difficult when they were willing to support the fight against the pandemic with low-cost, reliable syringes. It was an initiative consistent with Hanse's broad humanitarian agenda. Roberts became increasingly impressed with what could be achieved with a singular focus and without the compromise of corporate and political hierarchy. Roberts was delighted that his final role with Hanse was one that would make a meaningful contribution to the global fight.

Roberts turned as Kallis entered the office. Despite his advancing years, he always felt an aura of energy surrounding his friend and leader. Still in his outdoor gear, Hanse took off his Stetson - a gift from a previous US President and dropped it on the low table. He advanced to his old friend and embraced him in a bear hug.

'Hello, Pieter. Thank you for coming up here. I do hope you will be staying for lunch; we have a beautiful cut of our own aged beef being slow-cooked over coals.'

Roberts quietly smiled to himself, for while Kallis was a committed environmentalist and humanitarian–possibly the world's greatest financial contributor and certainly one of the leading forces for positive environmental change–he certainly hadn't left his South African heritage behind and gone all vegan!

'Of course Hanse. It is good to be back.' Roberts said as he dropped into one of the low leather and hardwood chairs.

Kallis said, 'I want to hear about your trip and our progress. And I need your opinion on some ideas for the forum this weekend. But first, how is the beautiful Angela and my godchildren?'

Chapter 50

THE TWO AGEING businessmen and modern-day humanitarians spent some time catching up and enjoying each other's company when Roberts moved the discussion to the work being done to fight the global pandemic.

'Our factories and third-party suppliers in China, Indonesia and Bangladesh have geared up production yet again. In the last ten or so months since the first vaccinations in late January and early February, we have distributed over four billion syringes, representing about half of the doses given globally. The financial benefit to us has been...'

Kallis interrupted, 'I'm not interested in the financials. They are inconsequential to the effort and imperative the pandemic demands.'

'Of course!' Roberts continued, 'The global rollout of the various vaccinations has been exponential, almost doubling every month. It's actually quite mind-boggling. Working with government agencies and pharmaceutical companies, we were ahead of everyone with your foresight, Hanse, so we have had the jump on production and distribution. Of course, the pharmaceutical companies and the vaccination clinics are delighted to have access to such low cost and reliable syringes.'

While impressive and at a scale never before managed in corporate history, Kallis continued to contemplate the bigger picture. 'How many will be delivered this month?'

Roberts knew his numbers, 'Another five hundred million this month, Hanse.' He continued, 'In saying that, what we are doing and what we have done has been an enormous effort, and while the business is profitable, the margins are very tight, and the pressure on people and equipment is immense. Perhaps we can leave some of the effort to others.'

Hanse seemed not to hear these last remarks. A strange expression crossed his face as he rose from his leather chair opposite Roberts. 'The new American President will arrive in a matter of hours. He is a keynote at the forum and will formally commit his country to some of the emissions and zero waste election promises we encouraged. At the same time, the President and I will be making a joint announcement to acknowledge the massive commitment and effort we have made in supplying syringes and applicators to his government-funded clinics and to the private vaccination facilities.'

Roberts nodded in assent. They had done a lot together in the decades building the company, but everything paled to insignificance when he considered the unprecedented scale of the delivery of vaccines they had now undertaken. He knew they were making a huge contribution to fighting the pandemic, and he was incredibly proud that this would be his legacy.

Knowing him so well, Kallis seemed to read his mind and his mood. 'You've done an amazing job, Pieter. I am certain the historians who write about this horrible virus will reflect on what you and I have done. There is no question our efforts have changed the world. How many can truly say that! Come - let us take coffee outside before lunch. I'll tell you what to expect at The Global Intervention Initiative. We are about to take yet another massive step in healing the planet.'

Roberts always felt renewed from the indefatigable purpose Kallis showed. He hoped his friend wasn't being naively optimistic about the forum. Politicians and 'big corporate' had only one agenda - their own. Roberts cynically felt politicians would sign up to Kyoto or Paris and now the Intervention Initiative without knowing how they would deliver the targets - or worse, never really intending to try. The halo of being involved with Hanse was seductive, and the politicians welcomed the opportunity to participate and present themselves as global leaders on the global stage. Having made such a massive contribution to fighting the ongoing global pandemic, Roberts was worried Hanse was going to have an enormous let down when his real passion inevitably failed at the hands of compromised politicians. They would only be attending as a means to their own end. Whatever that might be. And it was unlikely to be anything like the higher purpose Hanse had to truly drive change.

Then again, Kallis was certainly not naive to politicians' myopia, and he always seemed to be at least two steps ahead of everyone else...

Chapter 51

DR BENITA MORRIS brought her red-rimmed eyes up from the chart she was consulting in the Intensive Care Unit of the Royal London Hospital. She looked through her integrated PPE visor at the patient. Melinda Simpson was now experiencing chronic respiratory failure and was on a respirator. The patient had deteriorated at an alarming rate since presenting just hours ago. She had a pre-existing lung condition, which was why she had been a priority patient. However, her multiple COVID vaccinations seemed not to have worked. She was very sick. And they could offer no effective treatment other than to try and keep her comfortable as she and the vaccines and antivirals fought the virus in her body.

Pathology results were still being processed and nothing conclusive had been determined. However, Dr Morris was concerned not just about this patient but also about what it might mean. In just a matter of days, the number of patients presenting with the same symptoms had grown exponentially. One of the ongoing challenges of COVID-19 was that it would morph and evolve. But no one knew what form it would take or how to prevent it. The team at her hospital and innumerable facilities around the country and around the world were struggling just to deal with what was coming at them. They had almost no capacity to anticipate and prevent. If this was a new strain resistant to the vaccines it would present a confronting set of new problems. And no doubt inflame the panic of politicians and media - and the community.

She turned and exited the room. While waiting for pathology she figured she could post some observational notes to her network at hospitals and universities to confirm her nagging concern that this new event was becoming significant very quickly.

Chapter 52

ARRIVING BRIGHT AND EARLY, Daniel Walker was bunkered in his office working through his various and substantial duties as Chief of Strategy. Perhaps not so bright. But definitely early. He was ploughing through a raft of briefing papers and emails while simultaneously returning calls. And determining the meeting schedule and agenda for the President.

Whilst every day was frantic, today seemed supersized. He and the President would be flying out on the President's first international trip later that night. They'd be gone for several days and had a full media contingent traveling with them. Tempted to make this a multi-country tour, they had ultimately decided to keep it fairly short and focused. International travel had all but shut down in recent months for the general public due to restrictions applied to manage the pandemic. It would be a bad look to have a President galavanting.

The team was also concerned that whilst the President had had several vaccinations and boosters, it would expose him and all that travelled with him to a higher risk of catching the virus. So, they had limited the trip to South Africa to attend the forum - where they would commit the US to a range of environmental targets and protocols to address climate change. Followed by a brief but historic visit to Moscow. Both destinations were presented publicly as highly significant demonstrations of James Charleston's global position and leadership. For Daniel and the President, they were really nothing more than an expression of gratitude to those that had helped them secure office.

Or was that subservience, wondered Walker...

Walker reflected on the commitments they would be making at the South African forum and thought they represented economic mismanagement of the highest order. And if not scaled back, political suicide. But Hanse Kallis, like the Russians, had been crucial to them winning the election and the President was about to make good on his side of the bargain. It would represent the US's most aggressive targets for emissions, recycling, waste reduction and ocean cleansing. The President wanted to ensure it was the primary focus of the media. And hopefully distract interest in him heading to Moscow. So, today, they were cramming to free up for the next few days.

A bank of muted TVs mounted on his office wall were tuned to various news services, and he glanced up at them from time to time. His cell phone maintained an incessant buzzing with received messages, and he constantly checked the news alerts that populated his feed.

So robotic was his flicking between the papers in front of him, the screens on the wall and his phones that he almost missed the story. As he caught the images on the screens on the wall, he absently replaced the landline back in its cradle, as the person on the other end was in mid-sentence. He immediately turned the volume up on the screen that had caught his interest, showing a local affiliate news station.

It was reporting on an overnight shooting in DC at Navy Yard. Multiple shots fired and reports of a cafe patron killed. He knew that was the area Brendt lived in. A pragmatist and incessant worrier, Walker connected the dots and grabbed his jacket whilst reaching for the Nokia burner phone. He knew this would not be a coincidence. Fucking Boris had assured him they would be discreet and their little problem was only a little problem. Just removing a minor inconvenience. Guns blazing and multiple shots. Discreet. Sounds like they'd actually killed Brendt in public. Fucking idiots. He fired off a text as he exited through the door.

Chapter 53

HER PHONE SLIDING off her lap and dropping onto the hotel floor woke Alex Ward with a jolt. She had fallen asleep in a chair she'd positioned between the door and the window. Ward had picked a random hotel in a random part of the city at around midnight last night, and no one knew that she and Brendt were there. It was about the smallest possible space to fit two beds, a minibar and kettle and a tiny bathroom. It was enough. She hadn't even used the bed.

She nudged Brendt with her foot. So small was the space, she could reach his bed without getting out of the chair. He'd fallen asleep still fully clothed. Brendt had hardly said anything since the shooting at the cafe. Almost catatonic. But she needed to get him focused and determine her next steps.

'Get up, Thomas. I'm going to make coffee.' she instructed.

'OK.' his groggy response, indicating he was not really yet awake. 'Oh wait! What do you mean by make coffee? You talking instant?' he said, snapping a little out of his state and remembering where he was.

'I don't see an espresso machine here do you?'

'I don't do instant.'

'Well, good for you, Thomas. But you need something. That was intense last night. And we need to work out our next move.'

'Make me black tea. Strong. No sugar,' Brendt said as he stretched his long frame and pushed himself up to a seated position against the cheap backboard of the bed.

'Please!' she prompted.

'Please.' he offered.

At least he was coming out of his zombie state. Fucking coffee snob.

Ward started the kettle and got busy.

Quiet for some time, immobile in the bed, eventually Brendt seemed to come into focus, 'Who were those people? What was that tattooed monster trying to inject into me?' he asked.

'You don't know them?' challenged Ward as she poured steaming water from the kettle.

'What? No? How would I know them?' asked Brendt.

'There seems to be a lot of interest in you, Thomas. Government people watching you. Giants attacking you. I was instructed to contact you, to get information from you. And a large ugly man tried to stick a needle in your arm. Tell me why, Thomas? Why are you so interesting?' Ward asked.

'I really don't know. Why are you interested in me?' he countered, avoiding eye contact with Ward, looking over her shoulder through the filthy window.

Ward set hot, steaming tea before Brendt and sat opposite him with her instant coffee. She took a sip. He was right. She should have had tea. This stuff was shit.

Brendt gained a little courage and turned to look at her directly. 'Who are you? Really! You show up and tell me I need to talk to you and then I'm attacked. You shot that guy in the head without blinking. Maybe this was all a set up by you so I'd trust you!'

'Some setup, Thomas - I killed that guy and trust me, he wasn't there to take your sneakers. He was going to inject you. I assume it was going to be lethal. You need to think about that!' Ward knew he was super smart, so counted on him figuring this out and ultimately coming out on her side.

'Well, why were you there? Why were you sent to see me?' Brendt asked, revived by the strong tea.

Ward took a moment and considered her best approach. Her preference whenever possible was the most direct. She put both her feet up on the bed Brendt was using. Her proximity made him uncomfortable and he shimmied away a little. 'We are concerned that our new President had assistance in getting elected. By foreign governments. Russia mainly. And with his knowledge - his consent. That constitutes treason for our leader and terrorism by foreigners involved. And we think you assisted them.'

Brendt rankled at the unclean boots now resting near him on the bed and eyes widened. 'Are you kidding?'

'About which bit?' Ward asked.

'About me helping!' Ward was about to respond but sensed Brendt had more to say: 'Firstly, there is no doubt he was assisted in the election. He was assisted in 2016 to keep his senate seat. Plenty of candidates benefited in both elections - senators and members of Congress. The whole system is compromised. Manipulation is rife. Of course, he was assisted. Are you guys that far out of the loop!?'

'And secondly?' Ward asked.

'Yeah - secondly - I didn't assist anybody. I had nothing to do with this election, any candidates or any foreign anybody. Since the last election I have had nothing to do with politics. My life is quiet. And nice. And structured. Until last night. It's exactly how I like it. Exactly. And I want it to stay that way.' Brendt said.

'Bit late for that don't you think Thomas? So if you weren't involved, why are you so sure the election was compromised?' Ward asked.

'Because over four years ago, we invented how to compromise it. And it worked. And I'd imagine the same people have four years more knowledge on how to do it better. Seriously. Were you sent by the government to ask me whether voters have been misled and manipulated? My confidence in my government just hit a new low. And it was already rock bottom.' Brendt stared at Ward with disdain.

Ward decided to change direction, 'Somebody contacted an online blogger and fed them information about the election and how it was manipulated. The information was precise. We know that person was you.

It's made you a person of interest. That's why we had people watching you. Last time you were directly involved and then grew your conscience. We think that might have happened again. And that's why I'm here. To find out what you know. How it was done. And ideally, who is behind it all.'

Chapter 54

BRENDT WAS SILENT again for a while, 'You guys really don't know shit.' Brendt looked incredulous. Like a gifted child looks at his stupid sibling. He kept rolling, 'I don't work for anyone. I work for myself. Nobody else. I tried to tell your people about this last time and got shut down by some and ignored by plenty. People went after me. All sorts of people. So I moved on.'

Ward had been involved in interrogations and witness testimony many times. She knew it was important to keep the subject talking, keep questioning and to circle back from time to time, 'I think you're lying, Thomas, if you're not involved, why are people trying to kill you?'

Even as she challenged Brendt, something he had said was working away in the back of her brain. She tweaked on a comment he'd made earlier. Before Brendt could speak, she said, 'Hang on. What did you mean when you said you helped the President last election?'

Brendt looked down at the bottom of the bed. Then, across the room. A resigned look on his face. Like he was having to revisit a time he had wanted to forget. Brendt spoke in a veritable monotone, 'He was a Senator then. And barely hanging on to his seat. The people who hired me knew he was ambitious and would sell his own mother to keep his seat. They knew he'd want to make a run for the top job at some stage. And it wasn't just Charleston. We worked for all sorts of candidates. All willing to give something to get something. And then I got out. It was getting out of control. Even I was struggling to distinguish real from fake. I didn't know who was behind what we were doing. It wasn't what I'd signed up for.'

'I've been reading up on Cambridge Analytica. Wasn't that the whole idea? You guys were being paid to help parties and candidates get votes and win?' Ward looked at Brendt and tried to get him to make eye contact. She was drawing on her training in interrogation and reading the tells and wanted to be sure he was being straight. She continued, 'Did you ever think about who might be behind this and paying the bill? Whose interests were being served?' Ward asked.

Brendt leant forward, 'That's why I got out and why I was trying to tell people what was going on. I realised we were just a front. We never saw who was really involved. But I knew we were part of selling out the election. We just didn't know to who!'

'Whom' Ward said reflexively. She took a moment as pieces started to take shape. 'How did you do it Thomas - how would they have done it this time?'

Brendt's eyes went slightly out of focus as he seemed to withdraw into himself. He brought the cheap hotel mug to his lips and took another sip of the strong tea, 'It's pretty clear it was the Russians. And they understood that our elections are won and lost at the margin. A relatively small number of votes in a relatively small number of areas are decisive. So, we would focus on highly targeted geographic locations and on defined demographic and psychographic profiles. And use deep fakes, CGI, recruit influencers, create fake news, blanket social media, activate trolls and hack information. There are plenty of tools that can be applied and are almost impossible to trace back. Much of it can be done remotely or through legitimised or semi-legitimate cutouts.'

As a Geo-Political specialist, this was not new to Ward, but she wanted Brendt talking, and he seemed to be on a roll. He continued, 'Russia is highly motivated. Just look at their President and his agenda to restore the power and prestige of the Federation. They have almost unlimited resources. And they see this as much cheaper and much more effective than going to war. If the United States can be rendered impotent through a compliant President, Russia can move on their own political agenda with far less concern for reprisal.'

Brendt's eyes continued to have a vacant stare, 'Even if the authorities suspect or know it is going on it is hard to identify - differentiating real from fake. And even harder to stop.' Ward was about to speak, thinking Brendt had finished, then he added a final comment, 'We always thought the only way to really stop the interference and the compromise it leads to was for the politicians themselves to not participate and to call it out publicly.

'But politicians whose integrity is greater than their desire to be elected are rare!'

Chapter 55

'SO, WE HAVE a new President that might only be President because you re-wired the internet?' Ward provoked.

'I told you - not me - I bailed out.' Brendt retorted.

Ward continued, 'My agency gets actionable intel this may have been going on and is tasked to find out whether foreign countries have fucked with our election. Your name pops up as the person supplying anonymous information and then, wham, you have people trying to kill you. Sound about right, Thomas?'

Brendt still wasn't convinced about who this woman was. Since he'd met her, his life had been turned upside down. He wondered if everything had been orchestrated to make him believe in her. He figured he'd give just a little more and see what he got back. 'Yes and No.' He relented. 'Yes - I've been sending information to a bunch of journalists saying they should take a look at the election and that it was corrupted. Again. No, because it would take about two minutes to realise it wasn't me doing the corrupting.'

'Now we're getting somewhere, Thomas! So - why are they worried enough to kill you?' Ward asked.

'Can you stop saying that!' his eyes darted to the hotel door as if he expected it to burst open.

Frustrated at being inactive, annoyed with the lack of progress with the conversation she was having with Brendt and completely over sitting passively in a dingy hotel room, Ward abruptly stood. 'I think we need to find out who the two pieces of meat that came to the cafe were.' said Ward, as she grabbed her phone. 'Kristen better have some answers.'

Chapter 56

THE BURNER NOKIA buzzed in the centre console of Daniel Walker's BMW as he drove away from the White House and towards the meeting point. Only a few people had the number, and it was never good news. His already elevated heart rate spiked as he recognised the caller and connected old-school wired earbuds to the phone.

'Mr President. Are you calling from the Oval?' Walker was paranoid about cameras and microphones, which he was sure were in the Oval Office and throughout the White House. The President didn't share his concern and seemed to think he was untouchable. Walker held no such illusion. He demanded they use burner phones for calls and an encrypted message app. But still...

'I'm outside Daniel. In the Rose Garden. Getting some air. Relax. No one can hear me. I need some answers. I've just been made aware of a shooting last night in DC. Is this related to the fucking hacker you were taking care of?'

Walker closed his eyes and prayed again no one could tap their calls. He opened them quickly, remembering he still had to steer the car. 'I'm on my way to meet with our friends now.'

'So it is the hacker?' challenged the President.

'Sir, I don't know yet and it may be best for you not to know at all.'

'Fuck that. This guy connects me to the Russians. I know his name from the campaign four years ago. I don't want the CIA investigation to get any traction. It has to be a dead end.'

'Not sure that we should use that expression with these people!' Walker stated, realising how literal they could be. 'I don't have any information. It was supposed to be dealt with quietly. Apply some pressure and get him to stop talking and take a holiday. Out of sight and out of mind. The shooting might be a coincidence and I hope it is. But that neighbourhood is where he lives and they were activating yesterday. I'll know more once I meet.'

The President wasn't happy, ' Coincidence my ass. Don't be naive, Daniel. Hope is not a strategy. As soon as I get back from this state trip, I'm going to load the CIA up with so much work and get them so distracted they won't know their ass from their elbow. And I'm going to get our senior Senator to initiate inquiries. I want them jumping through so many hoops they won't be able to focus on this.' the President said, ' And Daniel, if the Russians have actually killed this hacker, you may have just created a much bigger problem than we had a few hours ago.'

Chapter 57

A MILD BREEZE carried the fragrance of native Freesias as it took the edge off the afternoon heat, gently fanning the terrace where Kallis and Roberts took their coffee. The buzz of a phone interrupted their conversation. Annoyed with the disruption, Kallis looked at the screen on the low table next to him and recognised the number. He stood, 'Excuse me, Pieter, I need to take this.' He stepped off the terrace and walked out into the open expanse. 'Yes.' said Kallis

'Our interception failed.'

'How?' he asked.

'The target had company. We thought it was just a girlfriend he was meeting for coffee. Turned out it was an operative or maybe he now has protection. One of our men is dead and one, injured.' The voice responded.

'Dead! Can they be traced to you?' asked Kallis.

'Not directly. We used cutouts. Unfortunately they were not trained operators. Our intel indicated the target was not being protected and this would be a soft operation. We instructed them to make it look like a drug deal gone wrong or an overdose.'

'Is the target also dead? asked Kallis.

'No. The operator got the target away.'

'This failed attempt will bring attention!' a frustrated Kallis stated.

'You wanted it to look like an amateur hit.'

'Well, it was certainly amateur. What will you do now?' prompted Kallis.

'We will no longer be pursuing the target. We are backing off. Too much attention.'

Kallis took his time responding. People who didn't think annoyed him. And he hated unfinished tasks. But he couldn't afford to overreact.

There would be other opportunities. 'Understood. I assume you will clear your tracks?' this from Kallis was not a question.

'Already taken care of.'

Kallis disconnected the call. He looked out at the wilderness before him as he considered the implications and how to best handle the situation. He figured it would take the American agencies days to pull the threads together and connect this to Charleston, particularly if the Russians do a decent job of covering their tracks. Real, actionable evidence would be non-existent. Was further action needed? It could make things worse. An option was to let it play out. He just didn't want the CIA or any of the American agencies getting stirred up and distracting Charleston. He needed his full attention and his commitment.

He only needed a few more days without distraction to ensure the Global Intervention Initiative became the focus of the world. Whilst he expected this would all take some time to wash through, the stakes had just risen. This was his moment. He wanted nothing to take away from the most important event the world would know. He thought this to himself with a genuine and complete absence of humility. He needed to find out where they had taken Brendt.

Kallis turned back towards the house and his phone started buzzing again. Looking at the screen, he recognised the number as James Charleston. As he pressed the button to answer the call, he knew he would have to keep the President calm and reassured. He needed him here and completely present this weekend.

Everything was so close.

Chapter 58

DIRECTOR KRISTEN THOMAS left Langley late the night before and had returned in the early morning while it was still dark. Seated at her desk, she could see the first weak rays of sunlight trying to push away the early fog. She got up and went to the credenza, where she poured hot herbal tea. Kristen blew the steam off the top as she took a cautious sip and walked across the thick carpet to one of the large windows. It promised to be a beautiful late Fall day. She was unlikely to enjoy any of it.

Alone in her office, she'd been consolidating updated intel from multiple sources. Now, she felt parts of the picture were coming together. So far, her operatives looking into the likely foreign electoral fraud had been passive. Working behind the scenes. Acquiring and consolidating analysis off the back of solid yet unsubstantiated intelligence threads. The plan had been to surveil Brendt to confirm he was the one supplying the blogger intel. Beyond that, to see if he was still an active participant. She needed a bulletproof case to take on a President and an administration.

The speed and aggression of last night's incident were not expected. Her concern that American leadership may be the focus of significant foreign involvement seemed well placed. What a disaster. It was time to get on the offensive.

While the assailant's BMW had managed to elude the surveillance team, her forensic analysts had descended on the Insider Cafe in the moments after the attack. Coupled with the information Alex had sent through and the ink on the body of the dead guy, they had identified him as muscle from Russian organised crime. He operated out of a series of seedy strip clubs, bars and tattoo studios north of the city. He was low on the totem pole. Or perhaps the stripper's pole. She thought without any real humour.

The clumsy attack was intended to suggest Brendt was mixed up with dealers. And that this was some sort of retribution. But seriously! They hadn't thought it through. Even if it had been successful, it would have raised a flag or several at the agency. They knew Brendt was not an addict. Nor a dealer. In fact, the opposite. He lived a stoic life. Despite his wealth, he avoided indulgence and favoured minimalism and discipline. His life was routined and incredibly healthy. And Brendt would not be easily bought - he made a substantial income from his investments and trading.

The CIA financial team had found his offshore LLCs and identified that he held a range of assets in the US. Including The Insider. The cafe he frequented and that was the location of last night's attack was actually his own. She thought cynically for a moment that in hipster Washington the news of the incident last night would likely make it even more popular.

It was also clear this was the SVR at work - her competition in the East. Typical of them to use Russian organised crime to do their grunt work.

If the intel from Ward was correct then Brendt had not been an active player in the recent election. Kristen needed more convincing and had her team deep-diving into Thomas Brendt. He definitely had prior links to the new President. The interest her agency had taken in Brendt had made him a target. That made him more interesting.

Kristen moved back to her desk. Time for Ward to pay the Russian organised crime syndicate a visit and see if she could find out who was calling the shots. Mack had been patched up but was not yet operational. He could run overwatch.

Typically unflappable, it burned at Kristen to think that Russia and maybe others had yet again interfered with America. And if they had a compromised President in place, then nothing he did could be trusted. He'd be a lame duck–completely ineffectual–or worse. American intelligence and security would be in chaos.

She picked up her ringing phone. Speak of the devil.

Chapter 59

ALEX WARD BROUGHT the Durango to a stop outside The Landing Strip. This was where the Russian muscle was based, according to their intel. She rankled at the site of the place in the morning light. It looked disgusting. Seedy and grubby. The building itself was a single-storey flat-roofed structure that had required no input from the sharpened pencil of an architect. It was positioned close to the curb with low, heavy power lines strung out in front. She couldn't tell what the original colour of the building might have been, but it had faded to a filthy beige. There was an eight-foot steel security fence wrapping around both sides. The street in front was cold and empty with overflowing and uncollected rubbish. She looked at the facade and thought that the mess of dirty, unlit neon only added to the depressing scene. To think that only two days ago she had been running carefree along a beautiful, sun-kissed beach in Australia.

Ward looked at the signs promoting 'Live Nudes!' and felt for the girls who worked there. With the Russian connection, they were likely migrants from their homeland and other Eastern European countries. Working off debts or perhaps, worse. She'd take pleasure in disrupting the morning of the assholes inside.

She took her time observing the place from the driver's seat of the car, looking for security and trying to get a read on how many people might be there. So far nothing. No movement. The place seemed deserted.

Satisfied that their security was lax - or non-existent, Ward told Brendt to stay in the car and to keep his eyes open. He was to text her if he thought they'd been spotted or that trouble was coming her way. Especially more steroid-enhanced giants. She exited and headed around the back of the place, skirting the security fence. She wanted to get the lay of the land and see what exits there were. Working her way down the narrow alley between buildings, she made it around the back and climbed easily over the fence into the rear yard of the building. The yard was a combination of cracked concrete and muddy dirt. There were more overflowing bins and all sorts of discarded rubbish scattered and dumped. She cautiously tried to look through windows but they were impossible to see through - opaque with layers of filth they were also completely blacked out. Unholstering and checking her Sig semi-automatic, she whispered to herself under her breath and approached the rear entrance.

Chapter 60

THE BACK DOOR of The Landing Strip was sitting slightly ajar and the exposed sliver of interior beyond was just a black void. Silently, Ward pushed her back to the wall to the left side and listened. There was music coming from deep within. Maybe someone was here. She appreciated the music - certainly not the genre - just the fact that it would help cover her approach. Gun in her right hand, she pushed the door with her left and entered quickly, hoping the outside light pushing into the empty hallway in front of her wouldn't draw attention.

No sign of anybody. As she slowly moved down the hallway, an open door on her left revealed a disheveled and empty staff break room. Mugs and plates littered the counter. There were closed doors on either side as she moved further into the building, the soft soles of her boots pulling at the sticky carpet. She contemplated breaking into each room to ensure there would be no one behind her but decided to push further towards the source of the music, favouring speed and surprise. She continued slowly into the building, constantly sweeping both forward and back as she went.

Ahead of her was a large opening with dark red curtains pulled completely closed and heavy doors hooked back out of the way. The music was getting louder. Ward figured this was the main bar of the club. Approaching cautiously, she crouched low to avoid a silhouette and pulled a corner of the curtain back. It was dull and gloomy in the room. Still crouched, she moved quickly into the room and immediately pulled the curtains closed, waiting for her eyes to adjust to the gloom. This room was definitely the source of the music. It was loud in here. She could see no one, and her honed, intuitive sense of danger was staying quiet. With her gun now held in front with both hands, she pushed on cautiously, sweeping her eyes across the poorly lit space.

What confronted her was something reminiscent of a war zone. Multiple bodies were scattered haphazard across the floor. She made out blood splatter on the walls and more blood was oozing and soaking the carpet. It was a massacre.

Ward completed a thorough sweep of the entire room, all the booths and the bar area. There was no one else here. At least not alive. She found the controls for the sound system and turned it off. The silence was an assault.

She counted five bodies and even knowing it was pointless still checked each for signs of life and a pulse. They were all cold and dead. Ward found concealed weapons on all of them. None had been drawn. Each body had wounds to their upper torsos and kill shots to their heads. One of the five was the body of the dead cafe giant's partner. The driver of the black SUV lay in a pool of his own blood at the back of the bar.

This had been quick, very professional and unexpected. A superior force, likely multiple shooters had entered and caught them off guard. Guns had blazed on full auto. There was carnage all around the walls and glassed areas of the room. This little corner of the Russian mob had been wiped out. It validated Kristen's intel. The Russian SVR had cleaned up and covered their tracks. The perpetrators were likely either back at the embassy or already on their way out of the country. No leads here. At least this horrible place was out of commission for a while.

Ward headed back to the car.

Brendt looked up as the driver's door opened, 'I thought that would take longer!'

'Dead end.' said Ward.

'So, what's next?'

'You're about to be put to work, Thomas.'

Chapter 61

KRISTEN PICKED UP her buzzing, secure cell phone. Without waiting for her to say anything, Ward jumped in, 'The strip club was a bust. The SVR had already cleaned house. Five bodies on site, all dead.'

'Jesus Christ!' she heard Brendt mutter from the passenger seat.

Kristen said, 'I'll get a forensic team sent there now to look for evidence.'

'Don't bother. It was a professional hit. The team that did this will be long gone and well hidden.' Ward responded.

'Alex, we need to get ahead of this and focus on whoever is giving the orders. I hate playing defense.' Kristen stated.

'Agreed. I'm heading back to the hotel. Thomas is with me and I'm going to make use of him while he's here to access his old files and contacts. We need to see if we can flush out a connection.' This was met with a grunt from the seat next to her.

'We may have an active lead on that.' Kristen said. 'The attempt on Thomas confirmed the internal leak. No one else knew about our plans. And that, knowingly or unknowingly, the President is involved. More likely knowingly. I have had analysts reviewing his meetings and communications over the last couple of days.' She continued, 'Secret Service logs indicate Deputy Director Robert Marshal attended the President's private residence two nights ago. An unscheduled meeting for both of them. Nothing in the official diary.'

Ward asked, 'Marshal - I've heard that name, what does he do? Does he work for you, Boss?'

'Well, technically, everyone works for me; he's Deputy Director of CIA Support. It's completely back office. But he has access to a lot of information. If it's on digital files, he can get to it.' Kristen elaborated, 'Robert Marshal is a CIA lifer. And a puritan. He believes his ethical compass is the only one pointing north. He holds his own counsel, but we know he is disaffected by the current CIA leadership. Including and perhaps particularly me. It points to a misguided and ambitious player who, on merit and talent, has already gone beyond his natural ceiling in the CIA.'

Kristen paused, still joining the dots and assembling her thoughts. 'But he plays the political game well. It seems he has a long-standing and close relationship with Charleston. Now that he has the ear of a President rather than a Senator it is possible he is building his case for change within the CIA. We have some work to do to prove it, but I'm convinced he is our leak.'

Ward considered this for a moment. ' So are you going after Marshall, or shall I?'

Kristen was intent on keeping them focussed; 'Neither. We can't go after Marshall yet. I don't have enough evidence. Besides, if he is the leak to The President, we may be able to use that. He's read in on a number of agency areas. Need to know. But he also runs the systems. We're looking into whether there have been protocol breaches allowing access beyond his clearance.'

'Shit!' said Ward. 'Is Marshall also in with the Russians?'

She could hear Kristen on the other end sipping a drink, 'We don't think so. He's too much of a clean-skin. Charleston will have played him. Played to his own sense of integrity. And his ambition.' Kristen continued; 'However, the Russian connection is becoming clear as well, as it happens Daniel Walker, the President's Chief of Strategy, attended the residence about 30 minutes after Marshal left. Agents on duty indicate he seemed more than a little inebriated. And there were elevated voices in the office. Seems whatever Marshall told The President caused some intense discussion.'

'Sounds like amateur hour in Washington! Though I can't place Daniel Walker. He's not ringing my bell. Too long out of the country I guess! And what the hell is a Chief of Strategy?" Ward said.

'It's an invented role he and the President came up with. Designed to give him access without scrutiny. And he doesn't have a security detail. They are making it up as they go. Walker is young and ambitious. And he's arrogant. A dangerous combination. He's consistently looked to position himself as the de-facto gatekeeper to the President with myself and the National Security Advisor. He believes he should have access to the full PDB and decide what the President sees. We've managed him to date. He's a pit bull. With the subtlety to match. Charleston's right hand. We have him under surveillance now. We're monitoring his communications and reviewing his movements and contacts over the last few days.'

Ward was aware that all of this was outside the CIA charter and technically illegal. And she supported it completely. This was pointing to the top. A senior member of the CIA. A senior insider at the White House. And the President himself.

'Time to pay Mr Walker a visit.' she said almost to herself.

'As it happens, he is not in his office. He just cleared his calendar and is heading out of the city. Seems something urgent has come up.' Kristen indicated.

'Even better. Ping me his location.' said Ward.

Chapter 62

ALMOST BACK AT the hotel, Ward figured she'd quickly drop Brendt off and head to Walker. She worked better alone. Having heard one side of the conversation, Brendt was putting some of the information together; 'Daniel Walker was all over Cambridge Analytica in 2016.'

'What do you mean?' Ward quickly looked across the console of the car at Brendt.

'He was hands-on, and I mean completely. He loved how we could leverage the news cycle and control the narrative. His candidate - the Senator was hanging on by a thread. He was desperate and willing to do anything to have Charleston re-elected to the Senate. And he seriously got off on seeing how people could be brainwashed and led. He was one of the reasons I got out and tried to leak what was going on to the media. His greed for power was horrible. His ambition was unfiltered.' Brendt replied.

'You think he would get into bed with Russia or others to get his man in the Oval?' Ward asked

'He did it back then to hold a narrow senate seat. I imagine he would do much more for the Presidency.' Brendt paused. His eyes went distant for a moment, 'OK, I want to help.'

'I thought you wanted to go home!'

'Well I thought I'd left this behind. But from what I heard just now, it has gotten even more out of hand. I've seen these people up close. Their wires are crossed. They will do anything to get what they want - to get into power. It's scary. And I helped give them the blueprint.' Brendt pushed his eyes shut and then opened them again and looked out his window as they pulled into the hotel, 'Tell me what I can do? And can we find a nicer hotel?'

Ward knew Kristen and the CIA analysts were onto Walker, but she figured the more information the better. And it would keep Brendt busy. 'OK. I'm assuming you can get online without being detected?' He gave her a look as one would a simple child. Unfazed, Ward continued, 'Go to the room. Talk to no one. And I mean no one. These guys are serious. If they work out where you are they will come after you. Get everything you can on Walker. If this guy is working for the Russians or thinks he's playing the Russians, I want to know. And Thomas, we'll be out of this hotel soon.'

Chapter 63

PULLING UP OUTSIDE yet another diner in yet another depressing outer suburb in Washington, Daniel Walker looked at the facade of the building and cast his eyes around the carpark. What the fuck was this place? Stuck in a 1950's time warp!

The exterior had large neon lettering tracking along an inverted, u-shaped curve of the front facade. The letters spelt out DINER. Were they being ironic? He doubted it. It actually looked like a preserved piece of history. Though with all the lights and neon he saw that it was actually clean and lovingly maintained. Literally beaming through the wheezy November light. Somebody really cared about the place.

Walker curbed his impatience and took a moment to check the place out while he sat in his car. There were four square windows on either side of the front door, for a total of eight windows. An individually lit booth was visible through each window, with a formica table and two facing red vinyl bench seats on either side. Every table was set up in an identical and perfectly uniform way, with cutlery, napkins, and condiments pushed to the window end. As he regarded the diner through his windscreen, Walker could see three of the eight booths occupied.

If he thought he'd been conspicuous at their last meeting place, this was another level. He hadn't seen a white face in miles. And the only other European cars on the roads were pimped up and blacked out. He opened the car door, went to the trunk and took off his suit coat and tie, folding it carefully into the cramped space and replacing it with a plain navy bomber jacket and New Yorker ball cap. On the drive over he'd worried he'd be recognised. Not now. These people were more likely to be streaming Netflix than watching Meet The Press.

He really thought Boris was screwing with him by picking these locations. Pushing his buttons. Well, he was about to give Boris both barrels, given he had fucked up royally with his amateur hit squad at the cafe.

He looked around again as he walked up the steps to the diner. Christ, he felt out of place.

Chapter 64

EAGER TO GET this meeting done with, Walker bounded up the four steps to the portico style entry, pushed the door open and headed in. He was hit with music being played at a noticeable volume - above the level of conversation. At complete odds with the 50's styling, it was pumping out some sort of hip hop. He quickly looked around. In addition to the three occupied booths, two central tables had customers, and a lone construction worker was drinking coffee and reading a newspaper sitting at a stool with his hard hat on the counter.

He felt eyes on him. He was the only white face in the diner. Including the staff. With no sign of Boris, he went to an empty booth, asking for coffee as he walked past the waitress. Fuck Boris, he wasn't even going to try and order food here. He pulled out his phone in an effort to look distracted and to keep his head low. As he did the Nokia burner started buzzing. He hoped not the President again. He didn't recognise the number.

'Hello Daniel.' said the voice as soon as he pressed the answer key.

'Boris, where are you? Are you outside?' asked Walker as he peered through the windows.

'Change of plan Daniel, I won't be joining you.'

'Fuck off Boris. You need to get here.' Aware his voice had crept up, he reduced it below the level of the horrible music. 'Have you been held up? This is important.'

'Daniel, I did warn you that we should tread softly with the CIA. The men that went to meet your friend were both shot. One is dead and the other is unaccounted for.'

Walker was seething. What a cock up. At least they hadn't killed Brendt. He hated not to be in control.

'He's not my friend dickhead. He's your problem. You need to get your ass here now so we can sort this out.'

'No, Daniel. Amateur hour is over. You already look completely out of place sitting there with your convertible parked out the front. Imagine the attention the two of us would draw.'

Walker again looked around wondering if Boris could see him. Or was he playing him. Boris continued, 'We have no interest in starting a war with the CIA on American soil. Brendt is not connected to us. We will not risk making this a bigger issue. You need to shut the CIA investigation down from the inside and ensure your boss is protected. Surely a President can command his troops? This would be fixed with a single phone call in my country.'

Walker closed his eyes for a moment. This guy could not be serious. The last thing they could do now was to order the Director of the CIA to shut down an investigation they didn't officially know about. This was spiralling. He needed to cauterise the connection back to the President.

Walker's voice was an intense whisper, 'Your operatives fucked up. They were supposed to scare him off. I'm starting to feel isolated here, Boris. First sign of trouble and you go to ground. Your superiors won't be pleased, Boris. Especially when we stop taking their calls.'

'Goodbye, Daniel.' Boris's line went dead.

Walker was fuming. He felt played five ways. He'd been sent out to this shit-hole just to yank his chain. He needed to think this through and find a way to stop the CIA looking any further. He was the right-hand man to the most powerful person in the world. This needed to be fixed.

Chapter 65

SITTING IN HIS booth, trying to calm down and focus, Walker absently accepted more coffee and turned his mind to the problem. Working with the Russians was tantamount to treason. Not tantamount. It was treason. If it got out and could be proven, that was the end. It would be over less than a year into their first term. He knew the CIA could not have much evidence yet, or they and the feds would be all over it. So far, everything was being kept quiet. He would know if this was an extensive investigation and domestic agencies were involved. It was still early days. The incident at The Insider cafe will have added fuel to the fire. But they still wouldn't have much. He needed to get them off the scent without anything official being required. He thought this would be Kristen Thomas at work. She ran the agency, was super smart, cold as an eel and completely non-political. It would be a waste of time trying to intimidate or influence her. At least in the short term. Any attempt to interfere would only draw more attention. Sitting in the diner, trying to focus on what he could do rather than what he couldn't, he flashed back to his mother when she wanted to stop the incessant fighting between him and his siblings. She'd find a way to distract them. Divert their focus. Give them something more interesting to do.

It sparked a thought. He smiled slightly as he formed the start of an idea.

Chapter 66

ABSENTLY, WALKER THREW some cash on the table and started to slide out of the booth. His progress was stopped as someone sat down on the bench opposite him and put a foot across his seat, blocking his exit. He looked up from under the peak of his ball cap. What the fuck!

'In a hurry Daniel?' Alex Ward asked.

'Who the fuck are you?'

'You're the second person to ask me that in a coffee shop in the last day.' she replied. 'That last person nearly got killed. Not by me mind you. Nonetheless, it was unusual. For him.'

'What are you talking about?' Walker stared at her. 'I don't know who you are and I'm in a hurry.' he pushed at the leg, which was still blocking him from exiting the booth.

'I just need a minute of your time. Perhaps a little more.' Ward said. Her leg not budging.

'Do you know who I am?' Walker stated without any apparent humility at using the tired cliche.

Ward went direct, 'But of course. That is why I am here. You're an important person. Daniel Walker. Chief of Strategy to the President. Whatever the hell that means! Strange to see someone of your invented station in the boondocks of Washington drinking what looks like stewed, unappetising coffee. Unless you're on the campaign trail, I guess! So, if you haven't travelled this far for an old-school Americano, why are you here?'

A little shaken at her familiarity but trying to stay composed, Walker deferred to type. As self-assured as he could manage, he looked at the woman across the table. 'I don't know who you are. But I will find out. And I certainly don't need to explain myself to you. Get out of my way. Now!'

He started to move again. The foot moved. But was only raised enough to come down solidly between his legs. Immediate and painful pressure struck him right where it hurts. Walker involuntarily yelped and flexed forward to take the pressure off. The foot stayed and bore down even more. Shit, that hurt. He didn't dare move. With a pained expression on his face, leaning awkwardly across the formica table top, he stared at the woman across from him. Seething. He wasn't used to being threatened. Not verbally and certainly not physically. And by a woman! In his world, he didn't get threatened. He did the threatening. Through his discomfort, he wanted to remember this person. He noticed she was quite young and very attractive. But with an angular hard edge. She wasn't particularly large, but she was definitely intense, and he felt diminished across from her. She must have been sent by Boris to rattle him. He was the only person who knew he was here. He needed to get back to the safety of the White House to think this through. Fucking Russians were out of control and needed a lesson in respect.

Chapter 67

THE POKER FACE of a Washington power broker was a veil that sat easily on Walker and he fought to get it back in place. It wasn't easy. He was hunched over trying to relieve the pressure off his balls. And he had both hands pushing at the leg causing the damage that wouldn't move. His attempts to re-assert his authority were almost comical. 'Identify who you are.' He demanded. 'You just bought yourself a lot of trouble. What you are doing is unacceptable. I'm a senior member of the United States Government. Threats like this are taken very seriously.' He brought one hand back up to the table, grabbing his phone, searching for the keys to activate the camera one handed. He wanted a photo of this woman.

Moving with lightning speed, she reached across and slammed his hand with the phone onto the tabletop. He felt something crack. Possibly the phone. Possibly his hand. He cried out, completely let go of his still threatened testicles and cradled his now damaged hand.

'Jesus. What the fuck!' Walker exclaimed.

She clearly was not intimidated. Assaulting the Chief of Strategy to the President.

Ward relaxed her grip on his hand and easily removed the phone. The screen had cracked. By the painful way he was holding his hand she may have broken that as well. She hoped so.

'I would've thought such an important person would have a sophisticated, secure and encrypted cell phone. Not an old-school Nokia you can buy at any drugstore! You a luddite Mr Chief of Strategy? Or do you want to keep your calls private and unofficial? Shall I just hit redial and see who answers?'

Holding her gaze, he straightened a little, reached across and took his damaged phone with his good hand. Pushing her leg out of the way he swivelled to exit the booth. Walker knew she could have stopped him if she wanted. With as much resolve as he could manage and a noticeable limp, he pushed his chin out and started walking. Without looking back, he opened the diner door, went down the steps to his car and drove away.

Ward watched him leave through the window as she made a call. 'He's just leaving, boss. He looked rattled. Let's see if cool Mr Walker is starting to feel the heat.'

Chapter 68

HE ONLY MADE it a few hundred yards before pulling over. Walker's composure had fractured as soon as he had got into his car. His mind was scrambled and racing. His balls hurt. His hand hurt. In just a few short hours, things had quickly spun out of control. And he liked control.

He was trying to work out who the woman was and where she had come from. His initial thought was that she had been sent by Boris. But now he dismissed that option. Boris had been definitive that he was cutting their involvement. If he really wanted to threaten Walker, he would more likely have done it in person. And the girl didn't make any direct threats. Didn't seem to know anything. It left him with two possibilities. Hanse Kallis was their link and cut out to Russian agents. Maybe he had stepped in. But Kallis wanted Charleston in power. He was more likely to protect than to threaten.

That left the government. More specifically, Kristen Thomas and the CIA. It was the option he didn't want to consider. But it was the most likely. They had been surveilling Brendt. He figured it was most likely the CIA that had intercepted and shot Boris' people when they had attacked Brendt at the cafe. And now somehow and in a matter of a few hours they had connected him.

'Fuck! Fuck! Fuck!' Walker shouted inside the car, his good hand hitting the steering wheel in time with each profanity. What was supposed to be a quiet interception to warn off a has-been hacker had become a shit show. Fortunately, the President was about to fly to South Africa, and Walker would be traveling with him. He put the car back in gear with his good hand and used the same hand to steer the convertible towards the White House. Holding the steering wheel with his knee, he fumbled for the cracked phone and started dialing. It was time for Robert Marshal to show them just how committed he was to the new administration.

Chapter 69

BENITA MORRIS had convened a Zoom call with several colleagues, both within the UK and from the US, Europe and Australia. They were spread across a range of time zones. All had responded to her emailed queries regarding COVID-19 vaccinated patients presenting severe viral respiratory symptoms. Unfortunately, there were masses of them. Dr Kidman from Sydney was currently speaking to the group.

'We are continuing a range of pathology protocols on more than 500 patients showing varying signs and symptoms. This is our control group. The symptoms are fast-acting and debilitating. The two prevailing theories are that this is a new strain of COVID-19, resistant to current vaccines. Or alternatively, that it is an entirely new Coronavirus. One not treatable by the vaccine and potentially more chronic and deadly. We are trying to determine how this variant or virus is transmissible. We need to determine how these people got it. Current protocols are not working. Patients are continuing to decline.'

As Kidman was speaking, Morris reflected on the quickly growing stream of patients who had presented over the last few days and showed symptoms consistent with Melinda Simpson. They needed to find an effective treatment. And most likely they would need a vaccine or booster to the current vaccines, to fight this off.

Benita Morris took off her glasses and rubbed at tired, black-rimmed eyes as she addressed the group, 'Thank you, Dr Kidman. That's entirely consistent with our experience.' Kidman had been the last to speak. And everyone was reporting variations of the same issue. The numbers were becoming a real concern and were tracking ahead of the early days of the

COVID-19 progression. This strain was virulent and not responding. They had learnt all too well how quickly things could scale and get out of hand.

While addressing the virtual group, her phone alert sounded, indicating a message. She picked it up and looked at the screen. 'Ladies and gentlemen, I believe we need to alert our respective authorities to this new strain or virus. Immediately. Our patient zero, Melinda Simpson, just died. We could not stop it. We have scores of other patients deteriorating rapidly. And many more coming into the wards. It sounds like that is happening everywhere. Just what we need. An even more deadly virus. I'll have my PA set up a time to re-convene in the next twenty-four hours.'

Chapter 70

HANSE KALLIS WAS effusive.

His executive assistant, who was tasked with leading the coordination of the Global Intervention Initiative, was walking him through the final touches for the conference. And everything looked perfect. Meticulous in his planning and exacting in his expectations, his team had delivered. This was his true pinnacle. The culmination of the work of his most important years.

Presenters and guests would start arriving that night and many more the next morning for the summit to commence. He had completed work on his own introductory remarks the day prior, and this morning, he had run through a private rehearsal.

The location for the summit was stunning. Deep in his conservation park he had created an ecologically sustainable resort with a range of accommodation for his guests. It had cost him a fortune. The most senior and important attendees would enjoy their own villa built from local re-useable materials, nestled amongst the trees and the dense native bush. For others, he'd created a temporary tent village. An eye-catching repetition of off-white safari-style hexagonal tents fitted with beautiful timber-framed beds, soft cotton sheets, hide-covered chairs and rattan floor matting. Ensuite bathrooms had been installed in each eco-luxury villa and shared amenity had been installed for the tent village.

An open air dining facility with seating for over 400 had been set up for the opening conference dinner tomorrow night. It was situated on the far side of the expansive grasslands across from the office he currently occupied. Guests would be seated under the stars and amongst roaming wildlife. A large covered outdoor auditorium for the presentations that would begin the following day would host many more with state of the art audio and visuals.

The symbolism and beautiful backdrop of the location would provide a wonderful vista for those attending and the world's cameras. It was living proof that the damage mankind wrought upon nature could be reversed. His Global Intervention Initiative was physically immersed in nature re-vitalised.

He expected the location would be confronting for many attending. Specifically for those who had spent a lifetime in busy and crowded cities discussing and debating the importance of reversing climate change and the devastating environmental damage man had caused. But having never truly experienced nature first-hand. A tailored power suit - the armour of many corporates and politicians would be entirely out of place here. They would be truly amongst dense forrest and herds of wildlife.

The Global Intervention Initiative went way beyond the stifled climate summits hosted by the UN and others. Where politicians and leaders sat in air-conditioned auditoriums. Ferried to and from locations in a fleet of luxury cars. Wrapped in the uniforms and regalia of their station. This location would bring home to every attendee and every camera the amazing beauty and wonderful interconnection of flora and fauna that only nature herself could deliver. Kallis had spent years planning and preparing for this. Knowing the world was running out of time to reverse the damage and make the commitments and changes necessary. In his view they had one chance to get this right.

And that theme was represented everywhere.

ONE.

One common goal.

One singular purpose.

One measure of success.

One planet.

One humanity.

One chance.

Kallis was completely committed in his view that there was only ONE absolute global imperative. Because if left unaddressed the other imperatives - economic, social or political would not matter. The world was beyond the tipping point. Beyond the point at which moderate and incremental policy would make a difference. The world needed an intervention. And given that man had caused the devastation requiring such fundamental change, he believed man must own the responsibility to fix it. Unfortunately neither political leaders, government or corporates had stepped up.

And he knew why. Their imperatives were different and not aligned with the bigger picture and the longer-term goal of fixing the planet. Politicians and governments were singularly focussed on getting re-elected, while corporates were inevitably motivated by short-term profit and the unfortunate adage of shareholder value.

For some time, he believed that it was now to him that the obligation had fallen. And whilst it weighed heavily, he had come to the view that a global intervention was the only answer. This was the culmination of his lifetime's work. A lifetime of progressive realisation of what the planet needed. A lifetime that represented the single most destructive generation the world had experienced. Of witnessing the massive changes in his own backyard and across the globe. A lifetime of building influence and orchestrating the right people into the right places. And a lifetime creating the wealth that he was now deploying.

Chapter 71

THIS WAS WHY Kallis had worked so hard and compromised so much to have the right people in key positions. Why he had become bedfellows with those he would otherwise detest. Why he had taken shortcuts and circumvented. Why he had spent millions and orchestrated electoral corruption at a scale never before seen. In his ninth decade, he was running out of time. The world was running out of time. Neither he nor the planet could let nature take its course. He needed people in place who owed him. That would do his bidding. He was completely aware that what he had done broke countless laws and compromised the political system of the United States and governments in other countries.

But the bigger picture was, in fact, the biggest picture. It was a necessary price to pay. It was all for the good of the planet. For the collective future - of everyone.

So, these next two days would see the assembly of the most progressive and informed humanitarian and ecological thinkers in the world. Together with political leaders representing many countries and corporate and financial executives from both public and private organisations.

And what none of them knew, though they would all soon learn, that their commitment to ONE was far more significant and far more powerful than they could have ever imagined.

Chapter 72

NOW BACK AT the hotel, following her meeting at the diner, Ward was reviewing what Brendt had found about Walker. Intel from Kristen was often slow coming through. She was loving having her own private source.

Brendt was talking, 'Daniel Walker was completely involved in the coordination of fake news and manipulating social media right through the 2020 campaign. He used the same cell phone for months. It's a slightly modern take on an old school Nokia that he thought must be untraceable. But these things have almost no encryption or security. He should have been changing phones every few days.'

Brendt continued, 'He also used standard messaging accounts to communicate. There are literally thousands of texts and emails to and from his accounts. And his phone records are extensive. This guy must spend his life on his phone talking and typing.'

Ward interrupted, 'Who were his primary contacts? Can you determine who he was calling and texting?'

'That is the tricky bit - many recipients were more secure in their communications and had anonymous, encrypted and untraceable user names and accounts. That will take a while. What I can see is extensive international traffic through calls and IP addresses. There are international numbers and locations involved. Russia definitely and China possibly - I'll dig further into these. Most of the comms are within the US, although South Africa comes up a lot.'

Ward had expected the Russian connection, but South Africa was unusual; 'South Africa! Why South Africa? OK, keep digging. I need proof. Enough to confront this guy and bury him. If he was the orchestrator of a president winning with Russian support, I want to know about it. Walker will be the key to Charleston. And send everything you have to Kristen so she can cross-check with her analysts.'

Ward stood at the window of their low-rise, low-rent room. There was no view to speak of. Just a fairly bleak Washington street. The curtains smelt musty. In fact, the entire room had that closed-off atmosphere of hotel rooms the world over. Old curtains. Old, thin carpets. And god knew when the bed cover had last been properly cleaned or replaced. Fed by air conditioning units with windows that won't open. She thought she could smell mould. Definitely mould.

She missed Australia. The fragrant sea air and the warm sun. And she missed David. She would call him soon. Ward moved to the bench that hosted the kettle to make coffee. Brendt had organised supplies delivered by Uber so they could make their own French Press.

Chapter 73

AS SHE FIDDLED around with the kettle and ground beans, Ward reflected on the last couple of days. Literally, in a matter of hours, she had been brought right back into a world she thought she'd left behind. From a tranquil summer afternoon spent running along the beach and contemplating the subject of her next lecture, to quickly being roped back in and transported across half the globe. Immersed back into another disgusting and unbridled quest for power and ascendancy. She wouldn't admit it to anyone - particularly not David - but the taste of action had her buzzing.

Ward allowed her mind to drift as she poured the coffee. Fortunately, most people - the broader American populace - those she had fought for and protected couldn't contemplate and rarely experienced first-hand the blind narcissism that drove the enemies of her country. Both within and outside her borders. And she hoped it would stay that way. Unfortunately, it had been her world for many years. The people - the monsters - she dealt with would do anything to get what they wanted. Literally anything. Justified by whatever religion, retribution or vision suited them. She couldn't stand it. And wouldn't stand for it or stand by whilst it happened. She had fought these wars willingly. Believing in her own moral compass. Willing to match them with ferocity and aggression. It was the only way. They followed no rules and no laws. And she had bent and twisted and often ignored the rules and limitations her own country placed on how they should deal with their enemies.

They were rules created by vague people in suits. Rules designed to mitigate blowback onto them. Rules that claimed to uphold the values of their country, whilst their enemy had no such limitations and attacked without observing any laws. It meant Ward and her colleagues were fighting with one hand tied behind their backs. Or worse.

The politicians and bureaucrats always had one eye on how they could defend their actions if ever brought to the public's attention. The other on how they could manipulate their legacy. Ward had no interest in the games. And felt that being motivated by legacy was pretty perverse when you were fighting against those who wanted to destroy your country and the way of life it stood for. She had no intention to bring terrorists and political monsters to justice when she was sent to deal with them. She simply believed the world was better and could only move positively forward if they ceased to exist. It was an attitude and approach she matched with both talent and determination. With amazing success. To the point her superiors did everything they could to stop her retiring. She was the tip of the spear and they didn't have too many spears.

Chapter 74

BUT FOR ALEX Ward, it had come at a cost. Chasing the enemies of her country had been unending. She literally went from one hot spot to another, from one threat to the next. And whilst her physical resilience was off the charts, she was burning out. And it was showing, with an ever-shorter tolerance and a growing disregard for authority and oversight.

And then David got sick. It brought everything into focus. A new perspective. They had been college sweethearts. He was an Aussie studying medicine on a swimming scholarship. She had moved from Austin on a track scholarship and majored in political science. Both at Stanford. Once she met him, she fell immediately and could neither contemplate any other person in her life nor life without him. They simply gelled. He got her and she got him. And they had no secrets. Once she told him she was being recruited by and ultimately joined the CIA and the fight against terrorism, he had her back. He knew this was her purpose. Her calling. And he supported her. Without waiver. She reciprocated by never holding back from him. She wouldn't compromise operations by getting specific - but he knew what she was getting into. Despite this being against the protocols of confidentiality and secrecy her agency demanded and to which she had committed. If they wanted her and trusted her, then they got him as well. Without David she could not be the person she needed to be.

But he started to see the effect the job was having on her. Always exhausted. Always going headlong into danger. He knew she was fearless but he started to worry about her emotional state. She was withdrawn. And quick to get angry. She hardly slept. He began hating her job. And it was affecting their relationship.

David's illness hit them quickly. And at a time when she hadn't consciously realised how worn down she'd become from the relentless pace. It made everything even more stressful. He had started showing symptoms - being tired, suffering from constant mouth ulcers and night fevers. He couldn't finish the endurance swim sets and intense gym sessions he had always managed easily.

They initially put it down to the demands of his surgical rotation at The George Washington University Hospital: working extended hours and still trying to commit to the training regimen he and Ward shared. They figured he was simply burning the candle at both ends and just needed a rest. She also knew how David was feeling about her job, and it was quietly undermining their relationship. She worried that stress was exacerbating his exhaustion.

They took a short holiday to Bali to relax and restore under the tropical sun. But the symptoms persisted. Then, when they returned home, got worse. So, at Ward's insistence, he conscripted a colleague to run some blood tests. Within a week, after extensive testing and referral, he was diagnosed with the blood cancer Leukaemia. He was lucky - they hoped. He was young, having just turned thirty and very fit, they had caught it early, and he was a resident surgeon at a hospital. Ideally located to get the very best treatment.

They started an aggressive chemotherapy program intended to blast the slow-growing cancer. His initial response was positive. But the effects of the cancer and the side effects of the treatment were debilitating. Not sure how this would all end up, David had wanted to get back to Australia to be near his family. In that way, the stars aligned. Ward knew she had to do something different. For herself and for their marriage. She had only her sister as family. And when David got well they wanted to start their own. Her current career was not ideally suited to being a mother. She requested a 12 month sabbatical from Kristen with no thought of ever returning - she just knew she couldn't tell her that. And with the connections of the US government, secured a teaching role at the University of New South Wales. Six months later, she told Kristen she would not be coming back - an easier conversation from a distance. David was responding to treatment and had cycled through four rounds of chemo. Still a long road, but the signs were promising. And she convinced herself she loved her new life. Which she largely did. No one shot at her and she wasn't killing anyone.

Taking a deep breath of the rank air in her tiny hotel room, she considered how easily she had reverted to her old self. Ward wondered if it was just the years of training and fieldwork. Muscle-memory! Or was it more than that? Was it deeper - part of her DNA. Whatever it was she knew she couldn't turn it off until she fixed whatever was going on. She couldn't stand terrorists and the killing they perpetrated and justified. And she equally couldn't stand the untamed power games. Destroying people. Manipulating people. Going to any lengths. Just to get into power. Unfortunately the world didn't change. And she was deeply wired to not let it happen. This time, the bad guys were operating from within. People from her own country. In some ways that was worse. Mack and Kristen knew the buttons to push. Her phone started buzzing. About time.

Chapter 75

WARD ACCEPTED THE call, 'Yes Boss?'

Kristen responded, 'Daniel Walker made two calls after your chat with him at the diner. The first was to Deputy Director Robert Marshal. We were not able to listen in.'

Ward jumped in; 'Are you shutting Marshall down? Confront him. Arrest him?'

'No. Not yet. I have an idea on making him more useful where he is.'

Silently, Ward conceded the point. The field of political strategy and subterfuge was definitely Kristen's wheelhouse; she voiced the obvious, 'If Walker called Marshall, he clearly connected me to the CIA and the links to Thomas.'

'Agreed. I have a team of analysts on both Marshall and Walker. The evidence is becoming overwhelming. The dots are joining. This won't end well for them.' Kristen responded.

Ward focussed, 'The second call?'

'Was to South Africa to a person named Hanse Kallis.'

'OK. This must be the South African connection! Should I know that name?'

'Only if you're involved with pharmaceuticals. Or an environmental activist.' Kristen continued, 'Kallis is a South African businessman and humanitarian. He's in his 80's. Spends all of his time now on environmental activism. A crusader to influence governments and corporates to right the ecological wrongs. And he invests a lot of his personal wealth. He was a substantial contributor to the Charleston campaign. The President is about to fly to Sth Africa as a keynote at a major environmental forum Kallis is hosting called the Global Intervention Initiative.'

'He sounds like he'd be a good influence over our boy Walker and his boss!' Ward said.

Kristen responded, 'On the surface. That's how he wants to be seen. But there may be more to Hanse Kallis. He has piqued our interest previously. His businesses and connections span the globe. Including Russia. I'll brief you in more detail when we have a better picture. However, our real concern is that the President of the United States is about to commit the country to a raft of emissions targets and environmental protocols that will make the Paris Agreement seem like a reformist kindergarten. It could flip the economy on its head and send us into a massive recession. All because it's likely he owes Kallis and the Russians the Presidency.' Kristen paused as her own words began to sink in and the implications reverberated in her mind. This could be just the start!

She picked up again, 'Meantime it looks to me like Daniel Walker is circling the wagons. He won't want any more digging into the election. The clumsy attack on Thomas Brendt shows he's desperate. It also shows their arrogance, thinking they can call in the Russians and not be found out.'

Ward considered the comments from Kristen, 'That clumsy attempt on Thomas would have been successful if we hadn't been there. He'd be a drug statistic. It was a desperate play - no doubt. But very close to working. We got lucky with the timing.'

'Quite right. And now it's backfired. The target is now on their backs.' Kristen responded.

'So, what do we do about the Russians?' Ward asked and Kristen could sense the rising anger in her voice.

'The local SVR has clearly looked to clean house. The Russian mafia won't take that well. Let's leave them with their own war for now. They will likely go quiet. At least for a while. I'll also make a call to Dmitri Volkov head of the SVR in Moscow. He won't be pleased.'

Ward would have preferred to go on a hunt but this snake had more than one head. 'So we focus on Walker?'

'Walker and Charleston. They are feeling the heat. Making mistakes. Let's amplify. I want to unravel the entire electoral scheme and take out all the players.' Kristen was reading the play and knew that unchecked this government and those that followed would be completely compromised. The United States could be brought to its knees.

Ward changed gears, 'Thomas has found substantial communication going back months from Walker to South Africa. I'll get him to cross reference your intel to see if it's Kallis.'

Kristen was not surprised Ward had Brendt digging independently. The agency security breach aside, the initiative to build information and validate made sense. She replied evenly, 'I've no doubt it will be.'

Ward was building and focusing her anger, 'This is looking like a cluster fuck. Power-hungry politicians in bed with South Africans and Russians. And who knows who else. Are they fucking mad? Russia won't need to invade us - they are running our President! I need to get to Sth Africa.'

'I agree.' said Kristen. 'Let's get eyes on these players. A jet is on standby. Mack will be your support here if you can't reach me. I'll brief him in.'

Chapter 76

FUCK 'EYES-ON' fumed Ward as she disconnected the call. If these pricks were doing what she thought they were, they would be getting more than just 'eyes on'!

Ward absently carried her now cold coffee back to the window with its dirty glass and depressing view and took a sip; she immediately spat it back into the mug and put it on the sill. She considered the various pieces of intel and was concerned Kristen might be stifled if Robert Marshal got wind of the fact that they were looking into his relationship with the President. As good as Kristen was, the political pressure these people could bring to bear could be overwhelming for anyone. They would tie the agency in knots and slow everything down.

Still looking out the window, Ward said, 'Thomas, get packed, you're coming with me.'

'What? Where now. No more Russian strip clubs for me!'

She turned to look at him, 'Johannesburg.'

'Whoa! South Africa?' Brendt looked up with his mouth open, forming his protest. He was ready to head home. He looked at Ward and thought the better of it.

'I need some gear from my apartment. And I need to see Nikki.'

Ward was tempted to override. She wanted to get in the air, but she also wanted Brendt to trust her—she had a feeling he'd be pretty useful. 'OK. We'll swing by there on the way to the airfield. We leave here in five. I want to be in Sth Africa ahead of the President.'

Chapter 77

DANIEL WALKER SAT across from James Charleston in the Presidential office on Air Force One. They were moments before take off. First stop was Texas to pick up The First Lady, then Florida for a donor's dinner before flying to Johannesburg overnight. A long haul twenty hour trip. The First Lady had declined to join them on the state visit. She'd stay in The Sunshine State. It would mean he and the President could get some work done. Deal with this nuisance CIA fascination with the election. And make a plan for the Russians. Fuckers. And maybe get some sleep.

Walker looked up from his phone, gathered his thoughts, then addressed the President, 'The CIA is sending the operative that saved Brendt to Sth Africa. Thomas Brendt is travelling with her.'

'You know this how?' asked Charleston.

'Marshall.' responded Walker. 'I've told him he has to show us his value and his loyalty if he wants to be bumped up. We want no surprises.'

'Is his intel reliable? I specifically warned Kristen Thomas that I'd heard they were operating on US soil and they shouldn't. They need to have their eyes on our enemies. She wouldn't want a 9/11 to happen if she wasn't doing her job.'

Walker simultaneously closed his eyes, drew a breath and shook his head. Charleston should not be issuing those types of directives to the Director of the CIA. It would only intensify the heat.

Walker carefully chastised his Boss, 'The CIA is working through a loophole. The threat of terrorism gives them broad scope. I'd say she's more fired up than ever. The operative they are using is not a CIA employee. At least not anymore. Alex Ward. Former CIA agent retired a little over a year ago and moved to Australia. She lectures at the University in Sydney in Geo Politics. Does a little government connected corporate consulting. Seems they have reactivated her and gone off reserve to avoid scrutiny.' Daniel was impressing himself with the information he was relaying to the President. Even though he'd done nothing other than pressure Robert Marshall to get them intel.

Charleston was starting to steam, 'Fuckers must think we're stupid. Seriously, Kristen Thomas is a dog with a bone. Why would she care so much about the election? Every election is warped.'

Walker mused for a moment. 'And I've met her. She pressed my nuts earlier today.'

'What? Who?'

'This operator, Alex Ward.'

'What? She did what?' asked the President. 'Actually, never mind. Let's focus on Kristen Thomas. We need to get her gone. I need a supportive CIA, not this mob looking under stones.'

Walker picked it up, 'She has an issue with you and the Russians.'

'Oh, you think Daniel!' the President dialed up the sarcasm. Then vocalised his own thoughts, trying to convince himself as much as Walker. 'She should realise - we use them. Not the other way round. Kristen Thomas and her gung-ho, flag waving cohorts need to realise that we take a straight line to getting things done. Leave it to the big boys to sort the world out. And get out of the way.'

Pleased with himself Charleston looked across at Walker, 'OK, here is what you need to do. Firstly, let Hanse know there is an operator heading his way. He needs to be forewarned. Could be a good opportunity to get this nuisance Brendt taken care of on foreign soil.'

He continued, Secondly, we need to activate a plan to replace Kristen Thomas. I want to run a full press on her. Get her so caught up in saving her own skin she'll forget all about the election. Let's get the Congressional hearings into the CIA announced as soon as we get back on US soil. And tell your man Boris they need to generate fake news stories about the CIA. Some interrogation convention breeches and killing innocents in Iraq and Afghanistan and anywhere else he can come up with would work. Taped interviews with sobbing Iraqi widows would be a nice touch. He owes us with his fuck up over Brendt. And you use your best press contacts to start leaking.'

'On it.' Walker was relieved. He preferred being on the front foot. And he'd been pushing since they took office to replace the leadership at all the major agencies - including the CIA. He wanted friendlies in place.

As Walker rose, Sandy Green, the President's Private Secretary, came through the door. For a moment he forgot their growing problems and gave her a once over. He'd always admired the tall, blond and, as far as he knew, single assistant to Charleston, but she had never given him any vibe that she was interested. In fact, she offered nothing more than a very professional and pretty cold demeanour. He figured he'd use the rest of their first term to see if he could wear her down.

'Mr. President, I have Dr. Fauci on the line. He says it is urgent. He's been trying to reach you since yesterday and has called six times since. Says if you don't take his call, you'll see him on the networks complaining about the inaction of our government to address a new virological threat.' Sandy had been reading from her notebook and now looked up at Charleston, awaiting instruction.

'For fucks sake. I'm so sick of Fauci and this fucking virus. It's old news. Should have been dealt with by now. It's all anyone wants to ask me about. I've got the CIA breathing down my neck, and he wants to go to the press about this hyped-up fucking Chinese flu! And he's a scaremonger. Getting his 15 minutes. Every time I talk to him, he wants more money, more equipment, or to shut something down.' Charleston stopped his rant, about to tell Sandy to fuck him off again. But he knew he'd keep at him and he was actually very likely to speak to the press. He blew a stream of air through is cheeks,

'It's OK, Sandy. I'll speak to him. Put him through.'

Walker gave one last look over Sandy Green and then left the President's airborne office, heading to his own corner of the plane to make his calls.

Chapter 78

NAVY YARD DID not give up parking spaces readily. Ward circled the block around Brendt's apartment twice and finally opted for a 'No Parking' space close to his building.

'We need to make this quick, Thomas. Get what you need and we get going.'

'Nikki's home.' he said looking at the lights in the windows above.

'You can't tell her anything. If you like I can talk to her.'

About to reject out of hand, the idea of a CIA operative talking to his girlfriend, he thought again about the series of events of the last few hours, 'Actually, you may need to. I've been texting her. And I'm not sure she believes me. Someone trying to kill me. A dead giant Russian at the cafe. Getting shot at. A corrupt President. The CIA grabbing me. That is quite a bit in a day or two. And now I'm off to South Africa.' Almost as a continuous sentence, he said, 'Yes, you definitely need to talk to her.'

Brendt punched the key code into his front door. As soon as he walked into the open living space Nikki ran from the kitchen and jumped into his arms. She buried her face into his shoulder for a moment, then raised her face to look into his eyes, 'Tommy, what is going on? Where have you been?' She then saw Ward coming into the apartment behind him. 'You were at the cafe last night!' Nikki said a little breathless over Brendt's shoulder.

'Hello, Nikki. I'm Alex. I'm sorry, but we need to be quick.'

'Tommy messaged me about you. What do you mean you need to be quick?'

Ward looked at Brendt, 'Thomas, why don't you get what you need and I'll bring Nikki up to speed.'

Ward and Nikki moved to the open kitchen. Ward took a moment to take in the loft and to create some space for the conversation she needed to manage. She admired the floor-to-ceiling windows and expanse of restored timbers exposed as part of the ceiling. The polished concrete floors juxtaposed with mid century furniture and the stainless appliances. The open plan living area blended the kitchen, dining area and living room. There was subtle tech evident everywhere. From the Loewe flatscreen seventy-seven inch TV on an integrated pedestal to the Bowers and Wilkins floor speakers. The large space beautifully and minimally furnished.

The pause had settled Nikki, and she broke the silence, 'Can I make you some coffee?'.

Knowing she was a very capable barista Ward quickly accepted. She could still taste the cold brew from the hotel. As Nikki moved fluidly around the stainless steel, dual group La Marzocca espresso machine, Ward offered a sanitised version of what had happened at the cafe and everything since - with just enough detail to ensure Nikki took this seriously. Brendt re-entered the kitchen. Taking a sip of the delicious espresso Ward commented, 'You've changed!'

Brendt had been typically meticulous in his selection. He'd chosen tapered khaki Stone Island cargos tucked in to Brunello Cucinelli nubuk hiking boots with an untucked Moncler Grenoble baby blue cotton shirt. He finished the ensemble with a tan Moncler bucket hat. And he'd packed a few other options in his Bennett Winch leather weekender.

Without a wisp of self conscious, Brendt responded, 'I checked my weather app for the destination. It's warm there. And I grabbed my passport.'

'Those boots look brand new.' Ward offered with the ghost of a smile. 'I've been breaking them in walking to the cafe.' Brendt offered, this time a little defensively. 'Uh-huh!' Ward raised a single eyebrow.

Nikki hadn't yet touched her coffee and was looking at Brendt with genuine concern.

She started speaking and it all tumbled out, 'I really can't understand what is going on. The cafe has been closed since last night. The police were there for hours. They sent us all home. Said we should be OK to clean up and re-open tomorrow. I don't know if I want to go back there. And this is all about you, Tommy! Why? And now you're leaving - where are you going? Somewhere warm? With your passport! Where is that?'

Before Brendt could answer, Ward jumped in. She could see Nikki trembling a little and her eyes were tearing up as she spoke. She was worried Brendt would reveal too much or lose his resolve. She needed to control this and get them moving,

'Nikki, Thomas has a history with the people who attacked him at the cafe. It's actually a throw back to his time with Cambridge Analytica. When he gets back he can properly explain everything. For now he's safest with me and my team. He could also be really important and helpful to us. He can access information better than almost anyone. He knows them. I need his help.' Her intensity left little room for challenge.

Nikki looked completely overwhelmed and uncertain about what to do. From what she had just heard, Tommy was in a serious situation. Ward had saved his life. It seemed Thomas trusted her. Nikki felt she'd have to trust her. And she appreciated that she had told her what she had. She doubted she needed to.

Brendt moved to Nikki and hugged her. Ward wasn't sure if that was for him or for her. Nikki edged back from Brendt and with a slightly glazed look she asked Ward, 'Who do you work for?'

Ward considered her response, 'I work for the government. We needed to talk to Thomas and I was in the right place at the right time. For him. We really need to go. Sorry Nikki. I can't say more for now. Thomas, I'll leave you two for a moment. Meet me in the car. Please make it quick. Nikki -

perhaps you have family or friends you can stay with for a few days?' Ward turned and left through the front door as Bendt pulled Nikki back into his arms.

'Perhaps you could visit your parents ...'

Chapter 79

HER FEET PROPPED on the executive table in front of her, Alex Ward rested the encrypted tablet on her lap. She was reading a classified overview of the travel plans for President Charleston and his entourage.

As the CIA jet started to accelerate down the runway. She summarised for Brendt, 'The President will leave Florida late tonight after a party dinner and land in Jo-Burg late Saturday afternoon local. He will then be flown on Marine One to the forum location to attend the opening dinner.'

She looked up at Brendt. It was just the two of them; they would be linking up with a local agency contact when they arrived. She addressed Brendt, 'You and I will land at KMI Airport in the Kruger National Park and be on the ground six hours earlier than Air Force One. Thomas, I want to know who is attending this convention. I'd like to think our new President is truly committed to the planet, but there are clearly other motives for him being there. Kristen is working on securing access and credentials to the forum. We're going to find a way to meet the President's important friend, Hanse Kallis.' Almost as an afterthought Ward added, 'He's then going to Moscow after the forum. The puppet going to meet his master.'

At just over Mach1, the CIA Gulfstream G650 was quicker than Air Force One. Equipped with long-range tanks, it could make the trip nonstop. Coupled with the President's stop in Florida and the Marine One ride to the game reserve, it gave them a few hours of advantage. And it had high speed, secure satellite internet connection. Brendt set up in one of the oversized leather chairs, opened the hinged table top and went to work. Ward found them some food in the self-service galley. She called David and caught him at home - morning his time. They had a short and slightly tense conversation, slipping back into the language of her previous life; he didn't ask any specific questions he knew she wouldn't answer.

Tired after having slept in a chair last night and with a long flight ahead she showered and changed in the on-board bathroom, putting on discreet and functional street clothes suited to the climate they would be landing in. Ward adjusted one of the seats in the rear of the plane so it laid flat, found a light blanket, put in some ear plugs and an eye mask and let the soft drone of the engines and motion of the plane relax her into a much-needed sleep.

Chapter 80

ASSOCIATE PROFESSOR MICHAEL Francis was head of the National COVID-19 Clinical Evidence Taskforce based in Melbourne, Australia. The months since the outbreak had been a blur. Francis had simultaneously been working with the Australian Medical Association, the Chief Medical Officer, and Federal and State Governments to manage the epidemic, establish protocols for containment and authorise and roll out the unprecedented vaccination program. All while being one of the critical points of liaison with the international virological community. Australia had been amongst the leading nations in their response to the virus. Developing and enforcing strict community protocols. Placing the states and country into rolling lock downs. And scaling a program of vaccinations at a speed never seen prior.

Like many - perhaps all, of his colleagues in the public health system, he was running on fumes. Sleep deprivation from weeks and months without rest coupled with unprecedented stress to lead the response. The distress of witnessing first hand severe illness and death across the community. Their lack of preparedness and consequent scramble for facilities and equipment. And the burden to inform the country and the politicians of the imperative to enforce community lockdowns and deliver the vaccine.

It had been an overwhelming period. One which he had never anticipated and had no time to prepare or train for. He just had to accept and adapt and act. Like everyone else. But unlike most, he was a leader in the fight. They looked to him and a handful of others for answers. It was a real-time response to a global crisis that they could only understand as they were dealing with it. It had been catch-up medicine and he was constantly fearful of the mistakes and missteps they were no doubt making.

Finally, he felt, seemingly after months on end, they could see some results. The restrictions, lock downs, protocols and vaccinations were having the effect they had hoped for. The rate of new infections had finally started to decline. The more extreme symptoms were moderating. Death rates were reducing. The surreal experience they had all been living, hopefully, coming to an end. Or, at the very least, dialing back a notch. The pre-covid lifestyle and freedoms they all took for granted may again be possible. The glimpses of light down a long tunnel - these positive signs he had initially, cautiously doubted had now given him renewed energy. Reinvigorating his determination and commitment and confidence in the course they had committed to.

Until now.

Professor Francis was part of the international virological team with whom Dr Benita Morris from London had been communicating. In the last days and weeks, she alerted them to what she felt may be a new derivative of COVID-19. A variant or strand proving to be highly virulent and less responsive or perhaps not responsive to the established protocols and medicines. This was not uncommon as a virus mutated over time. His colleagues took each piece of new information seriously and worked to stay informed and share ideas and research to mitigate. But the mutated variations had historically been inconsequential. Not taking a firm hold as COVID-19 had. And whilst often devastating to the victims had been tiny in numbers.

Until now.

Wrapped in full hazard grade PPE, Professor Francis was standing just inside the ground level entry to one of the large temporary hospitals the military had set up on a massive indoor sports ground in Melbourne. He reflected on how sad it was that this was now one of the central response locations to the pandemic. And not the place he would come to sit in the stands wearing the colours of the Demons and shouting along with thousands of others to cheer his team and admonish the umpires. Such a quintessential and now distant way to spend a Melbourne afternoon.

A week or more ago, the makeshift hospital had been busy but ordered, controlled and calm. Now it resembled something from an apocalypse movie. Every bed inside was taken. In fact, some of the narrow beds had two patients top to tail. Where only days ago, there had been mobile screening to provide privacy between beds, these had now been pulled down to create more space, and even the floor space in between had patients. It was a sea of bodies and people and beds. With PPE encased medical staff almost running to respond to voices and alerts. This had escalated at an alarming pace. In just days.

His mind flashed to the early, uncertain, manic days of the virus, and the experienced and field-tested Professor Michael Francis considered this scene to be the worst he had witnessed.

Chapter 81

PROFESSOR FRANCIS LOOKED across the paved promenade outside the sports ground, taking in the broad tree-covered and landscaped grounds leading into the sports arena and the car parks beyond. This was where the massive weekend crowds would congregate before a game. But the crowds before him now were very different. There were literally hundreds of people lining up to get in to the hospital. All in varying states of distress. Some on their own. Many with family or friends offering support and comfort. Some could no longer stand and were lying on the ground. Paramedics and medical staff were trying to triage the large number of people with crowd-controlling assistance from various military personnel. Unfortunately, the makeshift COVID hospital could offer them very little. There were no more beds. Medication to reduce pain and fever was proving ineffectual. Inside and outside the temporary hospital, sick people were getting sicker.

This scene seemed surreal. A nightmare playing out in front of him. How had this happened so quickly? All in just a matter of days. From what appeared to be a pandemic being brought under control to this. Initially, he had hoped it was isolated. Some geo-specific outbreak or vaccine contamination or perhaps something else. Something that would be a disturbing but minor blip. That they could work out a treatment for it and get it under control. Much like many of the COVID variants they had dealt with. But so far, that was not the case. What he witnessed here was being seen in a growing number of locations in Australia and around the world. He watched as more media trucks pulled up and reporters and camera crews, also wearing personal protection, started filming and recording. He had been trying to call Benita Morris for hours. No answer. All he had received was an email from Dr Morris to the full international virological group with a series of images very similar to what he was looking at.

Standing immobile for what seemed hours but was, in reality, only minutes, Professor Francis was torn. He wanted to get back into the hospital and work with the doctors, nurses, paramedics, and military staff to administer treatment and tend to those suffering.

But he couldn't. Instinct honed through years of practice coupled with the reports they were now receiving indicated this was not a variant strand of COVID-19. This was something new altogether. Something potentially more devastating than COVID-19, seemingly spreading at an accelerating speed. And not responding to the treatments they had developed. He needed to get back to the task force HQ and manage this new horror. They needed information. They needed to understand what they were dealing with. He needed to inform the political leaders. And they would need answers - a response. So far, he had none.

He dreaded to turn on the news or look at his feed. These scenes would be re-igniting the panic they had worked to contain since the early days of COVID.

Inside his enclosed visor, the overwhelming pent-up emotion of many months had tears of pain and frustration running down his face. The hope he had been building that this horrible pandemic was slowly being controlled was washed away as he watched a young resident doctor pull a sheet over another deceased patient's face.

Chapter 82

DR ANTHONY FAUCI had finally gotten through to the President. As Chief Medical Advisor, he was the nation's most senior infectious disease expert. He was leading the country, the medical community, the government and in many ways the world in the response to COVID. And he was brilliant. A lifetime in infectious disease had led him to this moment. The problem was Charleston found him a whining pain in the ass.

'Dr Fauci, I apologise for missing your calls. It's been a busy time. How can I help?' Charleston braced for the barrage to come - the demands for greater restrictions and accelerated vaccinations. It was already costing a fortune. Charleston felt the US and the world were overreacting massively to the virus. Every protocol the medical community required was going to stifle the economy. He was not going to be the President responsible for an economic spiral. It was just a fucking virus. And it mainly killed old people.

Fauci rolled his eyes at the comment that the President had been too busy! What on earth could be more important! 'Mr President, I appreciate you making time. I'll get to the point. There is a new virus hitting the community. It's hitting hard. We don't yet know if it's a strain of COVID or something else. It's not responding to treatment and current vaccines are ineffective. Symptomatic people are flooding hospitals and vaccination clinics. If you turn any of the news services on, you will see real-time footage. And it's not just in the United States. It's across the globe.'

For fuck's sake, thought the President. This guy had waited his whole life for a crisis like this. There was always a new virus. He needed to get him off the line and focus on the real crisis. 'Dr Fauci, thank you for bringing this to my attention. I hadn't been informed. Give me the highlights and your recommendations....'

The fucking highlights, thought Fauci. This was not a Monday night football recap - it was a fucking deadly pandemic!

'Of course Mr President....'

Chapter 83

UNITED STATES SENATOR Elizabeth Goldman stood with each hand lightly gripping the side of the podium. She was at the base of the steps of the Capitol. The familiar structure that rose elegantly behind her provided an imposing backdrop suggesting she stood with the full authority of the United States government and her country. Around her stood a large number of aids, officials and supporters as well as several men and women in various uniforms of service. The podium hosted numerous microphones and she spoke into these as she looked directly ahead.

'Good afternoon. Many will have seen the disturbing video footage of what appears to be United States intelligence officers conducting a violent interrogation of a hooded and restrained prisoner.' The Senator was speaking without notes or a teleprompter and now looked with intent into each of the various cameras in front of her and the the crowd of media beyond.

'This graphic footage follows numerous recent news stories and eye witness interviews indicating illegal detainment, interrogation and deaths of innocents at the hands of US serving officers.'

Watching the live press conference on one of the screens on the wall of her office at Langley, Kristen Thomas was disturbed. Not by the alleged actions of intelligence and other serving officers Goldman was speaking about. But by the blatant approach of the Charleston administration. She'd seen the video in question, had it analysed and it was fake. Not even a good fake. And the news stories referenced were also staged. Likely paid for with US currency funded by taxpayers. Kristen watched as The Senator continued.

'This administration condemns and repudiates such actions. Not only are they immoral, Enhanced Interrogation is in violation of United

States anti torture statutes, is contrary to international law and to the United Nations convention against torture. This government will not allow such actions to continue by Americans under our watch.' Again The Senator paused. An experienced orator she wanted to ensure the drama of the moment was captured. She had also given careful consideration to the sound bites she wanted used by the media.

'I am today announcing the formation of a Senate Select Committee on Intelligence, to specifically investigate the claims made in these reports. The scope, powers and membership of the Select Committee will be announced in due course. The United States takes it's role as a leader within the International Community very seriously. Acting legally, acting with oversight and acting under the moral umbrella of our faith is critical to who we are. We will not lower ourselves to the inhumane level of those we condemn.

'Our President, James Charleston is fully supportive of the investigation to be undertaken by the Select Committee and has committed to implementing all recommendations the committee makes. Such recommendations may include structural changes, oversight changes and personnel changes. And may also include criminal proceedings.' The full blush of the moment was clearly upon the Senator. Convention had it that one did not preempt the outcome of a Senate Committee of Inquiry. Or try to influence its outcomes. Convention was being flaunted. She now looked above the cameras and above the heads of those before her.

'The CIA is evidently complicit in the actions we have seen in these reports. I call for CIA Director Kristen Thomas to voluntarily step aside from her position as this investigation proceeds to ensure her full cooperation. And to ensure her leadership and her attention on a job that may be beyond her is not further diluted.' Without another word the senator walked into the nest of advisors and aids to her right and was ushered to a waiting black Cadillac Escalade.

Somewhere in Washington Deputy Director Robert Marshall was smiling in anticipation of the hearings that he was certain would be the final straw for the CIA Director. While he mentally crafted his Confirmation Speech.

And somewhere over the Atlantic Ocean, James Charleston took a congratulatory sip of aged bourbon as he acknowledged a multi-taloned strategy of political guile worthy of Frank Underwood.

In her Langley office Kristen Thomas muted the bank of TV's. Where the speech from Charleston's senatorial lap dog referenced the importance of legal due diligence and oversight, the irony of an unsubstantiated and singular accusation against the CIA and specifically herself laid the President's agenda bare. Kristen Thomas was well aware the politics of power knew no limits - or depths. And the politics of desperation was much worse. And it was a desperate politician that had formed an alliance with their historic enemy in turn led by a dictatorial tyrant, to manipulate and sabotage his own country and its political system to secure the country's highest office. Such a person would have few, if any boundaries in keeping it. The public sacrifice of her as the leader of the most important international intelligence agency in the country would be inconsequential. His only concern would be to optimise the political and public advantage.

The stakes had just risen. Her country was in it's weakest strategic position since federation. A realist, Kristen had always understood and become adept at the importance of politics and managing politicians. But she never thought her country's greatest threat would come from its own President.

Chapter 84

WARD LED BRENDT down the aircraft stairs to the tarmac of KMI airport. Having left a cold Washington DC just hours ago, the warm tropical air and humidity were confronting, carrying the fragrance of local flowers and reminding her of where she lived in Sydney. Traveling light, they cleared customs and were met by the local CIA agent. Sean O'Shea had been stationed in South Africa for over twenty-five years. A veteran, he intimately knew the landscape - both physically and politically. And he was old school CIA - someone Kristen could trust. His vehicle was a late model long-wheelbase Land Cruiser. Ideal for the environment, it could handle both city and bush conditions. O'Shea had left the V8 diesel running to keep the air conditioning going. His passengers tossed their luggage in the back of the SUV. Pulling out of the airport carpark, O'Shea dialled Langley on his secure satellite phone.

Chapter 85

'HI MACK.' SAID O'Shea. 'Is Kristen with you?'

'Hey Sean, No, I'm handling the briefing alone. Apparently, all hell has broken loose in Washington. The President has launched at the CIA. He's got us chasing fantasy terrorists in the 'Stans, demanding the CIA give him answers on an indicated threat that only he is somehow aware of. And the Senate is launching an intelligence inquiry - which is actually a CIA inquiry. The boss is bunkered down working out a response.'

Listening over the car's speaker system, Ward was a little surprised. Kristen was a master at multitasking. And had the bandwidth to manage numerous operations at once. Must be serious. And no doubt related. She put the question to Mack, 'I take it Kristen would have seen this coming?'

'She hasn't let me in on any of her plans.' Mack got to the point. 'We have secured your accreditation to the forum. You are part of the press - an American environmental journalist and photographic team. You'll have access to tonight's opening dinner and some of the sessions tomorrow. Sean has your details, new identification, passports, personal effects and credit cards. Leave everything else with him. Make sure you are otherwise clean going in. That includes anything personal, such as phones, computers, and other electronics. We have replacements in the satchels Sean will provide that align with your cover. No weapons. With the President and other heads of state and commerce in attendance, security is as tight as a fishes ass.'

As they listened to Mack, Ward noticed the road to the wildlife sanctuary had turned rural. O'Shea had advised them they would be taking backroads into the reserve to avoid unwanted attention and security. Narrow and rutted, it was slow going, and the verge was almost non-existent, with lush bushland encroaching at the sloping gravel edge. Ward briefly wondered about the logistics of hosting a global event in such a remote location.

She hit the mute button, 'Is this the only way in?' she asked O'Shea.

'Shortcut.' he responded.

Mack hadn't stopped the briefing, 'We need to know who meets with who. Or whom! The forum is legitimate, but we have to know who the President is meeting and it's likely Alex that you will need to go to Russia after this.'

'Got it. And Hanse Kallis?' asked Ward.

'He is the hub of the wheel. Seems to be at the centre of everything. We want to know what his agenda is with Charleston. Why he worked so hard and spent so much to get him elected. Is it just this environmental crusade? See what you can see. Photos and videos will help and we can run faces through recognition software.'

'Got it. We will report back tomorrow.' Ward changed the topic. 'What is going on back home, Mack?'

'Unsophisticated and old-fashioned politicking. Albeit in the digital age. Seems Kristen is now fully out of favour with the administration.'

'She can handle herself.' said Ward.

'Agreed. Our President may have just put his head in the hornet's nest. Suggest we just focus on our operation.'

'Copy......' Ward said, about to end the call.

At that same moment, they rounded a blind, slow corner and were confronted by a man in camouflage fatigues standing next to a military-style Land Rover blocking the track about 100 meters further along the road. He had a semi-automatic rifle over his shoulder and his right arm raised in the stance used the world over by law enforcement to indicate for them to stop.

Chapter 86

HER INTERNAL ALARM bells immediately started screaming and Ward shouted at O'Shea, 'Stop the car. Now!'

O'Shea had sensed the same trap and already slammed on the brakes.

'Is this an official checkpoint? We're sitting ducks in the open.' Ward said twisting around to look out each of the Land Cruiser's windows. 'This isn't right. Checkpoints are properly set up and manned with more people. This is a rural back road. Back it up. Fast.'

Before Ward had barked her orders, O'Shea had already started reverse navigating with the large digital screen activated by the rear camera. Then he turned to look back over his shoulder to get a better perspective to back down the road as quickly as possible.

'More coming out of the scrub behind us!' he shouted.

Men appeared from the bush on both sides of the track they'd just driven on.

'Any weapons on board at all? Ward asked as she frantically looked around to asses the tactical situation.

'Nothing. We had to come in clean.'

'Right. Ok. Try and drive at them, and if they don't move, take them out with the car.'

'Hang on!' yelled O'Shea. The dirt track was throwing dust everywhere, obscuring their view. He grabbed the automatic shifter in the centre console with his left hand and ripped the steering wheel hard right, putting the car into a tight spin on the gravel track. As he did so, he threw the transmission back into drive and gunned the V8 diesel engine. The big 4WD had all four wheels trying to find traction. On the slippery track, he managed to control the car's spin as it went hard to the left and reversed direction, facing towards the way they had come. O'Shea fought with the steering wheel trying to correct and stabilise. As the big SUV wavered on its suspension and began to straighten, he pointed it at the nearest of the gunmen and hit the accelerator.

The attackers now ahead and to their sides opened fire. The nearest were just metres away. Bullets were pinging off the metal, the windshield and side windows.

'Bulletproof.' grunted O'Shea.

Brendt unclipped his seat belt and dived into the rear footwell. Ward also unclipped her seatbelt, held onto the grab handle attached to the roof of the car above her door and reached for the door handle, ready to jump when they slowed. She'd counted four soldiers in front and to the sides as they had reversed and at least one, possibly more, back where they had first spotted the ambush. O'Shea had lined up two of the soldiers that were firing at them and standing adjacent to each other on the right-hand side of the track. One of them, he rammed dead centre with the large bull-bar attached to the front chassis of the car. The other leapt to his side as the SUV bounced off the track. O'Shea was pretty sure he'd clipped him as well. The first was definitely out of the fight. The second maybe. He didn't slow, driving the SUV hard into the high native grass lining the track. He couldn't see much through the vegetation and was pushing the big rig as hard as he dared, bracing himself for when they inevitably hit rocks or low trees. He was desperate to get distance from the attackers and hoped he might find them a way out. Ward had other ideas. She could do nothing from inside the car. As bullets chased them into the bush, hitting the rear of the truck, she opened her door and leapt out.

'Fuck!' momentarily stunned, O'Shea quickly recovered and pressed on; instead of going deeper into the brush as he'd planned, he started to pull left back around to the track.

Chapter 87

WARD FLUNG THE door open and dived from the bouncing SUV, tucking into a ball and rolling. The tall grass helped a little to soften her landing. She hit the ground on her right shoulder and her back, rolling several times until coming to a stop. It knocked the wind from her. Her right shoulder was numb. Despite the stinging pain, she fluidly rolled onto her feet, coming up in a crouch, and started scrambling. Trying to catch her breath. Shaking her right arm, hoping it would come good. Automatic gunfire continued around her.

Ward swung around to the left, searching for the attacker O'Shea had hit. Seconds later, she found him about ten metres off the track, partially obscured in the bush. Clearly dead, his body was lying at odd angles, broken by the impact of the SUV. She grabbed his weapon. It seemed intact. She wouldn't know until she fired it. He had spare magazines in his tactical vest and she pulled two of these out, her hand getting covered in blood. Ward wiped her bloodied hand on his pants. She unclipped his side holster and grabbed a Glock 19, tucking it into her waistband.

Now armed, she turned towards the sound of gunfire and went looking for targets.

Chapter 88

SEAN O'SHEA WAS re-calibrating plan B? His initial reaction on seeing the armed soldier with his arm raised was to reverse and get the fuck out. A soldier this remote was way out of context. It could be a local gang looking for bounty or hostages. Or it could be they had been made and these guys carefully positioned knowing they were coming. Either way, you just don't stop at a suspect roadblock in Africa.

Realising it was a full ambush, he kicked into survival mode and planned to ram through the bush and find a way out. However, with Ward jumping from the car and going on the attack, he had to back her up. O'Shea thought her action was incredibly brave–and dumb. He always favoured running and living to *not* fight another day.

All this seemed to happen in mere seconds, but was, in reality, maybe a minute or two. So now, Plan B! Find Ward. And help her. Which meant taking on the bad guys. With no weapons. Still driving the truck as hard as possible he was bringing it back around to the track and looking to find another attacker he could hit.

'Stay down.' he called back to Brendt.

'Not moving.' Was the muffled cry from the back.

So far, the SUV seemed ok. It had B6 armour installed as standard by the agency in this part of the world. It could withstand automatic and semi-automatic fire. But it had taken a hammering and wouldn't last forever. He hoped they didn't have any weapons more potent.

The Land Cruiser jumped back up onto the track. O'Shea picked up gunfire to his right and steered in that direction, accelerating as hard as he could to close the distance and panic the shooter. The attacker turned towards the fast-approaching SUV, bringing his AK around, and commenced firing directly at O'Shea. Out of reflex, O'Shea ducked even though the reinforced glass held. The movement wrenched the steering wheel further right, which was unfortunate for the shooter as he'd decided to leap to his left. The two point six millimetre thick steel tubing of the bull-bar caught the diving attacker flush to his head, making a popping noise O'Shea heard over the sounds of the engine.

Chapter 89

ALEX WARD WAS in a hyperaware state. She saw their SUV swinging back to the track in her right peripheral. She moved through the grass looking to get around behind and flank the ongoing gun fire. O'Shea was taking a lot of rounds. The enemy was not aware of her yet. She needed to take advantage of any surprise she had. She also needed to make it fast, as the Land Cruiser wouldn't hold out much longer.

With the enemy guns trained on the moving SUV, she broke cover and advanced towards multiple shooters. Emerging from the thick grass, she saw two attackers firing full auto on the SUV. The truck was now running on at least one if not more, flat tyres, had steam coming from the bonnet and was making a strange noise. She advanced a few more metres onto the track, stopped dead still, and assumed a firing position. From about seventy feet, she brought the nearest shooter into her sights and squeezed, firing two rounds in quick succession. The moment of truth as to whether the sights were still true and the gun worked properly. Barely aware of the gun firing, she brought the barrel slightly left, acquired the second shooter and fired another two consecutive shots. She saw these shots strike the attacker in the neck and one slightly higher in the back of the head. She quickly looked back to the first target. Also down. That took at least three out of the fight and maybe another if Sean had managed to hit one. It left at least one attacker from the ambush and the original a few hundred metres now in front of her on the track past the carnage. There was also the possibility of others as yet unaccounted.

Ward calculated the original attacker would be closing the distance by now, aware the fight was not the one-sided ambush they would have hoped for. The shooting had stopped. The remaining attacking force re-grouping. They would come again. And there might be more. The SUV was no longer running, stopped at an angled standstill some distance away, half on the track and half in the shrub. She could see doors open but no people. Ward knew the enemy would come for the truck and wanted a better tactical position. There was no near high ground. In fact, the track was slightly built up and was the highest part of the landscape. Run-off for the heavy tropical rains. The verge dropped gradually away, it was predominantly high native grasses with intermittent small trees that didn't offer any cover. There were hills in the distance. But they were way too far and of no use. It was just flat earth from here to there. Her ears ringed from the cacophony that had only just ceased. She figured the enemy would have similar sensory reduction and decided to move quickly to a position they would least expect. Back to the truck.

Ward moved fast and low through the shrub, swapping for a fresh mag. She didn't want to happen upon either O'Shea and Brendt or the attackers or have them come into contact with her. She figured the enemy would move to the SUV from the other side. And she hoped O'Shea and Brendt had exited the truck and had found some low ground cover. Encountering no one, she made it back to the SUV, took a position just a few metres from the rear and pushed herself down flat into the shrub as much as possible. About to look up and scope for targets, a barrage of gunfire erupted and bullets sprayed the SUV from back to front and back again. The shooters were really close. The noise was deafening. She put her hands over her ears and pushed her head and body as hard as she could into the ground and prayed for no stray shots or ricochets. Ward heard tyres deflating and glass breaking. The armour was giving out under the barrage. She felt bullets whizzing through the grass around her and thudding into the ground. After what seemed like hundreds of rounds, the shooting finally stopped.

Ward figured everyone in the vicinity would be as deaf as she was and abandoned the need for silence. She had a read on the location of the shooters. Putting the destroyed SUV between her and them, she broke from the shrub, assault rifle at her shoulder and her eyes aligned to the sights. She moved swiftly, closer to the SUV, crouched below the door sill's line. Once next to the truck, she raised her body and saw both targets, one about five metres in front of the other and just on the other side of the SUV. The first was close, walking towards the SUV along the corrugated track. The front shooter had lowered his weapon, allowing it to rest on its sling. The other shooter was slightly obscured to Ward behind the first but looked more alert.

Shooter one looked complacent, believing no one could have survived that onslaught, and was coming to check the damage they'd inflicted. He finally noticed her as she rose quickly above the window frame of the SUV and moved to grab his weapon and bring it up. Too late. With her gun on single-select, Ward squeezed twice, firing into the attacker, aiming for a headshot to mitigate any body armour. The first hit his forehead and snapped his head back in a pink mist. At this range, there would be little of his skull or brain left. The second struck just below the nose. The shooter behind hesitated, briefly obscured by his teammate in front, and then fired. By which time it was too late. Ward had waited for less than a heartbeat and then shot through the space where the first attacker's head had just been. She hit number two in the left cheekbone with a slightly upward trajectory. The impact took the top of his head off and threw him backwards as he reflexively fired his weapon. Her second bullet caught him just behind the left ear as he spun. Another two down. No others currently visible.

The world went silent. Ward's ears were buzzing and she had very limited audio sensory. The silence actually hurt. She stayed behind the SUV on high alert, looking for further unaccounted attackers. Ward swept her weapon across the track from side to side, repeatedly looking down the track and into the dense shrub on either side to acquire any additional targets. Nothing moved. Still, she held her stance.

'You got 'em all.' She heard the muffled words from somewhere off the track's left.

'Say again.' She said as she continued to sweep through the sights of the gun.

The voice rose a notch, cutting through her muffled hearing, 'You got 'em all. There's none left. Thomas and I are coming out.' O'Shea had called from their hide.

'Copy.' Ward replied but kept her eyes trained on the fringes of the track.

Ward watched, still alert and her head swiveling as O'Shea and Brendt emerged from the low grass. O'Shea was bleeding from a cut on his face. The blood running down and soaking his collar. Brendt clutched the laptop he'd been using in the backseat and looked dazed and shell-shocked. It had been a big couple of days for the introverted hacker. Both had been lying on the ground and were covered in grass and red sandy dirt. Nothing else moved. Ward circled the entire area through the gun sights until she was satisfied the danger was over. Convinced they had taken care of all the threats, she gave the two men her proper attention.

'I'm going back down the track and bring that Land Rover up here. Grab whatever gear can be salvaged from the Cruiser and sanitise the entire car.'

O'Shea nodded, 'These men are not from local gangs. They are kitted as paramilitary contractors.'

'Agreed.' said Ward. She threw him a piece of cloth from the Cruiser to stem the flow of blood on his face. 'This is not a coincidence. Let's go and find the fuckers that want us dead. You need to stop that bleeding and change your shirt. And stay on alert. No more surprises.'

Sean O'Shea looked up and down the track into the fringe of the shrub. There were bodies visible in multiple places and the Land Cruiser was destroyed. It was carnage. He'd taken out a couple, but she was a wrecking machine.

Chapter 90

SPECIAL AGENT MICHAEL Smart - known as 'Max' to his friends and colleagues was completing his final assessment as head of the Advance Team for the Presidential Protective Detail. This was Smart's second visit to South Africa in the last three months. The first to complete the preliminary threat and security assessment, where he met with the head of the Global Intervention Initiative security team. And now, just hours before the President's arrival, he was re-checking everything. His job was to liaise with the Presidential Detail Leader to establish all the required security cordons and measures, determine a minimum of two alternate exit routes and ensure first responder and medical treatment protocols were in place.

This detail was one of the few Smart had been required to manage in months, and it was the first international visit by this President. COVID had put a stop to a lot of travel - particularly international travel, reducing it to almost zero. Domestic travel for the previous President and now this President had continued, albeit at a significantly reduced level. But domestic travel - as infrequent as it had become, was relatively straightforward for the Secret Service and the advance teams that managed security for the President's itinerary. Security requirements to most domestic destinations and venues had been mapped over many previous visits and was more an implementation task.   International tours by the President were far more stressful. Dealing with local authorities and surveying local risk assessment and response options was challenging. Some countries and locations had similar standards and protocols - so they were easier to work with. Others did not go out of their way to assist the Secret Service. The COVID-led reduction in international travel for the President had made Smart's life easier. But incredibly boring. So he was energised by the President's trip. An opportunity to stretch his professional legs. And stop the taunts of his colleagues about his improving golf handicap.

The remote wilderness park location for this forum was a threat management mixed blessing. The security in place by the organisers was first-rate. To be expected given the calibre of world political and corporate leaders attending. However, the remote location and long distances to communications and support assets were a nightmare. If they needed to get The President to a hospital, it would be a thirteen minute chopper flight. Smart was finding it hard to shake the feeling that they were sitting ducks for some motivated, well-resourced, disaffected type. And there were plenty of those in the more militant pro-environment groups. And so his stress levels were peaking as he entered the accommodation quarters in the main building of the Kallis wildlife reserve the President would be using.

Chapter 91

DRIVING THEIR NEWLY acquired Land Rover, Alex Ward pulled up about half a kilometre from the entry to the wildlife park. They had managed to salvage their travel bags from the destroyed Land Cruiser and little else. The camera gear they'd brought for Thomas' cover as a magazine photographer had been mostly destroyed. All but one were unusable. They'd grabbed what looked intact, along with their communications gear and the weapons and ammunition the attackers had with them, and loaded it all into the rugged off-roader. Ward knew security would be too tight to get the weapons in. But she liked having them nearby. They were now as close as she would risk. Ward could see on the map of O'Shea's iPhone navigation system that they would soon merge with the main road into the game park, and it would be busy with all the attention of the forum and plenty of security.

She grabbed a canvas tarp from the back of the long-wheelbase wagon and the collapsible shovel from the roof rack. She and O'Shea then wrapped all the weapons and ammunition they had grabbed along with their personal gear into the canvas and headed into the bush. Brendt had actually nodded off in the back seat and just stirred as the vehicle stopped. Adrenalin crash, she figured. Fifty meters off the track, Ward found a sandy spot under a strange-looking tree with a massive bulbous trunk and large canopy and started digging.

'We should be able to find this tree again. It's distinctive. I'll mark the location as we head back to the truck.' Ward said to O'Shea.

'It's an ancient Baobab tree.' he responded.

'Thanks. I wasn't wondering.'

Completing their work, sweating in the heat and almost back at the truck, Ward stacked numerous rocks off the side of the track in an arrangement she hoped she'd remember, but that would not draw attention. She also marked their location using the GPS on her phone.

Back behind the wheel, O'Shea directed Ward to a small offshoot of the track they had been on, and shortly after, they bumped up onto a dry and dusty, fairly wide bitumen road. Moments later, they rounded a bend, and in front of them was the sanctuary entrance. A pitched grass-roofed canopied structure of round beams and timber framing provided a gated entry and exit with a central hut that serviced both those entering and those leaving. High chain link security fencing was attached to both sides of the structure and disappeared into the shrub, ensuring no way around.

The entrance had been converted to a full security screening compound with temporary booms and bollards allowing only a single vehicle through at a time. There were large banners promoting the Global Intervention Initiative and welcoming guests. There were more banners and signs with the simple word ONE presented in a bold and stylised font.

Most of the limited traffic consisted of identical small buses with aggressive tyres and elevated suspensions, clearly designed for the corrugated roads and no doubt ferrying guests in from the airport or other locations. Numerous uniformed and armed security personnel were working in a coordinated ballet and checking each vehicle thoroughly. Passengers all alighted and had to personally locate and bring their luggage forward. They were then run through body scanners and had security wands waved over them. All baggage was x-rayed, opened, and hand-searched. So much for personal privacy, Ward thought. Vehicles - including the official busses- were opened completely. All boots, bonnets and doors. Handlers with sniffer dogs went over everything. Security personnel were using extended undercarriage mirrors and then creeper trays to slide under vehicles to look for explosives or anything else secreted. It was as thorough as Ward had seen and validated their caution over trying to bring anything suspicious into the forum. And it was slow. Finally, it was their turn. A filthy Land Rover was not out of place here and didn't raise an eyebrow.

Eventually, they were able to re-pack their vehicle head into the temporary event car park and then walk with their gear to the registration area. Their credentials and cover held firm. O'Shea was traveling as Sean O'Lash, a freelancer, Ward, a journalist named Alex Walsh and Brendt had the cover Thomas Brown as her photographer. They were each assigned single accommodation in the area colloquially known as tent city. A four-seater modified electric golf buggy dropped them at their adjoining tents.

'Meet me in mine in five.' Ward instructed as they each went to drop their luggage.

Chapter 92

WARD ENTERED HER tent and looked around. She assumed there would be listening devices or cameras and spent a few minutes searching. The room, as far as her search revealed, was clean and as she worked around the space, she couldn't help but be impressed. The generous-sized, hexagonal-shaped canvas tent was beautifully appointed. Scented with fresh Freesias, the darkened interior was illuminated with soft yellow lighting from two lamps on either side of the queen-sized bed. The bed was set off to the left to allow for the central tent pole and a low day bed covered in soft blankets and cushions was to the right. On top of the bed, resting on the pillows, was a single, sturdy sheet of thick paper with the itinerary for the forum printed on one side and a map on the other showing the corresponding locations. Ward folded and put the sheet of paper in one of the cargo pockets of her fitted black pants.

Past the bed, she noticed a covered opening. She entered another connected tent containing a beautiful clawfoot bath with a freestanding shower riser in the middle of the room. A toilet was off to one side and on the other a mirror sat above a timber vanity with complimentary luxury toiletries. All the linen and towels were pure white and the timber floors were covered with sheepskin and animal hide. The beautiful bathroom serviced three other guest tents. Impressive to consider the quality their hosts had achieved with such a scaled event.

Ward looked longingly at the deep tub, briefly contemplated a long soak in a hot bath, and then shut it from her mind. She heard someone coming through the front entrance of her tent. She came back to find O'Shea entering and trailing right behind was Brendt.

O'Shea had tidied the cut to his face and it was almost invisible. Brendt had washed and cleaned up a little. He looked less shaken and a little more focused.

He asked, 'Do you think we're safe here?' a fair question figured Ward, given his last couple of days.

'I do. In fact this may be the safest place we could be at the moment. I doubt Kallis or his soldiers will try anything here. This is his career showpiece. He wouldn't want the world's press to be distracted by violence or any sort of incident.'

Brendt didn't look convinced.

Ward changed tack, 'There are a few hours before the opening of the forum and the dinner. Let's use them to get the lay of the land. Sean - you know the drill. Thomas, grab your camera and get shots of whatever you find interesting. If anyone asks, use your cover and say you're taking B roll and background. Just don't say too much. Let's get back here in an hour.'

'What's your plan, boss?' asked O'Shea.

'I'm going to look for our host, and if I find him, we'll get to know each other a little more.'

Chapter 93

KRISTEN THOMAS KNEW she was in the veritable hot seat. Called by the Director of National Intelligence for an unscheduled and urgent meeting, she had made the short trip from her office at Langley across to the National Counterterrorism Center.

Suspicious that this was more political than national security, her concerns were compounded as she was left waiting for the 'urgent' meeting in the ante-room adjoining Director William Jacob's office for over thirty minutes. Kristen had Senator Olsen threatening oversight enquiries and now this. Seems the growing investigation into a corrupted election had sparked a reaction. The games had started.

Director Jacob was a Charleston appointment. A former Republican Congressional Representative, he was an unashamed loyalist with no previous intelligence experience. None. He was there to represent the President and to control the seventeen agencies that reported to the office. More PR than terrorism operator Kristen Thomas had known since Jacob's appointment that she would be in his sights. The new President wanted friendlies in charge of all the key agencies. And whilst she respected the office of the DNI, she had no intent of subverting the crucial importance of her role. Charleston was her third President since becoming Director, and she had served numerous others in lesser roles as she'd climbed the ranks. Fortunately, some of Charleston's predecessors had been aligned with the critical importance of national security and managing the threat of terrorism. Unfortunately, others felt they knew better and looked to manage the geo-political maze themselves. Often with disastrous results. Kristen had taken the view, very early in her career and guided by her mentor, the previous CIA Director Harold J Pendleton, that the job was to serve the United States.

First and foremost. Presidents would come and go. The threats posed to their country would not. A trained analyst, she had moved through the CIA quickly, eventually following her mentor in running the agency. Kristen had become adept at both being the tip of the intelligence spear and reading the political winds and agendas of the White House.

And she was always prepared.

Now sitting in the DNI's office across the desk from Director Jacob, she had not been invited to the more comfortable and convivial opposing sofas.

She had just taken her seat and settled, and without even a greeting, Jacob immediately stood from his position at his desk across from her. 'Follow me.' Without waiting for her reply, Jacob pushed through his office door. Kristen was left with little choice but to trail behind. She followed in silence.

Eventually, they came to a door Kristen knew well–the secure entry to the National Counterterrorism Operations Centre. Jacob swiped his security pass and complied with the biometric scanner. Still following, still silent, Kristen did the same.

Whilst the CIA's Langley complex of buildings had undergone renovations and upgrades over the years, the relatively new NCTC was a modern, digitised masterpiece. The Operations Centre was its heartbeat.

Kristen entered the room on the mezzanine that looked down at a series of tiered theatre-style rows of manned workstations. Each workstation had three monitors, one centred and two more located to the left and right of the central screen angled into the operator. The room was hermetically sealed, soundproofed and impervious to electronic surveillance or listening devices. A little like her own office, it was unnaturally quiet - seeming to suck in its own sounds. Whilst there was no natural light, the cavernous vaulted roof showed exposed engineering, and the room offered a calm and focused ambience from the low blue-tinged lighting. It was all incredibly impressive. Futuristic. Kristen reflected that, whilst no luddite, she preferred the more collegiate and less intimidating environment of the temporary centre they had used prior.

Chapter 94

DNI WILLIAM JACOB bounded down the glass and steel spiral staircase from the mezzanine to the operational floor. Kristen followed, and as she got closer, she could make out the soft white noise of computers and keyboards at work, coupled with the subdued, neutral voices of operators communicating amongst themselves or with others in various locations over secure comms.

Kristen recognised the Chief of the NCTC Operations Centre. A new appointment since Jacob had ascended the directorship. And another stooge that had bypassed the tenure and capability of others far more qualified.

'Chief, an update on the recent threat profile from Iraq.' Jacob instructed.

'Director, we are continuing to monitor increased chatter emanating from Diyala, approximately one hundred and thirty clicks north of Bagdad.'

Kristen observed the Chief scanning uncomfortably around the room. A senior role, not typically stationed on the operations floor, security protocol dictated this type of briefing would never be openly discussed here, even amongst securely cleared analysts. She appreciated it for what it was. A staged berating in front of these senior intelligence operators. It didn't offend her. What concerned her was the clear breach in protocol and complete lack of regard for operational discipline, the need for which had been proven time and again.

'Go on.' Instructed Jacob.

'Sir, perhaps we should take this to a SCIF?' Requested the Chief, referring to a Sensitive Compartmented Information Facility. Essentially, a sound-proofed and secure meeting and operations room.

Jacob didn't hesitate, 'No need. Run us through the scenario.'

Idiot. Thought Kristen. When even your own lap dog is uncomfortable with these breaches, it should be time to take notice.

After a long pause, the Chief continued with his script, 'We have elevated this to a level four threat assessment and recommend we go operational locally and domestically. Diyala has been growing in prominence as a centre for training and funding coordinated missions to the US.'

Jacob turned to Kristen and well within earshot of numerous analysts doing their best to seem focused on their screens, spoke in a raised voice, 'Director Thomas, why am I not being made aware of this threat from you and your agency? It seems I need to go direct to get real intel. Are you guys asleep at the wheel?' Jacob paused waiting for a reply. He was getting frustrated at the lack of response from his subordinate. 'Director Thomas I am instructing you to make this your top priority. Whatever else you're doing, this threat in Diyala is your primary focus. We want analysis and options in the PDB tomorrow.'

Kristen had all but tuned out. She appreciated this was all set up for her–part of the deflection strategy Charleston was now initiating. But level four–severe–with an attack highly likely! Not only were they breeching all sorts of security protocols by having this conversation here, but worse, they were flagging a wasteful allocation of resources–one that would take operational teams and tech away from targets they should be focussed on.

Such a waste of time. And energy. The President and this fool Jacob were playing games. She needed to get back to her office. There were real threats she needed to manage. And this charade of a meeting and attempt to deflect the attention of the CIA made her more concerned than ever about how deep this administration was with their enemies.

In actual fact, she'd been watching Diyala for months. And it had been included some time ago on the PDB and then removed. The leader of the local Islamic cell in Diyala was a very wealthy Arab named Hassan Ahmad. He was not a member of the Saudi royals but had close ties and connected business interests. He was definitely funding activity and they were aware of ties to the US Islamic community, but they were highly disorganised and leaked like a sieve. And the CIA had a local asset within their inner circle. They were not an imminent threat. Yes, there was chatter. There was always chatter from these extremists. She had previously authorised the re-positioning of Sentient Intel gathering satellites, deployed both local drones, and put operators on the ground out of Bagdad. She was very aware of the activity in Diyala and was utterly convinced they couldn't organise a decent birthday party, let alone stage coordinated attacks on domestic US soil.

She took this for what it was. A goose chase. A chastising as 'public' as the DNI could make it in front of the Operational Center team. They wanted her attention and that of her agency elsewhere, and they didn't even have the political subtlety to do it properly. Without raising her voice or indeed looking at all concerned from the double barrel berating she was taking, Kristen held up her left hand,

'Chief, I'm going to stop you there.' she turned slightly and looked at William Jacob, 'I understand your intentions, Director.'

Jacob opened his mouth to say more, but Kristen didn't wait. Without another word, she turned her back on the two men, strode briskly up the staircase and exited the room.

Chapter 95

'THAT SKINNY BITCH just walked away from me. Brushed me like I was a crumb on her overly tight skirt. She acts like she doesn't take orders from anyone. Particularly not me. She has to go.' A steamed William Jacob was on the phone with the President, now somewhere in South Africa.

'I can't fire her without cause, Bill. Believe me, nothing would make me happier. She's becoming a pain in the ass.' President James Charleston sat in the forward-facing single chair on the upgraded Sikorsky VH92 Marine One helicopter. They were a few minutes out from Hanse's Reserve. William Jacob called via video conference after having an entirely unsatisfactory result with Kristen Thomas.

A frustrated Jacob spoke loudly down the line, 'You're the President, you can fire anyone.'

'She is the first female Director of the CIA. Half the press already paints me as some throw-back misogynist. If I sack her without clear cause, the other half will join them. Her time will come.' Charleston, in reality, was not overly worried about the response of the press. He knew he couldn't ever hope to win over those who already hated him and his party. He was far more concerned about what information the CIA was building on him. This needed to be done right.

Charleston continued, 'I'll work on Thomas from my end. But in the meantime, do not let up. In fact, let's dial it up. I want you to call an immediate head of agency meeting. Get all seventeen agencies in. Have the Chief brief them collectively on the Diyala threat. Instruct them that I want a response within forty-eight hours. She won't be able to ignore an all-agency initiative. It will tie them all in knots.'

'Sir, that is not really how it works.'

'I don't give a fuck how it works. You work for me. Get it done.' Charleston disconnected the call and tossed the over-ear headphones connected to the secure communications system on Marine One onto the table in front of him.

Sitting across from President, Daniel Walker, also wearing headphones, had heard both sides of the conversation. He started to feel like it was amateur hour at the White House. Charleston was already on his second FBI Director with the first appointment lasting just weeks. The Director of National Intelligence was a blatant party room appointment and had been targeted relentlessly by less supportive members of the press. Their Vice President was an expedient appointment only, intentionally kept completely in the dark and sent on all sorts of trivial errands. She had only ever been a partner of political convenience to secure them crucial electoral college support and to appeal to women voters. And now they were bungling the resignation or firing of the Director of the CIA.

Walker reflected that they seemed untouchable only months ago when they were in full honeymoon mode and orchestrating their own news. Coming into office, the pandemic had made them politically bulletproof. But now they were feeling the full heat of being in government. All these Boy Scouts in the intelligence community were completely out of touch. He and Charleston knew that doing deals with foreign powers was smart business. They could do so much more together than as adversaries. Charleston would have a special relationship with the Kremlin - much like his predecessors had with the Brits. A relationship that he and the President would stage-manage. No way would they be at the behest of the apparent puppet masters in Moscow. But the jackals were circling the White House wagons now. And he knew Kristen Thomas and her cohorts would not give up. Despite the poor political optics, he agreed they needed her gone and their own person in charge. And if they couldn't make that happen, Walker was wondering if he needed to find a new candidate to hitch his ride to and distance himself from the inevitable shitstorm that was on the political horizon.

The President interrupted his self-absorbed thoughts, 'Set up a meeting with our Senator as soon as we're back. I want the hearings fast-tracked and Thomas squirming.'

Chapter 96

DR DAVID MITCHELL sat down on the bench seat in the staff rooms of the temporary COVID centre buried in the stands of the converted sports ground in Sydney. The medical staff had taken over what would have been the change rooms for the football and cricket teams that played here. The masculine rooms styled with stained timber and brushed stainless steel had celebrated victories and consoled defeats and would undoubtedly have many stories to tell. They were spacious, tastefully done and well-equipped. As the stadium had been re-purposed in the fight against the pandemic, the rooms had been quickly and temporarily re-fitted to comply with infectious disease protocols.

And they were entirely depressing.

At the moment, the rooms had the tense quiet of a losing team after the game. He looked around. There were several of his colleagues spread around the space, both male and female. Some sitting, some lying on the floor. None were talking. Many were softly weeping. David was too exhausted to be emotional. He'd been going for over twenty-four hours and had finally been ordered by his director to go home and get some rest. It was the worst day of the pandemic he'd experienced. In fact, he was now convinced that it wasn't the COVID pandemic they were dealing with. He'd lost count of the deaths they'd pronounced today. They'd run out of space for the bodies and had been stacking them behind a temporary curtain until they were taken away. He didn't know where the bodies went from here. It made him feel sick in his stomach.

He pulled off the clear, full-face visor and reached around to untie the face mask. Sitting in his PPE scrubs, he reached into the locker and turned on his phone. He really wanted to talk to Alex. But he couldn't call her. Tiredly, he wondered if she had messaged him or left a voicemail and activated the screen. As his phone started vibrating, he was surprised at the number of messages he'd received. He scrolled through the notifications, looking for anything from Alex. Instead, he had several WhatsApp messages from a private medical group he and his friends set up as students and residents. They were all now working in various locations around the world. All the messages were referencing the exponential explosion in patients presenting with horrible symptoms. And dying. The most recent was from Dr Simone Laurent, a French native and fellow former international student at Stanford now working at the Institut Pasteur in Paris. Simone had posted several images that looked horribly similar to what David had been experiencing all day. Her message was direct and laden with emotion.

'This is not COVID! WHAT IS THIS?'

Chapter 97

ALEX WARD WAS moving around the main building of the wilderness reserve. She had found Kallis's private office location. The U-shaped design allowed her to look from one side of the building through the windows and across the courtyard. The structure she was in was all earthy stone, large timber beams, and masses of glass. His office took up a whole wing - the entire opposite side of the large building. She could see it, but she couldn't get near it. There was Secret Service everywhere. It seemed her President had arrived.

As Ward discreetly monitored the office across the courtyard, she took in the cathedral interior of the main part of the game reserve clubhouse. The rambling building was a fusion of contemporary style and furniture mixed with safari memorabilia and artifacts. The vaulted roof was emphasised by floor-to-ceiling windows looking out onto open grassed areas merging into the shrub and bushland beyond.

Even focused as she was, Ward was taken by the clever way the architecture enhanced rather than detracted from the stunning South African landscape. The design both framed the landscape and focussed the attention of those inside, dramatising the impact of the horizon line. Looking through the windows and across to her right, she could see the covered outdoor auditorium that would shortly fill with people for the forum's opening dinner. And in the middle distance, partially obscured by the undulating topography and the native bushland, she could see accommodation villas and Tent City.

Ward was blending in with the growing, buzzing crowd building for the formal opening. She politely ignored those who wanted to chat about the forum, staying focused and waiting for an opportunity to confront Kallis. She kept an eye on the exterior of the office wing as it ran at an angle off the main structure hoping to see movement. Most windows were draped, but a few were not, and she could see plenty of security and secret service personnel moving about. Ward felt the phone in her pocket vibrate and took it out to check the message. It was from David. Rare that he would try and contact her whilst she was operational. She hoped everything was ok. Ward fired off a short response indicating she would call when she could. She pocketed the phone and resumed her watch, hoping an opportunity would come.

Chapter 98

STANDING WITH PRESIDENT James Charleston, Hanse Kallis took in the view through the wall of glass at the far end of the long structure that held his office. Just the two of them looking out as dusk took the day's light into evening. Nobody else was in the office with them. No security. No aides or staff. Both men were relaxed in each other's company.

'It's beautiful here, Hanse. I can see why protecting this is so important to you,' offered Charleston as his eyes fell on a small herd of Springbok in the distance at the edge of the bushland.

'Mr President, it is wonderful to finally have you here in person.'

The President turned and the two men faced each other, Charleston, away from the US and the glare of the pressures he was under was in full charm mode, 'Please, Hanse, no formalities. Without you, I would not be here.'

'Of course, James. Please, come and relax.'

Kallis gestured to two large leather armchairs angled slightly towards each other, facing the large window. Charleston unbuttoned his suit coat and took the nearest seat.

He looked across and pointed at Kallis, 'Seriously Hanse. I owe you. Without your support and that of your ...network, I'm not President. Simple.'

'James, finding people that share my vision the way you do is rare. Supporting you supports our future. Simple.'

Charleston pushed back into the soft leather. This guy really was an idealist. He reminded Charleston of Steve Jobs and how the team at Apple described his Reality Distortion Field. These types believed they could make the impossible possible - invent the future through sheer force of will and relentless focus. And they had the money and resources to indulge their manifest.

Charleston was prepared to dial things down with Kallis and eventually disengage altogether. But Daniel believed they would need him again in four years. Daniel, he thought, was underselling his political ability! He believed he could win the people over without the external assistance they'd had during the recent election. As the people got to know him over the next few years, he'd have them clambering for more! Particularly the female voters. And more women voted than men! But Daniel was convinced elections were no longer a fair contest. He used a Lance Armstrong analogy - if your competitors were doping, you either did it better or lost. So Charleston was here to ensure the relationship with Kallis stayed strong. Mutually beneficial.

Chapter 99

BESIDES, THOUGHT CHARLESTON, this big show Kallis was putting on over the next couple of days was great for the cameras. And affirmed his position on the world stage. A welcome distraction from the turmoil that was brewing at home. As President he would make all the right noises and put his moniker on the meaningless protocols. But there was no way he was about to turn the US economy on its head to achieve some fanciful emissions targets and force industry to use renewable energy. He didn't plan to make blue-collar Americans sacrifice their jobs and jeopardise his second term for the sake of the fucking Pandas.

Kallis continued, 'Having you share the stage with me tonight in front of the eyes and cameras of the world and to have the largest and most influential economy commit to the One Initiative is everything I have planned for.'

Fucking misguided billionaire, thought Charleston, 'Hanse, I am behind you, which means America is behind you. The Paris Agreement has failed. We need to fill the void. The world needs the leadership and relentless commitment you've shown.' Charleston paused momentarily, 'There is, however, a problem that affects us both...'

Kallis knew this would be front of mind. 'The Russians?'

'Yeah. They have been sloppy. And now I have the CIA and god knows which other agencies breathing down my neck. That do-gooder Kristen Thomas couldn't see the big picture if I framed it for her. She's not like you and I.'

'It is already in motion James. Our friends know they have let us down. I feel confident the focus of the CIA will be on other matters very soon.'

Kallis reflected that this was partially true. He didn't really have a plan for the Russians or the CIA. Not specifically. And his local team had failed to stop Ward and Brendt on their way here. But he needed the US President focussed on the night ahead. And, he thought without self-deprecation, The Global Intervention Initiative would soon occupy the world's attention.

The President offered a toast, 'You have never let either me or the United States down. Here's to the One Initiative.' He raised his glass of South African KWV Twenty Year Old Brandy to Kallis and took a deep gulp. Charleston looked at the amber fluid in the glass as he savoured the finish on his palate. A committed bourbon man, but this stuff wasn't bad.

Kallis reciprocated as he raised his glass to the President and thought, 'Yes! Here's to it'. The culmination of years of planning. Cultivating relationships. A chess board and its pieces on a global scale. James Charleston had been crucial - without ever really understanding how. Kallis had ensured his re-election years ago as a very marginal senator. Kallis knew the payoff would come. And when the pandemic broke, and the next electoral cycle began, their approach to manipulating news and controlling the attention of the people had been even more effective. Landing them a President in office.

The new President had worked to secure even more contracts in the US and in many other allied and dependent countries for Kallis to produce and distribute a dominant share of the world's hypodermic syringes. The demand needed for vaccine delivery had exploded in recent months. And so had both his wealth and, more importantly, his scale.

It was ironic that the COVID-19 pandemic that had showed the world just how fragile our global health had become had also given him the opportunity and resources he needed to truly implement change.

Chapter 100

MACK STEWART REACHED to the other side of his Langley desk for the tepid remnants of his coffee and was abruptly reminded of the gunshot wound as pain shot up his side. He was avoiding taking painkillers to keep his mind sharp and to reduce the risk of getting reliant. But he was paying for it. In the last couple of days the dull intensity of the pain had increased. He told himself this was his body healing.

Since the firestorm at the Insider Cafe he'd been shadowing Kristen. Riding a desk wasn't his natural environment, but with the leaks and the pressure being applied to the agency and him not being fit for the field, she wanted trusted eyes and ears across a raft of operations.

Most notably, the team working to build a case on foreign electoral tampering. With Kristen caught up in all sorts of Washington politicking, he was front and centre with Ward and O'Shea. He found himself restlessly waiting to hear from them and what they could find with all the fuckers in one place in Sth Africa. Mack couldn't stand the thought of his country being infiltrated and overrun by those he had been fighting for years. Once they had actionable intel, he'd be out of this chair and would join the hunt. Whether his body was ready for it or not.

His computer pinged with an incoming secure message. He hoped that might be either Ward or O'Shea now.

But this was something new. Unrelated. Another issue to add to the pile. One of the Senior Analysts at Langley was trying to get to the boss and, having had no luck, was now coming to him. The analyst had consolidated multiple reports of a surge in cases presenting at COVID-19 centres in the US and across the globe. Mack had been vaguely aware of news reports over the last couple of weeks or so showing an unexpected spike in cases being presented. He had yet to really take much notice. COVID had been around for months, and like almost every other country around the world, the US had a vaccination and booster program that was showing encouraging signs, and clear protocols were in place to minimise infection. He figured it was just a temporary spike. Or perhaps seasonal. And it wasn't the remit of the CIA.

However, the analyst reached out to a number of COVID centres around the country and spoke to several leading virologists. They were all convinced this was not COVID and was not a mutation they'd be able to deal with. This was something else altogether. So far, it had proven un-treatable and, in many cases, lethal. Death rates were spiraling. The analyst felt the new virus may be synthetic. And the final line in the email - actually, it was just a single word, sent a chill down Mack's spine...

'Bio-terrorism?'

Chapter 101

FINALLY A DECENT coffee. Actually it was really good, much better than decent! The young barista at the coffee cart on the grassed expanse outside the reserve's clubhouse told Ward the beans were from Ethiopia. Ward was vaguely aware that Ethiopia was to the north and was heavily overpopulated. And very poor. But damn, their beans were good. Her fatigue and jet lag were put temporarily at bay.

She took her long black to the clubhouse interior and took up a position in a soft leather lounge chair. From her vantage point, looking through the glass of the main public part of the structure, she could see across the angled building to Kallis' enclosed office wing. Through several partially covered windows, she could see the Secret Service security cordon was on the move. It looked like the meeting was ending. POTUS was about to head out. She pushed back a little deeper into the leather chair.

'Patience, Alex. Patience.' She thought to herself. The opportunity to get to Kallis would present itself.

Chapter 102

THOMAS BRENDT HAD also found the same coffee cart. Harder to impress than Ward, he was thankful nonetheless that this remote part of South Africa could offer something so nicely refined. He had his fake press credentials on a lanyard draped around his neck, along with the strap holding the Canon EOS R6 camera that had survived the attack. Not as sleek as the Leica Q2 he used at home, the Canon was a beautiful camera for both stills and video. He'd captured some fantastic images. He was trying to blend in as one of the many international journalists at the forum. Though on close inspection his carefully considered wardrobe - James Perse linen trousers, Sunspel polo and suede Birkenstocks, whilst perfect for the climate were considerably out of reach for most freelance photographers.

The location of the wildlife reserve and the set-up for the forum were stunning. The level of detail was meticulous - impressing even a pedant like himself. He had no idea what Alex wanted him to photograph, so he just clicked away. He'd captured the repetition of the 'glamping' tent array and cropped in on some of the textures and styling of the interiors. He'd even noted for himself a few ideas he was going to implement in his own loft in Washington. At one point he found his way to the more luxurious and permanent eco cottages tucked into the undulating hills and tree line, but had been ushered away from several of the grand and impressive residences before he could get any decent shots. He'd caught glimpses of stunning stone and glass architecture with outdoor enamel and coated cast-iron baths on their decks and sunken lounges wrapped around central fire pits looking over the beautiful African landscape. These, he figured, were for the more senior political leaders attending. He wandered around the outdoor auditorium where the forum would be launched, capturing images of staff putting the final touches on the rows of long tables for tonight's dinner.

All the while he had photographed as many of the people attending the forum as possible. These he thought would be of the most interest to Ward. There were a few he recognised. Netflix documentary makers and some familiar Hollywood types turned eco-warriors. 60 minutes was here, rumoured to be shadowing a member of the British Royalty who was positioning to use the environment as his life's cause.

As far as he could tell, no one he'd recognised would agitate Ward's spy-antennae. The real A-listers would no doubt want to make an entrance and be hidden away, getting themselves ready. Twice, he thought he'd seen glimpses of Hanse Kallis moving through the main building of the game reserve and into the auditorium. Though he couldn't be sure. He'd zoomed in and snapped away anyway.

To his highly untrained eye, this looked exactly how it was promoted. A billionaire's passion project. Someone with enough money, enough political pull and enough cameras to attract an impressive cohort for a content fest. This would no doubt fill news shows, news feeds, newspapers, blogs, docos, and social media, the world over. Few would be brave enough not to support such a visible initiative to fix the world's biggest environmental problems. Unfortunately, very few of them would stay true to their commitments once they returned home. Through political pressure or commercial circumstance, Brendt knew the excuses would run thick as to why they could not deliver what they had fervently committed to in the picturesque jungle of Africa.

But Brendt figured that there was no real downside to such an event. Even if the most superficial and vacuous of politicians weaseled out of their commitments, at the very least the issues were once again laid out in front of the world. And positive change was still positive change. Even if not to the degree that was really needed. Or committed to! Perhaps this is why Kallis wielded his political influence - and capital. To get politicians in his pocket - to pressure and blackmail and cajole them into committing to his global environmental initiative. The optimist in him hoped that to be the case. That there was good intent at the heart of criminal activity. The realist in him figured it was highly unlikely. Particularly if Kallis was working with Russia. If Russia was involved in getting Charleston elected as President, it was not to fix the emissions and waste of the world's largest economy.

Brendt realised he had filled another memory card with images and video. Time to head back to the tent, send these to Mack back at Langley and get ready for dinner. His invite did not extend to a seat at a table, but he was very keen to witness the night through his lens.

Chapter 103

APPROACHING THE MASSIVE wooden doors to Hanse Kallis office, Ward noticed security, once the President had left was non existent. Even the desk for Kallis' assistant outside the office was vacant. Perhaps he had another way out and had left. Ward grabbed the handle and pushed on the large double door. It moved deceptively easily, opening to a stunning expanse of floor-to-ceiling glass looking down and out across the cultivated grassland and into the native bush way beyond. She was transfixed for a moment by the striking view. The darkening horizon seemingly melting into the hills in the distance. She caught herself. Taking in the view! Excellent situational awareness Alex, she thought.

'Come in, Miss Walsh. Or is it Agent Ward? I figured you would be my next guest.' a voice from the deep leather lounges facing away from her towards the glass windows.

Determined not to be put off balance by Kallis, Ward responded, 'Getting to you wasn't particularly hard; your security all seemed to scatter when the President left.'

'I've allowed them to pull back a little, given that they seemed redundant after seeing how you handled the security check on the way here.'

'Is that what it was? A security check. Seemed more like an ambush.'

'Will you join me agent Ward? The view is beautiful.'

'I think I'll stand. And keep you where I can see you.'

Kallis swivelled to look at her, 'Let us cut the small-talk, shall we. We can choose to dance around the edges, or we can choose to get face-to-face. My security is nearby, though I imagine you can take care of me before they get here. It would be the last act you perform, but you may be so motivated. Shall we talk before you make your move?'   Kallis paused to properly look at Ward. This person was causing ripples in his careful plan. She was taller, younger and much more attractive than he had anticipated. Though her expression was tight and her eyes were fierce. 'I realise you are here at the behest of Director Thomas. She has concerns about the relationship I have with your President.' offered Kallis.

'Her concern is that the President has been bought and paid for by the Russians. And that you seem to be the broker.' responded Ward.

'Let me assure you I am nobody's patsy. You may expect that I will deny your accusations, but I will save us all some time. Shortly I need to open this global event. Time is a luxury old people like me really don't have.'

Ward cut him off, 'Nobody's patsy! We know you're the cut out between Charleston and his merry band and the Russians.'

'You see what you want to see Agent Ward.'

'Phone records, emails, satellite imagery, recordings. We see what is clearly there.'

Despite her best efforts, Ward was off balance. She had, in fact, expected Kallis to be evasive in her presence. To deny and deny. She figured her surprise visit would cause some panic and lead to mistakes. And that they would ultimately catch Kallis and Charleston in their lie. But Kallis was not trying to hide his involvement. Was he taunting her into a misstep? She needed to reconsider her options - she was unarmed and had no real support or authority. She could no doubt take Kallis out - killing an old and unarmed man would not present a challenge. But to what end? It was Charleston that they needed to shut down. And then understand what damage had been done.

Still facing Ward, Kallis now smiled and swivelled once again back to the view before him. 'The job your agency is asked to do is becoming impossible, is it not? Where years and decades ago it was about finding information. Getting access. An intercept. An overheard conversation. A leaked memo or file. A planted agent or a disaffected and motivated official.

Sometimes even just snippets that would help identify and incriminate an enemy. Now you are overwhelmed with information. A proverbial needle within the haystack. Made so much more difficult because social media, fake news and artificial intelligence let us create many haystacks. What is right? What is wrong? What is real? What is fake? And what to act upon?'

Kallis seemed keen to talk. There was little Ward could do. She figured she would learn what she could. Confirm their suspicions. They needed a watertight case against Charleston and his conspirators.

Kallis continued, 'You think I'm rambling. Clearing my conscience. Or perhaps feeding my ego. None of those are true. I'm simply pointing out that you and your agency are looking under the wrong haystack. Let me leave you with this: I wanted Charleston to be President. But supporting him in becoming President was not about planting a stooge - or me working for the Russians. Why do I need the Russians? No, my motivations are entirely transparent and consistent. We need people in these positions who are committed to changing the world. To save the world.

'Honestly - I know your President has no appreciation for the ecological time bomb ticking ever more loudly. But he was committed to being President. And I made it happen. He is now repaying his debt. In so doing, we will turn the massive damage humanity has caused around. Now I really must prepare for the event. The world is going to seem very different tomorrow, Agent Ward.'

With that, Hanse Kallis stood, put his glass down and simply walked past her and out of the large double doors back into the main building.

Holy shit. No denial. Not even a deflection. It was as good as a confession that he had been the puppet master of a compromised election. Fucking eco warrior. Thought Alex. So full of his own agenda and self-importance. He really thinks this fancy camp-out in the bush is going to change the world. Well, at least she knew now without doubt that their President was not 'of the people'. He was in office because he had sold himself, the American electoral system and the American people to their enemy. All to get himself elected. She needed to talk to Kristen. They had to take Charleston down. And they needed someone in charge that would put America first.

She'd contemplated grabbing Kallis here and now but figured her attempt would be effectively shooting from the hip - no real plan or exfil strategy and the place was crawling with security. She needed Kristen to provide additional assets for a take-down of Kallis. They also needed a plan to get him to a secure location. He was the self-appointed conductor and the key to building the evidence against the President.

Chapter 104

SWEEPING HER GAZE across the beautiful open-air dining space, Ward was enjoying the still warm and slightly heavy evening. Now dressed for a formal dinner, albeit one with a dress code modified for their location, Ward wore a very fitted midnight blue dress with spaghetti straps and a long split up her left leg, almost to her hip. The dress had been provided by O'Shea. He told her he'd had limited notice and approximate measurements. She felt conspicuous. Aware of eyes on her. Not what she would have chosen to be discreet and blend. From her table near the back of the massive space she figured there were at least several hundred attendees - politicians, corporate leaders, scientists, journalists, influencers and many others, seated at beautifully laid tables, enjoying South African wine and entrees and buzzing with conversation prior to the commencement of the formal part of the evening.

She reflected on the secure call she'd had with Kristen. It had proven frustrating. Despite the admissions of Kallis, taking down a high profile foreign national on home soil and bringing down a sitting US President was not something to be taken lightly. Kristen was running through the evidence they now had. She needed more. Much remained circumstantial. An action against a President would need to be incontrovertible. Ideally they would be able to force his resignation and then prosecute. Much cleaner than a public and political fight. But forcing a President to resign was going to be complicated. Especially one who had been so desperate to get into office. It was going to take time. Kristen had agreed with Ward that the first priority was Kallis. To secure him at one of their safe locations and to pressure him into revealing the full details of his manipulative electoral strategy. That, too, was complicated. He was a South African national treasure. Billionaire businessman, environmentalist and COVID-19 global savior. And he was centre stage of the most significant event in the world at the moment. He would be incredibly well protected by his country and his lawyers.

Ward was steaming with frustration at the delay and seriously contemplated a much quicker resolution. It wouldn't be good for her career–or her future–but it would be definitive.

Chapter 105

WARD TOLD HERSELF to calm and to focus on her true objective in resolving an illegally elected and compromised President. She forced herself to tune in to the opening speaker of the forum. The teenage female climate activist, with a pretty face and a sharp tongue. An interesting choice to set the tone of the event.

The EMCEE completed his opening remarks and hen welcomed the teenager to open this milestone event. As she made her way across the platform, the massive outdoor auditorium was blasted with Fatboy Slim - Right Here, Right Now - accompanied by a laser and light show that danced around the room and into the night sky.

The female activist offered no preamble and was immediately on familiar territory admonishing the dismal record of countries and enterprise to have taken any meaningful steps to address environmental destruction. Many of her remarks were in fact targeted directly at those present. And their predecessors. These political and corporate leaders, many of whom had won their position on a platform of reform and progression.

Now, she intentionally named many present for their failures and inability to take definitive action. Ward admired her mettle. And her refusal to be intimidated. Her image in sharp focus on large screens surrounding the space and her accented voice clear and emboldened by numerous loud speakers. She expressed her fervent hope that this would not just be another forum of hollow words. Protocols and agreements without any real commitment or responsibility. Convenient speeches and ambitious visions that were never realised. She was putting this congregation on notice as was her style, in unambiguous terms. Her final words - imploring the generations in this forum not to let down the generations coming, was met with modest, uncertain applause.

Stepping down from the podium, she was met onstage and warmly greeted by the next speaker. The young British Prince - had been recently finding his voice, building his own brand by adding his profile and position to the imperative of fixing the planet.

As he stepped to the microphone, Ward turned her focus to the audience. In her periphery, she was aware of the more modest, self-deprecating and conservative British tone of the handsome and smiling royal compared to the previous speaker. She brought her eyes to the main table near the stage. Hard to make out at some distance from her position at the rear. She was ignoring attempts by others at her table to engage. She focussed on the President sitting to the right of Kallis, both men beaming, resplendent under the soft lights, in similarly coloured and informal open-necked shirts. Clearly very comfortable both in each other's company and the global attention.

The Prince was now fully engaged, energised and strident in challenging the world's sharpest minds and most influential leaders to re-direct their focus. To put aside the chase for headlines, wealth and superficial endeavours. And to make meaningful change. The world he admonished, was already broken. Sick and dying in many areas. It was this generation right now that must fix this. His message was clear - we cannot mortgage the environmental debt to our children. To not be obsessed with this challenge, with the priority of fixing the environment, was to misplace one's focus. Competition, he acknowledged, drove many of those in the room. Surely, the ultimate competition was to be the first to save the planet!

A geopolitical realist, Ward knew that these passionate speakers and generational agents of change were likely wasting their efforts. Despite her cynicism, she felt herself rise to the words and emotion. A firm believer in the need to address environmental destruction and climate change, she wanted this group to truly commit. But unfortunately, she knew that the words and the actions of many of those in this place were rarely aligned. Optics and self interest tended to be far more compelling drivers. Particularly given the short attention span of the media and the public. And the constant focus on getting re-elected. Politicians who, by necessity, had to lead the charge and force the change would never back their words with actions. The fear of the economic unknown was paralysing. The lobbyists and interest groups would hold sway. It would stay as it always was - with economic imperatives prioritised at the cost of the environment. She agreed with the first two speakers. The world could not continue like this forever.

She tuned out of the final words from the Prince as he introduced the American President and instead re-focused her attention on the job at hand. She stood from her table and made her way to the side of the room to move closer to the stage and to discreetly scope who was there.

Chapter 106

PRESIDENT JAMES CHARLESTON finished a well articulated albeit predictable and warmly received speech and introduced their host.

Dr Hanse Kallis stood, and as he approached, Charleston stood to the side of the microphone. He and Kallis embraced to the almost rapturous applause of the attendees. Their combined presence and stature contributing to a palpable aura.

Ward again tuned out and continued moving around the room's edge. She noted faces, languages and accents well familiar. Kallis really had drawn the cream of the world's leaders. She wondered who would meet with whom behind closed doors. Many agendas would be laid bare over the next couple of days. She took particular interest in searching for the bloated round face of the Russian President. She couldn't see him on the main tables. Perhaps there were other senior representatives from the Kremlin. She wondered if Kristen was right - that this was why they had orchestrated Charleston to the Presidency - to hold the US to ransom in some manner over the environment. The Russians would be happy if it crippled the US economy and caused internal disaffection. And Kallis would be happy to have his environmental charter supported by the world's largest economy.

The applause continued as Kallis stood in all white at the microphone. Ward thought his hair looked whiter and his skin more tanned than just a short while ago when she confronted him in his office. He had the presence of a TV evangelist. There was an almost iridescent halo around his whole body from the lighting around the stage. Ward was drawn to his magnetism and the surreal nature of this event in the South African Jungle as Kallis began his speech.

Kallis opened, 'The Global Intervention Initiative will mark the single most important moment in geopolitical transition. Ever.'

Not one for understatement thought Ward.

'I will not labour the facts and figures as nobody knows the historical devastation nor the grim reality of our future better than those in this auditorium. From the compromised Kyoto Protocol to the withering Paris Agreement we have failed and we continue to fail. To many of us, it is incomprehensible and irrational that we continue to fail. Because we are failing our own future. Our own survival. Our own children.

'Where I stand today and where we hold this forum, only as many years ago as my grandfather rode here on horseback, this wilderness was teeming with wildlife and thick with beautiful dense bushland. In just a generation and a half, there has been more destruction to our natural environment and to the balance and harmony of the planet since the ice age. And what will happen in the next generation? The forecasts are so grim most people cannot comprehend the true implication. Or perhaps they don't want to.

'We live in the moment. Focussed on our now. We look forward only as far as securing our own, personal future. The next few months. Perhaps the next few years. And yet we rip the heart out of the earth. Pollute and rape the oceans. The air so thick that in many countries we can see it. Taste it. In some, we cannot even see through it. If we continue on this path, the result is entirely inevitable. Inevitable. Inevitable. And the future will not be in our hands. It will be beyond our control and beyond our ability to fix.'

Kallis looked around the now silent room. He had gotten to the point very quickly.

He continued, the intensity shimmering from him, 'Waiting for somebody to invent the magic bullet that will solve all of this and secure a healthy planet and a bright future for us all........is a fools game.

Many of us here are truly motivated and committed - genuinely excited and hopeful of the changes we can make and commit to. Many others come here only to be seen. To propagate the veneer of leadership and authority. Looking for a photo opportunity or a sound bite to appease their constituency. But with no real appetite or commitment to drive their countries to change. This, we know, is how it is and always has been.

'In the past, whenever our leaders met in whatever forum was provided, the positive statements and good intent were never matched by real action. We have failed. Every time. Compromised by the imperative of short-term self-interest. It is why I have taken the steps needed to ensure we do not fail the future again.

'The Global Intervention Initiative will be different. I do not say this ironically. And I do not say this naively. I can sense the ripple of skepticism running around this forum and around the world. A rich man's self-indulgent crusade. But it *will* be different. Because while I know you have come here ready to negotiate over new targets and a new agenda that will be forgotten as quickly as you board your planes, in fact, I ask nothing of you. Nothing of your countries. Nothing of your companies. And nothing of your people. The Global Intervention Initiative requires nothing of you.'

Kallis paused, knowing there would be confusion - or perhaps an expectation of an explanation of his remarks.

'I ask nothing of you because I know that is the one thing you will be able to deliver. Nothing. Unfortunately, it is what you, as leaders, have always delivered. Nothing. No tangible, meaningful substantive change to address the problems we face. Since identifying the reality of environmental destruction and consequent climate change almost thirty years ago, nothing has been done to address the fundamental issues. In fact, worse than nothing. We have continued to advance - backwards and our position today is the worst it has ever been in living history. It will be worse again tomorrow. And next week, next month and next year.

'Were we to engage over the next few days and come to meaningful and aggressive new targets and commitments, yes we would be celebrated by some - many perhaps. We would clap ourselves on the back and congratulate ourselves around tables over great wine and food. Indulging in our leadership and our new place in history.

'And, of course, we would be lauded by others - those who think we have gone too far and those who think we have not gone far enough. But in reality, even with the best case outcome projected by the most learned analysts, we would at best slow the pace of devastation. At best. Where even with our most committed efforts the devastation we see today would continue to worsen. Perhaps slow, but certainly not improve.'

For the second time this evening, Alex Ward did not hear what she had expected from Hanse Kallis. He was telling everyone the Global Intervention Initiative - the reason they were here was a waste of time. A failure before it even commenced. Inevitably, a raft of hollow promises from those that want to be seen to be seen. He was voicing the scepticism she herself had for such forums and conventions. From the looks on faces and the total silence around the auditorium Kallis' speech was not what anyone had expected. But it was mesmerising.

'The stark, historical, brutal reality is that whatever we commit to here at this forum, at the Global Intervention Initiative will simply be vacuous rhetoric.

'When you are back in front of your constituents, your parliaments, your press and your shareholders, you will revert to what has always happened. Where the opportunity for true leadership is subverted by the more potent pull of self interest. The economy - money - drives everything. The environment - our own planet and its survival - and ours with it, remains subservient to economic growth and prosperity. It is an abhorrent and irresponsible misdirection.'

Kallis had not once looked at his notes. And there was no autocue. The emotion was real and raw. Coming off him in waves. And whilst still a long way from the stage, Ward thought she could see tears in his eyes and gleaming on his cheeks.

Chapter 107

HANSE KALLIS CONTINUED to rail the crowd. His intensity reaching new heights, 'In the lead-up to this event and now all around this place, you will have seen references to the theme of this forum. ONE!

'Of course - a singular commitment to a singular purpose. ONE planet. ONE goal. ONE focus. ONE chance! You will soon realise that the meaning of ONE is far more powerful than a marketing catchphrase to consolidate our focus and energise the world's media. ONE represents the problem. And ONE represents the answer.'

Now, he paused. Looked down briefly and then continued. 'Everywhere we look, the planet is sick and dying.'

Ward noted the change sweeping across Kallis's face. His energy and demeanour elevated even further. This clearly meant a lot to the old dog.

'Plant and animal species are dying daily. The air quality is universally poor. As is our water. The oceans are massively over-farmed and now have more plastic than fish. Much of the fish remaining are full of antibiotics or mercury. We are tasking our scientists and our public health organisations to find answers to the destruction. To slow the rate of damage. Documentaries populate streaming services, articulating the level of destruction the public is largely ignorant to. Imploring our people and leaders to make the necessary changes before it's too late. If it isn't already.

'There is a viral pandemic - COVID-19 - sweeping the globe like something out of a futuristic movie. This is the most potent and most explicit evidence yet of just how sick the planet is.

'But you all know this. It is well documented. And increasingly topical. After all. It's the reason for this forum.

Unfortunately, nothing of substance has changed. Despite the knowledge. Despite the damage. Despite the attention brought by many. The public - our various peoples - nod their heads and regurgitate the issues over dinner parties and barbecues. But the change it would require to how they live to reverse the damage is too big a step. The wealthy countries are too comfortable. The less fortunate countries, too busy trying to survive.

'Let us not kid ourselves, the politicians in this auditorium have probably already discussed how they will find the economic and political rationale to change their minds once they are back home.

'It is the undeniable and very uncomfortable reality that every single issue with our planet, with its deterioration and inevitable demise, is attributable to ONE factor.

Us. Humans. People. We are the most destructive force that has ever happened. And we're just getting started. We are the problem. And we are the solution. But not through words, protocols and arrangements.

'Prior to the mid-1800's, there were less than one billion people on the planet. By the mid-1900s, there were two billion. In the last 70 years we have added nearly another six billion. We have effectively added more people in just 70 years than has ever lived before. We are approaching eight billion people. We will be at 10 billion in another 30 years.

'Yes, population growth is slowing. The UN has initiatives in place. Particularly addressing reduced growth in less developed countries. But it's hard to stop people re-producing!'

Ward had made her way further forward and could see the emotions rippling across the face of Kallis.

He continued, 'Unfortunately, the problem is also the answer. There is only ONE action that can succeed. There is only ONE solution. It is not popular. In fact, it is never talked about. But it is the true Global Intervention. The intervention the world must have if it is to survive and hopefully to once again thrive.

'Bringing you to this place serves many purposes. Not the least is to see what can be done when we allow nature the space it needs. Look around you. Wildlife is again increasing. Species have stopped being wiped out. Harmony is truly happening.'

Chapter 108

HIS EYES SEEMED to bore into Ward from many metres away. Hanse Kallis prepared to deliver his final pitch.

'The ONE solution is ONE billion.

'ONE billion is the optimal number of people the world should have. Not eight billion as we have today. Not 10 billion that we will have in a few years. ONE billion.'

Ward took a breath. This had been a hell of a speech. Ripe with emotion. Quivering with energy. But where was he going. One billion people...

'A stable, zero growth, distributed global population of ONE billion. It is not a made-up number. I have had my best people model the optimal global population.

'Admittedly it is not ideal for economic growth. More people has typically meant bigger economies. But that measure is flawed. It's convenient. Good for politicians and elections. Good for balance sheets and bonuses. Good for the short term - one or two generations. But it is disastrous for the planet. Look where it has gotten us.

'The ONE goal we should all have is a healthy planet. Not a faster car or a giant TV. It is the only goal that matters. The only one that makes real sense. And the ONE solution to a healthy planet.

Is ONE billion.

'Unfortunately, if we let things run their course, there is no guarantee humanity will survive its own destruction. Our inability to act over the last 30 years will continue. By the time our own destruction is inevitable, it will be too late.

'I have initiated a plan to rebalance the planet and bring it into proper harmony, to see it thrive again–not in centuries, not in decades, not in years.

'Right now.

'To bring the population back to what it should be. ONE Billion.

'Many of you have unknowingly contributed to achieving this very necessary target, so I ask nothing more of you. The work has already been done.

'As the architect of this initiative - of this intervention I am saddened beyond words that it has come to this. That this most drastic of actions is required due to the absence of your leadership. Implementing this has taken many months of planning and for many moving parts to fall into place. So I have had a long time to consider these actions and am resolute that this is the only way our planet will not only survive - but once again thrive.'

Now, Kallis had Ward's full attention. As he did everyone in the room. Was his plan to reduce the world's population to One Billion? Was that what he was going to ask of all those present? What the fuck! A unilateral commitment to massive population reduction. But that would take years - decades. She tuned back in...

'The pandemic provided the opportunity to make this happen. At scale and at speed. And it has happened. Unfortunately, the brutality of the pandemic and the deaths and hardships it caused is not over - it has only prepared us for what will now happen - and is happening.'

Ward was fixed in place. Staring. The Pandemic! Is he saying he is behind the pandemic?

'I commend you now to make your way from this place back to your homes and your families. There is no forum beyond tonight. The Global

Intervention Initiative has already been implemented. The inevitable is inevitable. Almost all of us here tonight have at best days, possibly a week or two to live. I suggest you make the most of it. As I intend to.'

Kallis stood at the Podium and seemed to shrink. The palpable energy dissipated. The aura of moments ago; gone. He looked utterly beaten.

Then, the entire auditorium went pitch black.

Chapter 109

ALEX WARD INSTINCTIVELY took off as soon as the room went dark. She was following the most recent picture in her mind of where Kallis had last been on the stage and the route to get there. She was at least forty or fifty metres away. Probably ten seconds to get there. More if she tripped and fell. And she was in heels.

The auditorium was almost completely black. There was not a light visible anywhere. The temporary roof was a series of overlapping sails that let none of the moon or starlight through. There was some very minimal peripheral light coming in from the open sides. Not enough to distinguish shapes. No one had a phone - including Ward. They had been required to leave them in their rooms or deposit them in the cloakrooms before the event. They had been told it was to ensure no un-sanctioned photos. And she had nothing else on her. No light, no weapon. There was nowhere to hide anything in this dress.

Ward was blindly pushing stunned and confused attendees out of the way. She was aware of the shouts of the Secret Service agents as they moved to extract the President. They were to the left of the stage, and some agents must have been carrying flashlights as beams flickered around as they escorted Charleston away.

It sounded like the Prince and his wife were also being extracted by his SO14 Royal Protection Squad. Ward fell twice, landing heavily on top of another guest both times. She could not tell if they were male or female. People were starting to shout. Panic was replacing stunned silence. She figured at least twenty seconds had elapsed. She found the stage and leapt up onto it. Found the podium. It was empty. She peered to both sides of the stage and behind into blackness. She could make out nothing. She took a guess and went to her right back towards the main game park structures across the lawn. But she had no idea of the layout of this part of the auditorium and immediately fell from the stage three feet to the floor and hit it hard on her right hip, arms extended reflexively to break her fall. Ward sprung to her feet ignoring the pain in her hip, and took off into the darkness. She emerged from the temporary auditorium and could see the faint outline of the main buildings. It seemed the power was out everywhere. There were frantic shouts behind her. Ward pulled off her heels, hitched her dress and sprinted across the grassed expanse towards Hanse Kallis' office.

Chapter 110

CHEIF OF STRATEGY Daniel Walker had been sitting at the table adjacent to and immediately behind the President and Hanse Kallis. His mind was trying to process what Kallis had said in his speech. One Billion! An intervention to reduce the world to One Billion. What the fuck was he saying. Walker was staring intently at Hanse Kallis when the lights went out. He was still sitting in his chair. Oblivious to the commotion of the Secret Service detail extracting the President and of the other dignitaries being whisked away by their security teams.

Chapter 111

JUST OVER FOUR minutes after the lights went out, US President James
Charleston– Secret Service code name Stallion, of course, was being ushered
up the stairs to board Marine One. Rotors were already spinning up,
preparing for an emergency takeoff. They would fly immediately to KMI
Airport, where Air Force One had been alerted and was being prepped.

Special Agent in Charge Justin Breust was the head of Charleston's
detail. He seated the President in the single front-facing seat on the port side
and ensured he was strapped in. Charleston pushed him away.

'What the fuck just happened, Justin?' demanded a clearly winded
President.

'Sir, the lights went, and all power seemed cut. Our comms went
down. It presented a clear threat. We will immediately head to Air Force One
and determine the best evacuation location.'

Charleston felt off balance and confused. He'd been half listening to
Kallis as he started his speech. In his mind, he was trying to figure out how to
come up with some emergency that would get away from the forum early. He
couldn't stay at this talk fest for two days. He'd tuned back in when Kallis
started talking about the need to manage the environment by reducing the
population. One Billion. What was he on about?

The President looked at his security head, 'No, I mean, what
happened with Hanse Kallis back there? What was he talking about?'

'Sir, I can't comment. I wasn't really listening.'

'Get me Director Jacob on the line.'

'Mr President, I suggest we get you out of here and to the plane first,
then evaluate.'

'Now Justin!'

'Yes, Sir.'

Charleston was aware of the increased noise and vibration in the cabin and the sensation of lifting off. He looked around. Apart from the Secret Service agents, he was the only one in the main cabin. He closed his eyes. The takeoff was fast—much faster than normal. His stomach flipped. They seemed to lift straight up.

Chapter 112

'SIR - THE DNI.' Justin Breust handed the President a secure phone.

'William Jacob, Mr President.' said the DNI.

'Bill, are you aware of what the fuck is happening over here?

'I've been briefed that you were extracted from the international forum. An issue with the power blacking out. The Secret Service do not believe there is a serious threat, Mr President.'

'No Bill - I mean Kallis. What is he up to? Have you heard his speech?'

'No sir, I haven't.'

'Well, listen to it now. I want to know what Kallis is up to. He's off the rails.'

'Sir, I'll try and get a feed. And I will patch Director Thomas from the CIA in on this call. This is her patch.'

'I'll wait. Hurry the fuck up!'

'It should only take a minute.'

Charleston checked his watch - a vintage Omega Speedmaster he told everyone was his Father's. He'd actually bought it himself in Korea on vacation years ago but liked the story. It could only have been ten or twelve minutes since he'd left the auditorium. He was not sure if anyone would know what was going on. But he needed answers. He was tied completely into Kallis. He didn't need him to end up being a fucking madman.

Jacob came back over the phone, 'Mr President, you have myself and Director Thomas.'

Charleston launched straight in, 'Does the CIA have any idea what Kallis is up to? Is he making an actual threat, or has he just lost it?'

Kristen Thomas had watched the speech in full. One of her analysts had emailed it to her within seconds of the President being escorted away.

They had identified some patterns with Kallis through their recent investigation. They knew he was a wildlife warrior, and some of his historical speeches she viewed had him lamenting the demise of the natural environment and the devastation of species. But the picture was incomplete. Murky. The speech she had just watched from the Global Intervention Initiative spoke to extremism. Extreme extremism. Until now, they had really only been looking at his relationship with the Russians and his role in the election. She wasn't about to give unresolved intel or advice to an immature, newbie, panicking President. And an idiot DNI.

Kristen Thomas responded, 'Mr President, this situation is in real-time. We don't know where Kallis is. We want to get proper intel together and determine whether this is a threat and, if so, the nature of the threat. We have people on the ground and analysts deployed. I've watched the speech and it leads to more questions than answers. We will need some time to present a more actionable package.'

The President sounded frantic, 'Actionable package! Are you kidding! He clearly alluded to the pandemic and a massive global population reduction. What does he mean by that? Does he know something about the pandemic we don't? Is he referring to this new strain I've just been briefed on? I know this man. He doesn't take to idle statements. Or wishful dialogue. He's very private. And he just spoke to the world. It sounded more like a warning than a threat.'

Not one for political games, Kristen nonetheless took the opportunity to remind the President that Kallis was his friend.

'You may be right. You do know him better than all of us. But we can provide no real insight until we can properly pull information together. And certainly no proper response.'

'Director Thomas, I was a keynote speaker just minutes ago. I fucking introduced Hanse Kallis at this forum. I've now been ripped out of there in the dark in a panic. If Kallis proves to be some extremist nut job, I'm going to be tied right in. I'll be on every news feed, sitting right next to him. Embracing him onstage. I need to know what is going on. Yesterday.'

Ah, now the politician emerges. That didn't take long, thought Kristen, worried about the optics and how it will affect him. 'Mr President, I'm going to have to call you back once we know more.'

Charleston looked at the phone in his hand. Did she just hang up on me?

Chapter 113

SPRINTING BACK TO Kallis' office with only the light from the stars, Ward slammed into one of the event team sending them both flying. She grabbed the poor woman's small flashlight as she lay on the ground groaning and kept going. Ward added sore ribs to her already bruised hip.

Ward looked up from the ground as the sound of thrusting jet engines filled the dark night. She climbed to her feet as she watched the silhouette of three jets take off one after the other and turn in different directions. That was quick. Had to be Kallis on one of them, she thought. But she had no way of contacting anyone to let them know. She took off running again.

Ward got to the office and it was still completely dark. Blacked out. The small light from the torch barely penetrating a few metres into the room. It was empty. Silent. And there was nothing to indicate Kallis had been back here. She moved further in and could make out secure cabinets behind the desk and locked drawers underneath. Kallis' laptop was dark. She hit the enter key, and the laptop came to life, running on its battery, prompting for a password.

Ward figured their best chance of knowing where Kallis had gone would likely be somewhere in this room. In the distance, she heard the rotors of a helicopter taking off—no doubt Marine One. She needed help and wanted to get her phone. Ward quickly headed out the office door to run back to her tent and find Brendt and O'Shea. She almost ran straight into O'Shea coming out of the darkness towards her at the office door.

'I was just coming to get you; where is Thomas?' Ward asked.

'Right here.' Brendt said, emerging from the darkness behind O'Shea. 'Did you guys hear the speech from Kallis?'

O'Shea responded, 'Yep, we were in tent city, and it was being broadcast on screens. Until it all went dark. We figured you'd be over here somewhere looking for him. And that you'd need this.'

O'Shea passed Ward her secure phone, a small bag of clothing, and her boots.

'Thanks. Thomas can you get into Kallis' laptop? It's on his desk.' she pointed across the room with her small light.

'Yes, but only his hard drive while the power is off and we are offline.'

'Do your best. I need to know where he might have gone. He's had plenty of time to plan this, so we need to catch up fast. Sean - let's get his hard copy files open. Start with the desk draws. Do you two have any lights?'

'Only from our phones.' O'Shea responded.

'I wont need a light.' said Thomas.

'OK - Sean, use this.' she passed him the small torch she'd acquired.

Both Brendt and O'Shea moved to the large desk. Ward used her phone light and emptied the bag O'Shea had brought onto one of the sofas, grabbing long olive cargo pants and a black t-shirt.

'Any thoughts on his password?' Brendt asked.

'Try one billion,' suggested Ward

'Nice one,' the sound of a keyboard in the darkness. 'Actually no - that is not it.'

'Can't you just crack it?' asked Ward as she unzipped and pulled her cocktail dress above her head.

'No problem. Thought we'd try the obvious first. It would just be easier with power and a connection,' replied Brendt.

And with that the lights in the office snapped back on. The three of them looked up at once. Brendt and O'Shea were distracted with Ward standing beside the leather sofa in just her tiny bikini briefs and nothing else.

'Now can you crack it Thomas?' Ward asked, seemingly oblivious to the two men staring at her almost naked body.

'On it!' he said quickly, looking back at his screen.

Ward pulled on the cargo pants, snapped the buttons closed, and then put the t-shirt over her head. She quickly put on socks and boots and joined O'Shea at the desk. He had picked the lock off the first draw, which seemed to release them all. Ward pulled out a draw and started sorting through it. She had a bad feeling that this search would be futile.

Chapter 114

DR BENITA MORRIS was distraught. She hadn't slept in what felt like days. She hadn't been home to eat or, shower or sleep. A tsunami of new cases was now presenting at her hospital. And this was replicated in dozens of hospitals around the country and around the world. All with the same symptoms and story. They had all been vaccinated and yet all were suffering acute respiratory failure and not responding to treatment. People were dying. Within days, sometimes only hours of admission. And she had no answers.

Morris and her colleagues had initially considered that perhaps one of the vaccines was triggering some delayed side effects. But that was not the issue. These cases were not limited to one vaccine. This new strain or new virus did not discriminate. Collectively, they'd managed to keep the idea of a new virus from the press. They didn't want more confusion. Or panic. It had happened quickly and was caught up in the daily COVID reporting and cases. But that would not last. The death rates were too high. And now accelerating at an exponential and unprecedented rate.

Beds in ICU and throughout the hospital were filled. Hallways were filled. They could take no more. People were queuing outside the hospital and in the car parks. Many lay on the ground where they fell. Some dying where they lay. Non essential and elective surgery had been canceled. Medical staff across disciplines were being redeployed to assist.

Overwhelmed and exhausted both emotionally and physically from months of dealing with the pandemic, they now seemed to be dealing with some new and deadly virus. Just as there was light emerging in the distant tunnel after the vaccine rollout, giving them hope and renewing their energy and effort, now this. The health system and their own spirits were on the precipice. This may just take them over the edge.

Morris sat in her office and clicked on the Zoom link. They had hastily convened a meeting of virologists from around the world. As her video and audio connected, she entered the online meeting, where Dr David Mitchell from Australia spoke. He was screen-sharing devastating images. Hundreds of bodies in their temporary COVID hospital. More, many more on the grounds outside the tent walls. The gallery of voices on the Zoom call were chiming in, commenting that the scenes were similar at their hospitals. It happened almost overnight. Benita Morris sat in stunned silence, tears rolling down her face. The worst of the fears they had harboured during the pandemic now seemed to be happening. Like some terrible scene from a horror movie...

Chapter 115

KRISTEN THOMAS WAS in her office. Six analysts were with her putting together a full package on Hanse Kallis. They had already worked up extensive background as part of the investigation into electoral rigging, but the focus was now critical. She had to find him.

They now knew Kallis had taken off in his private jet from the game park moments after the place went dark. In fact, three jets took off one at once, and went in different directions. The satellites she had repurposed had caught the take off, but then the planes had disappeared. They were not set up to track plane movement. All the jets were dark, emitting no signals at all.

The more detailed picture they were building of Kallis, confirmed a massive and diverse pharmaceutical empire across the globe. His wealth was in the stratosphere and had grown massively during the pandemic. His passion was clearly the wildlife and flora of Sth Africa and more broadly across the world. The environmental focus of the Global Intervention Initiative was not a recent hobby horse. Kallis had been vocal about the massive damage being done to the planet for years - decades. He had consistently made the connection between the human impact of exponential population growth and the accelerating demise of the planet. And he had put his money where his mouth was - investing heavily in buying and quarantining massive parcels of land in Africa, Asia and South America coupled with programs to re-populate both animal and plant species.

His business and investment interests would take her team some time to unravel and connect. But he had the means, and it seemed the motive to take action. But what was the action? Was his threat real, or just the frustrated bluster of a motivated billionaire running out of time...

Chapter 116

'OH FUCK. OH fuck. Oh fuck.' Thomas Brendt was staring into the computer on Hanse Kallis's desk.

'Thomas! Have you found him?' prompted Ward.

'Ah...no, I don't know where Kallis is. But I think I know what he has done.' Brendt looked up from the laptop at Ward, 'Oh fuck.' he repeated.

Chapter 117

HANSE KALLIS WAS reclining in the leather seat on his Bombardier Global 8000. The extended range jet would allow him to fly without refueling to the private airfield in Wellington New Zealand. Then a short chopper ride to his island off the east coast.

He was alone in the opulent cabin, staring into the dark porthole window. Seeing only a dim representation of his reflection. He was contemplative and incredibly saddened that this was the culmination of the last few years of his work. In fact, his lifetime's work. It was out there now. And he felt emptied.

Kallis had spent the best part of the last decade doing everything he could to inform and engage with political and corporate leaders to have them understand the dire precipice they were inexorably approaching. And to act before it was too late. He had even resorted to funding candidates into seats and, more recently, manipulating elections, news and social media. All to get those who were aligned - and who owed him - to take the action needed. But to no avail. The near-sighted vision of leaders had them continuing on a path that had no alternative but a slow and painful global death. A man-made four horseman writ large.

And so he had started to make his own plans. A strategy reliant on no one else. The realisation that a world of ten billion or more souls was a world that would kill itself. The planet would be all-but destroyed. Humanity potentially wiped out. His strategy was the only one that he could see working. To bring the planet back into balance and for it to once again thrive.

It sickened him. But he had come to the view that there was no alternative. At least none that was likely to work. He had told no one the full plan. Had compartmentalised everything. He knew he would be regarded by history as its greatest monster. But he also knew he would be the world's salvation. Even though he would not be there to witness it. Nobody else had the foresight to do what was needed. Nobody else had the means to make it happen. And so he could tell nobody. Until tonight. He had orchestrated the Global Intervention Initiative as the forum where he would tell the world what was happening. He wanted to give leaders warning - time to get organised to manage what was coming. And he felt that if they were in one location it would make the message real and expedite their best collective action.

He knew it was more likely that the fight or flight response would kick in and that nothing positive would come from them being together. They would most likely panic, argue, and then return to their own countries and homes, wasting time and resources trying to stop what was inevitable. But he felt it important to try.

Chapter 118

WARD HIT THE preset number on the secure sat phone for Kristen Thomas. 'Boss, Kallis has left us a package of information about what he has done. He made it easy for us to find. He wanted us to find it. He's laid it out for us. Rigging elections was just a means to an end. Garnering favours that facilitated his plans. I'll give you a debrief, but first, can you get me a plane to follow Kallis?'

'I have a chopper coming to you to take you to KMI airport, where your plane is refuelled and ready to go. But we don't know where he has gone - we're working on it.'

'So are we. Thomas is in his laptop now. We have to find him.'

'What is in the package? What's his plan?' asked Kristen?

'I'm trying to get my head around it. I'll give you what we think we know.'

Ward paused and drew a breath, trying to comprehend the words even as she spoke them. 'Across his various companies, Kallis is now the world's largest producer and supplier of hypodermic syringes. When the pandemic hit, he scaled and bought other companies. He quickly became the preferred manufacturer of syringes to the pharmas producing the various COVID-19 vaccines. In some cases in developing countries he almost gave them away. His companies have supplied hundreds of millions of syringes for the global vaccination program.

'And Kristen, this is what we he says he's done - every one of those syringes carried an undetectable, synthetic and latent virus. Once triggered, the virus becomes lethal. It kills almost everyone it infects. And it's contagious. That is his plan. He's piggybacked COVID-19 to deliver a virus much worse. That will obliterate the population. Literally wiping out billions.' Ward stopped talking her breathing rushed.

'Alex, you need to get me everything you have right now.' said Kristen.

'Thomas is doing that as we speak - it should be with you any moment.'

'Do you believe this to be real, or is this about leverage - to shake the world into action?' asked Kristen.

'If I had to put my life on it, I'd say yes. It's real. The data he has left us is not some madman gloating. It's clinical. He wants us to know what we're dealing with. He wants us to know we can't stop it. And he wants us to get organised for what will happen - what is happening. That is why he brought these leaders and environmentalists here. To collectively consider a global response - to deal with the inevitable deaths of millions and to get ready for the aftermath.'

'Do you know the timeline?' asked Kristen.

'We haven't found anything on a timeline yet.'

'Have you spoken to David?' asked Kristen.

Alex was thrown a little by the pivot, 'What? No. I haven't exactly had time for a husband and wife chat.'

'Alex. He is right in the middle of this already. We've been getting reports of a massive spike in cases and deaths at COVID-19 facilities here in the US and in many other countries. We assumed it was an aggressive new variant. But now it seems highly likely it's the virus Kallis has released. Some of these reports are from Australia. Alex, you can't say anything to David until we know what is going on. And have a plan to deal with it. We have to contain who knows about this, or we will have unprecedented panic. Get to the chopper. I'll find out where Kallis has gone.'

Chapter 119

PRESIDENT JAMES CHARLESTON was sitting unmoving in his office on Air Force One, still on the tarmac at KMI airport. Since he'd been pulled away from the forum and flown here on Marine One, very little had been clarified. His security detail wanted to get moving but admitted there was no imminent threat so Charleston had demanded his Chief of Strategy Daniel Walker be brought to him. They had sent the helicopter back to get him. Charleston had no idea if he should return to the US, head to Moscow, or go back to find Kallis at the game park. He'd called Bill Jacob twice and he knew nothing. He'd called Director Thomas several times and was waiting on a callback. She was ignoring him. The Commander in Chief! He was sitting alone in his Presidential Chair behind his Presidential Desk on his Presidential Plane with his Presidential Dick in his hand and no idea what the fuck was happening.

Finally, the phone on his desk rang. He snatched it up.

'Yes!'

'James. It's Hanse Kallis.'

'Fuck me, Hanse. What are you doing?'

Chapter 120

A DISBELIEVING PRESIDENT sat and listened, his mouth agape as Kallis explained exactly what he had initiated. Kallis paused after he'd delivered the highlights waiting for a reply. He wasn't sure if he had been disconnected. Just the hollow static of an empty phone line.

Finally he heard breathing... then, 'This is something out of a bad movie. It is barbaric. Syringes contaminated with a virus. Why are you saying this? Are you playing me, Hanse?'

'I can assure you it is all true. And really James. You and I deal in the bigger picture. We have tried and failed so many times. We refuse to acknowledge and address the real problem. I'm running out of time. The planet is running out of time. We are all running out of time. This is the only answer.' stated Kallis definitively.

'Global genocide is your answer! You've taken the devastating coronavirus, and what......made it catastrophic?' asked an incredulous and reeling President.

'We are the virus James. An intervention is demanded. We must stop the decline and the destruction of the planet. In its place. Completely. By removing the cause of the destruction. Us - the eight billion people that now live here. The human mass is suffocating and obliterating everything else. We must deal with the cause. And then we must re-set.' Again, his tone was categoric.

'I'll stop you. I have to stop you. You're one man. One fucking mad-man!' A seething President responded.

Kallis continued calmly, 'When it happens, my death will make no difference. You're too late. My personal fate is sealed. And irrelevant now. I'm calling you and telling you this because the United States and countries around the world need to prepare. My company has already distributed over three billion syringes. Most have been used. The earliest infected vaccinations were provided in March, several months ago. For most people, the adaptation takes six months. Once it is triggered in the body, it only takes a few days to be lethal. There are reports of many deaths already. Doctors grappling, thinking it is a new strain. I have viewed some of the confidential communications between hospitals.'

'Three billion syringes!' Charleston softly repeated. The combined effects of the alcohol he'd consumed at the forum and his current state of confusion were clouding his comprehension. That and the preposterous enormity of what was being said. His body slumped further into the leather chair.

Kallis continued in his very reasoned, unemotional tone, 'And growing daily. You must also consider the infection multiplier. For everyone injected with the virus, the models show between one point five and one point seven additional people will be infected. It is not precise. There are a lot of variables. But it is enough.'

Kallis paused. The President said nothing.

Kallis continued, 'The offer of low cost syringes, in some cases donated completely free, held great appeal. It was an opportunity that presented itself with the pandemic. One that I acted on. And remember. You helped me with many of the contracts in the United States and with your allies.'

The President shouted down the line, 'I will stop you. We will find a cure. Another vaccine.'

'Perhaps. But it will take time. With more time to consider what I have put in place, you may determine another option. You are not here by accident. I went to a lot of trouble to have you elected. The right man in the right place at the right time. Let's see if I was right.' suggested Kallis.

Chapter 121

CHARLESTON FIGURED IT best to keep Kallis talking. Calls were automatically recorded. He would play this back when Walker arrived and come up with a plan.

'The right man....what are you talking about?' the President asked.

Kallis stood and moved around the otherwise empty aircraft cabin. Connected to the call via a Bluetooth headset, he thrust his hands in his pockets and looked into one of the dark aircraft windows. He could see a beautiful bright moon, which at this altitude was not obscured by city lights or polluted air. He paused for a moment and then again addressed the President.

'James. There is no stopping, turning back or reversing. The plan is well-advanced and absolutely necessary. I've no doubt this seems fanciful to you right now. Considered at face value I appreciate it is extreme and monstrous. But I am not going to defend the decision or spend undue time trying to explain it. I appreciate very few would ever agree with what I have done. But with perspective and time and the application of rational thought I have come to the view that there is no other way. No other way that will ensure the perpetuation of both humanity and the planet.

'I have spent years contemplating this, considering every alternative. Spending hundreds of hours and millions of dollars trying to get governments and corporations to change. Not only have we not made progress, the problems humanity has created are getting worse. Left in the hands of wallowing leadership and hollow promises the devastation we face for ourselves and the planet is many times greater than the intervention I have initiated. My plan restores the planet - and us.'

Charleston interrupted 'But those needles - your needles - are going into the arms of the elderly, children, mothers, fathers. How can you do that? How can you be so clinical and dispassionate about genocide at a scale never seen? Your legacy will not be that of a saviour, visionary, or humanitarian. You will be the greatest monster we've ever had. Your name synonymous with absolute evil.'

As the President spoke, he subconsciously rubbed his arm where he had received multiple vaccinations and boosters.

Kallis continued to gaze at the bright almost full moon through the window of his plane. 'So be it. There is no point trying to rationalise or win the argument.'

'So, why are you telling me?' asked the President.

Chapter 122

KALLIS PICKED UP his narrative, 'Because this is your moment. Or could be. The United States and every other country must now prepare and organise. As the leader of the world's most powerful and influential country, you must take charge and get everyone on board. This is all about saving the planet. Without leadership, it will get out of hand. Who knows what will happen. The next phase for the world will be horrible and unstable. Countries, cities, entire populations are about to be devastated. It will be horrific. In little more than a week the population will be quickly reduced by almost 90%. The social, political and economic framework built over centuries is about to be completely destroyed. To avoid complete anarchy, a new structure and system must be created.'

Kallis paused for a moment. Then, 'The world and its people will need leadership like few times in its history. The United States should take that role. You need to get off that plane and go back to the forum, gather the other politicians and be the leader the world needs.'

Flabbergasted, the President had somehow picked up on one comment Kallis had made, 'Hanse, wait a minute, you said before the virus sits latent in people for months. Now you're saying a week! How is that possible?'

The President, completely off balance, was sitting, squeezing the phone to his ear, waiting for an answer, finally realising it had gone dead some time ago.

Charleston felt like he wanted to be somewhere else. Anywhere else. To wake from this nightmare. Sitting here in the job he had fought so hard for, now on the precipice of complete disaster.

Chapter 123

WARD TOOK KRISTEN'S incoming call on her headset in the helicopter taking them from the wildlife park to KMI airport. 'Of the three jets that took off simultaneously from Kallis' private airfield, we are only tracking one with the satellites, and we don't know if it is the plane Kallis is on. The President is on Air Force One still on the tarmac at KMI. I want you to get on Air Force One and interrogate Charleston. Your primary objective is to locate Kallis and the President may know more. Let's pray to god he isn't part of this.' Kristen Thomas stated.

'Copy.' Ward disconnected. She recognised the situation for what it was. Barely controlled panic. With almost no information. Kristen and her team and who knows which other agencies were trying to get a proper picture. And to contain the public release of information, otherwise, it would move from controlled panic to uncontrolled panic. Good luck with that. Ward's approach was to consider the threat genuine until they knew otherwise and take action. Plan for the worst. That meant getting to Kallis - as quickly as possible. And The President was the best place to start.

She toggled the comms button on the headset, 'Lieutenant, how far out are we?'

'Three minutes, Ma'am.'

She pulled out her own secure sat phone and dialled David.

Chapter 124

DAVID MITCHELL LOOKED at his screen and recognised the number. 'Alex, where are you?' Despite their long established understanding that he could never ask, David couldn't help himself. The last few days had been the worst he'd experienced.

Small talk seemed utterly inadequate. Ward responded, 'I hear things are pretty bad there?'

'I've never seen anything like this. Not even the darkest days of COVID. This new strain - whatever it is - we can't seem to slow it down.'

Ward closed her eyes - the mental picture she had of David being at ground zero of a deadly and infectious virus was almost too much. 'David, we think...it seems this is not COVID. We're not sure. But it seems likely.'

'Yeah. That is our thinking as well. Not even an aggressive strain will do this.'

Ward continued, 'It's some new lethal virus. And it's infectious. You need to leave there. Go straight to your parent's place in the country. I'll meet you there as soon as I can.'

Ward closed her eyes, knowing the response she would get but also knowing she had to try to protect him.

David replied in a soft voice, 'Honey, you know I can't do that. I need to help these people. They are dying. We need to find an answer. It's my job. What are you not telling me?'

She paused. Considering what she could do to demand he listen to her. That he had to save himself. He'd only just beaten the blood borne cancer. And now this. But she knew he wouldn't listen - couldn't. It was not in his nature. She decided she had to jump straight in, 'If this is what we think it is, then it's synthetic - man made - intentionally introduced to millions of people.'

David's exhaustion felt like cobwebs in his brain, 'What - why. Synthetic! Intentional! Is this a terrorist thing?'

'I'm working on that. And also working on getting to the instigators.'

Ward's mind flashed for a moment. They had both been vaccinated and had boosters. She wondered what was lying in wait in her body and in David's. Were they both human time bombs...She took a deep breath.

'David - I only have another minute or so. You and your team - you need to look at the syringes. That is where they hid the virus. In the syringe itself.'

'In the actual syringe - how?'

'I don't know; information is pretty raw at the moment. And nothing is validated. But we need to know what we are dealing with and we need to find answers. Please do this quietly - people will panic.'

'People already are. Have you seen the news? The dooms-dayers are all over this. Supermarkets are being emptied.'

'I have to go. David - please be careful.'

'Me! Alex - you're in the thick of it..' but the line was already dead..

Chapter 125

EVERY CHAIR IN Kristen Thomas' office was taken. Around the conference table. The two facing sofas. The chairs facing her desk. More chairs had been brought in. And some of her team were standing. She needed to move this soiree to one of the dedicated operational rooms but hadn't had time. The sun was streaming through the windows. It was mid-afternoon, and outside was a beautiful day, a cloudless sky and bright sunshine. A mild, Fall day that many would be enjoying. Take an afternoon walk or eat outside somewhere. A day oblivious to the unfolding crisis.

Kristen coordinated the team to prioritise the most immediate tasks. They had to assume the Kallis virus threat was real and that he had, in fact, managed to taint the syringes he manufactured and distributed. Unfortunately, the early evidence indicated this to be the case.

She sent agents out to collect syringes from hospitals and vaccination clinics. They would be tested at USAMRIID Fort Detrick. If they found - as it seemed likely, that the threat was real, she wanted the information contained until they could come up with a plan.

She had analysts pull together a comprehensive data package from US and allied countries on the spike in virus cases, illness and deaths. The progressive and partial reports indicated the current numbers to be higher than the worst days of the COVID pandemic.

With the President out of the country and most likely compromised, Kristen Thomas and the Director of the FBI had briefed Vice President Michelle Anders on the current threat. They requested she instruct the Department of Health and Human Services to immediately and quietly stop the government vaccination centres. No explanation would be offered.

Thomas knew this would create an immediate public response - questions and speculation. But for now, she just wanted to ensure no more infections were happening. They needed a more comprehensive plan to shut down the subsidised private vaccination program, and for this, she asked Mack to work with a cross-agency team to coordinate. They could pause the government centres for a short time, but Kristen was of the view they needed to shut down the entire program indefinitely.

As soon as they did this, the government would be unable to contain the public response. Which she knew would be unbridled panic. It would take people and the media seconds to join the dots of the spike in illness and deaths, the Kallis speech that would whip around the internet and the shutdown of the program. But it had to be done. She had given Mack an hour to come back with the plan. They had no idea where Kallis-sourced syringes were being used. Based on the scale of Kallis' operation and the deals he'd done - largely through Charleston's influence, it was probable his syringes were everywhere. The fear a complete shut-down would create likely meant the vaccination program would never re-start. She wondered if that would even matter.

She had asked her Deputy Director of Intelligence, Tom Gillian, to work with the White House on how they would advise the country and their allies. Once they went public with the vaccination shutdown, they would lose control of the message. Current thinking was to allude to a small number of contaminated vaccinations and they were taking the more conservative action. But the conspiracy theorists and the less favourable press would jump all over it. It would take on a life of its own.

They also had a President, through his ties with Kallis that could not be trusted to lead the nation in its response to this emerging disaster.

There were so many balls in the air that it made their heads spin. And they hadn't yet contemplated how to respond to those infected with the virus itself. It had taken months to develop, test and ultimately release vaccines for the Coronavirus. From what Kristen was seeing, they didn't have months. It was happening right now.

Worst of all, they could not find Kallis. The jet decoy and speed with which it had happened caught them all off guard.

She was trying to remain calm and not show the sickening anxiety coursing through her body. Her team needed her to remain in control and clear-minded, particularly given that they really didn't know who they could trust and work with. Even to an experienced, world-weary operator like Kristen Thomas a mass synthetic virus seemed fanciful. The stuff of Hollywood. Until she looked at the growing deaths and over-whelmed hospitals being shown across all the news services. Reality was right in front of her.

The phone on her desk lit up - her assistant had been advised of the very few calls she would be taking.

'Kristen Thomas.' she answered. 'Director, this is Colonel Watkins from USAMRIID.'

Kirsten cut to it, 'What do you have, Colonel?'

'Director, these are preliminary results and require validation. However, we have confirmed contamination - a virus within the hypodermics.....'

The Colonel continued to speak, and Kristen was vaguely aware of him describing their theory of how this had been done. But she wasn't really listening. Her mind overrun with the implications.

'Sorry, Colonel, can I stop you there. The confirmation is enough for now. I'll have my assistant set up a secure video call in 15 minutes. I want you to provide a full briefing on what you have found and what you suspect.'

'Yes, ma'am.'

Kristen hung up as Mack walked into her office.

She looked at him.

'The whole COVID vaccination program has to be shut down. Across the globe. Right now.'

Chapter 126

THE MASSIVE 747 jet was almost empty. President James Charleston was still in his office. And still alone. Where it typically travelled with hundreds of staffers, guests, journalists and Secret Service, Air Force One currently sat idle on the tarmac with just the President, flight crew and his security detail.

Following his call with Kallis, Charleston had been lying on the leather sofa across from his desk, trying to process what he had been told and to come up with a plan to save his presidency. He'd only taken calls from DNI William Jacob and CIA Deputy Director Robert Marshall. Marshall had proven useless, was completely out of the loop and knew nothing. Jacob, at least, was being briefed by his agencies, and the emerging information indicated that Kallis had done precisely what he said he had. And it looked like the scale was massive - beyond the President's ability to comprehend.

He had pulled down the blinds on the porthole windows and dimmed the lights. He was in the semi-dark. A tumbler of amber liquid resting on his stomach. The door to the office burst open. Causing Charleston to jump and spill some of his drink on his dress shirt.

'Mr President, I'm here.'

Charleston cursed and brushed the liquid from his now-stained shirt. The lights in the room came on, 'Where the fuck have you been, Daniel? Have you heard what Kallis has done?'

'Of course. I was there. Do we think he's serious? It could just be Hanse playing us. Get everyone riled up for his eco agenda!'

'Don't be fucking naive. It's confirmed alright. I've had Bill Jacob on the phone every five minutes. And I've spoken to Kallis. It's a fucking disaster. Not only is this happening on my watch, he got me elected.'

A proper politician's perspective.

Walker didn't flinch at Charleston's misguided priorities. Like himself, he always had his political lens as primary.

'You spoke with Hanse? What did he say?'

'He told me he's put three billion contaminated syringes into people's arms. Three billion Daniel! Holy fuck! And I'm probably one of them - remember the photo op we did during the election...'

'Well, we're at arm's length from Kallis. He's just another donor.' Suggested Walker.

'Daniel - don't say another stupid word. How are we at arm's length? He got me elected. I introduced him onto the stage. I fucking hugged him.'

Charleston closed his eyes for a minute and sat back on the sofa.

'The American public is going to crucify me. I need a plan to take control of this mess. We are going to use the flight back to the States to work out how I stay President. And you keep your job!'

Charleston looked up from where he sat on the sofa. 'Speak to the pilot and get this fucking plane back to Washington.'

Daniel Walker turned back without another word towards the office door just as it burst open.

Chapter 127

ALEX WARD CAME through the door and almost knocked Walker over. She was tempted to barrel into the twerp and knock him on his ass. He literally jumped out of the way. For the second time, the President spilt his drink, this time onto his lap.

'Oh, for fucks sake!' said Charleston as he tried to brush the wet stain this time off his pants. 'Who the fuck are you? How did you get past the Secret Service?'

'I know who she is.' said Walker. 'She's the bitch that held me by the balls in the diner. She's CIA.'

'Get off my plane. And tell your boss to return my calls.'

Ward was determined to be calm, 'Sit down, both of you. This plane is not going anywhere until you tell me what I need to know.'

Walker stood his ground. 'You have no authority here. You're talking to....'

She'd had enough of this prick. Before he could finish Ward threw a straight left jab to his larynx and windpipe. Walker grabbed at his throat, unable to breathe. He flailed to the single leather seater and collapsed into it. Still clutching his throat. Trying to force his breathing. His eyes wide.

'Don't panic. You should start breathing again soon.'

The President took a step towards his desk, 'Do you know where you are? You just assaulted a senior official of the United States government!'

Before he could continue his obvious threat, Ward jumped in, 'If you take another step or touch that phone, I'll be assaulting a President next!'

'You wouldn't dare!' Charleston crossed the room and reached for his phone. Ward covered the ground in a blink, grabbed his outstretched hand, and pulled and twisted until she heard something crack. The President's glass fell from his other hand to the thick carpet and he cried out, grabbing his injured wrist.

So much for staying calm! 'You two are in a world of shit. Now sit down. Both of you. Together on this couch.'   Charleston glared at her, still cradling his hand. Walker was taking short gulping breaths. Beetroot red in the face.

'You're going to tell me everything you know about Hanse Kallis. And where he's gone. And don't think about lying. We already know quite a lot and learning more by the minute. Then you can take your pathetic asses back to Washington. And when you get there, I can tell you now, Mr President, it won't be you addressing the nation!'

Chapter 128

'MY FELLOW AMERICANS. Citizens of the world. I come to you tonight from the White House. I want to update you on the current situation with the COVID-19 vaccination program.'

Vice President Michelle Anders paused and looked into the camera directly before her. By agreement with the major networks, they had interrupted their regular program schedule to take the press conference live. She also knew this would be picked up by other broadcasters and streaming networks and recorded and replayed around the world.

They had decided to proceed with the press conference in the Brady Press Briefing Room - where nearly all day-to-day press briefings were done, rather than any of the more ornate rooms in the White House. And certainly not the Oval Office. There were screens on either side of the Vice President, both displaying the headline

'COVID-19 VACCINATIONS SUSPENDED'

The Vice President continued, 'We have taken the unprecedented and unfortunate, but necessary steps to shut down with immediate effect the national COVID-19 vaccination program. Further, we have urged our allies and all nations to follow suit.

'It has become apparent over recent days that there has been a marked increase in the presentation of serious symptoms at hospitals, COVID-19 clinics and medical facilities. In some cases, tragically resulting in death. We do not yet know the reason.'

Vice President Anders paused at this point to allow that point to sink in. As unsatisfactory as it was, people needed to be prepared.

'This may be a new and aggressive COVID strain. It may be a completely new virus. We are concerned it may even be a reaction to the current vaccines and boosters. We do not yet know. And until we do. And until we can properly and safely administer vaccinations, the program will remain suspended.'

Again, the Vice President paused and looked at the camera and then around the silent ranks of the attending press. She had been pulled from her calendar of school visits and ceremonial duties to be immediately briefed on the situation and to prepare for this press conference. Her head was swirling from an overload of short and intense meetings. Her agency heads were desperately uninformed about what was happening or what to tell the American people. She had the horrible sensation of being both overwhelmed and yet completely under-informed.

'Like many of you, I have been vaccinated. As has my husband, my children, and many members of my family. I know, like me, you will be concerned. I ask that you react calmly. We are working as quickly as possible to understand the situation and to restore the program. The safety and health of our community is paramount. I will update you as soon as information is available. I will take just a couple of questions.'

Chapter 129

THE PRESS ROOM exploded with reporters and journalists shouting to be granted a question. The White House staff had set up the three questions she would take. The Vice President pointed, 'Yes Monica'.

'Madam Vice President, people are dying across the country. We are seeing images of hospital staff unable to cope. Speculation is that this is a deadly COVID variant. Is it?'

'Thanks, Monica. That people are dying is tragic and our hearts go out to their families. We want to ensure as few families as possible have to deal with that. That's why we are temporarily suspending the program. We just don't know what is causing the spike in sickness. We also know the medical community has been pushed incredibly hard over recent months. We are activating additional emergency protocols, and we will have more information on that over the coming days.'

More shouting from the floor...

'William'.

'Madam, why are you briefing us and not the President?'

'The President is returning from South Africa and is in the air right now. We wanted to brief the country immediately.'

She didn't add that the connection between Charleston, Kallis and this virus would make his appearance explosive once it became known.

'Last question - Sally.'

'Do you have a timing on when the vaccination program will re-start?'

'Unfortunately, there is so much we don't know. More questions than answers. No, I do not have a specific timing. It will re-start when we are confident the new wave is understood and under control. Thank you everybody.'

Vice President Anders turned to her right and exited through the door into the West Wing. Her team and various advisors had decided to avoid directly addressing and connecting the spike in deaths and illness to the comments and threats from Hanse Kallis. They had orchestrated the press questions so they would not be raised. Despite their avoidance, they realised there was the beginnings of a feeding frenzy amongst the news services and across social media. They needed more time.

Her next stop was the Situation Room. It promised to be a long night.

Chapter 130

HANDS AGAIN THRUST deep in his trouser pockets Hanse Kallis was quiet. Pensive. He was now in the office of his private island off the east coast of New Zealand. He acquired the island several years ago when many wealthy families had identified New Zealand as their preferred doomsday location. He didn't buy into the whole doomsday scenario. He had just loved the stunning natural beauty of New Zealand environment. And the island was almost untouched. He was oblivious to the irony that he would become the instigator of a true doomsday scenario and that he was going to watch it play out here.

The island ownership was almost untraceable through a maze of corporations and entities. His office was in the main house he'd built on the island. The house blended into the cliffs and native trees. Over three levels, it offered generous living spaces, kitchens on two levels, a functional exercise room, an indoor pool and seven bedrooms, each with its own bathroom. He had wanted it to be a sanctuary for his extended family. A place to gather in complete privacy, amongst nature. Each level had full-height windows that appeared to hang directly over the South Pacific Ocean, providing an endless and uninterrupted horizon. The windows were double-glazed and soundproofed. When it wasn't too windy, Kallis loved to open them all and breathe the salt air.

Kallis brought his gaze back from the view towards the 80-inch flatscreen on the wall. CNN was connected via Starlink. It had now been a full day since the press conference from the American Vice President. The scenes reported by CNN were entirely foreseeable and gave Kallis no pleasure. He reflected that when the original COVID-19 pandemic broke months ago, people panicked. They stockpiled - emptying supermarket shelves. They dusted off old survival gear. Re-opened and re-stocked legacy basements and bunkers. Read and watched everything and believed the worst of it. The last few days had made that initial reaction seem moderate.

After the VP's press conference, the internet had gone into overdrive. The distinction between news, fake news and conspiracy almost impossible to make. The prospect of a new strain or a new virus or a reaction to the vaccine had amplified the public response. Links and opinions were being promoted regarding his speech and the consequent confusion at the Global Intervention Initiative. But that was just one strain of commentary amongst the panicked noise. And the American government was staying tight-lipped.

CNN was oscillating between various images of overwhelmed hospitals and medical facilities. And of growing numbers of people sick and dying. Families - mothers and fathers, husbands and wives desperate for help and answers as they cradled loved ones. The reports showing images of grocery stores and drug stores being emptied. Queues lining up and purchase limits being applied. Survivalist and camping stores being over-run. And not limited to the United States. The scenes were being replicated across the globe.

People were anticipating a severe and complete lockdown was coming. And they were freaking out.

Kallis knew all this would happen. Knew it was inevitable. He had hardened himself to be ready. But still, tears ran down his face. While politicians and commentators implored people not to panic - that answers would be found- Kallis knew it would only get worse. Much worse. It was the only way the world could heal and humanity, along with millions of other species, could survive. He looked at the images of these poor people. The dawning realisation of their worst fears was written all over their faces. And felt so profoundly sorry that they had been let down. That mankind had done this to themselves.

He picked up the remote to shut down the screen, unable to watch the scenes unfolding when the door to his office was flung open.

Chapter 131

'I'M LEAVING. TODAY. Now. I cannot stay here and see this and see you.' Meagan Kallis had burst into the room, finger pointing at the TV screen Kallis stood before. 'This is you.' she said - not for the first time in the last few hours. 'You've done this!' she glared at her father whilst the images on the screen played over his shoulder.

Kallis turned from the screen to look at his daughter. The last twenty four hours had been the hardest and most trying of his life. Even harder than the premature death of his wife some years before. He paused and reflected briefly. He had organised for his daughter, her husband, and her children to be on the island prior to his arrival. A celebration he had promised them - following the inevitable success of the Global Intervention Initiative. Once he had arrived some hours after his dramatic exit from Africa, Meagan had already joined the dots. It had resulted in a massive confrontation. And one that had continued to percolate in the long hours since as the full implications of his plan became apparent.

Kallis had done everything he could to explain and rationalise. The devastation the planet was experiencing. That this would only get worse. And would likely, inevitably, result in cataclysmic change at some point - without control. His approach was the only way they could ensure as many species as possible, including humanity, could survive and exist in a more balanced and harmonious way. To take the action needed before it was too late. He had forlornly hoped she would come to the same realisation. It had not happened. And her anger and exasperation had only grown. It seemed inevitable now that his final time on the planet would see him estranged from his daughter and grandchildren. Another price to be paid.

Meagan saw the emotions rolling across the usually inscrutable face of her father and the tracks of his tears. She softened her tone, 'This affects you so much. Yet still you have done this!'

'If you leave here, you will be exposed. And so will Michael and the children.' Kallis said. In one of their earlier arguments, Kallis explained that her family had been inoculated from the COVID-19 virus with untainted syringes. They were not infected with the synthetic virus he had created. Hypocritical, he knew. But he couldn't bring himself to do otherwise.

'I am leaving alone. Michael and the children will stay here. I need to help. I feel responsible.'

The big picture that he had focused on so resolutely in his mind dissolved before his eyes as he looked at the face that had been the most important and beautiful in his world for over forty years. Tears flowed again.

'I will not stop you. But it is most likely the virus will get to you.'

'Not the virus. Your virus.' She turned and left the room. Kallis left standing, looking at the empty space where she had been.

Chapter 132

ALEX WARD WAS standing in her kitchen in Avalon on the Australian coast. The exact spot where, just a few days ago, Mack had brought her back into the agency. Staring out the window towards the sea. The sky was a beautiful fusion of red and yellow, streaming through soft, fluffy clouds as the sun crept over the horizon. The promise of a warm day. Ward was oblivious to the beauty. She had a steaming tea in a mug in her hand, trying to calm the frustrated energy burning at her. She had spent hours and hours with Thomas Brendt and liaising with Kristen's team chasing sightings and leads of Hanse Kallis without success. He had disappeared. It was beyond frustrating. Infuriating. The best technology in the world had failed them. So she'd decided to come home. To see David and to re-group.

Since being home, the news cycle was constant, and the scenes were horrible. And the intel and briefings she was privy to suggested it would get worse. A lot worse. It was making her boil. She wanted to move. To act. To fix what was happening.

On top of everything, she was worried about David. In his job, he was exposed both to the physical infection and also to the personal and traumatic emotional impact on people and their families. She had begged him to take some time off and be home with her. He needed a break. Or he was going to break. He said he'd try but had to be at the hospital. He was sleeping there. When he slept.

She hadn't seen him since she got back. She felt a deep dread that it was inevitable he would get the Kallis Virus. He - they - might have it already. Lying latent in their bodies from the vaccinations they'd both had. She needed to locate Kallis and find a way to stop this. Now. She picked up her phone and was about to call Kristen again when it started to ring. It was a blocked number. She answered anyway.

'I think I've found him.' Alex recognised the voice of Thomas Brendt.

Chapter 133

PRESIDENT JAMES CHARLESTON and Chief of Strategy Daniel Walker had barricaded themselves in the West Sitting Hall in the Executive Residence of the White House. They hadn't left the Residence since returning from Africa. Charleston had cleared his diary and refused to take all but a few calls. Though he had been calling the party leadership constantly hammering them for a way out of this mess. Walker hadn't left his side. They were sick of the sight of each other but were in damage control and didn't have anyone else they could trust.

Charleston was in a rumpled T-shirt and hadn't shaved for days. He looked anything but Presidential. Walker, ever the egotist, was still pruning each day. He had the White House staff dry clean and press for him. He sat upright in a desk chair in a starched white shirt tucked into belt-less dress pants.

Walker punched the end key on one of the burner phones he loved.

'That was a contact at Langley. Looks like Kristen Thomas and one of her pit-bulls are heading our way.'

'She is the last fucking person I want to see. Tell the Secret Service she doesn't get near me,' whined Charleston.

'We need a plan, James. We can't hide up here any longer.'

'I've been hoping Hanse is yanking our chain. That this is just a bad dream. I can't stand looking at the news. It's completely out of control.'

'Hope is not a strategy, Mr President.' Walker offered in a sarcastic reversal of their conversation on Air Force One.

'Oh, thank you, Tony Robbins.' said Charleston, oblivious his words were being played back to him.

Walker continued, 'Seriously, sir, we know this is real. Kallis even told us this is real. We need to get on the front foot. The daily summary indicates we consistently see the number of serious cases and deaths at almost triple the worst of the pandemic. This is not a hoax. And you will have an investigation into your business dealings with Kallis to add to the one already looking into electoral manipulation. As the bodies pile up, it will be you, the public, is coming for. The news services are calling for you to be available. To be seen to be in charge. It will be completely out of our hands soon.'

'Fuck me, Daniel. That's a lovely summary. So - what's the bad news?'

'Mr President....'

'Point made Daniel. As you've done every hour and every day since we've been back here.'

Charleston moved to the large, ornate window, careful to be far enough back so no one could see him if they looked up.

'This is real, isn't it' he said wistfully.'

'Yep.'

'OK, Daniel.' the President forced the air from his lungs. 'If we're going down, we go down swinging. I want you to get William Jacob on the phone. He can fire Kristen Thomas and we will work on a more accommodating replacement. The optics can work. All the resources of the CIA and she can't find Hanse Kallis. The public will back me once it all comes out. Then get the Attorney General on the phone and he can do the same to that twerp at the FBI. Set up a press conference for 8pm Eastern tonight. Prime time. That gives you 10 hours to come up with a speech that is going to save us and clearly point the blame for this shit storm at those two clowns.'

'OK. I'll get on it.' Pleased to finally see the President taking action, Walker paused momentarily. In a softer tone, he said, 'Have you thought through all of this... maybe Hanse has a point?'

'What the fuck does that mean?'

'Well - the world is pretty fucked. And there isn't a political party or corporate leader in the world willing to make the changes that it would really take to fix the environment. Maybe he's right - we're heading to the cliff's edge and need a......correction - to bring balance back.'

Charleston stared at Walker for a moment.

'Where are you going with this Daniel?'

'Perhaps our best chance of keeping the Oval is chaos. Sure, we clean house and get some friendlies in place. But what if we also let Hanse's plan run. At least for a while. Rather than trying to find a fix, we pour fuel on it.'

Hands in his pockets and looking out the window, Charleston didn't turn around, 'Go On.'

'Think about it. We make sure the acronyms don't make any progress. The United States and the rest of the world go postal. To the public we are frantically trying to find a cure to the virus. Behind the scenes, we help blow the place up and then invoke emergency powers, and after a while, it's your leadership that rights the ship.'

Charleston interrupted, 'The place will be a mad house. People will die.'

'We don't even know if we can stop this virus - they are going to die anyway.'

'You're saying we let the virus run. Without trying to stop it?'

'I'm saying we go to war. And people love a wartime President!' Walker continued; 'It's a Hail Mary, for sure. If no vaccine is found, it won't matter who is in the Oval Office. But this way, at least, we're playing offense.'

The President turned his head slightly towards Walker, a slight smile playing on his lips, 'I'll think about it. Either way - I want both directors gone.'

'I'm on it.'

As Walker was about to pick up another burner, the doors to the room were thrust open.

'I said no one is to come in!'

But as Charleston turned from the window to berate his security detail, he saw that Kristen Thomas and one of her sidekicks had defied his orders. And there was no Secret Service in sight.

Chapter 134

THOMAS BRENDT SAT in his luxury apartment in Navy Yard in Washington, DC. He had returned home from Africa as Alex went searching for Hanse Kallis. A search that proved and still proved to be in vain. It had been surreal returning home. The whirlwind his life had been upon meeting Alex Ward had come to a jarring stop. He had tried to resume some normalcy. He rode his bike in the dark, cold morning and headed to the Insider for coffee, to work, and to chat with Nikki. But his mind was mostly elsewhere. He knew more than most and he knew what was coming. Whilst Washington and the US had gone into an immediate state of frenzy following the address from the Vice President advising the shutting down of the vaccination program, there seemed to be yet another new normal pressing down over the country. People had become so attuned to responding to unsettling news and restrictions over the last few months that this was just another unknown to deal with. And the responses covered the whole gamut. From calm preparations to hysterical blame and everything in between. And, of course, it triggered the truly disaffected, resulting in scenes of violence across the country, played out on the streets and showcased on their screens.

The news cycle was depressing. People sick and dying in scenes far worse than the darkest days of the pandemic. But the situation had not spiked entirely out of control. At least not yet. People were operating in what Brendt considered a delusional state of hope.

But Brendt knew that the situation was going to get worse. Catastrophic. Ward and the CIA regarded the threat from Kallis as credible and serious. Kallis had almost limitless means and a massive organisation to deliver on his threat. Brendt, like most, was shell-shocked and initially in denial when they considered what Kallis had claimed. The prospect of wiping out most of the world's population so mind-boggling as to not able to be comprehended. Everyone just wanted to reject the prospect as science fiction poppycock.

But they had all seen how COVID-19 had spread. From first discovery to a scaled pandemic had only taken weeks. In the days since the Global Intervention Initiative and Kallis mic drop moment, those in charge of their national security had collectively drawn a deep breath. They had come to the view that this was real. That a synthetic virus more contagious and more deadly than what had so far been experienced, surreptitiously introduced into the arms of billions through a vaccination program sanctioned by both the government and the most trusted health organisations on the planet, was happening. Biological warfare had been feared for decades. With good reason. Now it had been unleashed.

Brendt had spoken to Ward several times and even Kristen Thomas. He knew teams of people were being coordinated across agencies and international borders. Some to consider the restrictions and sanctions needed to limit the spread of the new virus. Some to plan for how they would deal with loss of life at an unprecedented scale. Others to consider the economic impact and how it could be dealt with. And many others trying to analyse the virus and find a vaccination or at least some kind of response.

Behind the scenes - away from the public eye - it was chaos. And it was going to get a lot worse. The fragile calm he observed during his daily visits to the cafe as people buried their heads in the lives they had previously cursed, would soon be shattered. It was a matter of when. Not if. Brendt was informed enough to know that the more time they had to understand the Kallis virus and the scale of his program - the more they knew Armageddon was coming.

No one had a clue what they were dealing with or how to stop it. The answer they clung to was to find Kallis and get him to tell them how it could be prevented. To have an answer before they had to lay it all bare to the American - and global, public.

Brendt had allowed himself a day or so of living in denial and reverting to his own world before he realised he just had to do something. And so he went to work. To find Kallis.

He knew there were agencies everywhere tasked to do exactly that. And most likely with their head start and their resources they would succeed. But Thomas knew they were also very distracted, likely operating in a cyclone of competing noise and restricted to conducting their search within the law. Thomas had no such distractions or limitations.

For the first day or so, he made little progress. Kallis' digital security and level of encryption were cutting-edge. When he finally started to make his way into the Kallis network, he was confronted by a maze of corporate complexity. Across countries, jurisdictions, and differing languages, there were connected and unconnected entities everywhere.

Finally, after hours and hours where he hardly slept or left his loft, he thought he'd struck gold. He'd been simultaneously tracking and aligning possible locations to the known flight paths of the three jets that left the private airfield in South Africa. He also looked to correlate with assets and locations owned by Kallis companies and entities and those of his family. It was a literal needle in a global haystack. But when he'd come across the private island located off New Zealand and discovered the extensive works that had been carried out there in the last few years, he thought it could be a candidate. When he then googled images of the island and saw the stunning natural beauty and its remote and isolated location he had picked up the phone to Ward.

'I think I've found him.'

Chapter 135

THE TWO-YEAR-OLD Tesla Model X could really move. Ward was driving well within the car's limits . And well within the limit of the law. Because there was traffic everywhere. And because she didn't want to have to deal with the local police. Ward was on her way into Sydney to the private airfield where a CIA jet was on standby.

She had left as soon as she'd taken the call from Brendt. She hadn't even rinsed her tea cup. She was unarmed and on her own. She'd tried calling Kristen from the car, but no answer. Same with Mack. She'd called Brendt back to work out the quickest way for her to get to Kallis' island and he was dealing with the pilots directly.

She tried calling David. No answer. In operational mode she left him a brief message with no details.

Her phone rang through the car audio system. 'Yes, Thomas.'

'Your plane is ready to go as soon as you get there. I hope you remembered your passport. It's a little over two hours' flight time to Wellington, and we're working on a chopper to get you to the island. That trip should only take around twenty minutes.'

'OK good. Keep trying Kristen. I want to get satellites over that island to confirm if Kallis is there and what sort of security he has.'

She disconnected. Frustrated with the idle time she'd have while in the air. But thankful she was finally moving.

Chapter 136

AT THE SAME time as Alex Ward was pulling up to the private airfield adjacent to Sydney Mascot Private Airfield, Meagan Kallis was entering the lobby of the Park Hyatt luxury hotel in Sydney. This was a billionaire's version of convenient, budget accommodation. And a place she knew well.

Wracking her brain as to what she could do to stop what her father had put in motion, she tried again to contact Pieter Roberts, her father's closest confidant and the person in charge of the hypodermic program her father had initiated. She hoped he would know something. She'd initially tried to call Pieter from the island without luck. She'd messaged him to meet her here. She'd not heard anything. She had no idea where he was or if he'd received the messages. And she was worried to the pit of her stomach that he had been a collaborator in this mad scheme and had gone into hiding like her father. She had no plan B.

Meagan Kallis received the key card to the Sydney Suite from the receptionist and headed to the elevators. Once in her room, she'd try Pieter again and keep trying until she found him. This hotel would be her base until, one way or another, she came up with a plan. With the massive resources of the entire Kallis empire at her disposal, she had to find a way.

Chapter 137

MEAGAN SWIPED HER key card to enter the suite. Pushing into the entry there was a hallway in front of her, and the entire wall at the end was a series of bi-fold floor-to-ceiling glass doors opening onto a private veranda. So caught up in her own thoughts, she took no notice of the stunning Sydney Harbour views in front of her or the iconic Opera House, almost close enough to touch.

She dumped her bags and moved further into the suite, pondering her next step. As she entered the open lounge, she stopped. Pieter Roberts was sitting in one of the single chairs gazing out the window.

He turned to her. They both just stared at each other without a word.

Eventually, Meagan broke the silence. 'I hope you being here tells me you were not aware of what my father was up to?'

Pieter looked at her, and she could see across the room that tears flowed from his eyes, catching in the crevices of his aging, weather-hardened face.

'Oh Meags,' his strong Afrikaans accent cracking with emotion, 'What has he done? What have I done?'

Chapter 138

DAVID MITCHELL WAS exhausted. Beyond exhausted. He'd thought he'd been stripped and laid bare before - during the darkest days of the pandemic. Before the vaccines became available. When people were panicking and sick, they looked to him and his colleagues in Sydney, across Australia, and everywhere around the world for answers and assurance. Bringing their children into the hospitals. And their elderly. At the time, he, along with the entire medical community, were scrambling. Just trying to stay ahead of the infections and the worst of the symptoms. They did their best. Dealing with the unknown and feverishly working to treat people, mitigate their pain, and get them well enough to free up beds. And for the really sick - to make them as comfortable as possible as COVID attacked their respiratory system and destroyed their immune resistance. All the while, they hoped for the researchers to break through and find them some real answers - medicine that really worked.

But this - this was beyond those dark early days of the pandemic by a magnitude. This was becoming something beyond even the darkest imagination of a horror movie. Covered in full Personal Protective Equipment, including a respirator, David was in the far corner of the makeshift COVID hospital at the Sydney Cricket Ground. He was treating a thirteen year old boy admitted two days ago showing the initial symptoms he, along with all of his colleagues had come to dread. Fever, coughing, skin irritation and rashes. They knew these symptoms were a precursor to much worse - every single patient that presented with this virus deteriorated in the same way. It happened quickly and so far without exception, resulted in their death. It was brutal. It was lethal. And they were completely unable to stop it. It was like Ebola on steroids. For this young boy, they were now just trying to manage his pain. His fever had continued to spike each day, and the rashes were burning his skin. His body was bleeding internally. They had him loaded with pain medication. David knew this poor soul was, at best, a day away from losing this fight. And he was all alone. Like everyone else here. They didn't have the space for parents or relatives to be with their loved ones. In some cases, entire families were admitted - only because they were sick and dying.

If he had any tears left, David knew he would lose it again - overwhelmed with both sorrow for this poor boy whose life would end in the pure innocence of youth and his own frustration at their complete impotence to do anything.

He looked up slowly from the face of the teenager and gazed across the massive temporary hospital. When they had first set up here they couldn't comprehend ever needing this much space. Now the beds were jammed in. In fact they'd run out of beds and space. People were even in the gaps between beds and under the beds. Sick family members and complete strangers were sharing single hospital gurneys.

The areas outside the main structure - in the grounds of the stadium and the parklands around were also starting to fill. These had been areas for car parking, a concourse for attendees at events and landscaped parks and recreation areas. The sick and their families had come here looking for help and had fallen when they were too weak to stand or sit. There was no room left in the hospital. Teams of medical staff, families and volunteers were tending to the sick. Inside and outside the hospital. Trying to make them comfortable. Providing them with pain medication. Inevitably picking up the bodies and taking them away.

It was happening so quickly, and it was a scene David knew was being repeated across the city and across the country, and whilst he hadn't seen the news for some time, he assumed across the world.

In the last couple of days this hospital and others like it around Sydney and the rest of the country had shifted their focus from trying to treat and heal, to just trying to manage the pain. And it got worse. They were now working on plans to deal with the unprecedented number of bodies. It was growing, and they feared it would grow even faster. They were completely unprepared and had started to set up temporary morgues and crematoriums.

As concerned as they were with being humane and respectful they had to 'process' the deaths immediately - for fear of more infections. And to use the space. Even before families could be contacted or given the chance to say their goodbyes. He'd even heard stories of live patients being placed amongst the dead bodies in the haste and the confusion. Those poor people would only have a temporary reprieve.

David looked through his visor and swept his gaze across the expanse of beds and bodies. The place was frantic. Medical staff were trying to move those who had died and bring the sick in as quickly as possible. It was like a constant, morbid, horrible conveyor belt. He flashed on the statistics they had all become so familiar with during the pandemic - across Australia around fifteen-thousand had died from COVID-19 over the last few months. By all accounts, they would have that many deaths again in a couple of weeks. Maybe less.

David felt he was no longer a doctor. He was a mortician. Could someone really have done this intentionally? It went against everything he believed in. He collapsed to the ground, sitting with his knees bent to his chest in a small available space between patients. He pulled off his visor and mask and put his head in his hands.

Chapter 139

KRISTEN THOMAS ENTERED the room, looked at the President's disheveled state, and ignored his threats. She was followed by Mack Stewart and behind him FBI Director James Peterson. Kristen said, 'Mr President, please sit down. We need to talk. You too, Mr Walker.'

Mack was there to ensure these two stayed in line. His injury was healing, and he could handle these two with one arm anyway. She doubted it would come to that. But she didn't have time to mess about. This needed to be quick and not open to interpretation or negotiation. Mack's physical presence and his reputation were intimidating. And these two were essentially bullies. With all the false bravado that was typical.

The President glared across at Kristen, 'Actually, I'm glad you're here. I was about to get William Jacob to fire your ass. But I'll do it myself. You're fired. Effective right now. So are you Peterson. Get out of my building.'

Kristen Thomas stared right back at the President and calmly responded, 'I'm afraid that won't be happening. Section 4 of the 25th Amendment has been invoked by the Vice President. Congress has received the declaration of the inability of the President to effectively discharge the powers and duties of the office. A majority of Congress has confirmed the declaration. The Vice President has taken the office of President.'

Kristen Thomas paused to allow this to sink in.

'Daniel!' the President said as he stood staring at Kristen Thomas.

Walker took the prompt, 'Clearly, this is unlawful. I'll contact the Attorney General and sort this out now. The President is here and in full capacity to discharge his duties.'

Walker looked at Kristen as he moved towards a desk phone. 'And once that is cleared up, our backstabbing and power-hungry Vice President can follow you two out the door.'

Kristen looked at them both in turn. She moved to the central couch and took a seat. FBI Director Peterson followed suit, taking a single upholstered chair. Kristen dismissed Walker's taunt, 'It's too late for that. You are no longer in charge. Vice President Michelle Anders has been formally sworn in. Sit down. Both of you.'

Mack moved further into the room, pushing into their space and blocking Walker's progress to the phone. The disheveled President stared at Kristen Thomas. Emotions played across his face as the realisation hit that what he had been fearing for several days as he locked himself in the White House had now played out. Grudgingly both Charleston and Walker took the only spare seats - sitting next to each other, legs almost touching, on a cramped sofa.

Kristen calmly continued, 'There are two options. Firstly, you can voluntarily resign. Effective immediately. You will relocate to your own houses and the Secret Service will become your minders. Not so much for your protection as to ensure you go nowhere and do nothing.'

As she spoke, Kristen opened a binder and laid photos and documentation on the table showing Charleston's long history with Kallis. She piled papers on top of papers showing the deals Charleston had approved as a Senator that secured contracts for Kallis's businesses. Many of these awarding supply of hypodermics across the country to facilitate the COVID-19 vaccination program. Still, more images and documents were placed on the table - these showing the myriad of news articles, interviews and events orchestrated by Kallis and his Russian contacts to manipulate the American people and skew the election.

'You will see here irrefutable evidence of your relationship with Hanse Kallis, the illegal and unethical financial payments made to your campaign and Russian involvement in the manipulation of the election that brought you to office...'

Kristen paused and looked at Walker. 'I have another package just like this for you, Mr Walker, and your close relationship with the Russians. I believe you know the head of the SVR in the United States as Boris?'

Kristen then placed the last of her photos on the table. These showed the devastation the Kallis virus was having. From over run hospitals and medical clinics, to the financial meltdown happening across the country, empty supermarket shelves, unrestrained looting and violence. And brutal close-ups of the dying and the dead.

Both Walker and Charleston who had been trying to ignore the mounting incriminating evidence being laid out before them, now quickly looked away.

'The second option is impeachment and arrest. The Vice President will hold the office of President whilst this is happening. The evidence, as you can see, is overwhelming. The public will crucify you both. You will go to prison. It will not be pleasant for either of you. Director Peterson is here to arrest and arraign you if needed.' Kristen paused as the depth and detail of what she had laid out seeped in.

She continued, 'I suggest you take the former option. The arrangements have been made. Your resignation letters have been prepared and are ready for your signatures. The Attorney General has authorised this as legal and appropriate.'

As she said this, Kristen looked in turn at both Charleston and Walker; she then cleared the table, laid two black and embossed leather folders on the surface and placed a single, disposable blue ink pen on top of each.

'In one hour, President Charleston, you will pre-record a brief address for the country. That speech has also been written. You will then leave and never return to the White House.'

Kristen Thomas looked at both men in turn. They were political animals, street fighters who never gave in and always looked for an angle. But now they looked defeated. She counted on their own self-interest to accept the inevitable and take the easy way out.

'The country - and the world - faces the biggest challenge we have ever encountered. We need leadership and we need stability. Our focus must be on finding a cure to this virus and minimising the damage. We cannot be distracted and become ineffectual by some sideshow as you look to cover your disgusting asses. You have an opportunity to do the right thing. But one way or another you will be removed.'

James Charleston clasped his hands in his lap and took another look at the piles of evidence now strewn around him. He closed his eyes and tipped his head onto the back of the sofa. Kristen looked across at Walker. Tears were in his eyes, and his face was contorted with emotion. Good, she thought. She wanted them to realise there was really only one way out.

Charleston straightened up, grabbed the pen, opened the folder before him and signed the historical letters inside.

'I need to shower and prepare for my address. And I'd like you all to fuck off.'

Chapter 140

THE BELL 206 Jet Ranger helicopter the agency had chartered was flying Ward from Wellington New Zealand to the private island owned by Hanse Kallis. Ward had originally considered a more covert entry to the compound. Concerned about security or warning triggers that might see Kallis flee again. She had tasked both Brendt and the agency team to find out what they could about the island. In the last few hours, the CIA had worked with the National Reconnaissance Office to re-purpose a next-generation Minotaur satellite to cover the entire area. It had found no evidence of any security. Brendt had also done his thing and could find no defensive systems built into the plans of the house Kallis had built.

So, she'd decided on the direct approach. Speed was paramount. She'd had the pilot do a complete circuit around the island and she'd had a long look at the buildings. He was now bringing them in over the water to the landing area. This would not be a surreptitious arrival. The island was relatively small and a lot of it looked uninhabited. There was a large flat area at sea level below an inland cliff, which was the location of the connected compound Kallis had created. The flat part of the island was right on the water with a u shaped sandy beach wrapping around a graduating headland. The rest of the island sat higher than the compound, was naturally forested and provided the impression of creating a barrier for protection and privacy - both from the elements and prying eyes.

As she got closer, she took in the large resort-style building of several levels that ran almost the entire length of one side of the beach. It was flat-roofed and very modern, and the facade to the ocean was all glass. Every room would allow access directly outside with shaded verandas at ground level dropping onto a soft green lawn leading down to the sand. Through the expertise of architect and builder the design was able at once to blend into the environment and enhance the surrounding beauty. There were several other buildings north of the large house, all with views across the water, and each looked like a smaller replica of the main house. Towards the cliff behind these homes and hidden by native trees and the topography of the island, were functional structures and storage sheds. In the middle of the main compound was a flat, landscaped, groomed lawn bordering a large rectangular pool with water almost the same colour as the ocean. There were lounges running down one side and a resort style shaded entertaining area on the other.

It was one of the most beautiful places Ward had ever seen. And there was not a single person around.

Ward continued to take in the stunning, peaceful island, the picturesque isolation, sympathetically designed buildings, and landscaping. It looked straight out of Architectural Digest. A boutique, expertly styled resort with no expense spared. She contrasted this with the horrors of what she knew David was experiencing and what was being repeated in countless locations around the world. How dare Kallis hide here while people were dying and the world was accelerating towards armageddon. All at his doing. The anger she felt was simmering to a hot boil.

The pilot of the chartered helicopter had seen the landing area further north of the compound where another, larger chopper sat idle. He brought them in next to it.

'Wait here.' Ward said as the chopper touched down.

Ward exited and looked around. There was still no one around. No other people and no security to greet her. She made a beeline for the main house a few hundred metres across flat grass. She didn't bother to hide her approach. Her arrival had been anything but discreet.

Chapter 141

HANSE KALLIS STOOD dwarfed before the massive windows in his island office. It was windy and cool outside. The native pine trees were swaying and the small waves hitting the beach were choppy, crested with white peaks. Deep in thought, staring vacantly at the mass of ocean before him, his hands clasped behind the back of his chinos. He heard the door to his office open.

'Dr Kallis. You're a hard man to find.'

'Agent Ward. I've been expecting you. Or at least someone like you.'

Kallis turned from the window and looked at Ward.

'I actually thought I'd be seeing you sooner. And there would be more of you. But then I assume everyone is a little distracted.'

Ward couldn't hide her intensity, 'This place will be descended upon. A whole world out there wants to tear you apart.'

Kallis, seemingly unfazed, 'Will you take a seat so we can talk.'

'I don't want to take a seat. I don't want to chit chat. I want you to tell me how to stop this. Before you're killed and the answers die with you.'

Still calm, Kallis replied, 'I do want to tell you what is going on. You won't like what I tell you. It cannot be stopped. That's how I designed it. At least not in time to make a difference. But I do want you to understand it so you, your agency, your government, and all governments can deal with it. If it's not handled properly, the world will be a horrible mess.'

Ward stared at Kallis. A horrible mess. It was already pretty horrible. She had to find a way to stop what he had started. She'd come here prepared to do whatever it took. She composed herself. She'd let him talk. He'd planned everything. No doubt he had planned what he was going to say.

His persona. His manner. His presence in this beautiful place was anything but that of the evil monster that meticulously planned and unleashed this devastation. He seemed smaller - shrunken since she had seen him on the stage in Africa. The contrast was disarming. She found her anger subsiding. And she didn't like it. She wanted the anger. She wanted the motivation. It would drive her until this was fixed. Any alternative would not bear thinking about.

Ward took a breath and slowly took a seat.

Kallis sat down opposite her, 'You might want to dial your boss in to this conversation.'

Chapter 142

WARD AND KALLIS sat facing each other on opposing sofas, the framed South Pacific to their side. Ward's secure sat-phone was on the table in front of them. Kristen connected in her office at Langley.

'I'll be as to the point as I can. Indulge me a little background. It's important. As a native African and someone with a few decades under his belt I can still remember the way Africa used to be. And I was told stories of an even more wondrous place. The stunning native environment. Our beautiful and magical country. Herds of wildlife, clear water, crisp air. Massive skies that we gazed at in awe both day and night. Over time, these have become rare, In many cases, non-existent. As I became more successful and as a result more traveled, the changes I saw across the globe were astonishing. No land mass and no ocean was spared.

'I vowed to act. To drive the changes to save the planet before it was too late. I started with my own personal projects - the game park and specific programs for the oceans off our coast. And it worked. I could see the regeneration that was possible when that was the priority. But it was just a microcosm. Encouraging but insignificant. And the rest of the world just got worse. Even more recently, when the environment and the planet became fashionable, it was just rhetoric. I was an advocate and driver of these initiatives for a long time with Kyoto, the UN, and Paris. You name it. But we just keep going backwards.

'And everywhere I looked, it was so clearly evident that we were the problem. People. And our incessant drive for more. The only thing we valued was a better, more prosperous and comfortable living. But the price was - and is - astronomical. In fact, the trajectory of damage and the projections my team and others have developed indicate that the price will, in fact, be absolute. It will cost us the planet as we know it. It is inevitable, and the speed at which we get to that point is getting ever faster. Not slower.'

Ward interrupted, 'You said you'd get to the point!'

'I asked for a little indulgence - but yes. I'll fast forward. Inevitably, with enormous personal conflict, I realised that the problem - people - was also the solution. Remove people, and we will see nature re-establish and regenerate. But the opportunity is not open-ended. At some point, the chance to regenerate is gone. The damage is beyond fixing. That point is on our horizon. So, my focus became how we control the population. But as much as we talked about it and hypothesised and tested and researched no one really wanted to listen. A bigger population meant bigger economies. Growth. Wealth. Opportunity. Demand. And that was far more powerful than the message of containment and reduction of an eccentric South African.

'But for me, it remained the only answer. I felt like I was possibly the only one who thought this way. So, I compartmentalised my research and R&D so no one would know what I was looking into. As abhorrent as it sounds, the answer is pretty obvious. We needed to reset. Eight, nine, ten billion people is catastrophic. Small adjustments to population growth rates are essentially useless. It's just a slightly slower death for the planet. We had to reduce. Massively. I'll finish with this and then tell you what is happening. If you think about it, at our most fundamental we are hard wired for survival. For our species to perpetuate. And a big part of that is reproduction. Centuries ago, with high death rates, it balanced out. More recently we have become too efficient at staying alive. Our numbers have exploded exponentially and we are now stripping and suffocating our planet. My whole purpose is to actually see us survive for many more centuries. And for many other species to survive with us. If we don't interrupt and reset we will not survive. We will kill the planet we need to sustain us.' Kallis finally seemed to finish his preamble. His conscience laid out before them.

'The intervention needed would only come with a massive one-off reduction to the population. I landed on one billion. A little arbitrary, but the models support it. The reset meant reducing the population by seven or so billion. It was never going to be precise. The virus or viruses that would accomplish this were impossible to accurately forecast. But I counted on some people having natural resistance and others being isolated. A modern take on natural selection.'

Ward again jumped in whilst Kristen held her tongue on the other end of the line, 'You call it a reset. It's murder on a scale without precedent, at a level impossible to comprehend. But it is murder. Genocide.'

Kallis nodded, 'No doubt the work of a madman - yes, I understand the perspective. It is only through context - truly understanding the devastation of the planet and through being honest about where we are heading that this intervention makes sense. I've looked at it every way. It is the only answer.'

Now Kristen interrupted, 'We will disagree on that. What you are doing is beyond comprehension. That's all I've been thinking about for days, and I still can't get my head around it. But we will stop it. Smart and determined people always find a way. We - the global community will find a way.'

Alex wanted to move this on, 'OK - now is when you tell us how to stop this.'

'Agent Ward - let me fast forward. When the pandemic hit - a little before it became public- I realised this was the moment. Initially, I thought the virus would do what is needed. But it became apparent that whilst it would be lethal for some, for most, it would be a variation on the flu - harmful to many but not deadly. Not in the numbers needed. But it was an opportunity nonetheless.

'My companies had been developing new science on the slow release of medications through a technology using fat cells in the body to house the medication and release it over time. I won't go into the science. However, the application looked very promising - for example, insulin management for diabetics and numerous other treatments. I realised this could work - if I could bury the virus, leave it latent in the body and then release it once the cells were triggered, I could get enough infections to get the scale needed. Whilst the virus sat in the cells of those infected early, millions of others would be infected. And it is contagious. The pandemic was a godsend. The virus and its distribution could be hidden like a trojan horse in the vaccination program for COVID. These are the poor infected people that are dominating our news services right now.'

'A godsend!' Kristen spoke - her voice synthesised and distorted through the small speaker on the sat phone. 'So, millions of people have just weeks and months to live before the virus activates in their bodies?'

Ward contemplated this question. She could see Kristen's point. The latent virus Kallis had injected would slow-release, effectively correlating to the rate of COVID vaccinations. It was both distressing and hopeful. The slow spread and people dying would be heartbreaking. But it might just buy them the time they needed to find a cure for those who were still alive.

Kallis responded; 'I thought the same Director. How horrid it would be for the bandaid to be ripped off so slowly. Months and months of illness and deaths. Watching loved ones. Waiting for your own inevitable passing. Governments and enterprise trying in vain to find a cure. The answer - again - was in the science. The emerging area of micro-robots - nano-technology is re-shaping medicine. In short, nano-robotics operate at the cellular or molecular level. I had another company at the forefront of this technology. I injected massive funds into the R&D, and we cracked the code. And the ability to scale.

'In short, I simply began to add a microscopic nano-bot to every dose injected through one of our hypodermics. The robotics are sequenced and connected. I did the modelling and worked out when the synthetic nano-bot virus would hit the right scale - that the right number of people had been injected and it has been programmed to then activate the virus. At this point, it is released into the host's body. Everywhere. Everyone. Simultaneously.'

Kristen and Alex were stunned into silence. Ward - the wife of a research virologist had enough knowledge to join the dots. There were hundreds of millions, if not billions of people walking the planet with a latent virus in their bodies that would be released en-masse at some point. Millions - billions of people would be sentenced to death in a single moment. Alex felt the sting of tears well in her eyes. She didn't cry easily. When she got emotional, she acted. But this was beyond her.

Kristen was the first to respond. Her calm, methodical mind skipping past the desire to lash out and rage, 'How long until we hit the number of infections and the virus releases? What is the date, Doctor?'

'The precise date and time is irrelevant. Another distraction. However it is less than a week from today.'

Ward spontaneously cried out; 'A week! A week! How do we stop this in a week? Tell me there is a vaccine for this. You must have contemplated the need. We have to be able to stop it.'

Her intensity and urgency were evident. She forced her composure. She wanted to launch at Kallis.

Kallis looked directly at Ward, 'Agent Ward, I admire your fervour, but I'm afraid not. I intentionally did not commission any research into a vaccine. And it would hypothetically take other pharmaceutical companies and research agencies months to develop a solution. This is why I am telling you this. It is not stoppable. It will not be months and months of bodies piling up. It will be a singular event all over in just a few days. I understand the emotional toll will be paralysing. However, I am more concerned about the physical. For this to work - for our species to survive and then thrive and for nature to be restored, it must be managed. By those that survive. Bodies will clog the streets, houses, apartments, hotels, and public places. They will petrify and spoil both land and water. The financial markets and economies will collapse if this event is not managed properly. Supply chains will shut down. Essential services will be crippled. And the prospect of people having to literally fight for survival could see the remaining population destroy itself. Once you have time to consider the full extrapolated implications, it is mind-bending.'

Ward sat in stunned silence. The fact that Kallis had thought of this - had imagined bodies literally piled in the streets was even more abhorrent. She was silent. How could someone visualise this and then make it happen! She thought of David and of both their families. Potentially - perhaps even likely that they would all be wiped out. Her initial denial and inertia were quickly being consumed with renewed rage. Despite what Kallis was saying, there had to be something they could do. Some way of stopping this new holocaust.

Kallis was still talking, and Ward tuned back in, 'I have the advantage of time. Knowing this would happen. And that solutions would be needed. I developed plans to deal with the intervention event and stabilise the planet. The intervention will only matter if the world that is left is a better place. Not some law of the jungle, post-apocalypse war zone. The plans I've created need to be provided to every government. Your new President must lead this. There is very little time. I'm counting on you to get these into the right hands and to ensure we bring new stability to the planet.'

Chapter 143

THE SIMMERING RAGE in Alex Ward finally bubbled over. Tears burned down her cheeks, and she leapt from the chair she'd been sitting in. Unarmed, she launched at Kallis and locked both palms around his neck. One knee pushing into his chest. He was a strong and vibrant man, given his age, but her sheer force overwhelmed him. He was pressed back into the sofa, his head pushed into the soft cushion. His face quickly changed colour with the lack of oxygen. Kallis grabbed the wrists of Ward, trying to break her hold and push her away, but was completely ineffectual.

Ward seethed, 'Listen, Doctor. I know there is a way to stop this. To fix this. No way you don't have a vaccine or some way to shut these micro-robots down . Tell me what it is. Where can I find it? How do I do it?'

Ward applied even more pressure. Her own eyes bulging with intensity just inches from Kallis face. He was fading quickly, his complexion now a stormy shade of purple. He was shaking his head from side to side. Whether to try and break her hold or simply indicate there was no way to stop what he had started.

Kallis' eyes gradually closed. Ward continued to apply pressure. Veins and tendons in her forearms popping. Feeling cartilage in his neck crack and give way. She was aware he was fading, and they wanted him alive, but she couldn't pull herself back. Her intensity shutting all else out. From somewhere she became aware of a voice, she heard her name...

'Alex, Alex, what is going on. What are you doing? We need him alive'.

It was Kristen Thomas's voice coming through the speaker on the phone on the low table.

Still Ward held her grip. Now, the voice was shouting,

'Agent Ward, can you hear me? What is happening? I need Kallis alive. Whatever you are doing, stop.'

Kristen Thomas's voice finally got through. Ward gradually released the pressure on Kallis' neck. She pushed back off him and let him go. Ward collapsed to her knees in front of the sofa, her eyes pressed shut, her breath panting, sweat and tears running down her face. She looked back up at him. He had slipped across the sofa, seemingly unconscious. Colour was returning a little to his face. He was still breathing.

'I'm here Kristen. He's breathing. Alive. For now.'

'There is a team on its way. Lead by Mack. Thomas Brendt is with them. They are in the air only a few hours out. They will find whatever is there Alex. There has to be an answer. There must be.'

'He said we have a week, Kristen. Maybe less.'

Chapter 144

WALTER MATHIESON HAD been bringing the news to Americans for over thirty years. He had been a field reporter through the nineties, a political correspondent in the 2000s, a fantastic five-year long-story reporter on a weekend magazine show, and now a senior anchor for CNN. He'd seen a lot, been through a lot, and reported on all of it.

From Bosnia and the 'Stans in the nineties. Being in Sth Africa when Mandela was released. He'd watched first-hand when the statue of Saddam had come down. Mathieson cried with his country after the domestic awakening to the horrors of terrorism during 9/11. He'd reported and suffered for many when the global financial crisis hit. And the sheer devastation of Katrina.

His career was a showreel of the political, economic and human stories of the last thirty years. But the biggest story he thought he'd ever witness and be part of and report on was the global COVID-19 pandemic. Until now. The emerging story of this new lethal virus, coupled with the shutdown of the vaccination program, threatened to bring the nation - and likely the world - to its knees. Every country had followed suit - immediately ceasing their COVID vaccinations. And now every country from the developed to the third world was sharing similar pictures and horrible stories of the suffering caused by this new virus.

As he sat in his office reviewing the various news services and most recent network coverage, Mathieson reflected on the early days of the pandemic. People panicking. Stockpiling. Supermarket shelves emptying. Some in denial. Many anticipating and planning for the worst - a real doomsday event. Some had bunkered down. Some had fled to locations they thought would be safer - temporarily, or for others a permanent new start. Many had ignored the virus and continued their lives as best they could. He had feared for his country and his countrymen. In the early days there had been limited information and no real plan. Politicians playing the blame game. As the pandemic took hold there were daily reports of increased cases and deaths. No individual or family was unaffected. The pandemic dominated the media and changed their lives.

Once the vaccination program started, people felt they had a plan— an answer. Gradually, life returned to a relatively normal state—a new normal.

But this new virus saw people's fears magnified way beyond the worst COVID days. It was exploding. It was exponential. And it was deadly. While deaths from COVID-19 were horrible, most people who caught the virus survived. Particularly once they'd had vaccines. Not with this one. The mortality rates were diabolical. Current reports had them at over ninety percent. Everyone was hoping this was an anomaly. That the virus was infecting the most susceptible first and they didn't have the immunity to fight it. The hope was that the death rates would plummet once virologists understood what they were dealing with and healthier people were infected. But the information Mathieson was seeing indicated that was not yet happening. This virus was steamrolling. He looked away from his screen for a moment, turning to the generous windows of his office. Looking vaguely into the middle distance as he contemplated this virus getting to his own family - his daughters - and his grandchildren.

Chapter 145

MATHIESON PULLED HIMSELF back from his reverie. On his screen was raw footage not yet reviewed and edited for broadcast. Images of hospitals and temporary medical facilities completely overrun. Morgues so beyond capacity they had taken to stacking bodies outside and in car parks. People sick and dying or already dead, literally in the streets. The roads out of cities were clogged. Those who couldn't leave were boarding their homes. The financial markets were taking a hit every hour and every day, the circuit breakers were being triggered constantly. Despite these safety measures a financial meltdown was inevitable. The Supermarkets were empty and now needed more security than staff to prevent vandalism born of frustration and fear. Schools and workplaces had closed. No one had been coming in anyway.

Mathieson saw the images, read the reports, and felt sick to his stomach at what his country and every country was experiencing. This was the worst he had seen at home, and it was accelerating every day. He dreaded that they were on the precipice, looking over a cliff, and the fall into an unknown oblivion was inevitable.

The President has gone missing in recent days. The announcement from the Vice President two days ago was the last senior press conference from the White House. There was little to no verified information. The White House was unusually tight - leak free. And without official advice, without the Chief Health Officer providing information and guidance, speculation, conspiracy and misinformation was filling the void. Even a veteran like Mathieson struggled to distinguish between what was real and what wasn't.

Now, the White House had advised all media outlets that there would be an address to the nation tonight at seven pm Eastern. Networks and websites had been requested to clear their schedules and provide the feed live. Mathieson was one of the two anchors for his network that would host a thirty minute special immediately after the broadcast. At this stage, they didn't know any specifics. Undoubtedly, it would relate to the new pandemic and the chaos being created.

Chapter 146

NEWLY SWORN-IN President Michelle Anders sat behind the Resolute Desk in the Oval Office. A large TV camera and teleprompter were staring blankly at her from the other side. A makeup artist was touching up her face, fussing over her hair and straightening her jacket. Her oldest friend, closest confidant and now newly appointed Chief of Staff, Tullia Carina–known as Tully or, more informally, TC–was buzzing around trying to ensure everything was perfect.

Michelle Anders was oblivious to it all. Her mind was elsewhere. Focussed inward. Swirling. Trying to deal with the historical achievement of the first female - and black - President. Yet being appointed in the most dramatic circumstances. The most traumatic and tumultuous post-war challenges her country and the world had faced. Her first address to the nation as President - to go live immediately after the pre-recorded resignation of James Charleston would not be a celebration nor a milestone for her country in the progression of women and minorities. Rather, it would confirm the worst fears that had been spreading across all forms of media. Her real frustration was that she had no answers for the questions she knew her people and the press would have. With all of this, she sat calmly before the camera and the chaos around her and resolved to herself that whatever it took, she would find a way.

Chapter 147

'GOOD EVENING'.

The freshly scrubbed, still-tanned, handsome face of James Charleston filled screens around America and the globe. He was not in the Oval Office - but in another room in the White House.

'It has become evident that America and the world may be facing the greatest challenge to our survival we have ever encountered. Shortly, you will be provided with the most current information on this horrible and rampant virus and the plans to deal with this deadly enemy.'

Charleston's voice had been strong and his gaze steady with his brief opening remarks - both now faltered slightly.

'However, I will not be your President to guide you through this dark time. Effective at four pm today I resigned as President of the United States. Vice President Michelle Anders took the oath of office and was sworn in. It has been almost fifty years since a sitting President resigned. And like my infamous predecessor, I can tell you that I have never been a quitter.'

Charleston allowed that line to hang for a moment.

'However, the massive challenges ahead need unified leadership with the support of all those in public office, our agencies across the country and our allies worldwide. Do not underestimate what lies ahead, nor the need to work together and to respect and commit to the difficult decisions that will come. President Anders is an outstanding and compassionate leader. I leave this office knowing that America is in excellent hands. I urge you to pray if you have faith, be kind to your neighbour and hold those dear to you close. God Bless President Anders. And God Bless the United States of America.'

Millions of screens faded to black and then froze on an image of the Stars and Stripes.

Chapter 148

MEAGAN KALLIS BRIEFLY stopped messaging, emailing and calling Michelle Anders to watch the historic broadcast from the White House. She stood in the middle of the suite staring at the US flag on the TV screen, oblivious to the beautiful morning on display through the large windows overlooking Sydney Harbour. Like millions, this latest news had stunned her. Meagan had been desperately trying to get hold of Vice President Anders to get a message to the President and, ideally, set up a video meeting. Meagan had met Anders several times at various events - particularly those supporting the progression of women in senior and important roles. And she really wanted to get access to senior leadership. The information she had from Pieter Roberts was crucial and possibly the only hope they had to stop what her father had done. And even that was a long shot. But the sooner she could get to those in charge the sooner they could see if an answer could be found.

No wonder Michelle Anders had been hard to reach. And now, as President, it would be near impossible. Anders would be enveloped in security, and any attempt to contact her would have to go through layers of staff. Her hands shook with adrenalin and frustration as she stared at the phone in her hands, tried to compose herself and to think about what she could do from the other side of the world. She knew better than anyone that this robotically encased time bomb was lying in wait in the bloodstream of billions. She had crucial information. And time was running out.

Chapter 149

OLD GLORY FADED from the screen, replaced by the image of newly sworn-in President Michelle Anders. And she was in the Oval. 'My fellow Americans and those joining this broadcast around the world. Some will see this as a historic day for America and for women's progress. I wish we could take a moment to celebrate and reflect on those who paved the way and encourage others as they carve out their own path. Unfortunately, there will be no celebration.' Anders paused and looked into the camera.

'The events leading to my appointment and the circumstances we now find ourselves in are the most dire in our history. Let me repeat that. Even with all the conflicts we have battled and the challenges we have overcome, the situation we now face is our most challenging ever..

'I intend that in my first address as President, as I expect every time I talk to Americans and the world, I will be honest and frank.

'With this in mind, let me clarify exactly where we are as a nation and as a global community. Our TV screens and our news feeds are becoming filled with images of the sick and dying affected by this heinous virus. News agencies, both credible and not, are overwhelming us with images of families in distress, of hospitals overflowing, and of people lying where they fall. And of course the panicked and opportunistic response of many. These same news services are engaged in constant speculation as to what is going on and what will happen next. Let me clarify. In my view, accurate information is our best approach to managing the situation and defeating it.'

Out of view of the camera stood Kristen Thomas along with other senior agency members, FBI Director Peterson, and newly appointed Chief of Staff Tully Carina. Collectively, they took a breath. There had been debate about what to tell the American people - the world for that matter. Many felt they should manage the message and protect the populace from what was happening. The panic and chaos this bombshell would cause may be worse than the virus exploding through their cities. But, much like the historical desk she now sat behind, the new President had been resolute. She would be honest and transparent and speak up to the American people. She would express to them the expectation of how they must respond to this as a unified country - in a truly American way.

President Anders continued, 'This is not a variant of, or more virulent strain of the Corona Virus. This is not COVID-19. In fact, this is not a naturally occurring virus attacking our bodies.'

She looked into the camera and then continued. 'This is a synthetic - man-made - virus introduced into the American and global community. In an unprecedented act of terrorism, we are dealing with an intentional, carefully planned and orchestrated campaign to kill.'

Despite her determination to be stoic as she delivered this news and spoke these words aloud for the first time, emotion washed over the face of the new President. Her voice threatened to break. She took a moment to compose.

'Many would have seen the address from Dr Kallis at the Global Intervention Initiative some days ago. Since then, there has been speculation about the meaning behind his words. I can confirm that the synthetic virus now rampaging through our cities was created and implanted by Dr Kallis.' she paused again.

'Hanse Kallis took advantage of his privileged position running a multinational pharmaceutical empire, coupled with the unique circumstances of the global pandemic, to implement a carefully orchestrated program to achieve his inhumane ambition to reduce the global population. Put simply, he has initiated global genocide.

'The vaccination program that was so successfully implemented to protect us from COVID-19 was his Trojan Horse. I know this will strike fear into people everywhere. However, I must tell you that, unfortunately, every hypodermic needle supplied by companies controlled by Kallis around the globe was infected with his synthetic virus. The numbers of infected vaccinations run into the billions.' again President Anders allowed this to sink in. She found it hard to contemplate the magnitude of the situation. And to consider the panic and devastation that was coming. 'It is a virus that lies dormant in our bodies for some time and is then triggered and released. We are still working out how it is triggered.

'This information will shock people around the world as it shocked me when it was uncovered only a few days ago. My extended family, my husband, my children and myself, like many of you watching, will likely have this deadly virus lying in wait in our bodies. We do not yet know how to test who has it and who doesn't. As you are aware several days ago we ceased the vaccination program. Unfortunately that was too late for many.

'I appreciate this is a lot to take in. It is a horrible situation. An enormous bombshell that people need time to consider and digest. Unfortunately there is no time.'

President Anders had images in her mind as to how people would be reacting. Most would be shocked into denial and inertia as the information sunk in. With the images and stories now appearing everywhere it was only a matter of time until they would see the full gamut of human reaction. From irrational panic to violence to Darwinian survival to communities rallying, to quiet acceptance.

She knew she would have to deal with all of that later.

'Now you know what we know. There is so much we don't know. It is very new and happening in real-time. We don't know the full extent of who is infected. However, we expect it to be millions in the United States and billions around the world. We don't know how to test for the synthetic virus.

We don't know how to treat the symptoms. We don't know when it becomes active or what triggers it.'

This was the first 'white lie' she had told - but the information on micro-bots was too new and too overwhelming to share just yet. Truth be told Anders herself was having a hard time with it.

'And we don't have a vaccine. I said at the start of this address I would be frank. And I have been. It is confronting. And it is frightening. We are working on all of this as quickly as possible. I will communicate daily and keep you informed on our progress and understanding. As your new President you will ask a lot of me and my team and our agencies and resources. And it is our job to deliver. Your expectations of me are also my expectations. My total commitment is that we will defeat this. But we need to be prepared. The scenes we are witnessing today will get worse, much worse, before they get better. The days and weeks ahead will be the hardest this country and all countries have ever faced. Everyone will be affected.

'So I need to also ask for your help - to enlist every person in our great nation to fight with me as we face our biggest and most deadly challenge. It is the only way we will survive.

'The State of Emergency enacted early in response to the pandemic will remain indefinitely. You will hear from the Secretary of Homeland Security shortly about the protocols, restrictions, and settings we will now employ to help navigate this situation. I ask you to work with us with the best possible intent. Every sector of our society and economy will be affected. We will be instigating the most severe lockdown protocols ever seen in the United States to slow the virus and reduce pressure on emergency services. Schools will be closed. Malls will be closed. Workplaces will be closed. As will airports and our roads. We are doing this to save our country not to punish our people.

'The days and weeks ahead will be hard. Incredibly hard. We will be exposed to heartache and hardship, the stuff of our worst nightmares and our greatest fears. This will affect us all. Through ourselves individually, our children, parents, siblings and friends.

'I realise the unexpected and the unknown can bring out the worst in people. Perhaps even in ourselves. This is a time to be better. To think of others as much as yourself and those close to you. I entered politics because I believe in America - the idea of America. And what I believe is that there is nothing we cannot achieve. That we cannot overcome. When we come together as a nation. To truly look each other in the eye and to selflessly work with each other.

'President Charleston asked you to be kind to your neighbour and to hold those dear to you close. I will ask that you do more; to hold you to a higher standard. To the standard we expect when we think of The United States of America. God Bless us all.'

Screens again went briefly to the American flag as networks scrambled to organise their post-broadcast programs. The Oval Office was silent but for the sound of quiet weeping from more than one person. Michelle Anders continued to stare into the camera. Her mind churning with visions of what would lie ahead. With the cameras now off, her emotions rose to the surface, and tears streamed down her face, leaving distinctive tracks in her freshly made-up appearance.

Chapter 150

MEAGAN KALLIS HADN'T moved while watching both the Charleston resignation and the address from the new President. She was standing dumbfounded and distraught in the middle of her hotel suite, staring at, but not seeing the American flag filling the large flat screen. While she had become aware of the monstrous actions of her father over the last few days, seeing it laid bare to the world was incredibly confronting. She felt overwhelmed with conflict and emotion. She thought she might be sick. Slowly, she brought herself back to the present. She had to act. She felt numb with the weight of the world on her. She felt that she alone had to find a way and may have the information that could help them all out of this advancing horror. Even worse, it seemed they were only aware of the initial infections and did not know about the nano-bots that would sequence a devastating virological event.

Her phone still in hand, she messaged her assistant in Africa. 'Who do we know in the White House?' She'd lost track of what time it was back home. She quickly did the calculation. Two am Wednesday morning. Her assistant may not answer for hours. She also sent the same message to Pieter Roberts, although she hadn't heard from him since they had met in this suite hours ago. Meagan determined to keep trying to reach the new President, feeling isolated and frustrated at how far away she now felt. She was desperate.

She knew her father was incredibly connected, but would he help her? Would he even answer her call? She had to try.

Chapter 151

THE LONG-STANDING President of Russia was alone in the massive and ornate bedroom at the modern complex he favoured on the coast of the Black Sea. Although he had always denied this to be his Residence, it had become colloquially known as 'The President's Palace,' and he spent more and more of his time hidden behind the fortress walls and regulated and protected airspace.

It was the early hours of Wednesday morning. He'd had a large flatscreen TV wheeled in. And had viewed both President Charleston's resignation and his successor's emotionally charged address.

The Russian President had ignored the calls from Michelle Anders earlier that night. At that time not aware of her ascendancy. He was now seething with frustration. Bordering on one of his infamous rages. Why had he not known about the change in the American Presidency? He was learning it from CNN. Worse, his own agencies had not briefed him on the magnitude of the actions of Hanse Kallis. He had been privy to the speculation since the farcical eco conference in Africa. And he had been made aware of the spike in infection numbers across Russia of the western virus that had spread to his country. He attributed the increase in infections and deaths to the relatively poor vaccination numbers to date. But now he bordered on rage that the connection to Kallis and the magnitude of the situation had not been presented to him.

This was becoming what the Americans called a Cluster Fuck.

Charleston was his man! He'd supported him financially through Kallis and various cutouts in the US. More importantly, he had approved and funded the program to manipulate American news and media to promote

Charleston and discredit his competitors. And it worked. He had his man in the White House. And he had so many plans for him. His American President was going to be pressured and cornered into unwinding the American economy. Creating a recession that would decimate America and in turn elevate the Russian Federation's resurgence. Now, Charleston was gone.

And Kallis! Kallis had been their most important conduit. He was the Russian President's personal instrument to coordinate and 'cleanse' their involvement in getting Charleston into office. They had used Kallis. Rewarded Kallis. The Russian President himself had ensured Kallis companies were the favoured supplier of hypodermics for their pandemic vaccination program. Now it seemed Kallis had, in fact, been playing them! Been playing him.

He didn't like being played. By anyone.

Pulling his robe tightly around him, the President pushed a button on the table beside his bed.

'Get the Security Council assembled. Now.'

He wanted to find Kallis. Before the Americans did.

Chapter 152

THE SCREEN BEFORE him was completely blank. Walter Mathieson sat staring at it. He was in his anchor chair. Made up and about to go live. The network was running a long ad break. Giving themselves time to get organised. The studio around him was frantic. Producers and staffers shouting at each other. The teleprompter had been turned off. The script options they had created did not anticipate a President resigning, a new one appointed and an armageddon scenario laid bare. His senior producer was now speaking to him through his ear piece.

'Walter, this will be a live and unscripted broadcast. Nobody does it better. No one speaks to America as you can. We are on air in 90 seconds.'

Words had always come easily to Mathieson, whether crafting a story or speaking directly to the camera. In fact, he was often better off the cuff, spontaneous, responsive and connected to the story. As he continued to stare into the TV screen, he was consumed by thoughts of how history was repeating and the actions of a single man could threaten to destroy his country.

At that moment, he had no idea what he was going to say to the American people.

Chapter 153

THE BRAND NEW Gulfstream G800 was an extended-range jet customised for the CIA that would take Ward from Christchurch to Washington without refuelling. Flight time was an interminable eighteen hours. Eighteen hours where she would sit and do nothing whilst the most significant crisis that had faced the world was unfolding.

A CIA investigative team lead by Mack Stewart was en route to the island to tear it apart. Brendt was with them. Ward had to get back to the US. She knew that would be the epicentre of the response to Kallis' actions. They had to find an answer. And she had to be part of it.

Ward had watched the respective addresses of the two Presidents on a secure tablet. It rammed home the dire situation they faced. She reflected briefly on the original mission she'd been brought back for - to determine whether their sitting President had actually been backed by Russia. And she had been asked to do so without official CIA support, given the leaks they knew were undermining the agency. Only to find that a puppet President and the massive security threat posed was an issue that paled against the situation they now faced. They had, in fact, been too late. The damage a compromised President could allow had already happened. And it was beyond anyone's belief. Charleston had opened the gates and let the Trojan horse right through.

Ward had shut down the tablet once President Anders had gone off air. She had no interest in the opinions of the talking heads. The US and the world were undoubtedly in a media-feeding frenzy beyond any previously experienced. She'd called David on her secure sat phone. But again, it went to voice mail. He was basically living at the hospital. God knows where he slept. If he slept. And how could he possibly avoid getting infected? He was surrounded by illness and death. She literally shuddered at the thought of him getting the virus. And she was now hurtling away from him at close to the speed of sound.

She grabbed her sat phone, agitated by the inactivity and the isolation, and called Kristen.

'Alex, we are heading to the Situation Room. The National Security Council is about to meet to work out our response.' Kristen offered without introduction.

'And what is our response?' asked Alex.

'We don't have one.' Kristen paused as she said this, feeling sick in her stomach at what confronted them. 'If Kallis really has put molecular robotics into the arms of billions, we have no answer as to how to stop them going off. The focus will be on mitigating infections from his earlier release - before he'd introduced the bots. And how we manage the panic, the carnage and the economic free-fall.'

'Jesus! When does Mack and Thomas and the agency team get to Kallis?' asked Ward.

'They are on the mainland in New Zealand about to board the chopper - they should land on the island in about 15 minutes.'

'He has to give us a way out, Kristen.'

'Alex, I hold little hope. I think he was being honest when he said he had never wanted to contemplate a vaccine. He is not holding us to ransom. He actually wants this virus to do its job.'

There was silence on the line for some time as both tried to come to terms with the situation that had landed on them. And how helpless they felt.

Eventually Kristen continued, 'USAMRID is coordinating the research into the Kallis virus and the nano-bot technology with the Chief Medical Officer and anyone we can get hold of. It's a race against time. Alex, I have to go. Try and rest if you can. If we find an answer, we'll need you.'

Ward disconnected. Rest. Yeah right. Her husband was in the viral firestorm. Her home country, her adopted country, and the rest of the world were imploding. And she was sitting in soft leather at fifty thousand feet. She threw her phone onto the seat next to her. Just as it vibrated with an incoming message. She thought it might be Kristen or perhaps David. She grabbed the phone and looked at the screen, not expecting the name that came up.

A message from Hanse Kallis.

Chapter 154

KALLIS STOOD BAREFOOT on the soft sand on his private island. The cool water of the South Pacific lapped at his feet. It was mid-afternoon and a perfect, if slightly milder than typical November day. Blue skies and even bluer water. He looked across the mass of ocean, vaguely staring at the point where it met the horizon.

Like most of the rest of the world, he had watched the historic broadcast from the White House. Afterwards, he wandered the island and ended up at the beach. Now, the hairs on the back of his neck tingled as he felt the eyes of his family and the island staff looking down on him. Disgusted. Confused. In just a matter of days his name had become the most famous in the world, blasting around the globe as the madman monster behind the horrible scenes of suffering and death they were seeing on their TVs.

He knew this day would come. When his actions became known. He had protected his family. Selfishly. Ensuring they had not been infected with the virus or the nano robotics. And he had nearly all of them secluded in this island compound. Set up to be self-sustaining for as long as needed - years if required. He knew this was utterly hypocritical. But he couldn't contemplate being the architect of the death of those he loved most. He also knew they would hate him for it. Hating what he had done. And hating that he had singled them out from the rest of the world. If there was anything that was going to give him pause and to reconsider the actions, it was how it would affect his family. Meagan, more informed than the others, had already left the island. She had rung him only minutes ago. Asking for his help. He'd told her it was futile, but he would indulge her.

As he looked across the mass of water in front of him and weighed the heavy burden of his family's scorn, he again considered the state of the world.

Out there, spread in every direction from where he stood, were eight billion people. And growing. Killing the planet. Destroying the environment, wiping out species by the hour and putting pressure on resources that it just can't handle. His resolution didn't waive. He knew this was the only way to save humanity from itself. And even if he did change his mind there was no vaccine or way of stopping what was now in place. It was too late. They were just days away from the true Global Intervention he had orchestrated. Not the faux forum he had briefly hosted. His carefully crafted plan was about to be realised. And he did not want to be around to witness it.

Kallis took his phone from his pocket. He crafted a message to Alex Ward.

'My daughter Meagan will call you. Please take her call. Goodbye. HK.'

He heard the swoosh of the message being sent.

He dropped the phone into the water at his feet.

And slowly started walking into the cold ocean before him.

Chapter 155

DAVID MITCHELL TURNED the mixer tap in the shower to full cold. He forced himself to stay under the freezing jet for as long as he could stand it. In lieu of sleep, he figured an icy shower and a change of clothes would make him feel human again. It was not his shower - he still hadn't been home in.....he didn't know how long. And they were not his clothes. Time seemed to have lost its meaning. He knew he'd missed several calls from Alex, and when he'd tried her just now, he'd gotten a busy tone. His last contact with her had been, what, a day ago and she was heading to New Zealand. His concern for his wife swirled in his stomach, the worry magnified by days of sleep deprivation, unbearable stress and extreme exhaustion. The toll of human devastation he now witnessed every day. He felt worlds away from their ritual of sharing a beer on their deck in the afternoons before dinner as they looked out over the ocean. He wondered if he would ever be back on that deck with Alex again.

Finally, David turned the faucet off. He was actually in the showers of the home team change rooms at the Sydney Cricket Ground. The stadium had not been used for any sport since the pandemic demanded an emergency and scaled response, and it remained a temporary hospital and vaccination centre. However, in the last few days, it had become more morgue than hospital. He stepped from the cubicle, grabbed a towel and pushed his face into it as he tried to squeeze images of the masses of dead and dying from his eyes.

At least with COVID, they had been able to treat symptoms, even in the early days when they were learning about the virus. And whilst deaths were happening, they were comparatively rare. The new virus - the Kallis

Virus as it had become known, defied every attempt they made at treatment. Mortality rates were the highest they had experienced. Nothing seemed to work. If you caught it, it would probably kill you.

David looked around the room as he dried himself. It was still laid out as a locker room. But it was a mess. Clothes, scrubs, towels and rubbish littered the place. It was like a teenager's mother's nightmare. And numerous male medical staff were sleeping on the wooden benches and floor. At least, he hoped they were sleeping. David had laid here trying to grab an hour or two of sleep in recent days. There were flat screens attached to the walls showing various news feeds. He looked away, not wanting to think about the implications of the news the new President had shared. He found what he hoped were relatively clean scrubs and went looking for some food before heading back to the hospital floor.

After a futile search through the staff kitchen and finding two empty vending machines, he gave up. He figured there would be a delivery of some sort for medical and emergency staff later tonight, and he'd eat then. He decided to head back to the hospital while he felt refreshed. He put on his full PPE kit, wondering if it was futile given he likely had the virus sitting dormant in the fat cells of his blood stream anyway.

David pushed open the hinged double doors and entered the main hospital room. He stopped cold. The images before him were altogether confronting. As was the noise. He'd only been gone, what, an hour? And the number of people and bodies seemed to have multiplied. People were crying and screaming. Medical personnel shouting at each other. There appeared to be a procession of bodies being wheeled and carried out of the hospital. To where he didn't know. He kept gazing around the room. His already jaded mind and body further shocked into inertia. He started to look around to find someone he could actually help. He spotted a clearly distressed mother entering the hospital from the outer foyer. She was crying - struggling to carry a child almost as big as she was across her arms. The child's head was tipped back at an angle. Unconscious. Maybe worse. He didn't know how she'd managed to get past the lines of people outside, all trying to get in. He rushed across the room, sidestepping bodies as best he could.

'Are you a doctor?' the struggling mother asked.

'Yes, I am.'

He looked through his visor at the large child in her arms. A young girl - maybe eleven or twelve, not quite a teenager.

'Please help my daughter. My husband died yesterday at our home. We couldn't get him to any hospital. He's still there. Lucy woke up with a fever this morning. By this afternoon, she was unconscious. She's our only child. She can't die. She is all I have. Help her.' She thrust the child towards him.

David took the child from the mother. He looked for a stretcher or a bed but could find nothing. He laid her on the floor where they were standing. She was cold to the touch. Kneeling beside her, he grabbed his stethoscope to check vitals, knowing it was too late.

'What is your name?'

'Kate.'

'Kate, I'm so sorry, but Lucy is gone.'

The mother looked at him for a moment and then, shaking her head, let out a wail of anguish, penetrating the cacophony of noise around them. Some people glanced their way momentarily. Then, they went back to their own nightmare. Squatting next to her daughter, David looked at the young mother. Her pain penetrated right through him. In just twenty four hours, she had lost the two most important people in her life. He felt completely helpless. All around him, he just felt death and despair. He looked down at the peaceful face of this young girl who had her life stolen from her. And he looked again at the shell-shocked, distraught mother cradling her daughter's face.

'How did you get here, Kate?'

She didn't respond.

'Kate!' he said a little louder. She looked up at him.

'How did you get Lucy here?'

'I carried her. From home. The streets were jammed. We live up the hill in Paddington'

'We're going to take Lucy home. She needs to be with her dad.'

David Mitchell lifted the child in his arms and carried her through the hospital, out the front doors and into the late afternoon.

Chapter 156

SITTING IN THE soft leather of one of the seats on the executive jet, Alex Ward's phone rang simultaneously in her hands as she was looking at the message from Kallis. She didn't recognise the number but answered, thinking it would be his daughter. 'Is this Meagan?'

'No, it's Mack. Who is Meagan?'

'Never mind. Are you on the island? Anything from Kallis?'

'Kallis is a dead end.'

'What! Why? You need to keep at him.'

'He's actually dead. His body washed up on the rocks on the eastern side of the island. Some of the island staff saw him swim out into the ocean. Fully clothed. Seems he just kept swimming. Until he didn't.'

'Fuck! Fuck! That weak prick. Lights the fuse but doesn't want to face the explosion. Fucking coward's way out. OK, you need to see if there is anything there that will help. Look at everything. Look everywhere. Thomas should be able to access his drives and his online accounts. The rest of the team can focus on a hard search. It's a race against time, Mack. Call me with anything.'

Ward hung up, thinking she had just dished out orders to the person who had always been her boss.

The satellite phone rang again.

'Sorry about that, Mack.'

'This is Meagan Kallis.' Shit, thought Alex. That's O-2!

'Is this Alex Ward?'

'It is.' she recovered. 'Your father said you would call, and I should take it. What can I do for you, Meagan?'

'You need to know my father's actions were not known to me and, as far as I am aware, not to any of our family.' said Meagan.

'I don't have time for a conscience-purging, Meagan.' Ward responded.

'That's not why I am calling. I'm not looking for sympathy. Or empathy. I just want to contextualise my position. I want to help fix this if I can. I'll deal with my father later.'

Ward considered telling her that her father was dead. But thought the better of it, not wanting to prolong this call. 'Why call me then?'

'I've been trying to contact Vice President Michelle Anders. I have met her before. I thought she would be the quickest way to the President. Now that she is President and with everything that has happened, it is impossible to reach her. I've been doing everything I can, anything to try and find a way to stop what my father has started. I have an idea - well, actually, the idea is from the molecular robotics R+D team that worked for my father. But I need to get this to the people that make the decisions. Am I speaking to someone that can do that?'

Chapter 157

THE EARLY MORNING start for Kristen Thomas was now extending into the night of a momentous day in Washington. She was in the Situation Room listening to a weirdly smiley nano-robotics specialist that had been rushed in from a Washington-based think tank called Cerebrum. She'd forgotten his name. He was starting to ramble and was using terms neither she nor anyone else in the room could understand. His initial summary essentially validated the technology Kallis had described. The whole area was cutting edge and an enormous field of innovation. The opportunity involving nano-medicine and the development of ultra-small machines at the cellular level was immense and likely to transform medicine.

In essence - what Kallis was saying he had done was theoretically possible. But the scale was beyond anything Cerebrum thought feasible. And this is where this specialist had started to get a bit long. He seemed in awe of what Kallis had claimed to have done with the technology, describing it as a Nobel-worthy breakthrough. That was enough for Kristen.

Kristen caught the eye of the new Chief of Staff, Tully Carina. Tully took the cue.

'Thank you, Doctor. Your information has been invaluable. We need to move on. We will be in touch as and when we need more information.'

The visiting expert stopped mid-sentence, his mouth still slightly open. Hi smile faded as he looked around the room, quickly collected his notes, phone and tablet and made his exit.

Kristen figured they really needed to form a plan of action, at least for the next few hours and days. Tully had commenced the meeting with a concise and comprehensive summary of the national situation with the Kallis virus. The picture was bleak. Kallis' hypodermics were responsible for over sixty percent of three hundred million COVID vaccination doses distributed in the United States. Estimates were bouncing around as to how many of these contained his original 1.0 virus delivered in fat cells and how many doses contained the nano-bot 2.0 virus that, in theory, would be released simultaneously in mere days. The estimates were complete guesswork. But even the most conservative ran into the tens of millions infected. The Kallis virus 1.0 was becoming active at an exponential rate, with hundreds of thousands of patients presenting across the country and mortality rates through the roof. Scenes of the dead and dying were now a constant on their news feeds. Emergency services had been unable to cope for days. This first iteration of the virus was devastating. Tully concluded by indicating that the next iteration - Kallis virus 2.0 was anticipated to be triggered in the next few days. The infections that would result, if Kallis claims were accurate, were beyond calculation. Kallis indicated they had less than a week. And that was over two days ago. No one knew for sure when it would happen.They really needed a more definitive deadline. Once triggered, it would truly be an Armageddon event. Unstoppable.

Tully's summary had been met with silence from the overcrowded Situation Room. President Anders had then prompted Admiral Jock Campbell, Chairman of the Joint Chiefs, to brief the group. The 5-star Admiral provided a tight and frustrated summary of the new settings they had undertaken under the continuing Federal State of Emergency. In a nutshell everything that could be shut down was shut down. Businesses, schools, shopping centres, airports, bus and train terminals, government offices, everything. People were being advised to stay at home and to stay indoors. The police, military and national guard patrolled to ensure only those with authorisation were out of their homes. His frustration was that all of their actions to date were reactionary. Responding to the developing, deadly, horrific situation and their grim forecasts for the coming days. People would be running out of food. Many could not get loved ones to hospitals. So many homes would have dead or dying family members. What they hadn't done to date was to enact a proactive plan. To get ahead of this new pandemic and stop its rampant progression. They didn't know where to start.

The nano specialist following Admiral Campbell was now out of the room, and the President addressed those assembled.

'Current information is we have four or five days. We have to find a way to stop the nano-virus from going active. We've all heard - there is no effective treatment for the Kallis virus. If it goes active, mortality rates are over ninety percent. It will be catastrophic - completely catastrophic - in America and across the world.'

She paused to gaze around the room, individually eyeballing every person present. Kristen held the President's gaze, aware that her phone on top of her leather binder was vibrating constantly. As Anders's gaze moved past her, Kristen picked up her phone to check the messages on screen.

The President continued, 'We need ideas. Now is the time to come forward. There is no judgement.'

'Madame President, one of my operatives is trying to get to me. If you don't mind, I'll take it outside and advise if there is anything to contribute.'

Kristen stood to move out of the room.

'Director, we don't have time. Formalities and protocol are irrelevant. Who is it?'

'Alex Ward, Madame President. She has been leading the search and interrogation of Doctor Kallis.'

'Do you know what she wants?'

'No, Ma'am.'

Kristen was uncomfortable discussing this with the President in front of others. It went against her preferred approach of properly vetting all information and managing and filtering its use.

'Put her on speaker.'

'Ma'am, it may be better if I....'

'Put her on.'

Kristen's phone was again vibrating with a call coming in from Alex. She accepted the call and connected her phone to the speaker system.

'Alex. You are on Speaker in the Situation Room.'

Ward either didn't hear or didn't care. She didn't hold back

'Kallis is dead. Took his own life on his island hideaway. The fucking coward!'

A buzz went around the room, quickly escalating as voices rose and arguments broke out. Many had believed Kallis would hold the answer to the virus he alone had created. Once they had him, he would be interrogated and forced to work with them. Now, their primary hope was dead. Emotions were threatening to take over.

Kristen looked at the President. Alex Ward, if she was still on the line, could not be heard above the noise.

In her first real show of emotion, the President slammed her hand on the table.

Glaring around the room, she demanded, 'Quiet.' The room gradually silenced.

'Agent Ward, do you have anything else?'

One the other end of the phone, still in the jet hurtling towards the United States, Ward recognised the voice.

'Yes, Madame President, I do. I have Kallis' daughter Meagan on the line. I am going to merge her into this call. You need to hear what she has to say.'

At the prospect of the daughter of this madman being given a forum, there were more murmurings, which, with a withering look from the President, quickly went quiet.

Kristen Thomas realised this was the real reason Alex had been so persistent in trying to reach her; she leaned forward in her chair.

The connection was silent for several seconds save for the faint crackle of static and white noise. The Situation Room was eerily quiet.

Alex Ward spoke again; 'Meagan Kallis is now on the call. Meagan - can you explain to the group what you have told me.'

Chapter 158

WALTER MATHIESON WAS still seated at the anchor desk at CNN's Washington studio. He was off the air. Briefly. They were taking a much-needed, extended commercial break that would run into a hastily edited summary of the last couple of hours. Mathieson was drained. He needed to refresh. He would be back on all too soon.

Mathieson spent the time on the air since the President's address updating America on the fallout and public response and any information - more like speculation - on the impending catastrophic event. They could get nothing validated - they were running with the short and explosive comments from the President and some hastily located experts on how a virus could lie dormant in fat cells and then be triggered. Opinions were bouncing around. And nothing was coming out of the White House. Neither official nor unofficial. The place was in lock down.

Despite feeling emotionally wrung out, Mathieson was spending the off-air time looking at new feeds from across the country and locations around the world. He'd been reporting for some hours now on the scenes of panic and anger. Gridlock on the roads as people ignored shut downs and tried to exit cities. Shopping mall carparks clogged. Loaded shopping trolleys contrasted with empty shelves as people panic-purchased anything and everything. Fights breaking out constantly, and now frequent reports of shootings. Closed and empty airports, bus depots and train stations. Distressed and upset people trying to get home from their offices and workplaces were left stranded as emergency procedures were mismanaged, not understood or simply, ignored.

And then, of course, there were the scenes of the sick and dying and the dead. These images were unlike anything seen during the worst of the pandemic so far. It seemed no city, no suburb and no street was left untouched by images of hysterical parents, grandparents, family and friends. Unable to get to hospitals or for emergency services to get to them. Helplessly watching as their children and their siblings and their parents perished in their homes and in their arms.

New drone images were sent to one of his screens. It was taken from a high elevation above suburban streets. He could make out a typical American pattern of rooftops, yards, and miniaturised people. With the high altitude, detail was lost, though he could see pools and some yards with fences and more substantial structures - lawn furniture and gazebos. He also made out what he thought were dark mounds of soil in various yards. Mathieson wasn't sure what was happening or why these images were newsworthy.

He looked up at one of the producers, 'What is this - are people now building backyard bunkers and panic rooms?'

'They are not bunkers.' the producer responded, 'they're graves.'

The producer paused as he watched the images with Walter.

'Oh my god!' exclaimed Mathieson under his breath. 'This is America!' both men stared at the images on the screen - hardened, experienced newsmen unable to properly comprehend the scenes.

Absently, the producer spoke again, 'The feds are considering creating mass gravesites like the old photos from World War One and Two in Europe. And we're getting reports of home made crematoriums - really just massive fires communities have started. People are carrying their dead to them.'

'Turn it off, Sam. We can't show that. Not yet. Hopefully not ever.'

Chapter 159

MACK STEWART WAS in paradise. Actually, it was more like Paradise Lost. This stunning, remote island off the coast of New Zealand was breathtaking. And now it was ground zero - the final hope in the desperate search for anything to help them beat the Kallis virus.

They had come here to interview Kallis. Or interrogate him. Or drug him. Or torture him. Whatever it took to get answers. Kristen had given him carte blanche. The only requirement was that it needed to happen fast. Finding Kallis dead, they immediately commenced a physical and digital search across the island, the structures and particularly Kallis' office. Langley was working remotely to break open Kallis' online world. Mack and Thomas Brendt and a small agency team were performing a more traditional search. Anything hidden, printed or on hard drives. They'd been at it for hours, working frantically, and so far had nothing. Thomas and two other geeks were hooked up to the laptop and tablet they'd found in the office. They'd even rescued his phone half buried in the sand on the beach and had managed to access that hard drive. To be honest, Kallis made it easy. Accessing digital files and hard drives had proven to be no challenge. It was as if he wanted them to see he had nothing to hide. They'd found nothing that would help stop the virus.

But they would not give up. Mack and a handful of other agents were working room to room. Challenging, given the scale of the place. They'd started on the ground floor - the main kitchen and various open living areas. They'd covered the second level, another service kitchen, and the massive office area looking out over the ocean. And worked their way to the top-level living quarters. Four bedrooms and four bathrooms. They were trained and knew all the obvious and less obvious locations used to conceal whatever someone wanted to hide. They'd been through the whole place twice. First, a quick search, hoping for obvious information. The second time was far more thorough. Still, nothing they could use.

Despite the mild weather, Mack was sweating. And tired. And hungry. And thirsty. And pretty frustrated. He felt the pressure of time. But he needed a brief recharge. He decided to get some water and see what food was in the kitchen. Then he would start again. They'd go through everything. Again. In case they'd missed something. He had no other orders from the boss. She needed information. He'd keep at it until he was briefed on new orders. Besides, he figured morbidly that if the end of the world was coming, this was as good a place as any to be.

The kitchen of the primary residence was a modern masterpiece. All stainless steel and stone. With massive floor-to-ceiling windows that looked out into the South Pacific Ocean. Mack looked across the expanse of water in front of him and felt isolated and removed from the horror he knew was playing out back home. And everywhere around the world. He grabbed the right-hand handle of the double-door Sub Zero fridge and was about to pull it open to grab a bottle of water when he froze. An old-school BBC Green Planet calendar was magnetised to the fridge door. He'd seen it earlier but hadn't given it any thought. Such a mundane item, variations of which were found in millions of kitchens around the world.

It was open to the current month and featured a herd of African zebra on the top half separated by a spiral wire binding, then laid out below, the 30 days of the month in a grid. There were a few notations of family and other events. He noticed a single thick red marker had been used to circle one of the days, and the word ONE was next to it, also handwritten in red. Mack reflexively checked his watch. He didn't need to. He knew the date circled was less than three days away. He had a sickening feeling, realising what it meant.

At that moment, Thomas came bounding out of the office with a phone in his hand. A little breathless, 'Mack, I'm in Kallis's online calendar. One date jumps out. It's...'

'Saturday', Mack finished.

'What - yes - Saturday. I think that means.....'

'It means there won't really be a Sunday!' said Mack.

He grabbed his satellite phone and hit the speed dial for Kristen.

Chapter 160

THE RUSSIAN PRESIDENT had thought his day could not get any worse! Now mid-morning, he was dressed in a beautiful tailored Brioni suit, his round face clean shaven and his thin hair neatly combed. He was seated at his desk in the opulent office of his private castle, staring out at unending views of the Black Sea. And whilst the world he most immediately inhabited seemed beautiful and at his command, the world beyond his horizon was in disarray.

The team he had sent to find Kallis had been recalled. There was no point. They now had solid intel from their American contacts that Kallis was dead. And US agents were swarming all over the island.

More importantly, Charleston was no longer President. And the new President had not been part of his plans. He'd had nothing to do with her election, he had no one at his whim in her circle. And he couldn't even recall ever meeting her.

He had invested so much in getting Charleston elected, and had a clear plan as to how he would unwittingly do his bidding. A weak America was crucial to his plans. The ascendency of Russia to reclaim its world position would be the Russian President's legacy. Economic superiority for the Federation would come from a declining America struggling with a spiralling recession that he would orchestrate through a President he owned.

His Federation would further be restored by taking back the states that had been lost. Either through political will or by force. Starting with Crimea, he looked to annex Donetsk, Luhansk, Zaporizhia, and Kherson. He and his Generals were now working on plans to forcibly take the rest of the Ukraine. To do so smoothly and quickly. President Charleston would be pressured to ensure no support to President Zelensky. But that too was now in disarray.

The carefully laid-out geo-political chess board he had planned for so long was in pieces. Despite advancing years and declining health, he had remained fervently committed to restoring Russia as the world's great superpower.

His war games underway to annexe the independent states and bring them back under Russia were crumbling. Even his own troops were deserting in large numbers. Worse, many Russian men the right age to be conscripted and to serve had been fleeing the country, relocating elsewhere to ride out the storm. The crucial next-generation, that would inherit his legacy and continue to re-build Russia to its rightful position were being ripped out of the country.

The long game he had played to manipulate US Presidential elections had been a fantastic success. And now it had been pulled from under him. His co-conspirators in Beijing were not responding to his calls.

Beyond that, the glory of having led the world in developing an effective vaccine for COVID-19 was disintegrating into ashes. The Sputnik V vaccine was the first to be released, proving more efficacious than any of the big Pharma releases. It had been a glorious achievement for Russia, and the President spruiked it constantly.

And refused to share.

Yes, they had had issues delivering a scaled vaccination program for some time. But the solution was presented in the form of Hanse Kallis. Kallis had come to their rescue, providing limitless hypodermic needles and assisting in the logistics and distribution across their nation.

Chapter 161

NOT ONLY WAS Kallis a hero of Russia for supporting their fight against the pandemic, the Russian President had discovered an even deeper bond over their mutual desire to have a favourable counterpart elected in the US. With his contacts and credibility, Kallis was the ideal foil to broker and deliver.

That the Russian President now realised Kallis had been playing him both ways had him fuming. His anger, never far from the surface, was now simmering, fuelling his emotions and clouding his mind.

It was now clear Kallis had no interest in the re-emergence of Russia. In fact, the Russian President himself had been used as the conduit for Kallis to implant his virus into Russian arms. Even more enraging, Kallis had been party to their election strategy in the US for his own agenda - not to assist Moscow as he had committed on countless occasions.

His own SVR had confirmed the Kallis virus to be real. Horrific scenes of sickness and death were being seen in Russia as across the globe. He couldn't ignore it or play it down anymore. The President had instructed his ministers to invoke the most severe lockdown across the country since the pandemic broke. He feared this would be ineffectual.

But whilst the new virus seemed contagious and had a devastating impact, the real issue was the Kallis nano-bot time bomb. Initially made aware through intel from their US contacts, it had been confirmed with his own agencies' scrambling analysis of the syringes. The threat of delivering the synthetic virus through molecular robotics was authentic. This morning, the Russian President requested the most current vaccination numbers for his country. The accelerated program - courtesy of Kallis - had in excess of eighty million of his people vaccinated.

The President, until now thinking he had time to restore his country and see his plans realised, viscerally counted off on his meaty fingers splayed out on the desk before him. His plan to fundamentally weaken the United States through a beholden President was a fail. His plans to re-take Russian territories were crumbling. And with a new President likely to offer American support, the Ukraine would be a massive challenge. China was not talking to him. And now, pulsing in the veins of his people, to be triggered in a matter of days, was a deadly virus that threatened to wipe out most of his country. It would leave, at best, a pitiful shell of a populace behind.

The legacy he had worked his life for. Paid for in so many ways. Was laying shattered at his feet. The realisation that there would be no resurgence of the Federation was a pill so bitter it felt like cyanide was in his mouth and eating into his stomach. Even if he could somehow manipulate and weaken the United States and as improbable as it was, re-take many of the provinces that were rightfully Russian, this virus would make it all redundant. There would be no Russia left to ascend to lead the world.

He slammed his hand on the flat hardwood table top.

The Russian people were more accustomed to discipline and authority and had not yet started to rebel. But that would only last until they got cold. And hungry. How had everything unravelled so quickly and so completely?

The President dropped his round head into his hands. He started coughing and grabbed a small bottle of pills, swallowing several with his now cold tea. These things made him bloated and puffy, but they were keeping him alive.

He had been racing against his own clock for several years. He now felt a rare, unfamiliar sense of defeat. In his mind's eye, he saw the hands on the clock coming together. His own time was running out.

His bitterness and rage consumed him. Defeat was not an option. Others winning at Russia's expense was not an option. He could still land some blows for Mother Russia. He lifted his head and picked up the handset of one of several phones on his desk. This one had no buttons and provided a direct line to the Chief of General Staff.

Chapter 162

MEAGAN KALLIS WAS on Speaker addressing the Situation Room. 'Before I left the island, my father confirmed the worst of my fears. That he had used his enormous resources and all of his reach to initiate this plan to reduce the world's population. I know he is my father, but I believe he truly thinks he is doing something for the greater good - saving the world. That this is the only way.'

Meagan Kallis' voice trailed off. She paused to catch her breath and to compose her thoughts.

The President jumped into the space; 'Meagan. It is Michelle Anders here. We have met before. I appreciate you getting in touch, but we know all this. And we are extremely time-sensitive. Agent Ward believes you have information that might assist...'

Meagan refocussed, 'I have done nothing but try and find answers in the last few days. Every hour. I managed to contact my father's right hand, Pieter Roberts. Pieter worked closely with my father to manage the global production and supply of hypodermics. Pieter set up a call for me with the head of our R&D in molecular robotics....'

Alex Ward cut across Meagan, 'Meagan, let's get to the answer. If anyone needs the backstory, we can take it offline!'

Kristen Thomas, whilst listening, immediately sent a message to Mack and Thomas Brendt, as well as her Langley team, to look into Pieter Roberts. As she did so, she saw a detailed message from Mack and didn't look up from her phone.

'Three days.' she said aloud.

'Sorry Director?' prompted the President.

'Three days. My team on Kallis Island believes they have information confirming our deadline to be Saturday. Today is Wednesday.'

'My God!' exclaimed the new President to deathly silence.

Frustrated at the lack of focus of this meeting, Ward jumped back in, 'Everyone, please listen. Meagan knows we know about the nano-bots, and that we have decided not to release the information to the public. Meagan, get to it.'

'OK,' Meagan drew another breath, 'The molecular nano-bot technology is real. My father cracked the design and coding challenges others were grappling with and kept it tightly compartmentalised. The short story is, nano-bots can be mass produced. Have been mass produced. They are limited in functionality. But they can do the job he has assigned them. God help us!'

Meagan continued, 'The Kallis molecular biology team and I emphasise that this is speculative, have identified a possible opportunity to corrupt the nano-bots. We think the circuitry of the robotics can be disrupted and shorted with a direct electromagnetic charge.'

Meagan paused at this point. This was the coup de grace. The only possible way out she had found. She wasn't sure what else to say.

The President took the room, 'How do we deliver an electromagnetic charge?'

Meagan responded 'A form of powerful magnetic energy introduced directly to the body, such as an MRI, would work.'

An emotional Chief of Staff, Tully Carina, jumped in, 'An MRI! Seriously! We are talking millions, tens of millions, more likely hundreds of millions of people. And we have three days!' She looked at Kristen Thomas and the phone she still held in her hand and then continued. 'Even with our best efforts, we could get to just a fraction of that number with our available MRIs...'

Admiral Jock Campbell, Chairman of the Joint Chiefs, had not spoken since his briefing to the group almost two hours ago. His deep voice resonated around the room; 'What about an EMP?'

'An EMP is what exactly?' asked the President.

The Admiral responded, 'An Electro Magnetic Pulse - it delivers an energy pulse that short circuits electronics. We've been developing weaponised versions of the technology for some time.'

The President raised an eyebrow. A hopeful gesture, perhaps. She looked back towards the central speakerphone on the table, ready to interrogate Meagan Kallis on the idea of an EMP, but before the conversation continued, Kristen Thomas interrupted.

Reading from her phone, she addressed the group, 'I have a flash one priority signal. Russia shows preliminary signs of increased activity at all twelve nuclear warhead storage facilities. And Gadzhiyevo Naval Base in the Arctic is seeing a spike in movement; they've started warming up their subs.'

She looked up from her phone to the President and then to Admiral Campbell.

Tully Carina asked reflexively, 'What does that mean, Director?'

The Admiral spoke up. 'It means Russia has moved their wartime readiness up a level.'

'What on earth is he doing?' asked the President - a little louder than she intended.

The Admiral stood from his seat, 'Madame President, excuse me. I need to deal with this immediately.'

'Of course, Admiral.'

The President closed her eyes. Just hours into her ascendancy to the role, she was dealing with a synthetic virus that could wipe out most of her country and the world's population. And a Russian President who looked to be going rogue and might just beat the virus to it.

Chapter 163

TULLY CARINA LOOKED at the President, 'Perhaps we should clear the room?'

Chairs started to move, and The President snapped open her eyes. 'No, Tully.' She paused for a moment and looked around the room. Her eyes came back to the man in Uniform. 'Admiral, don't leave - stay here, please. Use the Situation Room as your base. It's what it was designed for. And we need to minimise delays. We need to bring the full Joint Chiefs in on both scenarios. I want them either in person in this room or on the secure link within 10 minutes.'

The President again looked around. 'Only members of the National Security Council to be in attendance with the Joint Chiefs and the DNI and CIA Director. Everyone else, we need you back at your jobs. We will call you when we are ready.'

As the room started to disperse, the President knew that Alex Ward and Meagan Kallis remained on the open line. The President spoke directly to them, 'Agent Ward, the information coming out of Russia is an immediate priority. We will disconnect now and call you back when we can.' With a nod to Tully, the call was shut down.

Kristen Thomas had her head bowed and was frantically typing into her phone. About to address the Director, the President's thoughts were interrupted by Admiral Jock Campbell, 'Madame President NORAD is recommending we move to Defcon 2. NATO has issued an Orange Alert status and is moving to a higher state of operational readiness.' The Admiral looked up from his secure tablet and made eye contact with his new Commander in Chief. President Michelle Anders needed some time to consider the comments from the Admiral. Defcon 2! That put them on the precipice of war!

This was moving too fast. She now had two fronts to deal with. She knew the people assembled in the Situation Room but really didn't know them deeply. Who really knew anyone in Washington? Only Tully Carina was her appointment, and she trusted her implicitly. Given time, she would either vette and confirm those in cabinet positions or replace them with people she knew were capable and aligned. But there wasn't time. She definitely couldn't trust William Jacob, the Director of National Intelligence nor the Secretary of Defense. Both Charleston appointments and both his close allies.

Those in Uniform should be different - the various Joint chiefs were required to provide strategic advice and execute the lawful orders they received. And their appointments pre-dated Charleston. She knew Kristen Thomas from extensive briefings and previous dealings. She would have to trust her for now. This handful of people would form her circle as she navigated the next hours and days. It meant she needed a circuit breaker to remove any confusion or territorial wars amongst the cabinet and, more immediately, the National Security Council. With two critical emergencies, there was no time to defer to process and the layers and layers of government. She couldn't have anyone running interference or second-guessing what this core team decided and needed to do.

Chapter 164

THE PRESIDENT LOOKED at Tully, 'Brief the Attorney General and Secretary of Homeland Security - we need to activate Continuity of Government protocols and facilities with immediate effect. I want all delegates moved ASAP. I will stay here. Those still in this room who are part of the COG succession need to move. Now. Let's just hope my Russian counterpart is commencing unannounced war games or is setting up another of his infamous bluffs!'

Anders paused as Tully Carina used a secure line to contact the AG and Homeland Security. The room was again disrupted as papers and laptops were stashed, and people began moving. Secretary of Defense Henry Blake, a former Colonel in the US Marines, hadn't moved.

'Secretary Blake, you are sixth in line for the COG and must move to your designated secure facility. Fifth, actually, given we have no Vice President.'

Hearing this comment, Tully Carina made a note on the journal page before her. The Defense Secretary spoke with emotion, 'With respect, Madame President, I feel my role here is more important given both emergency scenarios are military issues.'

The President thought for a moment, concerned about this likely Charleston ally. She looked for the eye of Admiral Campbell. The Defense Secretary picked up on this and spoke again, 'Madame President, I'm military through and through. I was appointed by President Charleston, but I was never his..... first preference. I really cannot contemplate being hidden in some silo whilst our country is under attack.'

Admiral Campbell and Director Thomas were seated next to each other. She saw them both give a slight nod. 'OK, Secretary Blake. We need as many cool heads as we can .'

Chapter 165

THOMAS BRENDT HAD begun receiving text messages directly from Kristen Thomas. Shit was evidently hitting the fan. The Director wanted a full and fast background on Meagan Kallis. She instructed him to break into any of her personal email, social media and Google accounts he could find. And to dig for any that might be hidden, protected or filed elsewhere. The Director needed to know if this Kallis could be trusted or if she was sending them down a rabbit hole as part of her father's grand plan. Were father and daughter actually working together? And Kristen wanted a work up on a Kallis crony named Pieter Roberts.

None of the instructions sounded lawful to Thomas, but he figured desperate times.....

Chapter 166

ALEX WARD HAD also been receiving messages from Kristen. Ward was being ordered to Russia. She responded back to Kristen that she'd already turned the jet around. As soon as Ward had overheard the conversation in the Situation Room about the Russian President's aggressive military posture, she knew that was where she needed to be. The new threat from Russia would take priority. And Washington was becoming over-burdened and over-whelmed with challenges. They'd want someone on the ground in Moscow. She ordered the pilot to change course.

However the Russian President wasn't in Moscow and Ward was now working with CIA Ops to determine the quickest way into the very southern part of Russia - the location of 'The President's Palace' in Gelendzhik.

The Gulfstream she was on didn't have the range to get to Russia and, in any case, had already burnt a lot of fuel. She needed a new plan to get there. More importantly, she really needed a plan once she arrived.

Chapter 167

PRESIDENT MICHELLE ANDERS considered the reduced group of people now in the Situation Room. Just herself, Chief of Staff Tully Carina, Chairman of the Joint Chiefs Admiral Jock Campbell, CIA Director Kristen Thomas and Secretary of Defense Henry Blake. Everyone else had either returned to their posts or were being swept up in the urgency to relocate them into protective facilities as part of the Continuity of Government protocol.

Whilst she had enormous assets and thousands of people at her disposal, this was the group she had to trust to guide them through the unprecedented scenarios they now faced. She preferred it this way. There could be no deference of responsibility. Communication would be direct. Adding layers and protocol would slow things down. And they could bring in expertise and issue clear commands as needed. She realised she was probably breaking all sorts of constitutional laws and precedents. But she also knew that the current state of emergency and the COG protocols gave her almost unrestricted breadth.

She addressed the small group now. 'The two scenarios we face are as dire as any in our country's history. A lethal virus and a desperate Russian President. The people in this room need to work out how we resolve both of these situations. Either of which could be catastrophic. And we have almost no time. We need to work as a collective. No territorial behaviour and no holding back. There is no one else that will save the day. It is on us. Right now. If you have information or ideas, you share them. Period.'

She paused, realising she was talking to herself as much as the group around the table. 'OK, we need to understand the situation and determine our most immediate priorities. Admiral - I'll get you to brief this group on the Russian threat. Sec Def, let's get that nano-bot professor back in here to clarify the validity of the electro-magnetic option. And then we need our best expert on whether we can activate enough EMPs and how it can be done.'

The Admiral jumped in, 'Secretary Blake, I suggest you contact Director Vicky Hudson - she heads up DTRA and can brief this group on our weaponised EMP program. She will want to bring in General Alex Martinez, the commanding officer in charge of the EMP program. Marty is a good man and will cut through the BS.' Blake nodded to the Admiral, grabbed his phone and started issuing orders.

When Blake was off the phone, the President continued, 'Director Thomas, I need our most recent take on the Russian President. What is he planning, and will he go through with it? And what options do we have from the Agency? I also need you and Tully to develop plans for the EMP option if it's viable - how do we prepare the country, and how do we work with our allies and others. Read in whoever you need.'

The President paused and drew her breath. 'Now, what have I missed. And as I said, don't hold back.'

Kristen Thomas spoke up, 'Ma'am, I have people looking into Meagan Kallis to ensure she is genuine and not part of her Father's plan.'

Anders nodded, appreciating the experienced spy for not taking anything for granted.

Tully Carina then spoke, 'Madame President, we should consider appointing a Vice President immediately. While it needs approval from both houses, I am concerned about some of the options in the line of succession. We can appoint an acting VP and then work through confirmation. The Speaker is currently next in line but is not one of ours and has a very different agenda. Your appointment has left a gap at the top of the COG protocol, and I want to ensure that if needed, the right person is next up.' Tully looked up quickly, realising she was essentially preparing for the death or incapacitation of her friend Michelle Anders and tried to recover quickly. 'Sorry, Madam President, I didn't...'

Anders jumped in, 'It's fine, Tully. It's good advice. Though God knows we don't have the bandwidth to deal with that right now - but we will - I agree it is critical. Tully - read in the AG, and you and I will consider candidates.'

The President looked across the table, 'Let's deal with the Russian threat first. Kristen, the short version on my Russian counterpart please and then Admiral, you're up.' the new President shook her head. 'A Nuclear Russia. God help us!'

Chapter 168

ALEX WARD NOW had a plan to get her to Gelendzhik, Krasnodar Krai, Russia - the location of the President's Palace. Sort of. Her plan had some gaps. Big gaps. But they would work to fix these over the next few hours. Her Gulfstream had re-routed and was now on its way to the Japanese island of Okinawa, where the US Kadena air base was located. She would land there and transfer to an F-15 two-seater fighter bomber fitted with external fuel tanks enabling extended range. It would fly her directly to Abkhazia, just south of the Russian border. It was as close as she could get without crossing into Russian air space. Even with the extra tanks, they would need to refuel mid-air en-route.

The F-15 pilot would land, drop her, refuel again and leave - as quickly as possible. Whilst Abkhazia was a sovereign state, it was a hotbed of political turmoil. A virtual political and regional football between Russia and Georgia. The US was on good terms with Georgia, and they, in turn, actively supported the independent regime in Abkhazia. But it was all pretty flukey. And could change by the day. The agency was concerned a US fighter that close to the Russian border was going to get noticed and get a reaction. Particularly given the over-excited state Russia seemed to be entering.

Ward then had a long overland journey from Abkhazia to Gelendzhik that required her to cross the border and avoid being detected over several hours of driving through southern Russia. She started to think about what could go wrong in the next few hours. She was one single and unsupported operator, currently unarmed. She'd be traveling in a US Air Force Fighter hurtling at more than Mach 2 towards a country that seemed to be quickly moving to the highest state of military readiness since the Cuban missile crisis. If she didn't get shot down somewhere over one of the 'Stans, she'd have to survive 10 hours of driving across open territory, including a border crossing into Russia.

Then came the hard part.

She needed to get into the President's fortress, locate the President, and, if her orders came through - and maybe even if they didn't - find a way to stop him or kill him and then get out and somehow get back to the US. Or, better still, get back to David in Australia. In her mind, contemplating the impossible task ahead, she invoked a quintessential Australian saying she'd heard numerous times in the last year or so - one her husband often used with deadpan irony when telling her about some incredibly complex surgery...'Piece of Piss,' she thought as she pushed her seat back and closed her eyes. She'd call Kristen for an update in a couple of hours.

Chapter 169

KRISTEN THOMAS DECIDED she would be unusually direct. Her favoured approach was to be forthright and considered but always circumspect in her advice and dealings with a President. Whilst concise, she was never one to hold back or to mince words; Kristen was balanced in her approach and ensured the President always had informed and validated intel and recommendations.

Anders was brand new, untested and largely unknown to Kristen. When working with a new President, she would look to understand their approach and their intent. And whether they would make the right calls. In her experience, there were plenty that would not. Unfortunately, some of Anders' predecessors didn't understand or appreciate the agency's work and how it needed to operate. They saw it as part of the political game and looked to use the agency to further their agenda and to propagate popular advantage.

With the dual threat they now faced, Kristen had to believe that this president had the right intent and would make the right decisions. There was no time for anything else. 'Madame President, we believe the Russian President is capable, willing and has the authority within his administration to launch a nuclear attack. In reality, he is a dictator within the regime.'

Kristen looked at President Anders. 'In short, he is most likely not bluffing or posturing.' Kristen continued, 'Compounding this and adding to the evident urgency, we think he is desperate. There is a perfect storm that has taken him to this point.' again, she looked at the President, 'And we do not believe he will pull back.'

Kristen then quickly summarised the situation; 'Firstly, his plans for regional expansion currently focused on territories within Ukraine - to begin to regain the lost states of the former USSR are in disarray. He's already been showing signs of desperation and we have been of the view for some time that he will escalate to full military conflict to achieve his goals. He has threatened the use of nuclear weapons in the past. And these threats are not idle. He has shown a pre-disposition to use nuclear weapons for many years. To date he has not. But our profile of him indicates he would not be troubled by deploying nuclear weapons. His narcism and warped values are so different to those we live by that they are difficult to understand or predict.'

'Secondly, Russian manipulation of the US political and media landscape to ensure a sympathetic and weak, if not openly supportive and collaborative US President has now failed.

'Thirdly, they failed in their COVID-19 response, arrogantly disregarding the need to lockdown, restrict and manage, leading to millions sick and hundreds of thousands dead. The official figures supplied by Russia, much like those from China, are entirely false.

'Even worse, Russia actively supported Hanse Kallis and his companies and used them extensively, almost exclusively in supplying hypodermics and other pandemic medications and vaccine delivery systems. We now know this was to fund Kallis as the Russian conduit to Charleston, initially as a Senator and later as a Presidential candidate and ultimately President. This means that Russian exposure to the Kallis virus is amongst the highest in the world.

'There is a literal time bomb ready to detonate in the veins of tens of millions of Russians.

'And finally - he's dying. We've known for some time that the Russian President is terminally ill. Most likely, it is cancer of the liver. He has, at most, a couple of years to live. Not enough time to ride out his military failure and regroup. And, of course, there is the complete uncertainty of the virus.

'Madame President, every action he takes is motivated by a desire for Russia to be respected. His equivalent of Make America Great Again. As a leader, how he is seen and perceived is paramount. Hence the suits, the cars, riding horseback with no shirt, wild hunting, the palaces and the women.

'In his country, being respected and feared are one and the same. If Russia cannot regain its position as a world superpower - and the events leading to this point show that it will not - then he would rather take his enemies down than to see them succeed and fill the chasm of his failure.' Kristen finished and looked at Admiral Campbell to see if he had anything to add. He gave a curt nod. Michelle Anders looked at her CIA Director for some time. Her head was literally spinning. She contemplated defusing the tension a light-hearted remark about now being ready for the good news but dismissed the thought before it properly formed.

An incredulous Anders asked Kristen, 'How long do we have until he can launch?'

Kristen responded, 'That is a question for Admiral Campbell. However, before we are briefed by the Admiral, we need to discuss Operation Caesar.'

Chapter 170

GENERAL PAVEL ANDREYEVICH Ivanov had been the Minister of
Defense for Russia since the President returned to power over a decade ago.
Together, he and his President made a formidable team. In one of the most
volatile countries in the world, they maintained an iron grip across their
country's political and military leadership. They were philosophically aligned
in their determination to return Russia to its rightful place. And they had
been ruthless in seeing it realised, showing allegiance only to each other.

The General was alone in his office at the defense ministry in
Arbatskaya Square. The office was massive, occupying a large part of the top
floor. It had a line of windows overlooking the Frunzenskaya Embankment.
The building itself and the office he occupied were sparse. Very Russian.
Pared back and severe. It always felt like the plantings and landscaping that
wrapped around the outside of the building were an accommodation of
some sort. A tokenistic attempt that was done without heart or warmth.

The General was seated at the large Russian Oak desk he'd had
customised with an inlay of soft Italian leather. He was in his daily dress of
open-necked olive green military office uniform. The General had a steaming
glass of traditional sweetened Russian black tea his assistant had brought, to
his left. The tea glass was held in an antique brass podstakannik. He loved
and celebrated many of the traditions of Russia, including tea and icy vodka.
However, he found that other Russian habit of tobacco smoking abhorrent
and, much to the dismay of many in his department, had banned it
throughout the ministry building.

Andreyevich had his head bowed and the reading glasses that he
only ever wore when by himself perched on his nose. He was poring over
reports he requested that provided detailed, comprehensive information

about the Russian COVID-19 vaccination program. Specifically, the involvement of Hanse Kallis and his various companies. The program had never been part of his purview as he occupied himself with matters military - particularly the expansion and annexure of former states to advance the Federation. He had left this annoying virus to his ministerial comrades.

Just hours ago, his interest spiked when he watched a taped recording of the address from the new President of the United States and had his personal translator provide a full transcript. Shocked by the revelations from the US leader, his immediate thought was that the close relationship between Kallis and his own President ensured Russia would be protected from this new deadly virus. In fact, he contemplated that the Russian President, with his guile and cunning, may well have been a collaborator or even the architect of this plan from Kallis orchestrating a masterful subversive attack on the West.

The reports he had before him showed that not to be the case. The surge in hospital presentations and deaths in recent weeks indicated the new virus was rampant. And that would be just the tip of the iceberg if the intelligence was accurate and Kallis had implanted a molecular virus through his hypodermics. The General was a military historian and a masterful strategist himself, but the magnitude and planning of this attack from Kallis had him astounded, offering Kallis his silent admiration.

A short time ago, the Russian President had ordered the General to bring the entire intercontinental nuclear arsenal to attack readiness.

It seemed rather than find a way to beat this new virus the President had a different response in mind.

The General, on the President's command had activated Operatsiya Severnoye Siyaniye - Operation Aurora Borealis - Russian strategic command's full-scale and until now, theoretical plan for a full nuclear attack.

General Andreyevich had experienced first-hand the iron will of Russia's President for more than a decade. He could read his intention so very clearly. He was particularly aware that the massive military structure of his country was moving at his command on the orders of the President and at a speed that belied its mass. The President wanted to be ready to launch within hours.

The General would be complicit if this plan went ahead, and he needed to look his leader in the eye before they went beyond the point of no return. Locking the reports in a drawer of his large desk, Andreyevich picked up the phone on his left, 'Have my driver come around immediately. And prepare my plane for departure.'

Chapter 171

'I TAKE IT from the operational title that Operation Caesar involves killing a foreign leader - my counterpart in Russia?' challenged Michelle Anders

Kristen Thomas was all for direct language, but this was a little too upfront from the President. There was an unstated set of protocols when it came to this type of discussion.

Without answering directly, Kristen responded, 'The United States has, with one or two exceptions, determined not to undertake these sorts of operations in the last forty plus years.' she added, 'Not because we would fail, but because our experience was that it generally didn't lead to the outcome we wanted. Cutting off the snake's head just leads to another head growing in its place.'

'I take it you think in this case it would be different?' the President asked.

'Ma'am, we think at the very least the removal of their leader will give pause - slow them down. And ideally, yes - a change in leadership leads to a change in policy and action. Candidly, we have just hours before Russia can be ready to launch. We must assume the Russian President is aware of the same timeline as we are for the release of the Kallis Virus and its devastating impact. He is desperate. This is a highly emotional move from the president responding to an extreme set of circumstances. In this case removing him may well change their direction as more reasoned heads prevail. We need to throw everything we can at stopping him.' Kristen leaned forward and lifted her glass of water, taking a sip.

The President took the opportunity the pause offered, 'I'm not going to ask for operational details. I assume you are moving assets into position, and I approve of getting ready. However, I am not going to give approval for the operation. We are talking about killing a fellow head of state. A blatant act of war. And we have no conclusive evidence it will change anything. I want to take further counsel, and I need time to think it through.' As an afterthought and before Kristen could remind her, she raised her hand in the universal stop signal and added, 'And I know there is very little time.'

Chapter 172

ALEX WARD HAD been given a g-suit and was pulling it on over her tactical cargos, knit top and padded jacket whilst the pilot was giving her a very brief pre-flight briefing. He finished and passed her a particularly large and complicated helmet and several foil-lined vomit bags.

'Is there a parachute?' asked Ward.

'Well, it's in the ejector seat. But if we have to bail and parachute into the countries we're flying over, you may prefer it didn't open than to get caught down there. Ma'am!'

Ward had stashed in an empty bomb casing under the fuselage several weapons, tactical gear and ammunition, the base command had supplied. An M4A1 automatic carbine, her preferred Sig handgun coupled with a SOG folding tactical knife, along with a black tactical vest crammed with spare ammo and an encrypted satellite phone. That was it. Not only was she going into enemy territory very light, she was going in without a strategy. She'd spoken to Mack during her previous flight, and he was working with the agency ops team to pull together a one-person assault plan to first get her across the border and then assassinate one of the highest profile and most protected people on the planet.

'Suicide mission anyone?' she said out loud, muffled into her helmet as she climbed the ladder into the second seat on the jet.

Her final thought before the pilot hit the thrusters and she was slammed back into her seat was that she really should have told Mack to fuck off a few days ago in her bathroom...

Chapter 173

COMMANDER OF US Navy Seal Team Seven, Nathan 'Hawk' Mitchell, was seated with his XO, Lieutenant Commander Alan Turner at a small table in the officer's dining room of the USS South Dakota. The South Dakota was one of the more recent Virginia Class fast attack nuclear submarines to go into commission for the United States Navy. It was brimming with technology and weaponry. It was fast and incredibly stealthy, having been the Navy's test sub for a raft of acoustic enhancement and innovation. The futuristic design included new acoustical hull coatings, a series of machinery improvements inside the hull and the addition of two new large vertical sonar arrays—one on each side along with an improved enhanced hybrid propulsor developed with DARPA. All were designed to leapfrog the technology of other countries and ensure that The South Dakota could hear the enemy earlier than ever before - and certainly earlier than the enemy could hear them.

The sub's speed and stealth capability was being tested right now as they powered from the Mediterranean to the Black Sea.

Commander Mitchell and his Seal team had been using The South Dakota as a base whilst officially running joint training operations with the Italian Navy and roaming the Mediterranean. In reality - and unofficially - their job was to be on standby and ready to act should the regional war in the states adjacent to Russia escalate and require their particular set of skills.

He had cleared the dining room to the quiet dismay of the submarine officers enjoying a meal, and he and his XO were now poring over the most current top-secret version of Operation Caesar.

Caesar had been put together by the CIA Special Operations Group some years ago and had been periodically updated as new intelligence became available. The operational name was an intentional giveaway - it was a plan to remove - assassinate the President of Russia. The plan considered a raft of options as to whether the President was at his Moscow base, traveling domestically or, as he rarely did, internationally. It was the version of Caesar that focused on the President's Palace in Gelendzhik that had the attention of Mitchell and his XO. It was not the Navy's plan. But it looked like they were going to have to run it.

Several hours ago, they had been instructed via Extremely Low Frequency radio to go to communications depth to receive orders and confidential communication - an information package too large and too time-critical to be delivered with the limitations of ELF comms. The Sub Captain hated coming shallow given the detection risk but raised an eyebrow in a silent show of support to the Seal commander when he received his orders.

They'd been given coordinates in The Black Sea and had been running at maximum sustained speed towards their destination for several hours.

Mitchell and the Turner reviewed Operation Caesar and were updating and adding amendments with recent on-the-ground HUMINT and the constant SIGINT they received from satellites, high-altitude planes and drones. It was going to be a bitch of a mission - entering a remote and highly secure location without detection and then finding and eliminating the target. And they hadn't even considered how they would get back out. While it was the type of mission he and his team trained for constantly, in a moment of black humour, he wondered whether he was in the right place at the right time or the wrong place at the wrong time. They were the nearest special forces to Gelendzhik, and this mission, if given the green light, was time-critical.

The rest of the team were resting. He'd get them up in couple of hours, and commence briefing and prep. They were six hours out from their operational staging destination.

Chapter 174

HER MIND SWIRLING and her emotions threatening to overwhelm, Michelle Anders was trying to work as calmly as she could through the impossible challenges she faced. 'Admiral Campbell, you're up.'

The Admiral nodded to an aide who had entered the situation room, and a grid of faces appeared on the video screens on the wall at the end of the table. These were the other Joint Chiefs of Staff. There were five faces with their names under each. Which meant two were missing. Joining the briefing were the Vice Chairman, the Chief of Staff of the Army, the Chief of Naval Operations, the Chief of Staff of the Air Force and the Chief of the National Guard Bureau. The Commandant of the Marine Corps and the Chief of Space Operations had not been able to get to a secure feed on short notice and would try to join during the session.

Without preamble or further introduction, Admiral Jock Campbell began, he looked briefly at CIA Director Thomas; 'We have determined through the profiling of the CIA that the President of Russia is adequately motivated to launch a Nuclear Attack. In a word, he is desperate. And that is a terribly dangerous condition. The deterrent of Mutually Assured Destruction does not apply, given the current scenario.

'Their procedure is very similar to ours. The Russians have redundancies built in to ensure orders are genuine and validated. There are also redundancies built in to retaliate if they are attacked without the need for authorisation or intervention.

'In the last few hours, we have confirmed that Russian nuclear assets are being activated and positioned. Russia has six nuclear missile fields in Kozelsk, Tatishchevo, Uzhur, Dombarovskiy, Kartalay, and Aleysk; nuclear missile submarines patrolling from three naval bases at Nerpich'ya,

Yagel'Naya, and Rybachiy; and nuclear bombers at Ukrainka and Engels air bases. We are aware of fourteen land-based nuclear storage sites. All have gone active and are moving warheads to their launch and delivery locations. Russia also has nuclear missiles on trucks and trains. We have intel that of the eleven nuclear-armed subs, four are currently docked. Two of these - the aging Delfin Class are showing heightened activity indicating they are preparing to go to sea. The other two, we assume, are in maintenance and not currently serviceable.' The Admiral paused for a moment. 'Even with a couple of subs out of action, the combined land and sea nuclear capability of Russia remains the largest in the world. They have almost six thousand nuclear weapons, of which about sixteen hundred are actively deployed strategic nuclear warheads. It is beyond enough.'

Having reaffirmed the frightening nuclear arsenal and capability at the disposal of the Russian President, the Admiral changed focus.

'The Russian Central Command Post of the General Staff is located at Chekhov-3, some seventy kilometres south of Moscow. It is from here that they coordinate and authorise any military or nuclear attack. In a nuclear action, they communicate directly with the Strategic Rocket Forces Command. Authorisation - similar to the United States, is through a system of portable nuclear briefcases. One briefcase is with the President, one is with the Defense Minister, and one is with the Chief of the General Staff Command Post.

'The nuclear briefcase allows the President to transmit an order to launch missiles. The President must transmit the permission code. The permission code prompts the leaders at the Command Post to send out the launch authorisation codes, the unblocking codes, and a war plan to missile sites and land and sea-based mobile launchers.

'The General Staff Command Post turns on a special communications circuit, which connects the post to all missile sites and mobile launchers. The three carrying briefcases will confer with one another by phone. At this point, they will also communicate with the early-warning centres to determine if any enemy launch is headed toward Russia.

'The strategic launchers are prepared for launch. Safety procedures require that the commanding officers at each missile site confirm that the orders are genuine. They do this by comparing the final authorisation codes they received against those kept in a safe. Launch procedures commence. Land-based nuclear-launched weapons would reach parts of Europe within minutes, the UK in around 20 minutes and the US in 30 minutes. Submarine launches, depending on their location, will reach targets more quickly. If Russia determines to launch a full assault, we anticipate over 300 weapons to be launched. Within 30 minutes, NATO countries would have casualties in the tens of millions. And we would have automatically launched a retaliatory strike at Russia. I can take you through US and NATO retaliation procedures if you like?'

The President held up her hand, her head bowed, looking down at the dark timber surface of the table, ' No! That paints the picture.' She looked up. 'What options do we have to prevent the attack, and how long do we have - when could he be ready to commence?'

The Admiral responded, 'Let me take the last question first. Each stored weapon is managed by a three-man team. The Russians are much more hands-on than we are; ours is almost fully automated. With authorisations and their built-in redundancies, it will take some time to move the full arsenal to their delivery locations. We estimate around 16 hours. That clock started ticking two hours ago as best we know. Of course, there are land and sea-based weapons already launch-ready. However, our read is that he wants a full-scale launch prior to any retaliation.'

Tully spoke, 'So, we have fourteen hours to stop him?'

'At best.' confirmed Campbell. He continued, 'To your other question - our options - really, there are only three:

'Firstly, the diplomatic approach.' the Admiral looked to his President. 'However, while we can open every possible channel, the Russian President is not responding to any calls and nor is the Defense Minister. They are the gatekeepers. No one else in Russia's leadership will or can do anything contrary to the orders of the President. The diplomatic option is currently redundant.'

The President considered this and reluctantly nodded. She had tasked her inherited Secretary of State to hammer the Russian leadership with calls and messages. From the President and Prime Minister down. She didn't care how it 'looked' - even if it seemed desperate. That is precisely what they were right now. She herself had called her Russian counterpart several times in the last couple of hours without response. And they had impressed upon all allies and NATO to do the same.

Admiral Campbell continued, 'Our next option is Operation Caesar. Special Forces assets have been tasked to develop assault plans and are moving into position. On short notice, the resources we can have in an effective strike location are limited. The Russian President is at his residence in Gelendzhik on the Black Sea. Seal Team Seven has been operational on The USS South Dakota off Italy in The Mediterranean Sea and is steaming to a tactical location off the Gelendzhik coast. They are currently three hours out and will be deployed on your command. Chief of Naval Operations Admiral Sarah Lawson is with us and can brief us on Caesar in more detail.'

Kristen Thomas was acutely aware of the timing and situation of Operation Caesar. It was, after all, an Agency plan, and they were working with U.S. Naval Special Warfare Command Joint Special Operations Command and the Seal Team Commander to coordinate the assault and assassination. She also had Alex Ward en route to Gelendzhik. Ward's timing was unknown. Currently out of communication and traveling by land northwest from the Georgian border, skirting Sochi to Gelendzhik. At this stage, Thomas and the Admiral had intentionally not read either the Seals or Alex in on each other.

Admiral Campbell continued, 'Our final option is a more extreme 'blunt instrument' variation on Operation Caesar. We have nominated this as Caesar Alternate. This option is a tactical missile strike on the President's residence of enough destructive force to guarantee success. The South Dakota is carrying Tomahawk Cruise Missiles. Our operational plan is to hit the Palace with three simultaneous strikes. It is overkill. We want no margin.'

The very new Chief Of Staff, Tully Carina, responded reflexively, 'Jesus, three Tomahawks from a US sub in the Black Sea taking out the Russian President and obliterating several square miles - are we serious? Hundreds of innocent people will die. We really will have a war then.'

Campbell looked across the table at Tully, 'Yes - we are very serious. And I agree. It is a last resort. It would trigger retaliation unless we can get to the Russian Prime Minister and Defense Minister - it would be seen as an act of terrorism or war. We would need to do everything possible to convince Russia's leadership that it was necessary. And, of course, there is the risk that we miss him - that he has moved or he gets to his bunker, and it saves him. But we need options. We have very few. And this is one of them.'

The Admiral drew a breath, 'Of course, we must consider the scenario that Russia launches. You are aware of our Ground-based Midcourse Defense program. We have sixty Ground-Based Interceptors designed to bring down nuclear missiles mid-flight. The interceptors look to take out enemy missiles in space. This system is designed to respond to relatively small-scale strikes. sixty interceptors cannot deal with over three hundred missiles, and some may miss their target. It is effectively a bullet trying to hit a bullet. And by the time the GMD has launched, we will have automatically retaliated with our own full-scale launch. If Russia launches, we launch.'

'Unless I countermand the order to retaliate.' the President said, looking across to the Admiral.

The Admiral looked silently at the President for several long seconds, 'Unless you do that. Yes ma'am.'

The President summarised the briefing, 'So really, if he doesn't back down of his own accord, we have one option to avoid global nuclear war. Take out or stop the Russian President. And we have fourteen hours. Or less.'

Chapter 175

'MADAME PRESIDENT, OUR recommendations are as follows, Operation Caesar is given the green light and expedited.' Admiral Jock Campbell looked above the line of his reading glasses to ensure he had the attention of the room. He needn't have bothered. Every eye was fixed on him. The expressions to a person strained to breaking point. 'We give Seal Team Seven twelve hours to complete the mission. If we do not have confirmation, we approve Caesar Alternate - the launch of the three Tomahawks. It gives us a two-hour margin prior to what we understand is the operational time frame of their nuclear launch. It also gives our diplomatic and intelligence teams time to contact those in the Russian leadership team that would replace the President and ideally avoid retaliation.'

The Admiral paused to see if there were any questions. There was none. 'We also recommend moving from Defcon 3 to Defcon 1 immediately - there is now no question in our minds that a launch from Russia is imminent.'

President Anders held up her hand and looked at Kristen Thomas, 'Director, what is your assessment of succession in Russia? If we are successful in removing the President, will Prime Minister Ivanoski rescind the attack orders? Or will our actions exacerbate?'

Thomas contemplated her answer; 'We are in uncharted waters, Madame President. Ivanoski is a technocrat and businessman. Unlike the President, he has no military or service history and has shown none of the aggressive expansionism of the President. However, he was a direct and unchallenged Presidential appointment. So he is the President's man. On balance, his profile suggests he would not want to go to war. Not at this scale.

Not a war that ensures the destruction of the Russian Federation. We believe he is someone we can work with. We have to.'

Before the President could respond, or the Admiral continue, Kristen went on, 'Whilst the Admiral and his team have put together this briefing, we have been optimising intelligence gathering across Russia. Our electronic reconnaissance has seen radio communications explode across all Russian military installations. Optical imaging and radar imaging confirm that all known missile storage silos are operational. Liquid-fuelled missiles are being filled. We are seeing unprecedented movement of land-based launchers on both road and rail systems. The two nuclear Delfin class subs in dock have gone to sea. That has been done in record time, indicating they are neither fuelled nor supplied for long-range operations. What is interesting and highly concerning is that Russia has not officially changed its readiness status. We understand they have been at Elevated Combat Readiness for some time - essentially our Defcon 3. In preparation for war they would move to Full Combat Readiness - Defcon 1. They have not.'

The President asked; 'What is the implication? Isn't that good news?'

Kristen responded, 'Typically, it would be. However, our take is that The President and Defense Minister Andreyevich are not preparing for traditional combat. They are only activating their nuclear arsenal. In short, ma'am, we have no doubt they are moving to full-strike capability at their fastest possible pace and are not anticipating a protracted traditional war. It's a fairly transparent case of, 'if we can't succeed, no one will.'

President Anders looked back at the Admiral; 'If we move to Defcon 1, won't that be taken as a direct threat and push them beyond the point of no return?'

Campbell reasoned; 'We don't think it matters at this point. They are moving with all speed now. It will allow us to be as prepared as possible. All respect Ma'am. We have to defend ourselves and we need to do so now knowing the strike is coming. If we wait until they launch and retaliate, all is lost. America and all NATO countries will be wiped from the planet.'

'Sorry Admiral, when you say 'now', are you suggesting a preemptive strike?'

'It may be our only way to survive - a more tactical strike before they are fully operational and deal with a much smaller retaliation.'

Kristen Thomas caught herself staring at the Admiral. This had not been discussed offline. The situation, as tenuous as it was, threatened to get completely beyond anyone's control very quickly. She remained necessarily hopeful they could shut this threat down. And then they would just have the virus to deal with.

The President fought to control her emotions, in a terse tone, her eyes unblinking at the Chairman of the Joints Chiefs of staff she said, 'Admiral, I know we are running against a fast-moving scenario, but I am not willing to authorise a nuclear strike on Russia.' She paused, 'Caesar is authorised to go. Caesar Alternate is not yet approved; however, please have it prepped and ready to proceed on my word. Move to Defcon 2. And God Save us all.'

Kristen was relieved. It seemed there was a cool head running the show. For now.

Watching this all unfold and struggling with both the surreal situation of a rapidly unfolding nuclear threat and a deadly virus, Chief of Staff Tully Carina was grappling with both her emotions and her thoughts. Could this really be going on? This was like converging nightmares. She felt like she was on an express train and had no time to think or properly absorb what was happening. And she wondered how her long-time friend was dealing with it. It was beyond comprehension to have to contemplate and manage even one apocalyptic scenario, let alone two. Simultaneously. She noted the Admiral was now speaking to the other chiefs, who were still on the secure video link. Preparing her country for war. Tully leant across to the

President; 'Ma'am how about a fifteen minute break while we get the Professor back in here. Let's take a walk outside.'

Chapter 176

ALEKSANDRE DVALI WAS a Georgia native, having grown up outside Guria on the west coastline of the Black Sea. He moved away in 2006 to study at the University in Tbilisi, where he wanted to become a teacher like his father. His plans were thrown into turmoil when Russia and Georgia went into conflict in August of 2008 - subsequently known as the five-day war. His father had stood up to the Russians, passionately speaking out and discrediting the attack against their people, trying desperately to bring the attention of the world to what was happening. Then, the ethnic cleansing began in Abkhazia, close to his home. His father, being a voice of discontent, was singled out, and on August 10, 2008, he was taken along with his two younger sisters and his mother by Russian forces. Aleksandre rushed back to his village, narrowly avoiding skirmishes and full-blown fighting several times. But he was too late and had never seen or heard from his family again.

He now found himself at the wheel of his 2009 Lada Bronto no more than thirty minutes from their destination, the coastal town of Gelendzhik. After the loss of his family, his career changed, and for more than a decade, he had been an agent for the Georgian Intelligence Service. He was based in the northwestern region of Abkhazia. Agency work took him into Russia constantly. Four hours ago, he crossed the border - just another countless trip to the country that had taken his family. But this time, he had a passenger. A tall, very intense and attractive American woman dressed all in black who had hardly spoken. He had picked her up outside Abkhazia - she had come from Vaziani military base by helicopter. Abkhazia was as close to the border as they would risk to ensure no Russian interest. The route he had taken from Abkhazia to Gelendzhik was circuitous and indirect. They needed to be discreet.   His papers were solid. The papers he had secured for his passenger should pass scrutiny. But if she was asked anything in Russian, they were in trouble. Despite the time-critical orders he had, getting questioned and detained would help no one. So he had erred to the cautious and avoided the more likely places to be stopped. Or noticed. And his passenger had slept. He had woken her an hour ago and she had been on her phone and tablet ever since. His English not really adequate to follow the conversation.

Finally, the silence was broken, 'What was your name again?'

'Aleksandre'

She wondered if that was the male version of her own name in this part of the world. 'Well, Alexi, you are about to get new orders from your bosses.'

'Who is Alexi? Perhaps just call me Alek.' He said in heavily accented English, 'And who are you?'

Ward almost looked at her tablet again to remind herself of her identity on the fake papers, 'Katerina is fine.'

He paused to find the right English words, 'OK, Katerina, what are the new orders?'

'You are no longer just dropping me off. You are about to go operational. This little chickadee requires a partner.'

Alek looked at her like she was speaking another language. Which she was!

Ward had debated the roughed out plan heatedly with Mack and Brendt, preferring to work alone, but had relented when Brendt pointed out they needed someone fluent in Russian. Thomas Brendt had gone from obscure hacker and financial wiz to offering operational advice in a matter of days. In any case, as soon as she was properly inside the Palace, she'd ditch her new partner and move alone.

Chapter 177

RUSSIAN DEFENSE MINISTER General Pavel Andreyevich was seated alone in the main forward cabin of the wide-bodied Ilyushin Il-96-300PU aircraft - one of several in the Presidential fleet made available at his disposal. The interior had been custom-fitted and was incredibly luxurious, though he would use none of the large space and myriad appointments on this fairly short trip.

His departure from his office at The Defense Ministry had been delayed. The President wanted constant updates on the preparations for their nuclear readiness. He demanded that their full strike launch capability be ready in half the time that Andreyevich had advised. It simply was not possible. A more modest retaliatory strike could launch within minutes. But to bring over 1000 warheads online and active took several hours.

It was a massive undertaking. Unprecedented for the General, even in their more elaborate war gaming exercises. When not speaking with the President, the General had been in fervent communication with his commanders across the air-force, navy and the armed forces. They needed to be briefed and receive their orders.

In Russia, perhaps even more than most other military organisations, orders were given and followed without question. The General visualised in his mind the enormous activity underway across all nuclear sites in Russia - and in the oceans. The constantly speculated and invariably feared Russian nuclear arsenal was coming to life and would be primed and ready in just a few short hours.

Driving to the airfield in his state issued Aurus Senat limousine and now on the plane, he had been in continuous contact with the President through the Kavkaz-7 nuclear communications system that was part of the

Cheget nuclear briefcase that accompanied both he and the President everywhere. In theory, it required two of the Cheget nuclear suitcases to authorise nuclear weapons release. Upon which codes would be unlocked. And the countdown to launch would begin. Andreyevich had often speculated that his President had quietly changed that protocol and could authorise the release of the codes without the validation of a second Cheget suitcase. It was part of the reason he was heading to meet the President personally.

His plane had left Domodedovo Airport thirty minutes ago and was now some thirty minutes from Gelendzhik. It would then be a short ride to the residence. The President remained unaware that he was traveling to him. The General had ensured that only a handful of people knew of his whereabouts and his plans. His secretary, his driver and pilot and his security team. The President had eyes everywhere, but Andreyevich was confident his arrival would be a surprise.

He was counting on it.

Chapter 178

COMMANDER 'HAWK' MITCHELL on the USS South Dakota had woken his platoon of fourteen Seals some thirty minutes ago. They had dressed in their black combat uniform and consumed a pre-battle meal to fuel them for the next few hours. They were now ninety minutes from going active. Mitchell was briefing them on the mission parameters of Operation Caesar. The CIA had provided a 3D rendering of the Palace, which was as good as they could get for the operation. There was no time or space to run through any rehearsal and he and his XO had figured the men were better rested and fresh. Shortly, all 16 would change into black customised wetsuits made by Neptunic, and all would be using underwater re-breathers. The 'palace' was tightly secured. There were over 17,000 acres of woodland and a no-fly zone as part of paranoia-inspired security.

The tactical plan developed by the CIA was not a frontal assault. That would be destined to fail and impossible to deny. They might as well just launch a missile at the place. Commander Mitchell had no illusion as to the challenge that lay ahead for him and his team. He didn't have the context as to why this mission had been authorised, but he had been around. He knew something like this - to take out a high-profile political leader on foreign soil and on short notice - and with a pretty sketchy likelihood of success - meant shit had gotten serious. They were a small team entering an incredibly well-secured and isolated location. The CIA had identified only one way to covertly access the Palace. And even then, a lot of moving parts had to fall into place to make it work.

Chapter 179

ALEX WARD AND her new partner had pulled their Lada into an underground shopping centre car park in Gelendzhik. They were minutes from the Palace, and Ward was running Alek through the operational plan. She figured he would be a profitable poker opponent. The more she talked, the wider his eyes became. She had to admit, it was an ambitious approach.

The Presidential Palace commenced construction almost 20 years ago, in 2005, and never been finished. In part because it was a massive and challenging design. In part because this was Russia, and that tended to happen. But mostly because the high-profile resident of the Palace tended to come up with new ideas and new demands. Often demolishing and re-commencing large parts of the structure that had only just been completed.

As a result, teams of construction workers, designers, and landscapers were constantly on-site. Without exception, anyone working on the site had passed stringent security and background checks and had to comply with an entire two-week quarantine period before coming onto the site to ensure they carried no virus or disease. The CIA had been quietly planting eyes and ears into the construction crews for years. And setting up backstories. Today, they were being called upon.

Ward and Alek were now in the back of a white, nondescript commercial van made by Russian manufacturer Gaz. The van had been provided by one of the workers the CIA had been quietly paying for years. It was well known and would not be out of place on-site at the Palace. As they were changing into full hazmat suits, Ward tried to calm her new partner.

She didn't think his eyes could get any wider, 'So we are just going to waltz into one of the most secure and paranoid places in Russia?' His English had improved in direct correlation with his level of excitement.

'Well - they are expecting us, so that might make it easier!'

'Expecting us! What, some female CIA ninja - is that what they are expecting?' Alek exclaimed.

'Alek - this will work.' said Ward, desperately trying to convince herself. She continued, 'One of the senior construction leaders we have onsite has raised an alert that a mass of black mould has been uncovered in the President's doomsday bunker and is a health risk - to his team members and anyone who might need to use the bunker. He demanded that it be inspected and removed. That's us.'

'Black mould! That's your plan? That is what gets us into the Palace!'

'The President is paranoid. And we think he is already pretty sick. No way will they risk any chance of infection, particularly with an artificial air supply system re-circulating existing air. Just be confident, be demanding and scare anyone we meet. We'll be escorted right in there.' Ward looked around the van. There was a raft of equipment that would complete their cover, including backpack ventilation systems and a range of air quality testing devices. They had to pull this off.

Alek struggled to get his white suit zipped and closed at the front, as he continued to stare wide-eyed at Ward. 'And what do we do once we're in the bunker?'

'One thing at a time, Alek.'

Chapter 180

PRESIDENT ANDERS RE-ENTERED the Situation Room. The brief break and some fresh air had helped her reenergise. Though she wasn't sure for how long. It had been non-stop for hours. Or was it now days? She'd walked and talked with Tully outside into the gardens and taken in the cold Washington night.

She now needed to give her full focus to the original problem she'd been briefed on - the ticking time bomb of the Kallis virus and how they could possibly stop it. Trying to focus was not an easy task, given the raw, frightening prospect of a nuclear strike by her lunatic counterpart in Moscow.

'Admiral - before the Professor comes back in, remind me of the timeline for Caesar?'

'Ma'am, Seal Team Seven is preparing to deploy in two Shallow Water Combat Submersibles. These are brand-new covert delivery vehicles we have been testing as part of our operational cover in the Mediterranean. Once they go wet in about six minutes, they are eighteen minutes from landfall. We expect to be able to take the video feed of the operation at that time.'

Kristen Thomas was still in her seat in the Situation Room. She had not taken a break, having used the time to confer with the Admiral and her team, assisting Alex Ward. She had decided not to challenge the Chairman of the Joint Chiefs on his aberration in suggesting a preemptive strike. She figured that would become a distraction. Kristen was convinced their only chance of averting disaster from the hand of the desperate Russian President was to remove him. Permanently. And deal with any fallout that resulted. She had used the last few minutes to receive an update on Ward's progress. It wasn't much of an update. Information was not easy to get. Ward was not actively communicating, preferring to go dark and avoid any risk of detection. Her team advised her that, as best they could tell, Ward was still operational. They didn't really know where she was or how long until she reached the Palace. She and the Admiral agreed they would keep the Seal Team in the dark about Ward and vice versa. They felt it gave them a little more hope of success. And it might just cause distraction and delay if they tried to brief each operation in. The only real risk was if both Ward and the Seals were successful in breaching the bunker and came across each other not realising they were on the same side. Kristen felt the chances of one of the teams succeeding was extremely low. Let alone both.

The President spoke again, 'Let's bring in the Professor and get Director Hudson on the screen.'

Chapter 181

NATHAN 'HAWK' MITCHELL was in the port side seat of the submersible breathing through the oxygen line attached to the vessel. They were currently at four metres depth and had about fifteen minutes until they would get to their contact point. He was running through the plan for a final time in his mind...

The Palace sat on a bluff above the Black Sea and was protected by a mass of more than seventeen thousand acres of secured and protected land around the site and restricted and monitored air space above. Years ago, the CIA had secured architectural plans for the design of the massive residence and had validated and updated them whenever they could get new information, given the predilection of the Russian President to both continually remodel the Palace and to spend a lot of time there.

Operation Caesar focussed on the secure doomsday bunker more than fifty metres underground. It was accessed from the main building by an elevator shaft, or if out of action a steel and concrete stair case, both of which fed into dual underground tunnels that led further down to access the bunker. The bunker itself was constructed of 15-inch thick steel reinforced concrete. It had its own air supply, water supply, fire safety system and sewer and was some six thousand five hundred square feet. The President and other officials could survive in the bunker for weeks. At first blush, the agency rejected the bunker as a poor tactical option. It was a fortress within a fortress.

But then a smart young CIA analyst proposed the idea that the bunker might actually be the weak point in the whole structure. For two key reasons - firstly, it was generally unguarded until needed. And secondly, it used the Black Sea to feed the water supply, distribute treated sewerage, and provide an escape option for the president. The key to the whole plan was to get to the bunker first. Undetected. And then create an emergency situation that would bring the President to them.

Chapter 182

THE SMILING PROFESSOR from the Cerebrum think tank was back in the Situation Room. The President's core team were now re-assembled, to determine whether the EMP strategy - the only strategy they currently had- could actually work.

Once again, the invited Professor was babbling a bit, clearly enjoying centre stage in front of the new President and again seemed to be in awe of the scale and technology Hanse Kallis had managed to create. Michelle Anders looked across at Tully Carina, who immediately took the cue; she raised her hand and spoke loudly above the academic, 'Sorry Professor, I need you to cut to the chase - can the micro robotics be stopped by an Electro Magnetic Pulse?'

The Professor again stopped mid-sentence, his toothy smile faded and he stared at the Chief of Staff as if he'd been interrupted by a rude millennial student... 'Well, my expertise is not EMP's per se. My PhD is in robotics, and......'

This time, the President spoke up, 'Professor - please, we have very little time.'

'Of course, Madame President. In my opinion, yes - an EMP or any strong magnetic field will degrade the robotics. This will either be through wiping the programming, erasing information or frying and short-circuiting the electronics themselves.' He paused as if that was enough and then added, 'Or a combination of all of these. Our modelling suggests a strong enough pulse will be devastating.'

Chapter 183

THE PROFESSOR WAS once again urged from the Situation Room. Focus now turned to Director Victoria Hudson of DTRA - the Defense Threat Reduction Agency set up to respond to the threat of weapons of mass destruction. The EMP program was part of her remit. Defense Secretary Blake had briefed Director Hudson in. Everyone in the Situation Room was looking at the cluster of screens projecting the face of the Director into the room.

Unlike the Professor, she didn't feel the need for context or a backstory, 'The two biggest challenges we have in delivering an Electro Magnetic Pulse to impact essentially every person in the United States - and in fact on the planet are one; scale and two; managing the consequences and fallout.'

Listening intently, Kristen Thomas was pleased that the director was getting to the point immediately. They didn't need a history lesson or an EMP for dummies lecture. They just needed to know if it was possible.

Hudson continued; 'Scale will be an enormous challenge. EMPs are essentially delivered in two ways - nuclear and non-nuclear. Non-nuclear EMPs are preferred as they are delivered without the destructive consequences of nuclear EMPs. However, non-nuclear EMPs are designed to be highly focused rather than widespread - to take out a specific electronic target. The only way we can achieve the scale needed - to cover all of the US population will be a combination of both - we will use non-nuclear where we can, but will need to deploy high-altitude nuclear EMPs to get the coverage. And the rest of the planet will do likewise. For countries without EMP capability, the US and others will have to step in.'

Tully Carina spoke up, 'So the only way we can protect or save our people from this lethal virus is to set off nukes?' Without waiting for an answer, she continued, 'How many nukes are we talking about, and how destructive will they be?'

'This is new ground for us. I have our DRTA team modelling this now. But the vague answer is that it will be quite a few. Fortunately, the nuclear EMP's will be detonated in the atmosphere - this optimises their coverage. And atmospheric nuclear explosions will not cause direct destruction or death. Our non-nuclear capability is solid, but there will be gaps in what it can achieve. Enormous gaps.'

Tully looked to the head of the table to the President. Anders' face was awash with emotions. Her eyes wide and unfocused. Knowing her friend so well, Tully knew she would be struggling with the realisation that even the best-case outcome from this mess would see her authorising the use of nuclear bombs. And not dropped in retaliation to some far flung enemy. But on her own people. No sitting President had ever faced a decision like this. And within just hours of the momentous sequence of events that necessitated her to authorise the assassination of the Russian President. A fellow head of state. The leader of one of the world's Super Powers. The fallout from which they could neither predict or control.

The enormity of what confronted the new President and the horrible consequences of whatever she decided, whatever course they took - would all sit squarely at her feet. This intensified pressure would cause angst and uncertainly amongst the most seasoned of Presidents and political leaders. And Anders had barely been sworn in. No wonder she looked shell shocked. Tully decided she would watch her friend like a hawk to ensure she was protected as much as possible. And to ensure she made clear and considered decisions.

Hudson continued,   'We are proceeding on the assumption that this is our preferred - in-fact our only course of proactive action. Within the next few hours, I will have a recommendation on how we can best deploy both non-nuclear EMP's and the nuclear program we will need.'

She paused to see if there were questions. Admiral Jock Campbell nodded for her to continue.

Before she could go on, President Anders spoke - her eyes a little glazed and indirect, 'Director Thomas remind us all of where we are in the countdown to the virus event.'

Kristen Thomas responded without looking at her notes, 'We are working to a notional deadline of midnight Friday GMT. The information we have retrieved from Doctor Kallis indicated the synchronised release of the virus would be on Saturday. He did not specify a time. So we are taking no chances. We are working backwards from midnight Friday GMT, so we do not risk even a minute into Saturday.

'If we can remove the Russian President and secure a favourable replacement, the Russian military will need around six hours to re-direct their nuclear launch to an EMP launch. That deadline is Friday six pm GMT. It's currently just after midday Friday GMT. We have just under six hours to remove the Russian President and stop the launch. And then another six hours to coordinate a global EMP strike. If the Seal team is not successful in the next four hours, we will move to Caesar Alternate and launch the Tomahawk strike at the Palace.' She heard Tully Carina swear quietly. Kristen looked across to the President. She saw Anders now had her head bowed and buried in both hands.

The room was silent for a few moments. Director Hudson, herself reeling from the comments about removing the Russian President forced herself to focus. She read the silence and knew there would be a reaction from those expected to make these horrible decisions. If people didn't react to such stress she would be more concerned. Hudson stepped in again, 'The prospect of a non-nuclear EMP launch is daunting enough. To contemplate a nuclear launch is almost impossible to get your head around. I know how each of you are feeling. I've been thinking about this and modeling scenarios for years and, for the last few hours, preparing our facilities for launch. I want to give you the best, most dispassionate information and advice I can.' Hudson paused to ensure she had the full focus of the room.

The President looked up. Every eye was on Hudson, 'The situation, as I understand it, is that the Kallis virus is real. There are literally tens if not hundreds of millions infected with a virus that will be triggered in just a few hours and for which we have no vaccine and no cure. It will kill untold millions. Stopping this virus is our first and only real priority. And this is the only way it can be done.' It was a good and effective rally for those present. Hudson saw their expressions clear and their focus return. President Anders was nodding. Hudson, of course, was not privy to the other monstrous threat from Russia, that was driving the operation to remove their leader.

The President spoke first, 'You are right, Director. We need to acknowledge this is not some out-of-body nightmare but a situation in which we need our best selves to make the right decisions. Continue.' Anders had spoken firmly. Looking to galvanise the room. And herself.

Hudson nodded to the President, 'We must work on the assumption that our EMP strategy works. And we must then start to prepare for the fallout. To be honest - that is when the real work will begin. The fallout is part known and a lot unknown. Even with our modeling. A massive, nationwide EMP will have far reaching implications. Our country is almost universally powered by the grid; water supply requires power to operate and is controlled by automated systems managed by computers, and the food chain is the same. And our reliance on devices, software and the internet for our communications and to run every part of the economy is almost completely pervasive. Every electronic circuit will be either temporarily or permanently shut down by the EMP. The impact on our people, economy and country will be both immediate and ongoing.' Hudson paused. She had the attention of everyone in the room. Everybody here was desperate to stop the Kallis virus releasing. Desperately hoping this Hail Mary EMP idea would work. They hadn't for a moment contemplated the broader consequences of the detonations. The domino affect of what Kallis had initiated seemed unending. Hudson wanted to make sure that even with the enormity of the decisions sitting with this group that they understood that their problems would not end once the EMP strike happened.

'In a nutshell, as soon as we fire the EMP's, we risk returning to the Dark Ages.'

Chapter 184

THE MONSTROSITY THAT is The President's Black Sea residence formed in its full glory in front of Alex Ward. She and Alek were in the van heading into the aptly named Palace. She'd seen glimpses of it as they approached, and it was massive. Now within arms reach she was struggling to comprehend the sheer size of the place. And the enormity of the challenge before her. They were just minutes away. She decided to break operational security and call her husband. The current circumstances were extreme. In her mind, even the best case didn't see her surviving this. She wanted to talk to David. It had been several days. A lot had happened, and a lot was about to happen.

Her comms were secure, and even if compromised, the Russians wouldn't be able to respond in time. They were minutes away from being operational. She pulled out her secure and encrypted sat phone and dialed David's mobile, praying this time he would answer.

The sat phone connected. Without waiting for him to say anything, Ward jumped in, 'David, it's me.'

'Alex - where are you? Are you on your way home?'

The line was surprisingly clear; she closed her eyes for a moment, relieved to hear his voice, 'Not yet. Unfortunately, this is not over. There is more to do.' Before he could hit her with questions, she kept talking, 'David - how are you? What is happening there?'

The line was silent, with just a hiss of static for several seconds,'It's a nightmare. A horror movie. The hospital is no longer even trying to treat anyone. We are over run with bodies. We're nothing more than a morgue, and we're out of space. The bodies are everywhere, inside and outside. The kids, the families, the parents...' he couldn't finish.

'Oh God, David. I'm so sorry. What you're seeing...that must be...well, it must be horrible.' Ward struggled to find the words and comfort the man she loved.

'Alex, is there an answer to this? Do we know what is going on? Do you know?'

Ward held her breath. At any other time, she would say something vague that would tell David nothing but would still convey that they were on it. But not this time. It was beyond that...

'What you're seeing honey, as horrible as it is.....is the tip of the iceberg.'

'Is this what the President meant by the Trojan Horse..?'

He sounded exhausted. Beyond tired. Without energy. No doubt defeated by what he was dealing with.

'Yes.'

'What's happening, Alex? Do you know?'

'Yes, at least some of it.'

'Tell me'

'The South African - Kallis put a virus in every hypodermic his companies supplied to vaccinate against COVID.'

'I know that - it's what I'm dealing with. I mean, it's a nightmare. How could anyone be so callous and have such a God complex...it is beyond imagining... it's, it's...Sorry, I'm rambling.'

'It is a nightmare. Unfortunately, what you have heard is not the worst of it. The Trojan Horse Anders referred to is not just that he placed a virus in the arms of millions but that he evolved his method. It's Kallis Virus 2.0, sitting latent amongst most people. It is going to be simultaneously triggered.'

'What - how is that possible?'

'Molecular robotics. The virus is carried by nano-robotics that lie dormant until activated.' Before she could go on, David interrupted, 'Nano-robotics - what! That's in its infancy. It's borderline science fiction. The hospital participates in R&D in that space. But its years away from being proven.'

'Not for Kallis - he cracked it. And this is how he is using it.'

'Fuck!'

'Yep!'

There was empty air for a few seconds. Ward was conscious that her new mate Alek was listening to her side of the conversation as he drove the van, and he was rubbing his left shoulder.

David then spoke again, 'how is it activated?'

'It's synchronised and scheduled - on a kind of timer. I don't really understand.'

'Scheduled for when?'

'Literally hours from now.'

'Holy Shit! Then what?'

'Then nothing for a few days until people start dying. Exactly as you're seeing now. But instead of hundreds or maybe thousands, it will be millions. Ultimately billions..'

'Why - Alex - why would he do this?

'David - he truly thinks he's saving the planet - and us - from ourselves and our failures and a future that is inevitably bleak.'

'What... that's madness! It has to be stopped!'

Ward could see the Palace looming ahead. Alek was making his way around the structure to where the tradespeople and workers went through security and were cleared to enter.

'David, I have to go...'

'Wait - Alex - how will it be stopped?'

'You familiar with the Big Bang Theory?'

The call disconnected. David still held his phone to his ear, staring off into the distance - the Big Bang Theory! What? He knew his wife was deeply involved in this solution somehow - unaware she was on a desperate and likely suicidal mission and about to try and enter the heavily secured fortress protecting a desperate Russian President.

Chapter 185

'WHEN YOU SAY Dark Ages, what does that actually mean?' Tully Carina looked at the image of Director Victoria Hudson on the large screen at the end of the table in the Situation Room, struggling to try and synthesise the information and threats only this small group had been made privy to. She looked down at her notepad and saw the words Vice President circled by her own pen several times.

Director Hudson responded, 'Secretary Carina, when we set off these EMPs, every electrical device within range will be affected - short-circuited or completely fried. And given the scale we need to deliver, that literally means every single electrical device - in the country and on the planet- very few have built-in hardened EMP protection. For example, every hospital and aged care facility will go black. Redundancy power sources will also be affected. No power, no air conditioning, no water, no respirators, no monitors, nothing. People will die - some immediately, some over a few days. Consider that across every single part of our society and economy and it is catastrophic. I mentioned before, everything is affected by power, computers, and the internet. Everything. The electricity grid, communications, satellites, the internet, food supply, water supply, sewerage, shopping malls, gas stations, financial institutions and the market itself. Many cars will simply stop where they are, and even if mobile, there will be no traffic management. Ships and boats will lose their GPS and navigation systems or lay idle. Aircraft will literally drop from the sky. We have come to rely on computers and the internet almost completely. The relatively small number of people off the grid or with solar or other power sources may be better placed. At least for a few days.'

Hudson paused, having made this point previously. She then continued, 'In the hands of our enemy, an EMP strike is regarded as a weapon of mass destruction. In this case it will be self inflicted.'

Tully continued, 'How long until it is all reset and comes back on?'

Hudson stared at her, 'Days, weeks, months, years, maybe never. Everything will be different. Nobody really knows. Let me be really clear. It is a weapon of mass destruction. For a reason! It will decimate our country and everywhere else it is deployed. For years. Our modelling indicates deaths will be in the millions. Just in the US. People will get sick. People will suffer extreme dehydration and starve. And people will turn on each other. The country will never be the same.'

'My God!' said Michelle Anders under her breath.

Jock Campbell jumped in, 'What about the military - our assets, our communications?'

'Almost completely disabled. Some have autonomous power and systems - but most don't, and almost everything is integrated and relies on power, computers, or GPS.'

Campbell continued, 'So - we'd be sitting ducks?'

Hudson looked across the screen, 'Yes and no - if EMP's are deployed everywhere, then our enemies will also be shut down.'

Campbell sat in silence - pondering the madman in Moscow and inwardly shuddering at the thought that the United States would be rendered incapacitated and unable to defend itself.

The President now spoke up, 'Can we prepare for it - at least we know it's coming? Will that help?'

As she listened, Tully contemplated how the perspective of those in the room had changed so quickly. Just a few days ago they were all just managing their own lives and jobs - appointments, meetings, their people - all the daily tasks they went through - and thinking about what to cook their kids for dinner. Now, they were being dealt disaster after disaster. Each with implications beyond anything that had happened in their country before. And they were trying desperately to be focused and deliberate in dealing with them.

She was also conscious of feeling a soft tingling in her arm. Her left arm. Where the vaccine and the boosters had been injected. Was that just her imagination triggering a response? Like thinking about an itch and then needing to scratch. Or was it the virus and the bots warming up? She subconsciously rubbed her arm.

Hudson was speaking, 'To a degree. From what you told me, we have just a few hours now to coordinate the EMP strike - both here in the US and across the world. That alone will take a mammoth effort. Getting properly prepared before the strike will be incredibly hard - impossible actually.'

Anders stared at the screen Hudson's face occupied - prompting her to continue...

'Madame President - the best preparation is to turn everything off.'

The President repeated, 'Turn everything off? What on earth does that mean?'

'It means everything. Everything from our massive power grids, hydro plants, sewerage treatment, railways, hospitals and schools to every car, motorbike and bus and right through to every TV, radio and mobile phone in the country. Even the redundancies. In fact, especially the redundancies. Plenty of essential services and businesses have backup generators or solar or backup batteries. These need to be shut down as well. Everything.'

Hudson read the faces, 'Turning everything off offers the best chance of not being fried by the EMP and for it to work when we try to turn it back on. But we're guessing. We don't really know what will work and what won't. As I said - the country will never look the same.'

Tully Carina, again, true to her empathetic nature, asked the DTRA Director, 'Does that not mean people will die? A lot of people?'

'Yes, it does. The modelling has anticipated both direct and indirect deaths from an EMP event. However, we need to moderate the data as it assumes a surprise attack, with no chance to prepare as we can here. However, the impact is frightening. Direct deaths will happen with those that have dependencies of some sort and need support. Indirect deaths will occur from resultant dehydration, disease and starvation. Not to mention criminal activity and the lengths people will go to to survive.'

Tully had gone white and was staring at the Director realising that what she was describing was actually their best case scenario, 'How many people are we talking...?'

'Some of the modelling has casualty rates of up to ninety percent of America's population within a year of an attack. I stress that this is at the extreme end and considers a widespread and surprise attack. However, the deaths will likely be in the millions - tens of millions - before we can restore our systems.'

'Jesus Christ!' breathed Tully.

The room went quiet. Really quiet. The President stared at the desk top in front of her. Her eyes not focussed. She knew that they simply must stop the madman in Russia and then they had to stop the virus created by another madman. To fail was not an option. And the solution she was being presented seemed as terrifying and devastating as the virus it was intended to stop. It seemed Hanse Kallis would largely achieve his monstrous objective and see the deaths of countless people - either at his own doing or at hers. She silently prayed the efforts they could make to limit the EMP damage would be more effective than the modelling she kept hearing about, suggested.

She caught herself reflecting for a moment that the concerns the CIA and FBI had about foreign involvement in their elections and a compromised President and government now paled against the monstrous plan of Kallis. His plan did not discriminate. It would affect every part of the globe and every person on it. The Kallis virus had been the tipping point that sent a Russian President off the edge. And was sending her - an American President down a path where even the best case was catastrophic.

This was Sophie's Choice on a global scale. To not act would result in unmitigated disaster. To act - to take the only course available would see them self inflict damage of potentially equal devastation. Anders forced herself back to the present, even though as she started to speak, it felt like the words were coming from someone else, 'Director Hudson, I am authorising you to proceed. Please work with Admiral Campbell and Director Thomas on the timing of the EMP strike - as late as possible so we can prepare. And work with Chief of Staff Carina to ensure everything we can possibly do to mitigate the self-inflicted damage is put in place'

She turned to Tully, 'I need to address the nation again. Set it up for eight am Eastern.'

Chapter 186

TO CALL THE residence on the Black Sea coast near Gelendzhik a Palace was totally inadequate. A more apt description Alex Ward had come across in some of her research and briefing packs considered it its own city - or Kingdom.

Designed by Moscow-based Italian architect Lanfranco Cirillo, the main structure was an Italianate mansion perched on the edge of the Black Sea on one hundred and seventy forested acres. That parcel of land was then protected by another seventeen thousand acres of closed territory. The scale of the structure and extent of the grounds were incredible and included vineyards, a hockey rink and a Chapel - in what was previously a gambling room. The compound was incredibly secure - by impenetrable fences, its own harbour, hundreds of guards housed in quarters on the grounds, numerous checkpoints, a no-fly zone and its own border point. It was technically regarded as a separate state within Russia.

Officially, it was owned by Arkady Rotenberg. But anyone who thought your average garden variety Russian Oligarch would be afforded the security and exemptions this place received was kidding themselves. This was the President's Palace. No matter how many times he denied it. And he was in residence regularly - as he was now.

As she approached, the scale both amazed and appalled her. The main building itself was enormous, surrounded by much smaller buildings that, in most other settings, would be mansions themselves.

Construction on the Palace commenced around 2005 and was 'finished' around ten years later. And then they discovered mould. Sloppy workmanship, a massive multi-level structure with several underground levels coupled with a location next to the ocean and poor ventilation all contributed to mould being found behind the walls in many of the hundreds of rooms in the mansion. So they began tearing it all down again and rebuilding. Literally, billions of roubles of materials and fixtures were tossed into landfill. Still today, it was a veritable construction site. Albeit one they tried to obscure with tradesman accessing through hidden entrances, parking their vehicles out of sight and wearing uniforms designed to colour blend with the structure and help them be invisible.

Years of the daily arrival of teams of workers had made the attitude of security to the uniformed tradesman more and more lax. Providing they had the proper papers and had no phones and no cameras, they were waved through. It was what Ward was counting on. That and the mere mention of mould, given the history of the site and the secret but constantly speculated dire health of their President and primary resident, sent a chill through those that were running years behind schedule to re-build the Palace.

So far, so good. They were approaching the final checkpoint. The papers the Georgians had provided had held up. And their cover as a specialist HVAC team being brought in to determine the extent of the black mould issue in the doomsday bunker under the massive hill near the Black Sea coastline had equally worked. Until now.

Alek was in a heated discussion with the two guards who had come to greet them from the pitched-roofed guardhouse. The previous checkpoints had been a formality. These guys were more engaged and rigorous. The guards looked across at her a couple of times. She desperately hoped they didn't ask her any questions. She had almost no Russian in her repertoire. Ward was in a beige Dupont Hazmat suit with a full mask and respirator. She hadn't yet put the headgear on but was wearing a surgical mask over her face and had tucked her short hair under a netted cap. With the bulky suit and tightly compressed clothing underneath, no one could tell if she was male or female.

She felt sweat slide down the side of her face and under her clothing. Finally, Alek threw his hands in the air and one of the guards gestured to a driveway running down the side of the massive building. Ward quietly expelled the breath she'd been holding. As they slowly drove towards the driveway, she noticed the two armed guards in a small electric buggy fall in behind them.

Quietly, from behind her mask, she asked Alek, 'What's going on - what was that about?'

Looking in his rearview mirror Alek replied, 'The guards require anyone going to the bunker to be escorted. I told them it was hazardous and no one should come without full protection. They insisted. I couldn't push any harder. So we have tweedle dum and tweedle dee coming with us.'

'OK, Alek. You did well. So long as we get inside, we can take care of those two.'

'Really! They have Ak-47 rifles and Vektor nine millimetre pistols, and are wearing body armour. And there are hundreds more of them. We are in clown suits and have mould-detection equipment. But I like your confidence.'

Chapter 187

THE TWO SBP guards from the Presidential Security Service actually proved very useful. So familiar were they with escorting tradespeople and construction workers they basically ignored Alek and Ward and just smoked and argued with each other. They knew their way around the massive building. Alex figured it could have taken them hours to find the bunker entrance on their own. Even with the floor plans she'd reviewed on the drive from the border, she would have been lost within minutes.

Following the guards, Ward and Alek had exited the van and carrying their mould detection equipment, entered on the basement level on foot moving around endless corridors. They passed an ornate gymnasium with draped windows, a massage room, saunas, a spa area and staff quarters. She caught glimpses through open doors of a huge indoor swimming pool in the centre of the basement level, hosting a single, lone swimmer doing laps. At one point, she was sure she saw what looked like a Vegas strip club, including a stripper pole attached to the ceiling.

Finally after passing restaurant scale kitchen prep areas they arrived at a bank of elevators. One of the guards used a swipe card and punched a code into a wall-mounted pad, at which point the elevator lights went on, and an electric hum could be heard. Another reason she was glad they had their escorts. So far the only other person they had seen was the swimmer in the pool.

Chapter 188

THE RUSSIAN PRESIDENT was pacing in his private office. It was a replica of the Presidential office in Moscow. He'd had it intentionally designed and fitted so he could seamlessly work between the two locations. And more importantly, everyone who saw him on a screen or video link would think he was in his official office.

He continued to pace the room, his prominent round forehead beading with perspiration. The rage that had been building within him was now at boiling point. Kallis had single-handedly destroyed his careful plans. Only days ago, he believed he was on track. To progressively reacquire lost Russian states while an American President - his American President - looked the other way. Or, better still, publicly espoused his admiration for his strong Russian counterpart. His legacy would be to re-establish Russia's global influence as the most powerful country in the world. Now Charleston was gone, and his own country was just hours away from having the virus rip through millions of his countrymen. The house of cards he had been building lay scattered at his feet.

But he felt he still had a joker to play. As a student of the American psyche he fervently believed they would not have the courage to respond to a broad based strike. Particularly now with a woman in charge. His generals advised him that the response would be automated. He knew this could be overridden. And the Americans wouldn't have the stomach to allow the nuclear devastation to happen. He'd been thinking about this for years.

He had the Kavkaz-7 nuclear communications system that was part of the Cheget nuclear briefcase pressed to his ear as he waited to be connected to General Andreyevich. He wanted an update on the launch plans. The delays were unacceptable. It must happen sooner. Now. He didn't know exactly how long they had until the virus went live. And he didn't trust the Americans.

The thought of a decimated and diminished Russia was almost too much for him to bear. He would not stand by and allow any other country to take ascension while he failed.

As he gripped the phone more tightly in his frustration at the silence on the other end, there was a single knock on his office door, and then it pushed open. General Pavel Andreyevich, in his green uniform, strode into the room. The President put the phone back into the cradle within the briefcase.

'General Andreyevich - this is a surprise, I thought you were in Moscow.'

'President, I felt I should be with you. We approach the Federation's most important hour.'

The President paused and glared at the General. It conveyed an intensity the General had seen many times. One that looked into the soul of the person. An intensity that had caused many to falter and crumble. Like a circling shark, the President had a sixth sense for fear. And opportunity.

Finally, the President spoke, 'I take it you have favourable news on our improved timetable?'

General Andreyevich, as he had many times before, was aware of the sheer presence of the man he faced. The energy and power radiated. It was impossible to ignore and equally difficult to counter. He had seen many whither under the intensity.

He had come here to look his President in the eye. To gauge whether he was truly committed to this action - this insanity that would inevitably wipe out most of the world. Or had he succumbed to his illness. Had his incredible determination and sheer will been consumed by the medications he was forced to take or the cancer eating his body? Had reality been overpowered, and his inner rage intensified by some hallucinatory state that had infected his President. Whatever it was, he was leading his country and taking the world to annihilation.

As he stood facing the President across the room he realised it really didn't matter. The fact that he had ordered his country to a full and unprovoked nuclear attack - and one that would inevitably be countered in equal measure, showed that the President had crossed the line. And the General had to stop it. This was not the answer. This was an irrational ego gone mad.

He had come here hoping to be able to talk and reason. He and The President had been through so much. Had survived and thrived in the toughest political environment. They were the architects of their own ambition and the ambition they aspired for their country. He had supported his President without equivocation for decades. He, too, wanted his country to rise to the top again. But there had to be a better way than this last minute armageddon. The General would not give up on their shared ambition. But he would also not be a party to this cowardly way out. And this way was suicide. Assured destruction.

Now, in the presence of the President, he could see there would be no talk and no reasoning. Conscious of the protective detail pit-bulls the President had with him at all times - just outside the door, the General's fingers twitched and moved imperceptibly towards the holstered pistol on his hip.

Chapter 189

AS SHE ENTERED the elevators that would take them to the tunnels and ultimately to the bunker, Ward had put the full HAZMAT headgear on. She'd hoped that would ensure the two escorts they had would not notice her features, nor would they try and converse with her. She inventoried the guards' weapons and positioned herself so that she could incapacitate and disarm one of the soldiers and then take out the other. She just needed Alek to stay out of the way.

That would be her last resort. She didn't know what other security was ahead of them, and she'd prefer to keep her private escort for now. But she remained completely on edge and ready to move.

The elevators silently descended into the bowels of the Palace. The two escorts had stopped their chattering when they entered the elevator. What was it about elevators that seemed to require silence from those on board? Ward took the opportunity to map out her next steps. The guards would take them to the bunker. If they couldn't be convinced by the hazardous work to leave Alek and her at that time she would have to take them out and hide their bodies. Mack and the CIA were working on a security breach that would force the Protective Detail to bring the Russian President to the bunker. Ward then had to find a way to kill the President, make it known he was dead so the Russian succession process would kick in, ensure his death was not blamed on America and ideally exfiltrate and get out alive.

Piece of Piss!

At that point she stopped trying to plan ahead. The chances of all that going to plan were zero. In any case, no plan survived first contact. So she'd be winging it. Ward had no way of communicating with Mack, so did not know what the security breach would be, or when it was going to happen. They had simply agreed that it not happen before GMT four pm, giving her at least that time to get into position. She looked at her watch. That was just twelve minutes from now.

The elevator came to a slightly bouncy stop and the doors opened. The two guards moved into the narrow stainless steel tunnel without even looking back to see if their charges were following.

Chapter 190

THE TWO SUBMERSIBLES were parked in about eight feet of water near the shoreline of the Black Sea, ensuring they were out of sight. Mitchell and his team of Seals would need these for their exfil if all went well. If things didn't go well the Dakota would take care of them. Actually, if things didn't go well, it probably wouldn't matter.

The team were now tracking carefully and silently up the beach towards the location of the tunnel entrance. They were still in their Neptunik wetsuits, not wanting to use valuable time and possible discovery to peel them off. Information on the security and fortification of the beach was limited. In fact it was zero. Mitchell was sure there would be automated security to complement the guards of the Security Service covering the grounds and Palace. Although it was unlikely there would be mines given the prospect of small animals setting them off. He and his team were using thermal imaging and had avoided the infrared sensors crisscrossing parts of the beach. He hoped that would be all until they encountered the steel door from the beachside at the tunnel entrance. What lay beyond that was unknown. But he and his team were trained to adapt.

Leading his team, Mitchell silently approached the three-inch-thick steel door. They had to get through this door and into the tunnel and then make their way several hundred feet undetected to the bunker. And they needed to be in position in the bunker prior to the Russian President being brought in. The mission briefing had the security breech happening in about eight minutes. This was going to be tight.

He had one of his platoon carrying a classified prototype of a portable TEC Torch. The TEC torch spat metal vapour at an incredible temperature in excess of five thousand degrees and would literally melt the steel in front of them. Prototype and development versions had burnt through the fuel cells quickly. That problem had been partially solved, and this model had enough to cut a hole through which they could fit. And it worked fast. The Seal with him was an E9 and highly experienced. He bent low to cut the hole as close to the ground as possible to try and hide it from view. Though once they started cutting it would be game on. This thing lit the place up like fireworks. Mitchell kept his M14 pointed just past his teammate in case there were un-friendlies on the other side of the door. He closed his eyes just as the torch engaged. The rest of the platoon had fanned out and ensured no one approached from behind or to their flanks.

His E9 finished cutting and pushed the steel into the tunnel with a thud as it hit the cement floor. That was the only noise. Mitchell hoped the silence from the other side was good news and not an ambush in waiting. Taking a breath he bent low to look into the gap. The tunnel was stainless steel with low-recessed lighting. He could see about 50 metres ahead before it started to pitch upwards. It looked quiet and empty. Deserted. He didn't think it would stay that way. They needed to move quickly now. It was inevitable the torchlight and noise had generated some interest.

He called his team forward and held back to cover until the last man was through the gap. He urged the men into a crouched run up the corridor. From the blueprints the CIA had acquired it was at least a couple of hundred metres to the bunker. He wasn't sure if his comms would work inside the tunnel or the bunker so he triggered the mike three times in rapid succession. The signal to the Dakota to initiate the threat that would force the Russian President to his bunker. If they didn't get the signal they would initiate anyway in....six minutes.

Chapter 191

GENERAL PAVEL ANDREYEVICH started to inch his right hand towards the clipped holster. Just as he reached the pistol and was about to unclip the leather holster, a massive explosion erupted somewhere in the Palace. The noise was incredible, and the whole structure seemed to shudder. Plaster and dust filled the air. His nerves already on edge the General literally jumped in the air. Almost instantly the large dual doors were thrust open, and several members of the President's detail swept in. Two men grabbed the President under his arms and propelled him towards the door they'd just come through. The General was pushed by strong hands and then swept along with them as they fast marched almost at a run down long corridors.

Andreyevich had men all around him as they rushed towards a single elevator. As he was pushed he was trying to make sense of what had happened. He shouted questions at a couple of the guards, but there was no response. The President said nothing as he was half carried and half pushed down the corridor. His tight expression conveying both anger and frustration. The elevator door was standing open, and the General, along with the President and six guards, entered, and the steel doors closed behind them.

Chapter 192

THE AMERICAN PRESIDENT was with her core team in the Situation Room - Chief of Staff Tully Carina, Director Kristen Thomas, Defense Secretary Blake and Joint Chief of Staff Admiral Jock Campbell. They were in an informal u shape around one end of the large table. All looking at the matrix of screens on the wall. The screens were showing a live feed from the chest mounted camera of one of the men in Seal Team Seven. There was no sound with the images. Anders was unsure if it had been muted or wasn't available. It made the scenes she saw both surreal and confusing without the context.

To fill the void of the missing audio, Admiral Campbell offered commentary. 'The team is now moving as quickly up the tunnel as possible towards the bunker. Time is critical. It is expected they will meet resistance before reaching the entrance.'

As he spoke, the image on the screens before them shook violently, and dust clouded the vision. The camera seemed to hit the concrete floor.

'What just happened?' exclaimed Tully Carina. Campbell didn't immediately respond, but Kristen Thomas spoke. 'USS South Dakota launched a Tomahawk missile at the palace and it just detonated.'

Jock Campbell then took over, 'The Security Service will immediately move the President to the bunker.'

'Will Team Seven get there in time?' asked Defense Secretary Blake.

As he spoke, the camera image started to move again. The soldier it was attached to had pushed himself off the ground and started running at a full sprint up the tunnel.

Chapter 193

AS SOON AS THE ground started to tremble in the underground tunnel, Alex Ward was moving. Instinctively, she realised this was the threat to the Russian President the CIA will have initiated to flush him to the bunker. But they were early. Her mental clock told her it was not due for several minutes. She put these flashing thoughts aside as she closed the gap to the Russian guard in front of her and to the right. Despite the cumbersome hazmat suit she moved with lethal speed. Ward reached forward to the holstered MP-443 Grach sidearm and twisted the snap clip just as the full effect of the explosion hit. The explosion startled both guards, they hesitated briefly and then their training kicked in and they simultaneously reached for their weapons. All too late, Ward already had the pistol in her hand and clicked off the safety, drew it up to the back of the first guard's head and fired once at point-blank range. She then sighted the guard on the left as he was turning towards her and fired twice. The first shot entered through the upper jaw and a pink mist simultaneously appeared at the back of his head, the second hit under his chin as his head snapped backwards. There was very little of his skull left at such close range.

'Holy shit!' cried Alek in English as both guards hit the ground.

'Fucking Washington has gone early.' said Ward. She grabbed the AK-74M rifle that was slung around the first guard and started patting him down, looking for ammunition and other weapons.

'Alek, grab the pistol and the AK and any ammo you can find from that other guy'. Ward knew the Russian President would be moved immediately. They were now just seconds in front of them. She needed to move these dead guards before they came down the elevator or the protective detail would never continue to the bunker.

'Alek, get that guy and move.'

Ward grabbed the tactical harness on the first dead guards chest and started to drag him as fast as she could down the tunnel, taking care not to leave any more blood smears as she went.

Chapter 194

EXITING THE ELEVATOR fifty metres underground, The Russian President was forcibly propelled down the lengthy tunnel and firmly pushed into the large open room of the bunker. As he was released from the hands of the two guards, he straightened, turned, and pulled his jacket down. He paused, drawing his breath whilst he eyeballed each of the guards,

'Leave me.' he commanded. There was no point in asking the security service what was going on. They would as yet have no information. He wanted the chamber emptied so he could find out what had happened. The commander of the protective detail started to protest, insisting that they stay with the President. He glared at the commander and the message was received.

As the security service guards left to wait in the tunnel, General Andreyevich was also unceremoniously pushed into the room. Without a word, the two guards that had escorted him left the chamber, and the hydraulic steel door was closed. The room was unnaturally silent around the two men, save for the hum of the HVAC systems feeding and cleaning the air. The General felt his ears and sinuses compress as the impenetrable and soundproofed bunker was sealed and pressurised.

Ever paranoid, The President wondered if the arrival of his Defense Minister at the palace just minutes ago and the almost simultaneous attack were more than a coincidence.

He considered this for a few short seconds and decided they were not - The General would not put himself in harm's way given the lack of precision of such an attack. His thoughts moved on. The Palace was closer to the border than Moscow. Fucking Ukrainians, he figured. He looked again at the General. Perhaps it would be fortuitous to have his Defense Minister with him. It will expedite their retaliation.

Chapter 195

THE SMALL BATHROOM in the doomsday bunker was located between the main chamber and the sleeping quarters of the President and was now crammed with Ward, Alek and the two dead guards. They'd only just closed the bathroom door when Ward heard the guards enter the chamber. It sounded like half the Russian army had come in. There were multiple bodies moving around and lots of discussion in Russian. Then it went completely quiet. She had no idea who was in the bunker, where they were or what they were doing. If there were more than a couple of armed guards out there this would be a very short fight.

She looked across at Alek, trying to convey that she was about to move. His eyes were bulging, and sweat was pouring down his face under his visor. She hoped he didn't accidentally shoot her in the back when the action started.

Ward checked her weapons to confirm they were ready to go.

Chapter 196

DIRECTOR KRISTEN THOMAS sat silently, staring at the equally silent video monitors in the Situation Room. The only giveaway to the stress she was feeling was the tight grip she had on the cardinal red Mont Verde pen her father had given her when she joined the CIA. She had not had any contact from Ward since they had commenced their approach to the palace some hours ago. She was now watching the live feed from the chest-mounted camera on Petty Officer Jake Reynolds as he ran up the sloping steel tunnel towards the bunker with his team. The tunnel was offset to the right of the bunker, and she could vaguely make out a kink on the left, ahead of the seal team. Thomas held her breath as, at full sprint, Reynolds hit the corner and continued along the long, dimly lit, empty steel tunnel.

Suddenly, there was another bend in the tunnel ahead. They must be close to where it met the bunker.

Chapter 197

SEAL COMMANDER HAWKE Mitchell had taken point as they sprinted up the tunnel. It was now a race against time as the missile strike on the palace moments ago would have sent the Russian Security Service into immediate action. There was no time for subtle and cautious advance. They had to get to the bunker and find somewhere to hide before they got their President inside and closed the doors.

The tunnel was longer than they had expected. Their briefing drawings had it much shorter than this. They were now running past an inactive moving walkway - no doubt designed to take the President back the way they had just come to an exfil at the beach as quickly as possible. Their progress was hampered by the blackout wetsuits, vests and weapons.

Seconds ago, they had rounded a hard left bend, and Mitchell had galvanised himself for what lay beyond. Fortunately, it had been clear. But now they approached another curve in the tunnel, and he wasn't willing to chance his luck twice. They must be nearing the bunker. He signalled for the team to slow down and approach silently. Fanning out and pushing themselves into the sides of the tunnel, the team crouched with their M4s raised and ready and crept forward. Mitchell maintained point and pushed hard against the left wall as the tunnel curved that way.

He raised his first for the team to stop. Unfortunately, they didn't have a flexible fibre optic camera or borescope with them, so he needed to do this old school. He took a quick turkey peak around the bend and saw maybe six or eight guards in the tunnel and the massive steel door was being secured in position. He had to move. Before that door was shut tight. He gave another hand signal to his team, grabbed a flash-bang from his vest, pulled the pin, and tossed it around the corner. As soon as it exploded, Mitchell burst from his crouch and sprinted into the tunnel. Team members followed him on the right wall and in a wedge formation in the middle of the tunnel. Visibility was hopeless in the aftermath of the frag, so he relied on the mental snapshot and fired three round bursts continually to positions guards had been in seconds ago. The sound of his gunfire and that of his team was deafening off the steel walls. He couldn't tell if the enemy was shooting back. From his peripheral, he saw one of his team members go down. That answered that question. Still firing, he strained to look through the smoke from the grenade, searching for targets. In the still of the tunnel, the smoke hung in the air. He caught movement to the right and fired that way. Quickly, he was on top of the guards. Bodies were strewn across the entrance to the bunker. It was a bloodbath. There was no one left standing. There were eight guards. All down. These guards had not been expecting them. It was an ambush. He and his LT quickly checked each body for a pulse whilst the men covered them and their six. None of them were alive.

'Anyone hit'? asked Mitchell.

'Me Hawk.' CSO Ryan responded.

'How bad?'

'Took a ricochet off the wall and into my left leg. It's not bad. I'm good to go.'

'Jensen, look after Ryan. Get compression on that leg. Get him mobile.'

Quickly, Mitchell approached the steel door to the bunker. It looked like it was in position. He tried to push the thick door and grabbed the handle. He shook the handle. Pushed as hard as he could against the door. Pushed the handle the other way. Knowing the futility, he looked around for any mechanism to unlock it.

His team watched his efforts. Then saw him hammer his fists into the unyielding door. Locked tight. At this point, they knew it would only open from the inside. They were too late. He'd failed. The Russian President was locked up tight and safe.

Hawk looked into the camera on Reynolds's chest and shook his head.

Chapter 198

'FUCK!' ADMIRAL JOCK Campbell swore. He had enormous confidence in the men who made up the special operations units across the military. And the Seal Teams were as good as they got. But this mission had been hammered together without time for proper intel or preparation. And definitely, no time to plan or rehearse. It was a Hail Mary attempt to stop a rogue from going full rogue.

And it had failed. Despite their blind, optimistic hope, he realised it had been almost destined to fail. He prayed for the men in that tunnel as he turned his attention to the small group of people in the Situation Room.

'What did that signal from Commander Mitchell indicate Admiral?' asked President Anders, with a sickening dread in her stomach.

'It means they were too late. The Russian leader beat them to the bunker and is now inside.'

'Can they get that door open or cut through it with that torch?'

'No, ma'am. That door is fifteen inches thick. Air-tight, soundproof, bombproof. Even Tomahawks will be challenged to work through all that rock and steel.'

Campbell looked around at the desperate faces. 'We failed. I'm sorry.'

The President answered straight back, 'Do not apologise Admiral. Everyone is putting in a superhuman effort. Can the Russian President communicate from that bunker? Can he authorise retaliation when our EMPs are launched?'

Kristen Thomas picked up this question, 'He can Madame President. The plans we have for that bunker indicate enough copper wire and fibre optic cable to ensure uninterrupted high-speed communication. He's fully connected. And he has the Cheget suitcase.'

Kristen looked at Campbell, 'Admiral, I suggest re-tasking the seal team to try to sabotage the tunnel - the ventilation and communications systems. Or even an extreme action to destroy the tunnel completely. It could stop or at least frustrate their ability to act. We need to prepare for Caesar Alternate and make ready a missile strike on the palace. '

'Agreed.' Campbell picked up his secure line to start issuing orders.

Kristen Thomas took the opportunity to type out a message to Brendt and Mack, who were still holed up and searching for information on the island off New Zealand, requesting with forlorn hope that they try to hack the communications at the Palace and shut it down remotely. She already had digital specialists at Langley doing the same. Another world class hacker couldn't hurt!

While she would try anything and everything, Kristen Thomas was a realist. This was looking incredibly dire.

Chapter 199

THE TWO MEN inside the bunker were oblivious to the commotion outside. The thick steel door and re-enforced stone walls made it impervious to sound.

'Our country is under attack, Pavel Andreyevich.' The Russian President said forcefully. The rage that was never far from the surface was visibly rippling through him. He had barely moved from the entry to the bunker where he and the General had been deposited.

'Yes, Comrade President.' Andreyevich had no idea what had hit the palace nor who was responsible. He intended to find out as soon as he could. But at this point, it was prudent to agree with his furious commander.

The President continued, 'I am sure it is the fucking Ukrainians. With missiles supplied by the Americans. They will know I am here. We must retaliate. Immediately and with extreme force. They have drawn first blood. Enough is enough. We will turn the American cities to rubble.'

Andreyevich was aware that sitting on the ground between them was the President's Cheget - the Kremlin Satchel - the Russian equivalent of the nuclear football. One of the protective detail will have been tasked with ensuring it remained with their leader. And it would now be connected through the communications within the bunker. His eyes were drawn to it.

'I agree Pavel.' said the President, following his gaze.

General Pavel Andreyevich realised this was the moment. A moment he had never before contemplated. He had served this man loyally. He loved his President and believed in what he wanted to do for Russia. But this was the tipping point. His President, so filled with rage and sickness and so determined to restore Russia to its former glory, also misunderstood and underestimated their enemies. He had surrounded himself with those who only ever agreed with him. And anyone that spoke or acted against him tended to disappear. Permanently. As a consequence, his vision and actions became more extreme and flawed over time. He had the myopia of both a dictator and a narcissist.

But Andreyevich thought he at least had to try one last time to persuade his leader, 'Mr President, if we launch a tactical nuclear missile at Kyiv or towards the United States, the Americans will then retaliate. They will know the source of the launch. Despite the attack on us today they will see this as unacceptable and respond immediately. This will escalate to an inevitable nuclear war. Our forces will, in turn, respond to the American launch.' He paused as he looked at his friend and leader and tried to understand if his words were having an impact. 'Let us - let me - find another way to respond to this attack and deal with our enemies.'

'Nonsense Pavel, the Americans will not dare. They are the puppet masters of Kyiv. Cowards operating through others. They do not dare to attack us directly. How many times have their threatening words proven to be empty and worthless statements from a quivering bully?' The President, in turn, looked at Andreyevich now. 'I wonder, Pavel, if you have lost your nerve? Perhaps age has taken the fight from you. Tell me - are you still with me, Pavel, or should I look for a younger and more vigorous General?'

Andreyevich had stopped listening. He knew the President was trying to goad him. And he knew how this would play out. The explosion at the palace would be seen by the President as an attack. Already mobilising for a preemptive strike this would only serve to galvanise his resolve to launch at the West. Unlike his President, Andreyevich had no doubt the US and NATO would retaliate. And so the world would very quickly have hundreds of nuclear missiles hurtling towards each other, intent on destroying their respective targets. The General felt he was looking over a precipice and the void below was a burning hell.

As his President continued to talk, Andreyevich held his gaze and used his left hand to gesture to the Cheget to distract the President, while his right hand moved purposely to the holster on his hip.

Chapter 200

ALEX WARD COULD hear muffled Russian voices on the other side of the bathroom door. It was pitch dark in the windowless bathroom, and she was concerned that if she or Alek moved or made a sound, those outside would be alerted to their presence, and this game would be over. She had surprise and speed as her only real advantage. Ward had no idea how many people or guards were out there. She would come out hot. Anyone she saw would be a target. Ward had no way to tell Alek what she was about to do, nor to instruct him on how to help. Despite the dark, she closed her eyes to visualise the layout of the room they had rushed through earlier and how she would move. Ward grabbed the bathroom door handle with her left hand and prepared to apply pressure. Her right hand held the polymer grip of the AK-74 she'd acquired. Go time. She pushed down on the handle and burst into the room just as a single loud, unsuppressed shot from a handgun was fired on the other side of the door.

Chapter 201

GENERAL PAVEL ANDREYEVICH looked at the muzzle smoke drifting from the barrel of his Nagant M1895 Revolver. A gift from his late father on entering the service, and whilst regarded as a ceremonial weapon, he had always ensured it was in perfect working order. And at this range, it was destructive. His eyes were out of focus as he stared at the gun in his hand, his mind swirling with the implications of what he had just done. He was vaguely aware of the President lying on the ground a few meters away.

So distracted was he that he didn't hear or notice the bathroom door opening and a figure in a Hazmat suit coming into the room. The figure was looking at him through the sights of an AK-74 and shouting at him to get on the floor. Gradually, his senses started to restore, and his eyes slowly focussed. Who was this person yelling at him in English.....?

'Drop the gun. Drop the gun. Get on the floor,' continued Ward as she moved out of the bathroom into the main chamber, simultaneously focussed on the uniformed man holding the revolver whilst scanning for other threats. Having been prepared for a firefight, Ward could see the room was empty save for one man holding a gun down by his side and another form on the ground. She continued to swivel across the entire space, hyped on adrenalin and wanting to ensure there were definitely no more targets.

Despite what had obviously happened, the uniformed man did not present as a threat. He seemed out of it. His eyes gradually turned towards her and focussed. He looked at the gun in his hand and then dropped it to the floor. Still looking through the AK's sights, she cleared the main bunker chamber and confirmed the galley-style kitchen was also empty. She went to the closed steel door and checked it was secure. Only then did she check for a pulse on the man on the ground. She needn't have bothered, the third eye in the middle of the forehead of one of the most famous faces on the planet was a giveaway.

'Alek, pick up that gun from the floor will you?'

Ward took stock of the situation. She looked properly at the man in uniform and immediately recognised him as Russian Defense Minister General Pavel Andreyevich. His eyes were now clear and his expression neutral as he watched Ward move around the room.

'CIA?' he asked

Ward just looked at him and then powered up her encrypted phone. She removed her headgear while waiting for the for the signal to connect and then tapped the number for Kristen Thomas.

Chapter 202

STILL AT THE main operations table in the Situation Room, Kristen had been working feverishly with Admiral Campbell to coordinate the missile strike that would ensure the death of the Russian President and the demolition of the communications systems at the bunker. And she had her own team trying to compromise the Russian system remotely. Brendt had been making slow progress, and they needed to shut comms down before any instruction for military action could be issued. The Admiral had also instructed Seal Team 7 to set charges to try and blow the steel door. It was possibly all in vain. The Russian Nuclear Briefcase was likely to be well-protected and completely autonomous. But desperate times....

The main screen in the Situation Room was still taking the chest-mounted video feed and Kristen was half watching the grainy images of Hawke Mitchell instructing his team to clear the tunnel in readiness for the detonation when her secure phone rang.

After listening for a moment, Kristen covered the mouthpiece and looked at Campbell. 'Stand the team down Admiral. And stand down the Dakota. Caesar is down. I repeat, Caesar is down.'

Despite the shock of the news, his ingrained training and military discipline saw the Admiral respond immediately and issued instructions to the submarine captain and to Commander Nathan Mitchell, who in turn relayed the orders to his team.

Shell-shocked figures in the Situation Room all looked at the CIA Director as she continued her discreet conversation. Just moments ago, they had all considered the attempt on the life of the Russian President a complete failure. To a person, they were utterly exhausted. And had each been quietly contemplating the horror that was coming.

President Anders tried to interrupt Kristen, 'Director, what has happened? Are you saying the Russian President is dead? Director Thomas..'

Unfazed, Kristen held up a finger to the President as she continued to listen to Ward.

Ward was not one to trust any communications - encrypted or otherwise. Despite the assurances from the propeller heads at the CIA. But the need to be clear in this situation took priority..

'Boss, I have Russian Defense Minister General Pavel Andreyevich in the bunker. We need to manage our message here to ensure we don't light a new fire. And we need to get the right people in Moscow properly focussed. I suggest we hide Cyclops because that might become very distracting. The General seems to have gained a broader perspective. In fact, it was he who removed the blockage. I think working with the General is an opportunity we should not pass up.'

Kristen was listening intently, and she understood. The back half of the message was unexpected. Kristen had assumed Ward had killed the Russian President. But the comment about removing the blockage indicated Andreyevich had, in fact, assassinated his own leader. If they handled this the right way, that would be even better. He'd clearly decided his President was out of control. And he needed to be stopped. It was a drastic step. But in the dictatorship that Russia really was, this was one way leadership changes happened.

Kristen figured the General had the proper authority to communicate with Russian leadership and get them aligned with the real global threat. They needed the launch build-up to be stopped. And then re-directed as part of the worldwide EMP initiative. Russian leadership - particularly the Russian Prime Minister, would need trusted voices to be convinced.

But Ward was right - if Russian security found their President shot dead and a US operative standing next to the body, they would have an international incident - and World War 3 would be back on again. Kristen decided she had to trust their comms security more than Ward did to resolve this situation quickly.

'Seal Team 7 is outside the steel doors. They had the same orders that you did. They don't know you're there. Find a way to get them inside. They can exfil...Cyclops... they are led by Commander Nathan Mitchell. You then need to work with Andreyevich to re-direct the nuclear strike and get Russia on the EMP program. We can assist. I've met the General several times, as has Admiral Campbell. We have less than six hours now before the Kallis Virus goes live. Once the situation there is secure, I'll talk to the General.'

Chapter 203

WARD ENDED THE call. She didn't love such direct language over communications, secure or not. But she understood the need. So, Seal Team 7 was deployed on the same mission she had. A redundancy. Or perhaps she was the redundancy. It turned out they were both redundant, and a lone and concerned Russian Minister had done their job for them. She turned to face the General now.

'Minister Andreyevich, we have very little time, so I will get to the point. I work for the US government. I was tasked to remove your President so that your country and your allies immediately cease the intended nuclear launch and align with the rest of the world to coordinate the EMP protocol. We believe an EMP strike is our only hope to stop the Kallis virus.'

Ward paused to see if the General wanted to speak. He remained impassive and looked at her to continue. 'General, we believed it crucial to remove your President.' Ward paused and looked down at the body lying inert between them. 'It seems you had similar concerns...'

About to continue, Andreyevich interrupted Ward, 'An American came here to kill the Russian President? Even worse, they sent a woman! You will be arrested and shot.'

He started to move to the phones on the desk. 'Ahh, Pavel - you're missing the point here. Firstly, YOU shot the President - not me - though, to be honest, I would have done so gladly - you saved me the trouble. And secondly, I'm the only one now with a gun here...'

Andreyevich stopped and turned to look at Ward, 'I have done what needed to be done. My President was a great man but obsessed with his legacy. His obsession was about to cost us everything. Kill me if you must.'

While the General was talking, Ward started stripping the hazmat suit, 'General, we are on the same side here. We want to work with Russia to stop the virus. Not start a war. It is actually fortunate you are here. You can talk to your Prime Minister, and you, and he can work with us to save as many people from the virus as possible.'

'And what of my President? How will this be explained? I had intended to use a second bullet on myself, and then you came out that door. I have killed our leader. It is reasonable to say I will not be in my position much longer.'

'I agree. A President with a bullet hole in his head is not a good look. Show me how to open these doors. And we'll take care of the......former President and then get to work.'

'Are you mad? His personal security detail are on the other side of those doors. They see the body, and you and your friend will not last five seconds.'

'General, it's time to start trusting me...'

Chapter 204

US PRESIDENT MICHELLE Anders was back in the Oval Office getting her make-up and hair attended in preparation for another address to the nation. It had been just hours since the last one. It felt like a lifetime. She felt like she'd lived years since she'd been elevated to the top job.

The roller coaster of the last few days and the intensity of the last few hours had drained her. She couldn't remember when she had last properly slept or eaten. It had been before she was sworn in. Her body was aching, and her hands carried a visible tremor from exhaustion. Her mind had started to dip in and out of focus. She wondered if she could spare an hour of sleep after this address and before the countdown to the EMP operation properly commenced, or she may stop functioning altogether.

The make-up artist finished her work. Anders didn't dare look in the mirror that was offered. She figured a miracle to remove the bags under her eyes, and the fatigue in her skin had not been performed. Sitting behind the President's desk, she looked at the polished, almost reflective, aged hardwood of the cleared surface. She visualised those who had sat here before her - all men - to conduct state business and deliver some of their most important speeches. Well, none of those previous speeches held a candle to what she now had to tell her people.

Tully materialised by her side. 'Thirty seconds, Madame President. Are you ready?'

Anders looked up at her friend and offered a partial smile, 'None of us can be vaguely ready for what is about to happen.' Anders gave her a wan look and then visibly steeled herself, 'OK, let's do this.'

The US President drew a deep breath and put her palms flat on the surface. She looked into the camera and saw the director progressively close three fingers to count her in.

'Good Morning America. And to the citizens of the world.' Anders paused very briefly. She and her team had considered whether they should address the death of the Russian President. They had quickly agreed it would not be appropriate. The message today must be singular and focused. 'Today I bring you devastating news. The deadly virus developed by Dr Hanse Kallis and delivered through the tens of millions of syringes his companies produced is scheduled to become active in our bodies in a matter of hours.

'The virus is incredibly destructive. We have seen the effects of what we now know as the Kallis virus on those unfortunate enough to have been infected early. We know the mortality rate once infected approaches ninety percent. And we have neither a cure nor a treatment.

'It is an abhorrent action from the sick mind of one individual. We have worked tirelessly over the last few days to double-check and confirm that the threat is real. And it is. This one person took advantage of the panic and confusion surrounding the global pandemic to realise his incompressible plan to reduce the world's population.

'We trusted this person and his companies to act in good faith to deliver the vaccination for COVID. And now our bodies carry the treachery of his deceit.

'As we face the unthinkable, we cannot allow ourselves to give up - either through the inertia of trying to understand what is happening or through emotional and physical outbursts of failure and frustration. We must work and fight and find a way.'

Anders paused and looked hard into the camera. She knew that providing some of the context - some of what they knew would help people cope and trust the action she was about to order. 'Allow me to give you some brief chronology. It seems Dr Kallis identified or invented this new and deadly virus some time ago, and when COVID spread around the world, he mobilised his companies to take advantage of the opportunity. The first release of the virus was through infected Kallis-produced syringes. It lay dormant in the fat cells of the people infected for some time and then, after a period of time, released and very quickly killed almost all of those people. Many of you have witnessed or been directly affected by this first phase of the virus over the last few weeks.

'Unfortunately, I say 'first release' intentionally as there is a second virus phase. The second phase of the virus is the one most of us are likely to be infected with. Dr Kallis, through his network of pharmaceutical companies, was able to leapfrog the rest of the medical world and perfect the use of microbiological robotics. This technology was being pursued by many R&D teams as a new frontier in medical science. This area of medicine and robotics is best known as nano-robotics. The robots are smaller than the naked eye can see - almost at the cellular level.

'I won't labour the science - I know this sounds like the stuff of Hollywood. However, nano-robotics are at the very cutting edge of molecular technology. Kallis managed to scale the technology and placed the virus in these nano-bots and, in turn, delivered these in his syringes. The nano-bots are programmed to release his deadly virus simultaneously into all host bodies.'

Again, Anders paused. She kept her palms flat on the desk, concerned that if she moved them, her shaking would be noticeable. 'The companies Kallis controlled were responsible for tens of millions of the syringes used in the United States to deliver the COVID vaccine. And many hundreds of millions around the world. The abhorrent implication is that tens of millions of Americans and hundreds of millions more now carry the Kallis virus.

'So - and this is the crucial part. As I said, the nano-bots have been programmed to release the virus simultaneously. In other words, the Kallis virus will go live in every infected person around the globe at the same time. Millions of people - in fact, billions of people will have the virus released into their bodies at once.

'And the timing for this simultaneous release is very soon - in just hours..

'If it is allowed to happen, the release of the virus will be devastating beyond what we can imagine. The simultaneous release planned by Dr Kallis was intended to deliver the maximum possible damage. Minimising the time medical teams and authorities would have to develop any treatment or cure. And overwhelming emergency services and hospitals to prevent effective treatment. His plan was to deliver such scale and such chaos as to ensure most of the people on the planet would be wiped out.'

President Anders shuddered involuntarily as she spoke these words. She still grappled with whether this could possibly be real. 'I should tell you now that Dr Kallis is dead. He died at his own hand. And was found washed up on the shores of an island in the South Pacific. He took any forlorn hope that he may have a cure or a vaccine or a way to stop the release of his virus with him.

'Dr Kallis rationalised this inhumane action, believing that the progressive and accelerating environmental destruction of our planet could only be stopped and reversed by removing the most destructive force - us - its people. Kallis' stated intent is to reduce the global population from eight billion to one billion. A level he believed to be both manageable for the planet and sustainable.'

President Anders and her small trusted cohort had debated as to how forthright and graphic she should be in this address. However, given how extreme their response was going to be, they felt being open and direct was the only way people would be galvanised to properly react.

Anders continued, 'Our best estimates are that he has likely infected enough people to both directly and indirectly achieve this level of genocide.'

Anders' focus and intensity seemed to elevate and carried down the lens of the camera. 'Let me repeat that, though I probably don't need to. We believe the direct infections across the globe from Kallis syringes run into the billions. Kallis companies have been the single largest supplier of hypodermics throughout the COVID-19 vaccination response. Coupled with secondary infections and the devastating effect of so many dead, the numbers are impossible to properly comprehend.' She hesitated again as if trying once again to comprehend this herself.

'People of America and the world, I implore you to listen to me carefully. We believe the nano-bots will release the virus in just a few hours. We also believe we can stop them.'

Chapter 205

IN THE BUNKER deep beneath the Presidential Palace near Gelendzhik, Alex Ward had spent the hours since the death of the President liaising between Langley and the Seal team to extract the body back to the coastline where the tactical submersibles had been hidden on the ocean floor. And to construct a story that would explain the disappearance of the President and the need to listen to the newly elevated General. The body had been taken with the Seals back to the Dakota and would be put on ice. They were yet to decide what to do with it. Ward favoured loading a torpedo bay and firing it into the depths of the Black Sea.

She had contemplated returning with the Seal team and making a slow trip home on the Dakota, but her value to Kristen and President Anders on the ground and working with the new Russian leadership was too great. Having a trusted and quite lethal set of eyes and ears in Russia may, in fact, prove invaluable.

Returning to the bunker, she thought the General might have locked her out. But the steel doors remained wide open. The bodies of the Russian security team lay where they had fallen in the tunnel near the bunker entrance. He had ordered that no one come near the bunker. And he'd been on various phones ever since. Working with the Prime Minister and his military leaders to convince them of their President's death and to systematically rescind the orders issued by \the fallen President. And to coordinate with the United States and countries across the globe to deal with the Kallis threat and coordinate the EMP launch - which itself would require a high-altitude nuclear strike. Under normal circumstances it would be a lot to work through and the layered cogs of the socialist government would turn slowly. But with a country moving to an unprecedented war footing and a trojan horse killer virus about to be released into the arms of millions of Russians, these were not normal times and the hierarchy of Russia came into line.

While the General continued working the phones and shouting in Russian at whoever was on the other end, Ward had tapped into the US Presidential broadcast on her secure tablet. Her encrypted phone rang; she looked at the number on the screen, 'How is it in Washington, Boss?'

Kristen Thomas had briefly stepped away to check in with her agent, 'Whatever it has been in the past, it is about to go stratospheric. As is the entire country. And the rest of the world. Are you catching the address from the President?'

'I am. If I hadn't witnessed some of this firsthand, I'm not sure I could comprehend what she is telling the world. Or how to deal with it. Boss, any idea how I'm getting home?'

Kristen spoke quietly down the line, an almost fatalistic tone in her voice, 'In times of crisis, we see the best and the worst. I think we are going to see a lot of the latter in the next few hours and days. I need to get back to the Oval Office. Alex, where you are is as safe as anywhere right now. And I might need you. Stay there.'

Chapter 206

PRESIDENT ANDERS HAD increased the intensity in her voice, intent to convey and implore her country and all countries to respond as they needed to this threat, 'Unfortunately, the response to the virus will have massive consequences. We believe we can shut down the nano-bots before they go active. The only way we believe this can be done is through a large scale and globally coordinated series of electromagnetic pulses.'

As Anders continued her address, the Oval Office was brimming with people, and none were making a sound.

'An electromagnetic pulse or EMP is a short and intense burst of electromagnetic energy. It will effectively short-circuit any electronic device or signal in its path. It will not harm people, but it should render the robotics completely disabled.' The President paused to let that information hang in the air. After a while she continued, 'I said earlier the idea of nano-bots carrying a virus in the bloodstream of billions of people is the stuff of Hollywood. And the way to disable these tiny robots is similarly the stuff of science fiction.'

Anders changed her delivery slightly, trying to implore her country to rally, 'I know many of you won't believe this is happening or just won't want to believe it. Alternative news stories are running across platforms almost unchecked. And conspiracy theories are rampant. I appreciate the conspiracies are easier to digest and to rationalise than the reality I'm presenting. But that is all they are. Think about your own families, your own neighborhoods and your own communities. Look at the images flooding our most credible and reliable news sources. This virus has already touched all of us. It is not fake news. It is not a conspiracy. And we have to act. Now.

'We are working with every country across the globe. Some have Electro Magenetic technology, but many do not - particularly not at the scale needed. The United States, our allies and others will consolidate our resources to cover as much of the globe and the global population as possible.

'The electro magnetic pulse can be delivered through nuclear and non-nuclear devices. We will be deploying both to achieve the coverage required. Again, I repeat, our response will be to blanket the planet with electromagnetic pulses from both nuclear and non-nuclear devices.' It flashed again in Anders's mind she would be the first President to deploy nuclear weapons on her own country.

'Nuclear detonations triggering the electromagnetic response will be set off in the upper atmosphere. This is intended to both maximise the reach and impact of the EMP and to limit any fallout of a nuclear explosion.

'We are confident that EMPs delivered at this scale will disable the infected robotics dormant in the bodies of most of us. And in so doing render the virus destroyed.' President Michelle Anders realised she had just informed her country that she had authorised a nuclear launch. On themselves.

'Implausible as it is, that's the good news. At least as good as it gets. To sit here today, look into this camera and inform America and the world that we are about to detonate nuclear missiles was, until just hours ago, unimaginable. But it is the only way. Kallis left no alternative and no time.

'So, we need to get prepared. These EMPs do not discriminate. They cannot be targeted. They will affect every electronic device in their path. In some limited circumstances, electronics are insulated and protected against the effects of EMP. However, this is rare. In a nutshell, the electromagnetic pulse that will disable the bots that carry the virus will also disable everything. Everything.

'The implication of disabling almost every electronic circuit and device in our country and across the world is enormous. We don't have time to go into the details - but consider our lives without power, without the internet, without running water and without transportation. It affects everything. But it is the only way to save the lives of billions. And we are running out of time.'

Chapter 207

ANDERS KNEW HER address would be causing confusion, all sorts of uncertainty, and panic. It was too much for most - in fact, anyone, to properly comprehend. But she felt she had no alternative. Because what she needed the country and the planet to do to have a chance at survival required some explanation.

'The United States and every other country in the world will activate a synchronised EMP detonation program in a little under four hours. Before this, in around one hour we will begin turning everything off. Let me say that again, everything is going to be turned off. In some parts of the economy, this has already commenced. We want to ensure all planes and public transport are properly secured on the ground or in stations. For the rest of the economy, we will progressively go dark. This includes power, water supply, the internet and all transportation.

'Turning off anything that is powered or has circuitry is the best - the only way to try and protect it against the Electro Magnetic Pulse. We are very aware of the implications this action will have. To say it will be disruptive is an understatement. There will be pandemonium. In hospitals, on the roads and in public and private locations everywhere.'

Anders and her team had decided not to tell the world they had no idea what would happen when they tried to turn everything back on...'I repeat, the systematic and complete shutdown will commence in an hour. So, here is what I am asking each of us to do - it is as simple as two things:

'Firstly, turn everything off. This is the best way to protect anything powered or with circuitry. Turn it off. At the source. This means shutting down your household, office or business at the circuit box. Disconnect or remove batteries. As soon as possible. Doing it now would be ideal - as soon as this address concludes. But absolutely within the next two hours. Whatever you have on or leave on when we release the EMPs will be rendered useless.

'And secondly, help each other. Be with your family. Be with your friends. Support each other. Now is the time. We are all brothers, and we are all sisters.

'That is all I have. Good luck to you all. And God Bless America. And Gold Bless this planet.'

TV and digital screens in all forms around the United States and around the world now went to a pre-organised information image that provided simple instructions on how to properly shut down everything that was powered.

Chapter 208

AT THE BACK of the Oval Office stood Kristen Thomas. She had wanted to stay rather than return to Langley. To show her support for the new President in an unprecedented time. And if she was honest, to witness history. Minutes before the address, she had called home, spoken to her husband, and had him wake their teenagers. She had told them to stay at home. To fill the bath tub. To watch the address and to then shut everything down. She would not be home prior to the EMP launch.

As she listened to the President's address, her mind wandered. From her own family preparing in their home in Georgetown to images of the widespread public uncertainty and pandemonium that she imagined was now being unleashed, to the protocols her agency was currently running through.

With the address from President Anders now complete, TV stations were running frenzied and constant news services reinforcing and interpreting the information the President had provided.

Kristen was tapping on her secure agency phone as she hurriedly moved through the White House back to the Situation Room. There was no time to get to her office in Langley. The Situation Room provided a secure and quiet location to direct her team on how to utilise the next couple of hours. CIA flash communications were bouncing across the globe - to agents and embassies in every country to ensure they did everything they could to protect their assets and information. Standard protocol ensured a lot of sensitive information was already backed up to autonomous hard drives. In addition, they were reverting to old school hard copies, which had printers whirring and safes being filled in every CIA office. At the last possible moment before the EMP detonations, all strategic communications satellites would be powered down.

Chapter 209

IN THE BUNKER below the late Russian President's Palace, Alex Ward closed the secure tablet on which she'd been watching the address from President Anders. She didn't need to tune in to the various news services and get swamped with opinion and hyperbole. She knew what was likely to be happening in her country. It would be complete chaos. Still early across most of the US, the country would be coming awake to the most confronting Presidential address since Franklin D. Roosevelt called December 7th 1941, 'A date that would live in infamy.'

Not typically emotional, Ward found her stomach and her mind swirling. She was consumed by thoughts of David, his family, her mother, and her sister and what they would all now be confronting. And for her countrymen and women. It would bring out the best and the worst. She was thousands of miles away and unable to help. She looked across the bunker and saw her new Georgian colleague in an emotional conversation on one of the desk phones.

Ward looked around the room. It was just her, the General and Alek. She noticed the dark stain on the deep red patterned rug where the President's body had fallen. The General had briefly paused his frantic activity to watch an interpreter relay the Anders address on Russian TV. He was now back on the phones urgently coaxing his generals and ministers to be ready. Russia was the last country to fall in line with the EMP operation and was scrambling to get their nuclear and non-nuclear launch plans in place. And they had to shut their grids down. One advantage of a centralised economic and political system was that orders would be issued and followed immediately and without question. Ward prayed they would make it in time.

If she had Hanse Kallis' little robotic fuckers in her body - and she probably did - she was relying on the Russians to ensure they were destroyed.

Ward had spoken with Kristen earlier as she liaised between the White House and the bunker and knew that almost every head of state around the world would now be following the US Presidential address with one of their own. Essentially delivering the same message to their own citizens. The Russian Prime Minister was just moments away from his address to the Federation.

Ward picked up her encrypted phone and walked to the bunker's entrance. The large steel door stood fully open. They had decided to leave it that way. They didn't know how it would react to the EMP strike and didn't want to be sealed inside an underground concrete and steel tomb. Not the grave she had in mind.

She stood in the bunker entrance looking at the bodies that still lay there, dialled David's number and held the phone to her ear. It didn't connect. Not even voicemail. She still had a signal to the satellites above her, so she assumed the Australians had already started shutting down their networks and grid. It was the middle of the night in Australia. Many in that country would have caught the late news or been alerted by the emergency messages delivered across internet-connected devices. Many more would be oblivious. She wondered what their world would be like in the morning. And she wondered where David might be.

Ward put her phone into one of the side pockets in her pants. She looked back into the bunker. The General was still yelling into one handset whilst holding another in his other hand. Alek was sitting on an easy chair, still talking into the phone. Ward wondered if he had a wife or girlfriend he was talking with back in Georgia. The General had ordered all security staff to not come near the bunker some hours ago. This part of the palace was deserted. She looked forward into the tunnel and figured she'd walk down to the beach to the edge of the Black Sea and wait for the EMP strike. She didn't want this steel tomb they were in to protect the bots in her arm from the pulse that would render them disabled. And she figured the beach would be a peaceful place to watch the world come to a stop as every country now inexorably shut down their grids and networks and prepared for the big show in a little over an hour.

As she saw the coastline appear at the end of the tunnel, she thought the beautiful and peaceful scenery felt like the calm before the electromagnetic storm.

Chapter 210

PRESIDENT MICHELLE ANDERS was still seated at the Resolute desk in her office. For the first time in hours - days - she gave pause to what her next move needed to be. The adrenaline of her address to the nation was washing away, leaving her feeling drained and depleted. Department heads were working feverishly with the bureaucracy and private companies to progressively shut everything down. In a little over thirty minutes, everything would stop. She wondered what the world would be like when it went quiet.

Admiral Jock Campbell working with the Director of DTRA, Victoria Hudson, and the various military chiefs, were finalising the sequence and protocols for the EMP initiative. There was now nothing she could add or offer to assist. She hadn't done it in a long time, but she felt that now might be a good time to pray.

Her Chief of Staff, Tully Carina, and the US Secretary of State had worked frantically to coordinate with heads of state across the world to ensure they covered as much of the global land mass as possible with the EMP strike. Particularly ensuring the more densely populated areas were covered. It boggled her mind to think that there was currently a multi-nation, global undertaking to coordinate a series of upper atmospheric nuclear explosions. Incomprehensible as recently as just a day or two ago.

Russia had been the final piece to the jigsaw. Their dictator would never support the global imperative - even worse, they realised he would use the actions of other countries as they desperately fought the implanted virus to justify his war. His manic desire to re-create Russia and the limited time he had left amplified his danger to the world. The Seals sent in to assassinate him had been too late. However, the CIA operative Director Thomas had mobilised had managed to get into the bunker, and had been ready to take out the Russian President. How fitting that even she had not been needed as one of the President's most trusted men had taken him down. Despite her misgivings at such action, she did not lament the passing of another global head of state. What needed to be done had been done.

Anders figured all the wheels were in motion. All the balls were in the air. The EMP strike against the nano-bots would either work or it wouldn't. Her job now, in the final hour or so, was to lead her country. To communicate with the American people while she still could. To reassure them, to empathise with them, and to continue to ask - demand - that they support each other and to bring their best. Nobody knew what lay on the other side of the electromagnetic pulse.

She cast her eyes around the crowded Oval, looking for Tully. She wanted to work out a plan to get back on the air shortly in whatever form would reach the most people - TV, radio, online - whatever it took. Conveniently, she saw Tully enter the side door of the Oval. She was in a hurry towards Anders. Something wasn't right. She looked visibly distressed.

Chapter 211

CHIEF OF STAFF Tully Carina was oblivious to the crowded Oval Office. She was focused entirely on the President sitting at her desk. The President's eyes tracked Tully as she crossed the room.

Tully went around the desk and bent to the side of the President to speak confidentially into her ear. She was both conscious of not wanting to be overheard by the onlookers as to be clearly heard by The President.

'Madame President we have a situation coming out of Congress.' without waiting for acknowledgment, Tully continued, 'The Speaker of the House has initiated the 25th Amendment to have you and the Joint Chiefs declared unable to discharge your duties and to be replaced. Effective immediately.' Now, Tully paused and looked at her friend to ensure she had her attention. Wide eyed, Anders turned her head towards Tully and gave a slight nod.

'Speaker Hawthorne has drafted a letter he will table to Congress for their support. The letter will provide a declaration indicating the unprecedented actions to both shut down the country and to initiate a nuclear and non nuclear strike on our own people to be unconstitutional and completely without justification. Congress will be...'

'Stop Tully. Not here. Not with all these people. Get the Attorney General to the Situation Room right now. And set up an emergency Cabinet meeting via video link in five minutes.' Anders stood and moved to the door to head immediately to the Situation Room. On top of everything else. Now this. My God. Fucking politics! This needed to be stopped. Right now. They were in the final countdown.

Chapter 212

KRISTEN THOMAS SAT in the Situation Room, sharing the space with Admiral Jock Campbell. They had briefly acknowledged the unorthodox but ultimately successful mission in Russia to remove the President. And had then been at either end of the long table focussed on their work. Both had a lot to do. Particularly the Admiral, who ensured the EMP initiative was as organised and coordinated as it could be. Meanwhile, Kristen was still working with all CIA offices, in addition to Langley, to protect their data and assets. She harboured real fears that the unprecedented EMP strike would expose them to hackers and data leaks and a nightmare of security issues.

She looked up as President Anders and Chief of Staff Carina came steaming into the room. Thomas had not expected to see the President again until after the strike, and they started turning the country back on again - if they could!

Tully spoke first, 'Sorry Director, Admiral, can you give us the room?'

Kristen began closing her laptop, 'Of course....'

'No, the Admiral should stay,' stated Anders, 'Admiral, your work is critical - we won't interrupt. Director Thomas - can you join us in the conference room next door?' The President spun on her heel and left as quickly as she'd arrived, moving into the adjoining room. Tully Carina was right behind her. Kristen Thomas grabbed her things and joined them.

Before they had seated, Anders quickly briefed Kristen on the challenge to her and the Admiral from the house speaker. 'It's why I don't want Admiral Campbell in this conversation. Nothing can disrupt his focus on coordinating the strike.' She looked at Kristen, who remained silent, her expression taut with tension. Then to her Chief of Staff, 'Tully, do we have a plan?'

'With the exception of your appointment to the Presidency just days ago, the only time the 25th Amendment has been invoked since Reagan has been to temporarily transfer the power of the President to the Vice President, whilst the sitting President has undergone surgery - typically a routine colonoscopy.' Anders felt that last bit to be unnecessary! 'The protocol is for the VP to initiate the 25th. However, we don't currently have a VP. I'm kicking myself we didn't get that appointment sorted. Even temporarily! I had a feeling it would bite us.' Tully paused every so briefly, 'So the next in line is the Speaker.' as Tully spoke, the image of the Attorney General appeared on the video monitor in the conference room.

'Perhaps I should take it from here?' offered Samuel Pierce - the US Attorney General appointed by former President James Charleston. Anders looked at the craggy face of the aging AG and hoped he wasn't one of the good old boys Charleston had doled out favours to. She didn't know him well enough to truly appreciate where his loyalty might be.

Anders nodded at the screen, 'Please proceed, Sam.'

Without preamble, the AG began, 'Speaker Hawthorne has already contacted Sec Def to immediately revoke the orders for the EMP indicating the President and the Chairman will be replaced and new orders forthcoming.'

Tully interrupted, 'Is that lawful?'

The AG continued, 'In a word no. Hawthorne knows this and is trying to circumvent the protocols of the 25th given the short window of time until the EMP launch happens.'

Anders just wanted to get to the answer but bit her tongue. Attorney General Pierce continued, 'Section 4 of the 25th Amendment allows the Vice President, or in this case the Speaker and a majority of the Cabinet or another body designated by Congress to declare that the President is unable to discharge the powers and duties of the office. This declaration would temporarily transfer the powers and responsibilities of the presidency to the Vice President - again, in this case, the Speaker.

'However, this process is not straightforward. It requires specific actions and the involvement of key officials in the executive branch. If the President disputes the declaration of incapacity, the issue would go to Congress for resolution. Congress would need to vote with a two-thirds majority in the House of Representatives and the Senate to uphold the transfer of powers to the next in line.'

Anders interrupted this time,'We definitely dispute the declaration of incapacity. Let Hawthorn send it to Congress. By the time the vote happens, it will all be over.'

AG Pierce nodded on screen, 'I agree ma'am. In fact, I think we can circumvent it more definitively. The amendment asks for "a majority of Cabinet, or another body designated by Congress" and we know he cannot designate "another body". So the key is to manage Cabinet. I know the current Cabinet are not your appointees and were installed by your recent predecessor. However, I've quickly called a couple of them, and I think we can proceed with an understanding that they are on your side. The imperative is to ensure the Speaker doesn't pause or derail the shutdown and the EMP protocol whilst this distraction plays out. If Hawthorn succeeds in holding things up even for a short period of time it will all be too late.'

Tully now jumped in, 'We have an emergency Cabinet meeting commencing now. Let's get this mess resolved there and then.'

As Tully spoke, the numerous screens in the conference room started to come alive, and a montage of images of the various cabinet members was created. The location of each member was displayed under their names. With the continuity of government protocol in effect, the Cabinet members were spread across a number of secure facilities around the country. The protocol had been updated significantly since it was last invoked following the September 11 attacks.

Anders prepared to take control of the meeting. While she waited for the rest of the Cabinet to join, she muted all but Secretary of Defense Henry Blake. She looked at Kristen Thomas and back to the Sec Def. 'I'm hoping this meeting will be done very quickly. When it's over I want you two to stay on.' Both nodded.

Again, hitting more buttons, Anders now only addressed the Attorney General, 'Samuel, once this is done, let's get the ball rolling on removing and replacing the Speaker.'

'Of course, ma'am.'

Chapter 213

THE FINAL MEMBERS of the Cabinet filled the screens. As Anders was about to speak, the door to the conference room burst open, and Speaker of the House Sterling Hawthorne came into the room, a single piece of paper in his hand. He was followed by a young female in a Washington power suit and a younger male with a camera. Without an invitation to speak, he walked directly to the President, ignoring the eyes following him within the room and on the screens. It seemed he was enjoying this moment. And given the camera now focused on him, he would ensure it was captured for the news anchors and historians.

'Madam President, I am invoking the 25th amendment. It is apparent from the decisions you have made to cripple the economy of our country with this unprecedented shutdown, coupled with the insanity of the impending nuclear strike that you are unfit for the role to which you have recently been appointed. I have with me a declaration signed by a designated Congressional body confirming your incapacity.' Looking across the numerous screens, Hawthorn found the one he was looking for and continued, 'I would ask Attorney General Pierce to confirm the legality of this document, and you will be removed from your office immediately.'

President Anders stared at Hawthorne as if having yet another out-of-body experience. She'd lost count of them over the last few days. She hoped the assurances of the AG were right and that the support of the Cabinet would fall in her favour. But she really didn't know. This uncertainty and delay could cost them precious minutes, or worse, hours. Which in turn may in fact cost the country everything. She felt perspiration form on her forehead. They really didn't have time to go through these ego driven political maneuvers. She needed to do something. Now!

While Hawthorne was focused on delivering his self-important speech, Kristen Thomas had a Secret Service Agent remove the cameraman. Only the President could authorise a camera in the Situation Room. She walked over to the Speaker.

'May I look at that paper?' without really thinking, Hawthorne handed it over to the CIA Director. Kristen looked it over, noting only a handful of signatures on the page. Hardly a compelling quorum. Though it wouldn't matter if, over the next few hours and days, this attempted coup proved unconstitutional - as she was certain it would be. By then, the damage would be done. If the EMP initiative did not launch in the next few minutes, they would miss the deadline. At that point, it wouldn't matter who presided over the remaining entrails of a decimated United States.

All the signatures were in fresh blue ink. She took a gamble that this was the original and only copy the speaker had brought with him. The whole coup would have been hastily organised and frantically executed. It may be the only copy in existence. Such was the urgency of his opportunistic takeover of the Presidency. Thomas held the paper for a moment more. She looked right into the Speaker's eyes. Then proceeded to tear it into shreds.

'It seems we have misplaced your declaration. Do you happen to have another copy for the Attorney General?' His mouth agape, Kristen could see the boil beginning as the Speaker began to move his mouth.

'You...you bitch. That is a historical, constitutional ....' He looked around the room and across the screens. 'Attorney General Pierce, you witnessed this. It's unlawful. Probably treasonous. You need to have this woman arrested.' His finger jabbing at the CIA Director. 'And you need to have this woman removed.' This time re-purposing his jabbing finger towards President Michelle Anders.

The Attorney General Samuel Pierce unmuted his screen, 'I see no constitutional reason for either of those actions. Do you have....' before he could finish, another person walked into the conference room. Chief Justice Eleanor Vaughn of the Supreme Court looked around, trying to understand what was going on.

What a circus, thought Kristen as the room went silent. Hawthorne had no doubt asked the Justice to come to the White House to swear him in once his coup had been effective. Hawthorne addressed the Justice, his fury growing, seething, 'Justice Vaughn, I have lawfully invoked the 25th amendment to remove the President from office. You are here to swear me in as the new President of the United States.'

Calmly, the Justice looked to Anders and then to the screen hosting the United States Attorney General, 'AG Pierce, do you concur with Speaker Hawthorne?'

'I do not. He is here without reason and without any apparent adherence to constitutional due process. As you can see, the United States Cabinet is assembled. None of those I have asked have been signatories to any such declaration. There is no constitutional foundation for his claim. I can attest we have a President with full and complete faculty. And she is duly steering us through this most horrible time.' In a departure from his typically formal and considered tone, the AG finished, 'Unfortunately, it seems our Speaker has come unglued with the stress of the moment.'

Justice Vaughn held the gaze of the AG and then eventually shifted to look at the President. Anders raised an eyebrow. The Justice then addressed Hawthorne, 'Under what constitutional protocol are you enacting the 25th amendment?'

'I have a lawfully signed declaration from a designated Congressional body that enacts the 25th Amendment and immediately removes the President.'

'Where is the declaration?

'Well I did have it. But SHE tore it up.' pointing at Kristen Thomas, Hawthorne was really working himself into a lather. 'What she did is treasonous! I'll get another declaration signed. But that is irrelevant. The President needs to be removed. And replaced. Now!'

The Justice then looked briefly at an enraged and silenced Speaker, turned and exited the room.

Kristen Thomas followed the Justice and moved to the door of the conference room. She had a burly Secret Service agent waiting just outside. She caught his eye and nodded. She'd been communicating with the head of the President's detail via text over the last few minutes. Speaker Hawthorne was about to find his anger fuelled trip back to the Capitol would face some significant delay.

Anders addressed Hawthorne, 'This is a formal, emergency meeting of the US Cabinet. Of which your are not a member. You need to leave.'

Hawthorne paused for a moment. He pushed his chest out and his chin up. 'This is not over.' he stormed through the door, his very short lived Presidential coup thwarted, now intent on returning to his cohort of collaborators and having the declaration properly executed. An agent in a dark suit gently grabbed him by the elbow. Too preoccupied, he didn't realise this man was not one of his own appointed security detail.

Chapter 214

ANDERS LOOKED ACROSS the various screens. She breathed in and breathed out. She caught the eye of Kristen Thomas, 'Not exactly a textbook response Director!'

A flicker of a smile crossed Kristen's face, 'No, Ma'am. But it bought us some time. Our deadline is almost here!'

Anders nodded silently, she figured this had only delayed an inevitable showdown with the political opportunist Hawthorne had always been. But a delay was all she needed. She wasn't sure she wanted this job much longer. The next few hours would see the most devastating series of events any President had ever ordered on their own country. That might just be enough for her. She was convinced it was the right thing. And it was almost too much to bear.

'Indeed! Well, since I now have my Cabinet assembled, there is work to be done. Will you excuse us, Director?'

With that, Kristen Thomas left the room.

Chapter 215

DOCTOR DAVID MITCHELL walked towards the exit of the large temporary hospital at the football ground in Sydney. He went past the last of the hundreds of partitioned beds installed under the stadium roof. All the beds had patients. Some more than one. The floors in the partitioned rooms had patients on them. Even the passageways had patients.

The massive, temporary room was in half darkness and was getting warmer. Power had progressively been shut off. They were now using the emergency generators as the state and national power grid was wound down. Even the generators would be switched off shortly to protect them from damage during the EMP. And they desperately hoped they could turn them back on afterwards. But no one knew what would work after the big pulse.

He exited the door, walked to the stadium concourse, and looked around. Temporary stanchions were lining the paved grounds, installed initially to manage the entry of new patients into the hospital. Over the last few days, they had simply become arbitrary dividers for where the sick and dying had fallen. There was no room for more people inside. Bodies were everywhere out here. Some under sleeping bags and blankets. Many just lying where they had fallen. He had no clue as to whether they were alive or dead. It had become pointless to check.

David's tired mind wandered and he thought about the events that led him to be standing, surveying this horrible scene. COVID-19 has been horrible. A virus they didn't understand and were in some ways slow to respond to. Highly infectious and deadly for many, the medical community and the various levels of government had scrambled to develop treatment protocols and community mitigation settings, with countries states and cities all responding differently. It had been real-time crisis management. However, with trial and error and tireless effort from medical and health workers, they managed to avoid an uncontrolled plague. Then the vaccinations started, and there was a distant light of hopeful promise.

And then this new virus hit. Kallis 1.0. A deadly, synthetic, intentional virus that was untreatable, infectious and with unprecedented mortality rates. It had hit them hard, and it had hit them quick. And David Ward stood amongst the horrific fallout.

By all accounts, what they had borne witness to and failed to stop over the last weeks and days would soon be surpassed by a new horror. For days and weeks now, they had been witness to hordes of people coming to them - desperately hoping for their symptoms to be treated and to be made well again. The sick and dying. Bodies jammed into the temporary tent hospital. Many unable to even get into the hospital. The crushing sea of dead. Cadavers literally stacked outside the rear of the hospital, waiting to be taken to mass graves or to be cremated. These scenes of suffering and death would soon be eclipsed. David could only speculate on the devastation that would come from shutting down the entire city and the entire country. The initial virus would continue on its devastating path. And it would be joined by the impact of no power, no water, no sanitation, no communication and no transport. And no one knew if anything would be restored quickly - or at all.

But David also knew this was the path they had to go down. As hard as it was to knowingly bring suffering, the alternative was beyond comprehension. The human devastation they had experienced so far with the pandemic and Kallis 1.0, and even the suffering that would be brought on by the shutdown and the EMP strike was minuscule compared to what would happen if the Kallis Nano Virus went active. The thousands - tens of thousands that had suffered and died so far would literally become millions and ultimately billions if both the shutdown and the EMP strike didn't happen.

The hardest thing to deal with was that he could now do nothing. Many of his colleagues had been sent home from the hospital, as new teams were brought in to manage the bodies. The unwavering commitment and determination to help the sick that had kept them here for days and weeks on end had finally been supplanted. The impending shutdown and the EMP strike to follow also forced many of them home. To be with and care for their own families.

Exhausted and with his emotions brimming to the surface, he pulled his phone out of his pocket as he walked, hoping to be able to call Alex before the phone network went dead. He looked at the screen. Too late. No connection. No signal.

And he had nowhere to go.

Chapter 216

CHAIRMAN OF THE Joint Chiefs Admiral Jock Campbell sat alone in the Situation Room - oblivious to the historic, failed showdown just down the corridor. He was facing the myriad of screens on the wall connecting him to the six other members of the Joint Chiefs, General Alex Martinez, head of the EMP task-force at DTRA, and The Director of DTRA, Victoria Hudson. Just coming back online now was Secretary of Defense Colonel (ret) Henry Blake.

A further two other screens held his primary focus. One of these screens was connected to JSOC - Joint Special Operations Command out of Fort Bragg, North Carolina. It was there that Brigadier General Ethan Blackwood coordinated the non-nuclear launch of the EMP strike.

The second screen was shared by Army General Mitchell Stone and Air Force Lieutenant General Lucinda Ramirez. Located in United States Strategic Command (USSTRATCOM) headquarters based at Offutt Air Force Base in Nebraska, these were the two senior officers responsible for the Dual Key System that would authorise and launch the nuclear EMP strike.

For about the thousandth time in the last half hour, the Admiral looked at his IWC Pilot watch and then double-checked the time on the array of digital clocks on the wall of the Situation Room. He offered what would not be his last prayer that the strike they would shortly launch would effectively stop this robotically delivered virus. And the damage the HEMP caused and the damage from the shutdown would not be as devastating as the projections.

President Anders walked silently back into the Situation Room with a cohort of staffers trailing her. She gave the Admiral a reassuring nod, and he returned the unspoken acknowledgement. The Admiral activated the audio link for both the screen connected to Fort Bragg and the screen connected to USSTRATCOM,

'General Blackwood, General Stone, General Ramirez, I have a lawful, authentic and properly verified order from the President of the United States to proceed with Operation Lightning. Acknowledge.'

As previously determined, Blackwood, controlling the non-nuclear strike from Fort Bragg responded first, 'Copy Admiral. Operation Lightning is Confirmed.'

The two Generals in Nebraska then repeated the acknowledgement.

'On my mark, you will commence the twelve-minute countdown to operation lighting.' the Admiral paused, again looking across at his President, he drew a breath as he considered the significance of this moment. 'Three, two, one, mark.'

As a professional military officer, Blackwood responded without hesitation and was followed with an identical acknowledgement by the two Generals in Nebraska, 'Roger that. Operation Lightning is go in twelve minutes.'

The admiral stayed motionless in his seat, closed his eyes and ran a hand across his face. They determined that the verification for Operation Lighting - both the nuclear and non-nuclear EMP strike- would be pre-authorised by twelve minutes to mitigate the risk of interference to communications from other EMP strikes from different countries.

Opening his eyes, Campbell leaned forward and spoke into a microphone connected to all screens, 'We will proceed with minimal operational communications. Unless anything unforeseen, I want to focus on the countdown and launch from Fort Bragg and Strategic Command. Thank you everyone. I'll see you on the other side. May God Bless us all.'

Chapter 217

ALEX WARD SAT with her knees pulled to her chest alone on a sandy ledge overlooking the pebbled beach below and the Black Sea beyond. The winter sun would soon appear over the horizon to the East. The night had been bitterly cold. She pulled the borrowed Russian military coat tight around her. A small number of boats sat at anchor spread around the bay, their running lights twinkling across the luminescent water. The view was beautiful and calm and peaceful. And belied the shattering events that were just moments away.

She had tried calling David again without getting through. The satellite phone lay next to her on the sand. She figured that whilst public communications were now offline, military and strategic communications would be the last to be shut down. Ward picked up the phone and dialled Kristen Thomas' secure number. She was a little surprised when the call was picked up.

'Hello Boss. Been busy?'

'Hello, Alex. A little! Much like yourself, I expect!' replied Kristen. A rare display of exhaustion was apparent in her voice.

'It's frightening, don't you think, that one man can bring the world to its knees?' Ward gazed pensively across the water as she spoke.

'History is unfortunately littered with the devastation of a single misguided individual!' Kristen countered, 'Alex, thank you for coming back in. We would not be where we are without you.'

Ward asked her, 'Is this going to work? Will the virus actually be shut down?.

'We're counting on it. But I'm not sure the cure will be better than what we're trying to prevent. We're about to send the world back to the 1800's.'

'We had to try and stop him, Kristen. And we had to stop that Russian tyrant. One of them or both of them were going to try and kill billions'

'They still might. But yes. We had to stop them.'

Ward paused for a moment. The rising sun was creating a false dawn. She asked Kristen for the second time, 'Any idea, boss, how I'm going to get home?'

But there was no response. The satellite link had dropped out.

Powering down the phone, she placed it beside her. The flickering lights below her in the village houses and stores all extinguished at once.

Chapter 218

UNIT COMMANDER COLONEL Rachel Turner looked around the palpably tense room in the operations centre at Strategic Command (USSTRATCOM), Nebraska. She made silent eye contact with the various operators at their digital stations as they went professionally and systematically through the final protocols before the nuclear launch, now just moments away.

The room was dimly lit to protect the eyes of officers and staff, spending countless hours looking into banks of monitors. There was only the low hum of machines at work. And low voices in soft exchange speaking just above the computers.

'Status report!' commanded Colonel Turner. The nearest officer responded immediately, 'Ma'am, all systems are online and operational. Silos A through F are ready for launch.'

On cue, the next officer mirrored the response, 'Submarine fleet is on standby, awaiting your command.'

And so the responses echoed across multiple stations.

A career officer, this was all very familiar, almost automatic for Rachel Turner. She had been through innumerable training exercises and simulations and had countless hours of preparation for this very moment. And whilst calm and focused on her team, she felt consumed with nerves and could feel the adrenaline pumping from her heart. This was different. This time, it was real.

Colonel Turner spoke in a controlled voice, audible across the room, and a green light appeared on her console. 'We have a duly authorised and authenticated launch order. Countdown sequence is confirmed. Commence firing sequence now.'

She looked up at the massive screen that showed a map of the world. There were blinking lights everywhere. The scale of what they were about to do in the US alone was more than they had ever undertaken. The lights she could see on the map represented the launch stations going online and active around the globe.

Turner was aware of the quiet, synchronised movements of the officers at their stations around the room. Each second felt like an eternity as the final protocols were being implemented.

A measured voice to Colonel Turner's right spoke, 'Launch is in five, four, three, two, one. Launch sequence initiated.'

This was followed by a series of the same measured statements as multiple launches were almost simultaneously confirmed.

Colonel Turner shifted her focus, as did everyone in the operations centre, to the central bank of screens. Land and sea-based launches were displayed from numerous locations punctuated by plumes of smoke and flaming rocket-propelled engines as an unrivaled and unbridled display of power and destruction screamed into the sky.

She softly spoke a quiet prayer under her breath, 'Godspeed to all.'

Chapter 219

STILL SITTING PERCHED on the rocky platform above the Black Sea, Ward thought about the invisible high-altitude electro magnetic and nuclear explosions that would be happening above and around her. She sensed a tingling in her left arm. She wondered if that was the bots being disabled. Or, more likely, her mind being overactive.

The darkness was slowly giving way to weak winter light. The coming dawn enhanced the lights emanating from the ocean whilst the night sky changed with the fading stars in the moonless sky. The absence of any man-made light reminded her of times in the desert. It was quiet and peaceful and serene here. But she knew that would not be the case elsewhere across the skies and across the globe.

Ward heard someone approach behind her, coming through the bush. She felt their presence, turned and looked up to see the Russian General.

'What happens now, Agent CIA?' he asked.

Ward extended her arm, and the General obliged, pulling her to her feet. She stood close facing him through the gloom; 'Well, General, I think we should go and find a beer. While they're still cold.'

THE END

Printed in Great Britain
by Amazon

63744272-ecec-4e28-8b9b-580034b84be8R01